The Celestial Twins

The
Celestial Twins

POETRY AND MUSIC
THROUGH THE AGES

H. T. KIRBY-SMITH

University of Massachusetts Press
AMHERST

Copyright © 1999 by
H. T. Kirby-Smith
All rights reserved
Printed in the United States of America

LC 99-15157
ISBN 1-55849-225-9
Designed by Steve Dyer
Printed and bound by Sheridan Books, Inc.

LIBRARY OF CONGRESS CATALOGING-IN-PUBLICATION DATA
Kirby-Smith, H. T. (Henry Tompkins), 1938–
The celestial twins : poetry and music through the ages / H. T. Kirby-Smith.
   p. cm.
Includes bibliographical references and index.
ISBN 1-55849-225-9
  1. Lyric poetry—History and criticism.   2. Music and literature.   I. Title.
PN1356.K54 1999
809.1'4—dc21   99-15157
CIP

British Library Cataloguing in Publication data are available.

To the memory of Paul McConnell,
    organist and choirmaster for many years at the
    University of the South,

and to Richard and Mary Alicia Cox, and Connie Kotis,
    and all who make music a living presence in our lives.

Das Dichten eines Volkes beginnt nicht mit der Zeile, sondern mit des Strophes, nicht mit der Metrik, sondern mit Musik.

—W. MEYER,
Gesammelte Ablandlungen zur mittellateinischen Rhythmik

Contents

Acknowledgments · xi

Introduction · 1

1. Initial Synthesis and Separation · 9

2. From Latin Verse to Sacred Song · 25

3. The Transition to Vernacular Song · 45

4. Oral-Formulaic Beginnings · 61

5. Nature and Artifice · 82

6. The English Renaissance · 101

7. Arranged Marriages · 118

8. "God-gifted Organ Voice of England" · 137

9. "Can Empty Sounds Such Joys Impart!" · 166

10. The Revival of the Lyric · 195

11. A Second Renaissance · 213

12. Three American Originals · 236

13. Some Moderns · 258

Afterword · 300

Appendix · 303

Bibliography and References · 309

Index · 319

ACKNOWLEDGMENTS

As I have done three times in the past, I express thanks for helpfulness on the part of most departments and many persons in the Jackson Library of the University of North Carolina at Greensboro. Anne Mahoney of Boston University gave me useful suggestions on the introduction, and Hugh Parker corrected my Latin translations and offered valuable advice on what I say about these poems. James Wimsatt saved me from several embarrassing mistakes in my comments on Chaucer and Machaut, and William Moore performed a similar service for my discussion of blues. Kathleen Mather offered an acute critique of the discussion of Valéry's "Le Cimetière Marin," as a result of which, among other more important things, I learned to spell the poem's title correctly for the first time in about forty years. By her diligence and interest, Angelique Wheelock revived my interest in this project at an important stage of its development, reading and editing most of the manuscript; Tara Gorvine worked over the last chapter. Many people in the office suite where I am located made my life pleasant during the writing, but I would especially mention Libby Bailey and Laurie White as active promoters of delightful sociability and as leaders of my unpaid claque. The prompt and warm welcome extended to my manuscript by Bruce Wilcox, director of the University of Massachusetts Press, and by its first reader, Paul Mariani, reassured me that I had not been wasting my time. Edward Doughtie's generous comments as second reader were also most welcome, as were his specific suggestions for revisions, all of which I have tried to incorporate. Leonard Trawick read the entire manuscript with much care, and it has greatly benefited from his advice and corrections. The author's proclivity for consorting with the Beast of Error, however, will always exceed the best-intended ministrations of his friends and assistants.

I thank my wife for putting up with things that are too numerous to mention.

Except in one or two instances—where an English version of a critical work was the most accessible—all translations, poetry as well as prose, are my own.

The Celestial Twins

Introduction

THIS IS A BOOK about poetry, not music. Originally titled "The Emergence of Poetry from Music," its purpose is to locate some of the more important moments in European literature when poetry and music went their separate ways and to show how poetry thenceforth developed as an independent art form. The question of whether there remain any relationships between poetry and music—like the question of just what makes a metaphor, or what free verse is—will never be settled to everyone's satisfaction. Contemporary views include a neoformalist extreme that simply dismisses the possibility (or desirability) of any residual connection; in the other direction are vague vestiges of nineteenth-century aesthetic confusion that assume that poetry is forever approximating musical expression—or that it ought to do so. Similar divisions, or attitudes, go back to ancient times. (For succinct historical treatments one may turn to entries in the *Princeton Encyclopedia of Poetry and Poetics*: "Music and Poetry" by James Anderson Winn and "Scansion" by T. V. F. Brogan.)

It has been common to speak of the "music" of poetry—and even of poetry that "sings"—and discussion of the relation of poetry to music is fraught with Baconian idols, making it difficult at times to employ terms that express precisely what one means. It is tempting, for example, to speak of "tonal" music to designate music that has no connection with poetry and that depends purely on the relation of sounds, or tones, to one another. But "tonal" has already been preempted for several other purposes. "Sonic" will not do. I am therefore left with "actual music," hoping that this will not irritate those for whom the "music" of poetry is as actual as any other.

The present study tries to mediate various conflicting claims, arguing that as a matter of historical fact all poetry can be connected directly or indirectly— sometimes only very distantly—with a musical context, but that the art of poetry is an art of words (just as Mallarmé said it was). Merely to trace all the different ways in which poetry written in English owes something of its rhythm and form to music would require many more pages than I have devoted. To attempt a survey of the same for the literature of the West would result in a series of volumes in which eventually senile confusion would come to a merciful end with the death of the author.

I have tried to supply enough examples from various languages and periods to support the general contention that poetry that continues to be read and remembered always retains some connection with music. The connection may be very tenuous. The poems of Keats, for example, cultivate a revived Miltonic and Shakespearean poetic music of a sort that had been already well distanced from actual music by 1580. Delicate reversals and counterpointing within Pope's closed couplets marked the culmination of another variety of poetic art that Chapman and Jonson were among the first to cultivate. Other examples are easy to think of where the connection with music was closer; seeking examples only in English, one comes up with Wyatt, Herrick, Burns, Dickinson, Hardy, and Langston Hughes.

At the same time, as I have already implied, I would insist that poetry is forever separating itself from its origins in music, developing rhythmic and structural principles of its own that have little to do directly with actual music. The separation may be instinctive (as in the poetry of Burns and Hardy, where the implicit model for a poem may be a song that the poet knows) or self-conscious (as when Dante or Langston Hughes composed poems as if they could be sung to music, but which are in fact offered as verbal art). Once the separation is well established, as in Latin poetry of the Golden Age and later, or much English poetry from the 1580s onward, actual music may become an increasingly distant memory.

My arguments both for indebtedness to music and for separation from it are naturalistic and evolutionary and, I hope, favor the idea of organic progress in the arts—even organic form, provided we understand that the process that produces the form involves conscious and learnable human artistry rather than the unaccountable impulses of transcendent genius. In no sense do I mean to act as a matchmaker for a remarriage of poetry to music, or to lend support to any form of Romantic confusion of the arts; nor do I think that poetry gains much by cross-fertilization, multimedia happenings, or experiments in syn-aesthesia—although to believe in such things has sometimes made possible extraordinary poems, made possible, indeed, the entire Symbolist movement. No new theory is being advanced, nor is any older theory being defended. I do take some things for granted, such as that time runs in only one direction and cannot be reversed; that human beings are not self-created; that we live in a physical universe that brought us into existence but that is indifferent to our survival; and that some human beings invent aesthetic objects that amuse, please, and satisfy in various ways, enriching life and putting it more in conformity with human needs and ideals. In a word, my aesthetic principles, such as they are, are naturalistic and pragmatic.

There is no contention here that a poet needs to be musically gifted or even needs to know anything about music. W. B. Yeats, whom many a contemporary free-verse writer might think of as hopelessly "musical," was tone deaf. On the other hand, the struggle to extricate poetry from music that we see (or hear) in Thomas Hardy, who was very musical, sometimes results in a cacophony that spoils his poems for some readers. Musical education does not do much to help the reader of a poem to appreciate its metrics or structure; it is interesting to listen to Beethoven's late quartets in conjunction with studying T. S. Eliot's *Four Quartets*, since one does come to understand how the shifts in theme and tempo suggested a strategy to Eliot as he listened to them, but doing so adds little to the enjoyment or comprehension of those poems. Where music is really important to the poetry, as in the songs of Thomas Campion or Thomas Moore, the poetry itself seems correspondingly weak. Yet meters and stanzas that were originally musical can be adapted to nonmusical poetic purposes, a prime example being the odes of Horace. Expectations imparted by formal and rhythmic patterns challenge and inspire the artist. Emily Dickinson's resources were much more limited than Horace's; she relied mainly on the hymns she had heard as a young woman before she ceased attending services in Amherst, but apparently that was sufficient. The best poetry, it seems to me, has always been that which, while not attempting literally to reproduce the effects of the other arts that occupy a temporal dimension (music and dance), has nevertheless succeeded in retaining some analogical awareness of the rhythms and harmonies of its sister muses.

In a few instances I use quasi-musical notation, but in doing so I do not mean to imply that the application of musical scansion to poetry is likely to make its rhythm any more understandable than other kind of marking. Although I have not worked it out in detail, I do think that such notation might be helpful in identifying what the Imagists called "the rhythm of the musical phrase" in free verse. In connection with syllabic meters, however, it is meaningless, and in accentual-syllabic prosody it leads to pointless overspecification. Even with quantitative meters, half notes and quarter notes tell little more than do macrons and breves. As applied by J. C. Pope to Old English alliterative meter it achieves some usefulness as a corrective for overingenious foot-scansion of the type invented by the German philologist Eduard Sievers, though even with Old English it is impossible to claim that the poetry can be fitted exactly to musical measures.

There are many other ways of looking at the problem. Mark W. Booth, using physiological psychology, argues that while a memorized song or ballad involves the right hemisphere of the brain, speech and literacy employ the left hemisphere (66–70, 112). The transition from song to speech, or to written poetry, is therefore a radical—almost physiological—change. But perhaps a metrically complex poem can involve recollections of rhythms from the right hemisphere against which are superimposed more linear texts dealt with by the left hemisphere.

Poetry may distance itself too far from music in more ways than one. It may abandon all claims as an audible medium (as some prescriptions of Imagist criticism, especially those of T. E. Hulme, seem to have expected it to do) and appeal primarily to other kinds of imagination, especially to the visual. Much of what is published as poetry at the end of the twentieth century fits this description. A hundred years ago, however, poetry often went too far in the direction of subtlety and ingenuity in its sound effects, a situation in which the temptation is strong to speak as if one literally heard music. I am thinking of something like "The Lady of Shalott"—or, descending a step or two, Poe's "The Bells." Poe put it this way in his essay, "The Poetic Principle":

> Contenting myself with the certainty that Music, in its various modes of metre, rhythm, and rhyme, is of so vast a moment in Poetry as never to be wisely rejected—is so vitally important an adjunct, that he is simply silly who declines its assistance, I will not now pause to maintain its absolute essentiality. It is in Music, perhaps, that the soul most nearly attains the great end for which, when inspired by the Poetic Sentiment, it struggles—the creation of supernal Beauty. It *may* be, indeed, that here this sublime end is, now and then, attained *in fact*. We are often made to feel, with a shivering delight, that from an earthly harp are stricken notes which *cannot* have been unfamiliar to the angels. And thus there can be little doubt that in the union of Poetry with Music in its popular sense, we shall find the widest field for the Poetic development.

The entire aesthetics (though happily not the practice) of French Symbolism perched unsteadily atop assumptions such as the necessity for musicality in poetry. This precariousness was partly due to the Symbolists' excessive reverence for Poe's poetry and ideas.

Poetry that aspires to the condition of music is different from poetry that emerges from music. Even to admit to such an aspiration may be to betray anxiousness about the distance by which poetry has separated itself from music. The most imposing examples of such anxiety in English verse are the works of Swinburne, who, as it happens, also gave us the most protracted— which is not to say successful—efforts at recapturing the spirit and the rhythms

of the classics. Of Swinburne's achievement the best I can say is that it provoked the writing of a fine elegy in sturdy accentual meters by his contemporary, Thomas Hardy, whose own poems owe much to West Country folk
rhythms and melodies:

> —His singing-mistress verily was no other
>   Than she the Lesbian, she the music-mother
>   Of all the tribe that feel in melodies;
>   Who leapt, love-anguished, from the Leucadian steep
>   Into the rambling world-encircling deep
>   Which hides her where none sees.
>
> (*from* "A Singer Asleep")

One admires Hardy's generosity of spirit toward his contemporary, but Swinburne's poetry was a major catastrophe in the history of English verse—ingenious without fascination and "musical" without real metrical interest.

For the last several centuries, poets, musicians, and critics have periodically
tried to bring the "sister arts" back together. Well-meaning discussions of the
twinned history of poetry and music, however, sometimes fall apart when
further evidence is presented. Take, for example, these sentences from O. B.
Hardison's *Prosody and Purpose in the English Renaissance*:

> The effect of the renewal of the alliance between music and poetry is appar-
> ent in the earliest northern French treatise on prosody, the *Art de dictier* by
> Eustache Deschamps (1392), which opens with the statement that poetry is
> "natural music."
>
>   Much renaissance discussion of music and verse is, one feels, conven-
> tional. Much, however, is not. Musical poetry in sixteenth-century England
> can be said to begin with poems like Sir Thomas Wyatt's "My Lute, Awake,"
> which continues the tradition of the courtly poetry of the trouvères into the
> reign of Henry VIII. By midcentury, Protestants were singing hymns writ-
> ten in common meter, and at the turn of the century, the English school of
> lutenist-songwriters, led by Thomas Campion, achieved a marriage of po-
> etry and music that remains impressive today. Campion also sought deeper
> harmonies in quantitative poems that attempt to revive the ancient alliance
> between poetry and music. (22)

Although the sentences just quoted are, taken one at a time, mostly correct,
the argument as a whole is, if one can say it gently, preposterous: it puts things
in backward order. The implication of these statements is that a movement
began in the fourteenth century, and continued through the sixteenth, that
resulted in a "marriage of poetry and music." Actually the opposite occurred:

poetry freed itself from music and became an independent art, and this separation began in England with Wyatt. Jerome Mazzaro took it for granted that this was the ordinary view: "As critics are quick to explain, the sixteenth-century English lyric changed from structures that once permitted a 'perfect' union of words and music to what in musical form became, in the Caroline court, formal aria and narrative recitative and to what, in literary form, became poetry written so as to exclude the possibility of its being set to music" (1). Though as Mazzaro notes, such a generalization may be stated so as to seem too facile and oversimplify literary history, still it remains a fundamentally accurate perception. While it is true that Deschamps's distinction does depend on the earlier "alliance of poetry and music," as Hardison puts it, Deschamps in fact argued that the alliance was a mistake and that the two arts should go their own ways. His treatise serves more as a description of what had already occurred (more than a century earlier in Italian poetry, a half-century before in French poetry, and contemporaneously in the work of Chaucer): the estrangement of the two arts. The significance of Deschamps's essay, as we will see, is the opposite of what Hardison says it is. Deschamps wanted poetry to have its own music separate from melody; he was not musical himself and he did not write poems for music.

Musical poetry (by which Hardison means poetry that was sung to music) in sixteenth-century England did not begin with Wyatt; it ended with Wyatt. This may seem a startling statement at first, in light of the vogue for madrigals and airs that adorned the later sixteenth century with such lovely musical inventions, but others go further; John Stevens even makes the extreme argument that Wyatt wrote nothing for music (*Music* 132–39). C. S. Lewis apparently thought, as I do, that Wyatt intended that some of his poems be sung (230). But even if Wyatt did accompany himself with a lute, his songs, as music, were the last fading notes of older traditions, not a Renaissance innovation—even while his poems initiated a tone and meter whose development one can trace through Sidney, Raleigh, and others to Donne. It is easy to show (as I will in Chapter 5) that there existed fifteenth-century songs that are precursors to Wyatt, and that are continuous with even earlier English lyrics, as well as songs from France and Italy. In Wyatt's poetry we see the very moment when a purely verbal art established itself as something that could exist independently from music; even some pieces that seem intended to be sung possess a rhythmical and rhetorical structure that make the music a secondary adornment. (One cannot say the same of Dowland's poetic lyrics, for which music is essential.)

Hardison's statement regarding psalms sung in common meter also needs to be modified by taking a retrospective look. Morrison C. Boyd asserts that pre-

Reformation psalms were sung to melodies derived from Gregorian chants (37–38); these, which survived in modified form in Anglican liturgy, are not what Hardison is speaking of. But Boyd suggests even more pertinently: "It is possible that psalms were sung in metrical English before the Reformation, at least outside the church. Sir Thomas Wyatt the elder and the Earl of Surrey had translated several" (38). Boyd makes clear that he is speaking of metrical psalms, the fourteeners that split so readily into ballad meter or common measure. Also one finds in Rollins and Baker's *Renaissance in England*: "Versifying the Psalter was a favorite exercise of sixteenth-century poets and poetasters. In England, the practice goes back at least to the early fourteenth century" (160). The metrical psalters had to give way to those of the Book of Common Prayer and to the King James Psalms, but in the end some good poetry did emerge from these efforts, most notably the versions of George Herbert. Although the Protestant emphasis on participation by the congregation encouraged versions of the Psalms that could be sung to easily learned strophic melodies, the metrical psalm itself is not a post-Reformation invention, and it is not a stage in the courtship of music and poetry.

Campion's achievement (when he used quantitative meters) had nothing to do with Wyatt, except that Campion was reacting against native English versifying in accentual meters that employed rhyme. In the attempt—which he abandoned in the end—to accommodate English to classical meters, Campion failed, but he did succeed in adapting English to the temporal rhythms of his melodies. The loveliness of his songs is undeniable, but his method is discontinuous with the evolution of accentual-syllabic meter in English poetry; at its best it is a fulfillment of the ultimately fruitless attempt—which went on for half the century—to convert English poets to classical meters. That attempt did serve the purpose of sharpening poets' awareness of what could be done with English, though in itself it was a failure. The lute song, or air, of the later sixteenth century tried to continue, or to revive, the strophic song of earlier times, giving it a more refined and elaborate musical treatment. In both the madrigal and the air, though, the poetry was subordinate to the music; Morley, Dowland, Campion, and others composed beautiful art songs but what they did was not a culmination of anything initiated by Wyatt. Their songs were partly an effort to revert to what existed before Wyatt—to rediscover a synthesis that Wyatt had moved away from, though not as a reaction against Wyatt himself. Campion's was among the first of many such projects (Augustan odes for music, opera, nineteenth-century art song, Beethoven's use of the human voice in his last symphony, and so on) aimed at recovering a *mousike*-like synthesis. When he wrote songs in accentual meters, Campion was more in the line of his contemporaries. As Edward Doughtie said in a reader's report for this book, "I'd argue that Campion's method in his English songs—not his quantitative experiments—is continuous with Sidney's discovery of how to vary the iambic pattern by degrees of stress and by employing the natural quantity of English (e.g., 'From that smooth tongue whose music hell can move.')"

In brief, Hardison sees poetry as merging with music in the course of the English Renaissance, while I see it as extricating itself repeatedly from its musical entanglements. A strong alliance between music and poetry had developed during the millennium following the collapse of the Roman Empire, and somewhat weaker alliances were a consequence of the importation of music from Italy and elsewhere. These broke apart in the Renaissance—but now I am getting well beyond the beginnings of my story.

1

Initial Synthesis and Separation

ALTHOUGH IT WOULD BE HELPFUL if we could listen with perfect comprehension to a musical performance from ancient times, we need not be conversant with Greek to understand the meaning of *mousike*. Even though there is no English word to translate it, a fusion of word, music, and dance makes its way into ordinary experience. Our problem is that we may identify such a fusion with either vulgar or childish examples, or else with some self-conscious attempt to constrain the now-separate arts back into company with one another. The triumphal dance and lyric utterance of the young Sophocles, or the stately strophes and antistrophes of the choruses in his mature plays, seem distant from the rock musician flourishing his electric guitar, the singing and clapping games of children, Wagnerian opera, or coffeehouse poetry-cum-music happenings. Yet all these help to illuminate the idea of *mousike*, that consort of the Muses.

Closest to the original Greek synthesis in contemporary America may be Native American dances such as those that I saw performed by a group of Hopis at Mesa Verde in June 1989 (part of whose purpose was to reclaim for themselves the title of Anasazi, the ancient people). Even when we do not understand the words, and even though the movements and melodies may be simple and repetitive, here is a sanctioned and shared union of what we now take to be distinct, or at best complementary, media. Other examples are easy to think of—but none that can be taken as serious expressions of ideals for our own culture. There are the lyrics and melodies of popular music, other than rock, to which people dance, and the numbers in stage and film musicals where words, singing, and dancing occur simultaneously. To children's singing games one might add performances of, for example, "*Sur le pont d'Avignon*" or "Oats, Peas, Beans and Barley Grow." In America we have patriotic songs, but none that anyone dances to and few that one can even march to. Processionals have completely replaced dance in religious observances, except for a few sects. In some parts of the world one finds much greater continuity with the distant past than in our own culture, but even there it may be difficult to cultivate an appreciation for what had been, in *mousike*, a much less self-conscious blending of music and poetry. Most fortunate in this respect, among Western nations, is Iceland, where a lively and continuous poetic tradition reaches back to the Middle Ages and where people today can sing their ancient alliterative *rímur* with greater ease than we read Chaucer. English speakers are not so lucky; because of the rapid evolution of English that occurred after the Norman Conquest, the language of *Beowulf* is as difficult for us to master as German, Dutch, or Yiddish.

In understanding the meters of a language, problems arise that have to do with changes not just in the pronunciation of individual words but in the entire character of the spoken language. Modern Greek poetry, for example, depends on stress—changes in volume or emphasis—whereas the ancient language used little or no stress but instead employed syllables of differing temporal lengths, or quantities, together with some sort of pitch system. These duration-units lent themselves well to—were in fact identical with—rhythmic patterns in music. The same situation (the transformation of a language in the course of centuries) prevails in India, as William Beare explains:

> Verse continued to be quantitative [after the appearance of stress patterns in the spoken language]. In the recitation of Indian verse at the present day this stress-accent is said to be observed, though it has no relation to the metre and hinders rather than helps the perception of the metre. The reciter almost always beats time with his hand, sometimes snapping his fingers or drumming on a table. Indian verse is almost invariably sung, so that it is not easy to say whether the words by themselves provide a rhythm. Indian theorists nowhere take any notice of stress-accent in their language, and the only rhythm of which they seem conscious is that imposed by the music. (46–47)

Elsewhere Beare makes the point that although it is difficult to know how the meters of ancient Vedic hymns (1300 B.C.) work, or what their connection with music may have been, Sanskrit (beginning some centuries B.C.) was definitely quantitative and musical in character: "The time unit, both in verse and in music, is the *mātra*, equal to one short syllable; and classical Sanskrit, like Greek, developed the principle that in some metres one long is equal to two shorts" (66–67).

Even though the music itself is irrecoverably lost, most accounts of ancient Greek culture insist on the centrality of music. Some competence in playing a stringed instrument—a lyre or kithera—and an acquaintance with numerous musical modes preceded reading and writing as an essential, or at least highly desirable, acquisition of a civilized person. The musical modes, which were distinguished from one another by the position of the controlling pitch to which the melody returned most frequently, were thought to express or encourage differing mental states. Performance in different modes required different tunings of the four- or eight-stringed kithera; we still recognize such tunings in contemporary music theory, where "blues mode" is added to those still called by their ancient names: Dorian, Phrygian, Mixolydian, and so forth. Ancient scales in which the controlling pitch, called by some the *mese*, occupied a central position gave the impression of resolve and balance. Plato, Aristotle, and others argued that scales that required that the melody constantly soar back to a higher *mese* could seem convivial or even irresponsible and self-indulgent, while those that sank regularly to a low note suggested melancholy. No doubt there is much room for argument as to the psychological accuracy of these notions, and conflicting or inconsistent interpretations of the emotional effects of modality can be instanced, but Plato accepted the idea of the formative and moral function of music, for good or ill, in a well-known passage in the *Republic*. The main line of Athenian philosophers set themselves against what they saw as a weakening and irrational influence, at least of certain modes. Socrates, at least as Plato represents him, had no use for any part of *mousike*. Plato countenanced only the more bracing or enlivening modes, the Dorian and the Phrygian; Aristotle, who could make room in human life for certain of the more relaxing modes, preferred the Dorian for serious purposes, seeing in its centrally located *mese* an emblem of the golden mean. It is also possible that there were qualities of the melodies associated with these scales that could be identified with different areas of Greece and with communal values imputed to the peoples occupying those areas (Lydia and Phrygia). Beyond these general comments it seems best not to go; as Donald Jay Grout put it, "No field of musicology has produced a richer crop of disputation from a thinner soil of fact" (34).

For our purposes, though, we can be confident that musical and poetic measures of duration were identical, resulting in a poetic meter that shared with music the same temporal, or quantitative, differences—the duration of a syllable being definitely long or definitely short. Such a meter, perfectly natural to ancient Greece, poses problems for an auditory imagination trained in English poetry where stress, or emphasis, is an organizing principle as well as a natural part of our language. Stress values, as we have noted, were originally of no importance to Greek meter. Quantity is not important enough in English to be the basis of a meter, but from time to time, beginning with the English Renaissance, poets have attempted quantitative meters in our language, in hopes of adding ancient dignity or greater mellifluousness, or in a spirit of playful experimentation. A handful of interesting examples exists, one of which (by Tennyson) I will make use of later in this chapter. But the method has never really worked. Native speakers of English show some sense of quantity when they imitate the pronunciation of foreign speakers of English, especially when they mimic an Italian accent by drawing out syllables unnaturally. But this in itself is further evidence of how unimportant temporal duration is in ordinary English speech. And efforts to scan English poetry using musical notation have not worked very well because the temporal component of such notation does not correspond to the actual character of the language.

In Greece, melodic singing took precedence over poetry and dance both in order of invention and in dignity. Poetry, when it did come, accommodated itself to the tempo and also, though not so strictly, to the pitch of the music that it accompanied, not only in choric or solo paeans but even in the recitation of epics. The degree of subordination of the word to the melody or rhythm differed both in nature and complexity, of course, and the subject affords materials for endless discussion, elucidation, and argument. Only those who are at home in the ancient language and who are thoroughly grounded both in the study of metrics and in musical theory are competent to discuss this in detail, but the rest of us may accept their conclusions, where one finds a solid consensus behind the idea that Greek poetry did grow out of Greek music, after having come into existence united with it and with dance. Scansions of Greek poetry coincide exactly with inalterably long or short syllables and poetic scansions are identical with Greek musical rhythms.

Acceptance of this identity, however, does not preclude controversy over scansion itself, considered as an analytical technique. The controversy began as soon as orderly minded scholars—as opposed to poets—tried to describe or account for what had been done to language to turn it into poetry. This effort may be the earliest instance in the West of the bad effects of spurious theorizing about art that accompanies the decadence of art itself. Grammarians observed that a spoken phrase could be subdivided into parts of speech, and in similar fashion prosodic analysts—the so-called *metrici*—found that a line of poetry could be separated into feet. Opposing the *metrici* almost from the start were the *rhythmici*, who argued for a more flexible, quasi-musical understanding of the line. This debate occurred in Hellenistic times (ca. 350–100 B.C.), culminating—for the *metrici* point of view—in the *Enchiridion* of Hephaestion from the second century A.D. Applying modern terms borrowed from electronics, one might call the methods of the former digital and those of the second analog. A polarization of opinion that is roughly comparable has reappeared in this century in the "cooked" versus "raw" opposition of schools of poetry, and most recently in the efforts of New Formalism to rehabilitate relatively rigid foot scansions. For our purposes the most important implication of the *metrici* versus *rhythmici* disagreement is that poetry had by that time already begun to separate itself from music and seemed in need of a rationale of its own. This separation had been anticipated centuries earlier with the appropriation of the performance of passages from Homer by the *rhapsodes*, who eventually substituted impassioned interpretive delivery in place of bardic chanting accompanied by a lyre. That is, poetic metrics began to become distinct from musical measure. Even in the later performances, however, where a staff was flourished or pounded in place of a musical accompaniment, the language itself retained the counterpoint of musical pitches against quantitative values that characterized Homer's metrical art, and the poetry remained close to music.

But one cannot put the blame on grammarians, critics, or performers for disrupting the chorus line of the muses and sending them off in separate directions. That estrangement—which need not be viewed as an undesirable development—is a natural consequence of increasing complexity and sophistication in all the arts. When Achilles took to his tent, he consoled himself by framing words for songs, accompanying himself on a lyre. His melody and his vocabulary of poetic formulas were relatively simple, permitting him to extemporize according to preestablished conventions. He did not, like the far more intellectual and leisured Sherlock Holmes, get out his violin to perform a complex musical composition preserved by musical notation and performed only after much study and practice. The lyre, or kithera, was more rudimentary than most toy instruments of today, in its ultimate development capable of covering only four conjoined tetrachords and in its beginnings much less. The range of its most advanced versions was comparable to two octaves on a modern scale, and each string was dedicated to a single pitch; the fundamental simplicity of the music possible on earlier instruments—initially having only four strings and only four possible pitches—made it easy to accommodate poetry. In the performance of oral epic poetry, for which the kithera in its simpler forms had provided an accompaniment, there had been a large degree of improvisation.

Or so goes the consensus of speculation. In a few manuscripts the use of alphabetic symbols and accents to indicate pitch and to hint at the direction of a melodic line does suggest that music was developing toward a self-sustaining intricacy that required notation for its preservation and possibly even for its composition. The use of written scores tends to separate word from melody, as does the written composition of poetry; the latter preserves the force and sense of the prose meaning and also makes possible a greater ingenuity of speech, resulting in poetry not suitable for music. The great Greek dramatists found in this incipient separation a valuable resource, allowing the intellectual power of pure language to show itself in the stichic parts of the plays and the totality of *mousike* in the choruses.

One effect of increasing technical virtuosity on the kithera was to inspire needless—though supposedly parallel—elaboration or ornamentation of the poetry. The dithyrambic poet Timotheus, though admired and perhaps imitated in some respects by Euripides, not only added a second set of strings to his lyre but also invented tropes and periphrases for his poetry that were objected to in his own day and that strike even modern readers of his poems as preposterously ornate—somewhat as do "Clevelandisms" of seventeenth-century English poetry, which consisted of absurdly elaborated "Metaphysical" imagery. Much contemporary American free verse, which in some respects resembles Timothean dithyramb in its rebelliousness against received forms and its Dionysiac abandon, has taken the opposite direction in diction: away from Victorian ornamental excrescence and toward a simplified, even vulgarized vocabulary. One wonders what poetry of the 1990s would be like if Tennyson had, for some reason, taken Wordsworth as his sole model and had written consistently in the unnaturally plain style of his "Dora." Would modern poets then have felt it necessary to cultivate a florid style? In any case, in Greek poetry, exercises in the style of Timotheus encouraged the separation of poetry from music by making the poetry, in its tasteless flashiness, a sort of baroque addition to the music; thus both music and poetry became self-conscious and exhibitionistic. A passage preserved from a lost play by Pherecrates (a contemporary of Aristophanes from the late fifth century B.C.) has a personification of *mousike* deliver a speech in which she complains in graphically suggestive terms that she has been abused and prostituted by dithyrambic poets. She complains especially of her treatment by Timotheus, saying that he has completely worn her out with his

> Weird extra-modal ant-runs—when he's done,
> What with his high-falutin quirks and squirms
> I might as well be a cabbage full of worms . . .
>
> (*trans.* Edmonds 1.265)

Mousike goes on to say that Timotheus's solo passages make your clothes fly right off you.

The overriding fact is that from its earliest beginnings to its decadent and reiterative phases (especially as the Roman Empire established itself), Greek poetry of all sorts was always connected with music, and the language itself observed temporal quantitative rhythms and exactitudes of pitch that were intrinsically musical. Literacy, written records of plays, never did replace the vast oral heritage in any of the genres—epic, dramatic, or lyric. Dance, or at least rhythmic movement, fused with word and melody, and this fusion remained the ideal. The seductive tones of the *aulos*, an oboe-like instrument with a greater range of effects than the lyre, offered temptations toward pure and nonverbal expression. More than two millennia later it occurred to Mallarmé to characterize free-verse writers of his day as those who went off by themselves to play on their flutes; perhaps the solitary woodwind calls attention to itself so insistently that it not only discourages use as an accompanying instrument but makes a natural metaphor of self-preoccupation.

Cultivation of meretricious rhetoric in the schools of the Sophists, adapting poetic effects to public speaking, pulled at *mousike* from another direction. That is, even as wordless melody established itself as an independent art, verbal rhythms and figures of speech borrowed from poetry were put to practical and even vicious uses. But the lyric poets and dramatists who saw themselves as the conservators of tradition kept the Muses together, and the composers of odes, following the example of Pindar, aimed at a new and even more exhilarating combination of effects. It remained for the Romans, assisted by the analysis of Alexandrian grammarians, to abstract from the Greek synthesis a schema that, though derived from music, was applied externally to the Latin language to force it into meters that were recognizable simulacra of Homer and Hesiod, Sappho and Alcaeus. Aeneas made his way from the ruins of the Hellenic world bearing on his back a quantitative Anchises.

One finds widespread agreement among linguistic scholars of early Latin that, despite the fact that almost the entire corpus of Latin poetry was deliberately composed in the quantitative meters of the Greeks, the Latin language itself, as spoken, employed accents or stresses. Stress-accent seems at work in the earliest recorded poetry and that in itself suggests that stress was a natural property of spoken Latin. Accent seems to have been more marked than in, say, contemporary French, where the last syllable of a polysyllabic word tends to receive a slight emphasis; but French may be a good model to keep in mind, being slightly more accentual in nature than some language teachers recognize. The Penultimate Law of Latin pronunciation stipulates that any long syllable occurring in the next-to-last position in a word shall be stressed, but if the syllable is short, the stress shall fall on the previous syllable. In words of two syllables the accent falls on the first syllable. This practice may have been to some extent preserved, or reverted to, in the hendecasyllabic line employed by Dante, where a stress on the tenth syllable of each line serves as punctuation, being followed by one, and occasionally two, unaccented syllables. It has even been argued that Latin pronunciation in ordinary speech was not that different in character from modern English, which has fairly well-defined habits in the placement of accents or stresses. Yet quantitative values—of a sort that find little place in English—also existed and lent themselves to the use of Greek meters, which could be allowed to overlay the language with a poetic grid. Something analogous has occurred several times in English poetry, beginning with Chaucer, when syllabic referential grids, borrowed mainly from French, have been applied to English, resulting in the accentual-syllabic compromise.

Only about 140–160 lines of Latin poetry exist that were composed previous to, or independent of, the Greek metrical models; these are mostly inscriptions. The meter used there is called Saturnian; the fact that it was a recognized meter is supported negatively by the denunciations of it by Virgil, Horace, and others. To them it must have seemed outlandish, uncouth, and rough, as the native English alliterative meters and folk rhythms seemed to the courtly Chaucer; one of the many explanations of the meter is that it could have been based on a three-beat dance (*tripudium*) of a sort that I have heard called the Mare Hop. Judicious authorities are reluctant to pronounce definitively on the Saturnian, but one guess is that it could have been a loose accentual meter, employing a marked caesura, with three stresses in the first half-line and two in the second. As such it would somewhat resemble old Germanic rhythms (even making use of alliteration as an organizing principle)—or possibly it was even closer to Hebrew poetry, to the loose hemistiches of the Psalms for example. So little is known about the Saturnian that speculation on its connection with music may be worse than useless, but at least its rhythms seem not out of keeping with the semimusical delivery of an Anglo-Saxon *scop* (poet/minstrel), or Old Testament psalmist. William Beare's treatment of the Saturnian in *Latin Verse and European Song* (114–31) seems unlikely to be surpassed for vigor, intelligence, thoroughness, and a willingness to consider the thing from all angles. Offering numerous specific examples, indeed analyzing nearly every known Saturnian line, Beare concludes that it was just terribly rough poetry and that the only thing regular about it was a break in the middle of each line. In any case, it was not quantitative. F. H. Whitman, bringing the controversy up to date in *A Comparative Study of Old English Meter* in preparation for studying the Anglo-Saxon line, makes clear that no definite consensus exists about the Saturnian and essays a compromise between those who insist it was purely accentual and those who discover quantity in it (29–34).

Another possible analogy to the Saturnian in English is the "tumbling verse" of the early Renaissance, which some prosodists see as a rough-and-ready survival of Anglo-Saxon meter. Tumbling verse appeared in comedies of the mid-sixteenth century (such as *Ralph Roister Doister*) and was revived periodically in later plays to accompany scenes that burlesqued the more serious action. Just as Ennius (239–169 B.C.) displaced the Saturnian with the more civilized hexameters borrowed from Homer, so sixteenth-century English poets, beginning suitably enough with Surrey's translation of the *Aeneid*, renewed Chaucer's invention of iambic pentameter. That accentual-syllabic compromise seemed to most poets an adequate step away from the remnants of Germanic barbarity heard in tumbling verse—though certain poets and critics, and grammarians (Roger Ascham, Richard Stanyhurst, Gabriel Harvey, William Webbe, Thomas Campion), insisted that English should break completely with rhyming and accents, cultivating in their place quantitative meters. We will review that controversy at length in a later chapter.

Adapting Latin to the Greek patterns required much concentration and revision, and could only be accomplished by writing the poetry down, reading it aloud, and varying the diction until a satisfactory accommodation of native stress to imported quantity had been achieved. Horace's poems give every evidence of being carefully labored, and Virgil is said to have spent an entire day reducing ten or twelve lines into a perfected one or two hexameters. In place of an hour's oral recitation—a mixture of memory and improvisation—one finds a year's meticulous labor as the literary epic took the place of the authentic, or oral, epic. The connection with music disappeared almost entirely; little surviving poetry in Latin is known to have been set to music, a rare exception being Horace's *Carmen Saeculare*. Horace may have announced an occasion for singing and dancing—as he did in Ode 1.37 that celebrated the defeat of Cleopatra's forces at Actium—but the poem itself was meant for quiet reading. The "music" of Horace's poems was a delicate counterpoint of stress and quantity, even more refined than the restrained modulations that make Pope's closed English couplets so various—and certainly more sophisticated than the *ore rotundo* performances of Victorian poets described by Ford Madox Ford in memoirs of his childhood (110).

Discussion of the rhythms of Latin poetry provides a convenient point at which to introduce the third constituent that was part of Greek *mousike*, from which Latin poetry emerged, or extricated itself, mainly by changing the meaning of two or three important words. This is the element of dance, or measured pacing back and forth across the stage, in the performance of Greek odes and choruses. Dance movements were coordinated with the audible part of the performance by the lifting and clumping down of an enlarged shoe worn by a leader, or by the raising and lowering of a staff. This practice led to the use of three words that are still a source of misunderstanding and controversy: *ictus*, *arsis*, and *thesis*—which can be translated as beat, lifting, and lowering. In Greek performances the *ictus*, or beat, coincided with the lowering of the foot or the staff—or of the hand, if hand gestures were being used to direct the dance. Lowering a foot is ordinarily a more emphatic action than raising it.

Although these conventions of choreographic direction caused no problems for the Greeks, the explanation of them was troublesome to Latin poets. To talk about the *ictus* (a Latin word that has been used to designate the heartbeat, or pulse, as well) in connection with the poetry—the only part of the performance that was regularly transcribed—is to suggest that there was an accentual component. That is, it does not seem natural to use a word that suggests the impact of a foot unless one intends to suggest an emphatic rise in vocal pressure, or volume—not a drawing out in length of a syllable. But unfortunately, grammarians and prosodists did introduce all three terms into the discussions of metrics that were known to the later Latin poets. As we have noted, in Greek performances the *ictus* came on the *thesis* part of the dance step; but when the Latin poets considered their own practice, in verse, they misunderstood the terms to refer to something intrinsic to the poetry. To them, *thesis*, or lowering, could only mean a lessening of emphasis; they took it to mean a lowering or diminishing of verbal stress, a lowering of the voice. The meaning in Latin use, therefore, became reversed. Latin *did* retain a degree of stress emphasis lacking in ancient Greek and therefore for Virgil and Horace the *ictus* had to come on the raised voice, the *arsis* part of the poetic foot. This confusion is even more significant in English prosody than in Latin, because grammarians, notably Richard Bentley—Pope's great enemy in the eighteenth century—imported the concept of *ictus* as designating the accent or stress, which in English accompanies a raising of the voice, and increase in emphasis. Bentley used the same symbol (/) to designate both *ictus* and word-accent in his analysis of Latin meter, thus completely confusing the issue (see Beare 61). For Bentley, the *ictus*, or beat, of a perfect iambic pentameter line in English is always on the *arsis*, the raised second syllable of each foot.

The point of restating and laboring these distinctions is to emphasize how completely Latin poetry had separated itself from the conventions of music and dance that had been an essential part of its Greek models. Latin poetry replaced a choreographic synthesis with a linguistic one; to do this with confidence it retained certain concepts from the Greek but modified, indeed, reversed, their meaning (the *arsis-thesis* switch) in order to rationalize its own achievement. Yet in separating itself and in modifying the terms, it retained the most important—if unstated and perhaps even unrecognized—concept, of an ordered and harmonious accommodation: "the complete consort dancing together," to borrow T. S. Eliot's phrase. In its formal aspect Latin poetry emerged from Greek music and dance, and, rather than rebelling against it or shaking it off, employed conventions of what we now consider as independent performative disciplines as analogies upon which to construct a purely verbal art of a complexity not seen before and seldom equaled since in Western literature. Latin poetry, as an independent art, emerged from Greek *mousike*.

A degree of confusion as to what one is accomplishing in establishing the conventions of a new art form (or perhaps a confidence that one is acting according to sound principles even when one may not be) is sometimes essential to artistic success. It is not important that Latin poets did not realize just what they had taken as a model. In quite another context, the self-forgetfulness that W. B. Yeats imagined might be found in fifth-century Byzantium was of great help to him although it was a skewed view of history. A little learning may be a dangerous thing, but a little theory seems positively salubrious for poetry, with the emphasis on "little"; a scrap of superficial theory that a poet can hold to without bothering too much over its logical consistency or historical accuracy often provides comfort and reassurance. Over and over one finds poets borrowing hints or concepts from other arts and from earlier poets, from other languages and literatures, imagining themselves to be acting on definite principles when in fact they were devising completely new forms of art. I am speaking of the successes. Much very bad art, in the eighteenth and late nineteenth centuries, was a consequence of genuine slavishness to conventions; some unsuccessful productions of the twentieth century, on the other hand, have been obsessive attempts at spurious originality.

The remainder of this chapter will examine the interplay of musical values and natural linguistic emphasis in a single poem of Horace's. Because there is much disagreement on questions of Latin prosody, it is hard to account for the poem in a way that will satisfy everyone. Contradictory statements and inconsistent notations appear in the comments of learned and meticulous scholars, together with occasional typographical mistakes. Such flaws are inevitable and excusable in light of the complexity of both the material and the symbolism used to analyze it. There is also the problem that a reader may hear the rhythm of a particular passage of poetry in one way on one occasion and in a slightly different way on another.

Below appears a diagram of the alcaic strophe as supplied in C. A. Bennett's venerable Loeb Classical Library edition of Horace; my purpose here, unhappily, is to show the incorrectness of the diagram. Bennett's convention is to mark shorts with U-shaped marks, longs with bars, and those where either is correct with both symbols. Feet are separated by vertical lines, and a double vertical line marks a definite recurrent caesura, or break. What is being notated here is length, duration, or quantity of the syllable, not stress or accent. Also, this is a musical pattern, a tempo, borrowed from Greek songs, and not a rhythm natural to Latin.

$$\underset{\smile}{-} \mid -\smile \mid -- \parallel -\smile\smile \mid -\smile \mid \overset{\smile}{-} \text{ (twice)}$$

$$\smile \mid -\smile \mid -- \mid -\smile \mid -\overset{\smile}{-}$$

$$-\smile\smile \mid -\smile\smile \mid -\smile \mid -\overset{\smile}{-}$$

To get a feel for the actual ebb and flow of quantity in Latin poetry (and to see where Bennett went wrong, as well), one might read a stanza or two of Tennyson's "Experiment in Quantity," the alcaics entitled "Milton." The best way is to read this aloud, making an effort to keep the quantitative rhythm going

DAH DAH di DAH DAH ‖ DAH di di DAH di DAH

or

♩　　♩　♪　♩　　♩　　　♩　♪♪　♩　♪　♩

for the first two lines of each stanza:

> O mighty-mouth'd inventor of harmonies,
> O skill'd to sing of Time or Eternity,
>   God-gifted organ voice of England,
>   Milton, a name to resound for ages;

> Whose Titan angels, Gabriel, Abdiel,
> Starr'd from Jehovah's gorgeous armories,
>   Tower, as the deep-domed empyrean
>   Rings to the roar of an angel onset!

> Me rather all that bowery loneliness,
> The brooks of Eden mazily murmuring,
>   And bloom profuse and cedar arches
>   Charm, as a wanderer out in ocean,

> Where some refulgent sunset of India
> Streams o'er a rich ambrosial ocean isle,
>   And crimson-hued the stately palm-woods
>   Whisper in odorous heights of even.

The paradigm that appears above, before Tennyson's poem, is explicitly connected by Bennett with Ode 1.9, the "Soractian Ode." But actual scansion of that poem reveals that without exception the isolated syllable, or anacrusis, found at the beginning of the third line of each strophe is long, not short. Also long are almost all the anacrustic first syllables of the first two lines in each stanza. Bennett's diagram, then, is not accurate for the Soractian Ode; neither does Tennyson's poem follow it exactly, making the first syllable of each stanza's third line long (as in "God-gifted organ voice of England"), and also consistently beginning the first two lines of each stanza with a long. *Long*, not *stressed*: in the line beginning "The brooks of Eden," the word "The," which almost never takes a stress in English poetry—certainly not here—is lengthened in quantity by having it surrounded by three consonants. Tennyson did not risk this particular line, however, until he had got his quantitative pattern well established.

Bennett's scansion is included here because many readers first encounter the alcaic in his edition and the scansion is still there to mislead a casual student of Horace. Other scansions have been more accurate; here is William Ross Hardie's diagram (260):

$$\overset{\smile}{\bar{}}\; \bar{}\; \smile\; \bar{}\; \bar{}\; |\; \bar{}\; \smile\; \smile\; \bar{}\; \smile\; \smile$$

$$\overset{\smile}{\bar{}}\; \bar{}\; \smile\; \bar{}\; \bar{}\; |\; \bar{}\; \smile\; \smile\; \bar{}\; \smile\; \smile$$

$$\overset{\smile}{\bar{}}\; \bar{}\; \smile\; \bar{}\; \bar{}\; \bar{}\; \overset{\smile}{\bar{}}$$

$$\bar{}\; \smile\; \smile\; \bar{}\; \smile\; \smile\; \bar{}\; \smile\; \overset{\smile}{\bar{}}$$

Useful as Hardie's version may be, though, there does seem some value in recognizing the breaks—be they caesuras or diaereses—in the first two lines of each stanza, and some value in marking off feet, rather than dipodies (units of two feet) or metrons (units of three to six syllables).

I have therefore scanned the Soractian Ode as follows:

ˇ|– ˇ |– – ‖ – ˇ ˇ –|– ˇ | ˇ
Vides ut alta stet nive candidum
–|– ˇ| – – ‖ – ˇˇ–|– ˇ |ˇ
Soracte, nec iam sustineant onus
– |– ˇ|– – |– ˇ|– ˇ
silvae laborantes, geluque
– ˇ ˇ|– ˇ ˇ|– ˇ|– –
flumina constiterint acuto?

– |– ˇ|– – ‖– ˇ ˇ|– ˇ|–
dissolve frigus ligna super foco
– | –ˇ|– – ‖– ˇ ˇ|– ˇ|–
large reponens atque benignius
– |– ˇ| – – |– ˇ|– –
deprome quadrimum Sabina
– ˇ ˇ|– ˇ ˇ| – ˇ|– –
o Thaliarche, merum diota.

–| – ˇ|– – ‖ –ˇ ˇ| – ˇ |ˇ
permitte divis cetera, qui simul
– |– ˇ |– – ‖– ˇ ˇ|– ˇ |–
stravere ventos aequore fervido

– | – –|– –| – – ~ | – –
deproeliantes, nec cupressi

– ~ –|– ~~ |– –| – –
nec veteres agitantur orni.

– |– ~ | – – ‖ – ~ ~ –| – ~ | ~
quid sit futurum cras, fuge quaerere et

– |– ~ |–– ‖ – ~ ~ –|– ~ | –
quem Fors dierum cumque dabit, lucro

– |– ~ | – –|– ~ | – –
appone nec dulces amores

– ~ ~ |– ~ ~ |– ~ |––
sperne puer neque tu choreas,

– |– ~ |– –|– ‖ – ~~|– ~ |–
donec virenti canities abest

–|– ~ |– – ‖ – ~ ~ –|– ~ |–
morosa nunc et campus et areae

–|– ~ | – – | – ~ |– –
lenesque sub noctem susurri

– ~ –|– ~~ |– ~ | ––
composita repetantur hora,

– | – ~ |– – ‖|– ~ ~ –|– ~ |–
nunc et latentis proditor intumo

– |– ~|–– ‖ –~ ~ | – ~ |–
gratus puella risus ab angulo

– |– ~ |– – | – ~ |– –
pignusque dereptum lacertis

– ~ ~ |– ~ ~ |– ~ ~ |––
aut digito male pertinaci.

[Do you see how Soracte stands glistening with deep snow, how the struggling forest no longer holds up the burden, and how the streams freeze up with the sharp cold?

Melt the cold, piling wood on the hearth and, more generously, get out the four-year-old wine in the Sabine jar, Thaliarchus!

Leave the rest to the gods who, soon as they have calmed the winds that make the ocean seethe with their struggling, neither the cypresses nor the ancient ashe trees are stirred.

Avoid asking what tomorrow will bring, and reckon each day that
   Luck sends you as added profit, and do not disdain sweet love and
   dancing, my young friend, in your green years,

as long as gloomy age is far away, let the park and the piazzas be visited
   now with gentle whispers at the agreed twilight meeting time,

now seek out the pleasing tell-tale laugh of the girl hiding in the angle
   of the street, the love-token snatched from her arm or her finger
   which scarcely resists.]

Critical commentary on this poem usually neglects the metrics and settles
on the issue of whether it consistently develops its subject. One reads indig-
nant objections to the idea of sending some young man out into the streets in
the dead of winter in hopes of picking up a girl, or suggestions that Horace
simply meandered away from his original intention of evoking a winter landscape and contrasting it with the consolations of a roaring fire and a drink.
Others, more sensibly, suggest that as Horace turns from himself to his young
friend he imagines a more hospitable season—of life as well as the year—when
the perils of senescent hypothermia are less threatening.

In the first stanza, Horace shares the exhilaration of a crisp winter scene. He
gives us a familiar landscape transformed by the snow, which adds an Alpine
excitement and novelty to what is really only a relatively modest peak on the
outskirts of Rome. There is in this just a hint of metaphor (age as the season of
snow)—or perhaps the metaphorical possibility only emerges as the poem
develops. The reference to storms on sea and land remind us that we could
well find ourselves in natural situations even more inhospitable to human
comfort than a quiet winter day in Rome. The transition to an imagined
springtime tryst in the last two stanzas is not as great a departure from the
winter scene as it may seem. We are listening to the voice of the poet in
conversation with his friend, and as in an actual conversation he allows himself
to make transitions that are guided more by what he wishes to communicate
than by some internal imagistic or thematic consistency. The entire speech is
also modulated by a complex interplay of metrics and natural speech; it is a
poetic performance despite its apparent casualness. I continue this argument
in the Appendix, where one may find a more detailed analysis of exactly how
the natural emphases of Latin play against the Greek meter.

In its highest development, then, Latin poetry had used rhythms of Greek
music, or metrical models borrowed therefrom, as part of its structure, although the poem itself was usually not intended for musical performance. The
art of the Latin poem was emergent from Greek *mousike*. This emergence,

however, lasted no longer than the Roman Empire itself. As we will see again with Provençal poetry, large-scale political events are remarkably effective in changing the direction of prosodies along with everything else. The direction of prosody reversed itself in a manner that one might see as analogous to other reversals that characterized the decline of Roman civilization into the so-called dark ages. As we follow the further development of poetry written in Latin, and as we take up the fortunes of languages derived from Latin, we shall see how completely retrograde the movement was, and how in the course of a millennium poetry, music, and even dance once again joined forces and made themselves into a single expressive medium.

2

From Latin Verse to Sacred Song

WELL BEFORE A.D. 1250 lyric poetry—both religious and secular—had again assumed its status as coadjutor to music and in some cases to dance as well. How this came about is not easy to explain. Whether this reunification resulted from the combining of music and words in Church services over the period A.D. 300–1100 is hard to determine; it is equally difficult to know how Church music affected secular songs, or vice-versa. Records of songs in the vernaculars are scarce. In all likelihood there were songs that provided models for the troubadours. James Anderson Winn, among others, assumes such influence:

> [T]heoretical treatises as early as the late ninth century mention *organum*, the practice of singing in parallel fourths, fifths, and octaves, and the earliest troubadour poems we have reveal a highly stylized art, *doubtless the result of centuries of unrecorded tradition* [my italics]. The sequence and the trope, in which text and melody had been closely related, may be connected with the origins of both sacred polyphony and vernacular poetry, but the two arts developed in contrasting and somewhat independent ways. (*Eloquence* 74)

Ruth Ellis Messenger, however, proposes that the hymn, and especially the sequence, were antecedents to popular songs. (The piece of music called the sequence, the nature of which I will explain at greater length, was so named because it followed some other part of the Mass.) Messenger says: "The evidence offered by secular lyrics, Latin or vernacular, in the early Middle Ages points to an outstanding growth from the sequence rather than a creative source for the sequence. As a matter of fact the sequence breaks away from the church and itself becomes secular, as the history of poetry in the later Middle Ages bears witness" (44). John Stevens is likewise quite definite on this subject: "Some of the new 'songs' [additions to the liturgy in the early Middle Ages] were deeply influential upon the nonliturgical songs which are the main subject of this study. Indeed, some of them—the sequence in particular—were more than merely influential; they provided models, often actual melodies, for so-called secular songs" (*Words and Music* 80).

Again, Winn offers a point of view that conflicts with this to some degree:

Some patterns of rhyming and other kinds of repetition in the secular poems bear a family resemblance to such patterns in sequences and *versus* forms, but it is not possible to show a precise evolutionary development of the troubadour and trouvère forms out of earlier combinations of Latin poetry and music. The music of secular Latin songs might provide some hints, but too little of it is accessible to us: even the well-known thirteenth-century codex called *Carmina Burana* shows the music in indecipherable neumes, so we are able to reconstruct only a few melodies from later sources. Surveying this meager harvest, J. A. Westrup [*The New Oxford History of Music*] concludes that "no valid distinction can be made between the religious and secular Latin songs of this period; the same types of melody, the same forms occur in both." (*Eloquence* 77)

In support of Winn's position one may quote Richard Leighton Greene, whose profound immersion in the popular literature of England qualified him to speak with authority:

The tendency in Goliardic verse to irreverent parody, of which so much has been made, must not be allowed to obscure the probability of its having acted as a transmitting medium for the influence operating in the other direction, from vernacular folklyric to sacred Latin. Surely the authors of the Nativity songs (just quoted) knew well the accent of amorous student songs!

One of the most telling pieces of evidence for the fact that medieval Latin lyrics were sometimes indebted for their verse-form to popular songs in the vernacular is provided by the "Red Book of Ossory" now in the Episcopal Palace at Kilkenny. The collection of religious *cantilenae* in this manuscript was composed by a bishop for his clerks to replace light and worldly songs, and at least those Latin pieces which have the tunes indicated by a few lines of English or French songs must be in the verse-form of the vernacular lyrics. (xci)

Nowhere is the problem of defining the nature and identifying the source of various kinds of medieval song more confusing than in discussions of the *conductus*. This word is applied to all sorts of vocal music from the eleventh to the thirteenth century, and its meanings are multifarious. The consensus is that the *conductus* originated as a description of a liturgical function—that it was something sung while someone or something was being conducted from one place to another; perhaps, for example, it preceded the reading of the lesson and was sung while the reader approached the lectern. But the word apparently metamorphosed into a purely musical term, as did "sequence." Earlier *conductu* were monophonic; later examples were polyphonic. Some were sacred; some were secular, but full of pious sentiment; and some were purely secular. Some authorities insist that a fundamental property of the *conductus* was that it was an original musical composition; some assert that these sacred pieces were imitated from the secular, and some the reverse—as we have just seen argued in connection with the sequence. Examples of such conflicting discussions follow, beginning with Donald Jay Grout's:

> Another kind of monophonic song written in the period from the eleventh to the thirteenth century is the *conductus*. Conducti are outstanding illustrations of how vague the dividing line was between sacred and secular in the Middle Ages. . . . [T]heir connection with the liturgy was so tenuous that by the end of the twelfth century the term *conductus* was applied to any non-liturgical Latin song, generally of a serious character, with a metrical text, on either a sacred or a secular subject. One important feature of the conductus was that, as a rule, its melody was newly composed, instead of being borrowed or adapted from Gregorian chant or some other source. (64)

John Stevens more or less agrees, except for the grammar of the word:

> Roughly speaking, the historical shift is from functional definition, *c.* 1100, to broader generic uses during the twelfth century; first religious, or at least serious, secular song; eventually secular dance and love-song. I use the form *conductus*, *conductūs* (fourth declension) following classical usage (see also Arlt); the form *conductus*, *conducti* (second) is common in the Middle Ages. (*Words and Music* 50 n9)

But should not a piece of music that is permitted to accompany an action in the Mass be called liturgical, even if not recognized as an essential part ("tenuous," according to Grout) of the Mass?

Harper's Dictionary of Music calls the *conductus* "a type of song of the eleventh to thirteenth centuries. Its text was a poem in the Latin language, religious or secular (nonreligious) in subject, and its music was not, like that of most other medieval musical forms, based upon a pre-existing melody." Richard Leighton Greene was of a contrary opinion:

> A "condute," Latin *conductus*, was a two-, three- or four-part song of which not all parts were furnished with words. Its distinctive feature was that the melody of the tenor, if not an original theme, was taken from popular song and not from ecclesiastical music as in most other part-songs, such as rotas or motets. (xix)

Theodore M. Finney's *A History of Music* provides further modifications and differences:

> [The *conductus*] was differentiated from all of the other learned forms of the period by the fact that the tenor part was not a plain-song melody but was, on the contrary, either a composed subject or a secular tune. The latter was

more often the case. It is important to remark here both that the influence of secular song was beginning to make itself felt and that a practice which gained great momentum in the succeeding two centuries, namely, that of using a secular melody for the subject around which a sacred composition was built, here comes to our notice for the first time. (104)

The problem of understanding what is meant by *conductus*, then, is complicated for several reasons:

1. The word originally identified a liturgical function, not a type of music.
2. *Conductus* continued to be used as music itself became more complex, monophonic compositions giving way to polyphony, so that it was applied to compositions that differed greatly from one another.
3. The word was also applied to different kinds of music in different geographical locations, at different times, and in different contexts.
4. Musicologists have attempted to use discussions of the *conductus*, as well as references to it, that date from the Middle Ages, and in so doing have modified the meaning of the word in various ways that depend not only on differences between the original discussions and references, but also on differing interpretations of those original comments.

Some recent discussions converge toward the view that the *conductus* originated in southern France simultaneously with the vernacular songs of the troubadours, and was the expression within the Church of a similar impulse toward original composition. A rhythmic and rhyming text in Latin was set to music; both text and music were essentially different from established hymns and chants. The occasion or opportunity for the composition was some moment of transition within the Mass. As compositional technique became more complex, the *conductus* as a piece of music tended to separate itself from the words and may even have become instrumental rather than vocal (see Winn, *Eloquence* 96–97; D. F. Wilson 182–83; Cattin 112, 153). All these discussions still leave unresolved the question of the relation of sacred to secular, of Latin to vernacular. Happily for my purposes precedence is much less important than the fact that, for both sacred and secular songs, melody and text became inseparable.

Whatever the source and nature of the *conductus*, that the sacred and the secular were not very different from one another is clear in Carleton Brown's charming retelling of a much-cited story recounted by Giraldus Cambrensis:

Before the close of the twelfth century, as we are told by Gerald of Wales, the folk were accustomed to sing as they danced in the churchyards. In the *Gemma Ecclesiastica* he tells the story of a parish priest in Worcestershire who had been kept awake all night by these churchyard dancers so that when he began the early morning service, instead of the usual "Dominus vobiscum," he startled his congregation by singing the refrain which had been ringing in his ears, "Swete lamman dhin are." [Sweet mistress, thy grace] So great was the scandal caused by this slip that Bishop Northall (1184–90) pronounced an anathema upon any person who should ever again sing that song within the limits of his diocese. (xi)

In order to trace the fusion of word and music that occurred and to consider the role of the Church in bringing this about, we now turn back again to ancient times and to Latin poetry. Although the evidence is scanty, there are those who argue that the accentual rhythms of archaic Latin never really died out and were preserved in popular songs, including coarse "soldiers' songs" that the Roman legions sang while on the march. Greene was quite definite in his arguments for this survival:

> In the years when the literary lyric was coming to light in the vernacular tongues of medieval Europe, there existed another important tradition of lyric poetry which must not be overlooked because of its almost complete disappearance in modern times. This was the tradition of accentual Latin verse, which had risen with the lapse of turbulent centuries from the low estate of labourer's chant or soldier's marching song to the highest possible use, the service of God. Like the other expressions of medieval Latinity, it took little heed of boundary lines or of national cultures; it shared the universality of the Church by whose servants it was mainly fostered. It could, and did, flourish undisturbed in England while the Germanic speech of the island was assimilating huge doses of Roman vocables and rhythms. (lx)

But before this could occur there had been further transformations of Latin prosody, which had always tended toward a refinement that distanced it from ordinary speech. William Ross Hardie offers explanations, remarkable for their succinctness and clarity, of what happened in Roman verse:

> In this period [the Golden Age, first century B.C.], as in the earlier one, the Romans modify Greek forms of verse to suit their own language. But now the modifications are *within* Greek rules and involve hardly any transgression of them. New laws are imposed. Horace enacts a number of new rules for his lyric metres, sometimes obeying them with absolute uniformity, sometimes deviating once or twice from his rule, as if to show that it is after all only an enactment of his own. . . . Horace's rules, as far as we know, were regarded by his successors as absolutely binding. Statius [ca. A.D. 61–96] was not free to write an Alcaic line [like one of Horace's]. (208)

Hardie goes on to argue that precisely because the later poets were metrical imitators of the Golden Age poets, they were more rigid in their versification. Even by the time that Virgil set about condensing elements of the *Iliad* and the

Odyssey into his own epic, earlier Latin imitators of Homer had produced works much more mechanically perfect than Homer had ever been. Hardie also contends that the very existence of a stress accent in ordinary Latin made it necessary for later poets to impose strict rules on their poetic language:

> A second cause [of this strictness] was undoubtedly the nature of the Latin language, its fibre or texture, and in particular the nature and incidence of its accent. A stress accent, even though slight, came into competition with the ictus or beat of the verse, as the Greek accent did not. . . . It seems certain that the more complex and variable types of Greek lyric were found to be unworkable in Latin. The language could not be poured into moulds so exact and so elaborate. The reader could not follow so subtle a structure, partly because the Latin accent would lead him astray. The Latin accent also had perplexing effects upon quantity. (209–10)

The first century of the Christian era, the so-called Silver Age of Latin poetry, saw the cultivation of new modes, such as the satires of Persius and the epigrams of Martial, as well as attempts to replicate the earlier achievements, as in Statius's epic, the *Thebaid*. The metric of the poets, however, was now at a double remove from the original Greek models and, rather than representing an accommodation of native Latin to an imported musical scheme, had become more an effort at *correctness* according to the examples of Horace, Virgil, and Ovid. The Silver Age was, furthermore, increasingly an age of criticism, even what we might call literary theory—although the full expression of that tendency only unfolded in the two succeeding centuries. Latin use of Greek models, as we have noted, had from the start resulted in a poetry that was more strictly controlled than the original Greek had been; with the prescriptions that Horace codified in his *Ars Poetica* to look back upon, later Latin poets became even more careful about observing the rules. One may trace comparable developments in English and American metrics—such as the excessive regularity of much late sixteenth-century English poetry (especially Gascoigne's pentameters), the high polish and restraint of eighteenth-century couplets, and in our own times the recidivism of the New Formalists in the direction of Longfellow. In each of these situations adherence to a preestablished metrical standard at times resulted in poetry that was more meticulously regulated than the examples it was emulating.

Coinciding with the ossification of Latin meters were theoretical discussions in which metrics were anatomized to the point of extinction. Prosody, as an extension of grammatical studies, had begun to flourish in the schools of Alexandria during Hellenistic times and achieved degrees of subtle elaboration never equaled since. It was at this time that the concept of the poetic foot was first employed, and that the system of marking syllables still found in handbooks and prosodic introductions was invented. A manuscript dating from the ninth century includes a short discussion of poetic feet by an author identified there (but otherwise unknown) as Julius Severus. Severus uses the notation that is still familiar: macrons and breves, longs and shorts. To judge from references in the text, Severus was writing at the end of the fourth century; his treatise, then, was contemporaneous with Augustine's *De musica*, which did not use symbols for scansion. But Hephaestion may have done so; in his *Enchiridion* itself the markings do not appear, but in a marginal gloss, or scholium, they seem to have been used.

Even after the fall of the Western Empire, on into the fifth and sixth centuries, poets continued to produce works in those quantitative meters that had long been separated from musical associations—a separation that was paralleled by the distancing of literary language from ordinary speech. In these later times, every generation saw the composition of some new concoction in hexameters. There was also a great deal of experimentation in applying other quantitative meters to subjects for which they had previously been thought inappropriate, such as pastoral poetry written in iambics. As often happens when a vigorous culture is protracted into decadence, there were increasingly intricate displays of poetic technique, such as anagrams and shaped poetry. If there was anything resembling twentieth-century free verse, however, it does not seem to have survived.

Between A.D. 500 and 800, literary Latin ceased to have any connections with the vernaculars. The spoken language underwent a linguistic diaspora, first differentiating into dialects and then into many independent Romance tongues. The phonological transformations that occurred were of such complexity that a lifetime could be spent in tracing the evolution of a single dialect. In *The French Language*, Alfred Ewert devotes eighty pages to the shifts that occurred as vulgar Latin ramified into the languages of northern France. The modest *Chrestomathie du Moyen Age*, a pocket-sized volume edited by Gaston Paris and E. Langlois, contains only 366 pages of poetry and prose, but more than eighty pages of succinct explanation of Old French grammar and phonology, much of it in terms of its derivation from Latin. Preservation of Latin as the official medium of the Church, and as the repository of Roman high culture, actually hastened its transformation as a spoken language. That is, serious writers continued to use Latin rather than the vernaculars, which were left to go their own illiterate ways. Any language not stabilized by a written literature evolves and subdivides very rapidly. This occurred with the vulgar Latin dialects, each of which rapidly developed its own idiosyncrasies until the speakers could no longer understand one another. Only Sardinian, protected by its literal isolation, remained close to what had been spoken when Horace and Virgil were alive. Even within what we think of now as a single country, barriers to oral communication could be severe; Provençal—the *langue d'oc*—was almost as different from the *langue d'oïl* of northern France as English is from Dutch. The presence of a definite frontier—whether political or geographical—encouraged radical divergences; Portuguese is more remote from Spanish than many people imagine.

It seems altogether likely that during these centuries the human habit of making up words for melodies or melodies for words never died out anywhere, and that cultural fragmentation left the way open for new developments untainted by literary tradition. Untainted, that is, by Greek or Roman high culture. Hymns modeled—possibly—on Latin vernacular poetry made their way into the liturgy of the Church early on as part of an effort to involve congregations in the services, and many have argued that this liturgical poetry eventually did serve, hundreds of years later, as a model for writers in the vernaculars. Although sacred poems were composed in the established quantitative meters on into the fifth and sixth centuries, their actual rhythm—as distinguished from whatever quantitative patterns they may have satisfied— was closer to rhythms of vulgar Latin than to rhythms of literary compositions. It seems probable that Christian congregations could not easily be led to make passionate and personal statements of their faith in the Greek-based meters of Catullus. Christianity was in any case inimical to Roman sophistication, and the languages of Christianity were at first those spoken by ordinary people. At the risk of repeating the point too often, we may note that spoken Latin was originally, and continued to be, a more accentual language than a study of classical literary Latin might lead one to believe. Some of the earliest compositions in Latin for Christian services were composed in accentual iambs or trochees, even though those who invented the hymns did not recognize this accentuality and in most cases continued to observe quantitative values as well.

Perhaps it is useful to restate and clarify the above developments and relationships in a more schematic way:

1. Hymns composed for use in Christian services, beginning about A.D. 350, often made use of classical quantitative meters, but showed a tendency to revert to the accentual rhythm that was naturally present in spoken vulgar Latin, perhaps even being modeled on secular songs current at that time.

2. As the Roman Empire fell apart, and especially after A.D. 500, vulgar Latin broke up and disseminated itself in a variety of dialects, some of which became modern Romance languages. Whatever songs or poems may have existed in these dialects do not survive, though references to such popular literature exist.

3. Meanwhile, well-educated writers, both secular and religious, continued to employ the language and poetic forms of classical Latin literature; they produced little of lasting value, but as Latin ceased to be the spoken language of ordinary people, and became instead the universal language of the Church, such literary efforts, together with the reading of the classics, did enrich this ecclesiastical tongue. Serving as the international language of scholarship in the Middle Ages, it did in some sense remain a living language, and still does. Even in the mid-twentieth century, when an American scholar found himself in a train compartment with a Catholic priest with whom he shared no modern language, they managed to communicate in Latin.

4. Hymns in this Church Latin continued to be composed over the entire thousand-year period (350–1350), and the earliest efforts at conscious poetic composition in Romance vernaculars—and, by imitation, of those in Germanic ones as well—could use these hymns as models. In a sense, then, Church Latin could have provided the medium whereby some remnants of popular culture were preserved and transmitted from Roman times, providing the basis for new popular literatures of the Middle Ages, with the intermediate steps of Goliardic verse and student songs such as "Gaudeamus Igitur."

5. The thousand-year association of strophic hymns with music in Christian services, then, achieved a reimmersion of poetry into music—and even helped to make possible a merger once again with dance. In the absence of written versions of vernacular poetry (in the Romance languages) before the twelfth century, one can only speculate on how well such poetry survived and provided a continuous oral tradition.

The earliest hymns attributed to a specific person are those of Hilary, Bishop of Poitiers (ca. 310–366). These are so long and complex that they could not have been meant for congregational participation, yet the rhythm lends itself easily to melodies familiar even today. In the terminology of English poetry, each line is an unrhymed catalectic trochaic octameter, with accentual stresses like those of Tennyson's "Locksley Hall":

/ ⌣ / ⌣ / ⌣ / ⌣ / ⌣ / ⌣ / ⌣ /
Comrades, leave me here a little, while as yet 'tis early morn

The first line of a hymn attributed to Hilary is:

/ ⌣ / ⌣ / ⌣ / ⌣ / ⌣ / ⌣ / ⌣ /
Hymnum dicat turba fratrum, hymnum cantus personet.

[The brotherly throngs sing hymns, their singing makes the hymns resound]

The passage is marked this way because the placement of accents does correspond fairly well with the penultimate law of Latin pronunciation discussed in the preceding chapter. Another way of describing the line is to call it trochaic tetrameter catalectic, using the concept of the *metron* as the unit rather than the foot (see below). One could also treat it as divisible into two lines, as in the Anglican hymn,

> Christ is made the sure foundation,
> Christ the head and cornerstone.

The first hymns composed for congregations were those of St. Ambrose; "Deus creator omnium" is one of four that are universally attributed to him:

Deus creator omnium	God, the creator of everything,
polique rector, uestiens	governor of the axis of the heavens, adorning
diem decoro lumine,	day with comely light,
noctem soporis gratia,	night with the gracious gift of sleep
artus solutos ut quies	that peace may restore relaxed limbs
reddat laboris usui,	to enjoyment of labor,
mentesque fessas alleuet	and relieve weary minds,
luctusque soluat anxios,	and disperse tormenting grief,
grates peracto iam die	thanks, now that day is over,
et noctis exortu preces,	and prayers, as night is falling,
uoti reos ut adiuues,	that you help those bound by vow
hymnum canentes soluimus.	we repay, singing hymns.
te cordis ima concinant,	You, from the depths of the heart, let them praise;
te uox canora concrepet,	you, let the harmonious voice loudly exalt;
te diligat castus amor,	you, let chaste love choose above all;
te mens adoret sobria:	you, let the sober mind adore:
ut cum profunda clauserit	as when the deep gloom of night closes
diem caligo noctium,	the day,
fides tenebras nesciat	faith knows no shadows
et nox fide reluceat.	and night is radiant with faith.
dormire mentem ne sinas,	Let not the soul fall asleep,
dormire culpa nouerit,	to sleep would renew guilt,
castis fides refrigerans	let faith, cooling the chaste,
somni uaporum temperet.	temper the hot fumes of sleep.
exuta sensu lubrico	Having put aside sensual dangers,
te cordis ima somnient,	let them dream of you from depths of their hearts,

nec hostis inuidi dolo	nor let fearsome quaking from the deceit
pauor quietos suscitet.	of the hateful enemy disturb the peace.

Christum rogemus et Patrem,	Let us pray to Christ and the Father,
Christi Patrisque Spiritum,	to the Spirit of the Christ and the Father,
unum potens per omnia,	one all-powerful power,
foue precantes, Trinitas.	hover round us as we pray, great Trinity.

(Latin text from Walpole 46–49)

In contrast with the complexity of scansion in Horace, the Ambrosian hymn appears at first to many English readers simplicity itself, and seems scannable throughout with the use of accentual iambic feet:

⏑ / ⏑/⏑ / ⏑/
Deus creator omnium
⏑ / ⏑ / ⏑ /⏑ /
polique rector, uestiens
⏑/ ⏑ / ⏑ / ⏑/
diem decoro lumine,
⏑ / ⏑ /⏑ / ⏑/
noctem soporis gratia.

The words seem designed to be sung to some simple melody, and the whole hymn is short enough to be easily memorized. Many have offered the reasonable supposition, mentioned above, that the melody was either borrowed from a popular tune or modeled on one. Those who wish to believe that the stressed syllables were also lengthened argue that it could have been a 3/4 rhythm:

♩♩ ♩♩♩ ♩♩♩

Deus creator omnium

Such a musical scansion could also be applied to Hilary's hymn—reversing the placement of the quarter and half notes, of course.

And yet, despite what one might imagine at first, the scansion of these hymns by Hilary and Ambrose is not nearly that simple. Such a metrical reading of them is possible, as is evident from James Anderson Winn's statement about Ambrose's hymns: "Each consists of 32 lines in a meter the ancients called iambic dimeter, but which we would consider tetrameter: it consists of alternating spondees and iambs; an iamb may substitute for a spondee, but not *vice versa*; the normal pattern is $|--|\smile-|--|\smile-$" (*Eloquence* 27). But William Beare argues:

It is a striking fact that the first Latin hymns which secured wide popularity were not those written in the rhythmic measures or influenced by them, but

those which followed the strictest rules of quantity. The best-authenticated
hymns of Ambrose are purely metrical; they obey the Dipodic law; they
show elision, not hiatus; there is no sign of an attempt to make the word-
accent coincide with the metrical beat, either in the interior or even at the
end of the line. (228–29)

In order to make clear what Beare means, and to explain an additional comment by A. S. Walpole, we must take up the definition of dipody in classical
verse. The term literally means "two feet," and refers to the concept of line-
measurement in Greek verse in terms of the *metron*, which could have more
than one foot in it. A *metron* of four syllables would be either iambic or trochaic; the notion of employing the *metron*, rather than the foot, resulted from
the frequent substitution of the spondee, two longs, in place of either an iamb
or a trochee. In order to define the true character of the line it was helpful to
think of it as composed of units containing at least one definite iamb or trochee
in the second position. In each four-syllable *metron* there were two possibilities
(for example, ˘ – ˘ – or – – ˘ – for iambic; and – ˘ – ˘ or – – – ˘ for trochaic).

In common English foot-based prosody, when we say "iambic dimeter" we
mean a line based on the recurrent pattern of two iambic feet. But often
enough in discussions of classical meters "iambic dimeter" designates a line
made up of two iambic *metra*; such a line in English accentual meter would be
called iambic tetrameter. This is the meaning when Walpole writes, "In the
next place we note that the four hymns were all written in the 'Ambrosian'
metre, the *iambic dimeter* as it is called. The laws of metre are carefully observed,
almost as carefully as they had been observed by the great metrists Vergil,
Horace, and Martial" (23). How are we to reconcile the insistence of these
authorities on the obedience of Ambrosian metrics to classical rules with the
widespread perception that stress values did matter in these early hymns and
were even more important in later ones? One of the authorities quoted by
Beare—a very great authority, none other than Gaston Paris—states this quite
forcefully:

[L]a quantité s'effaçant peu à peu à l'époque de la décadence, et son af-
faiblissement rendant l'accentuation de plus en plus marquée, on imagina de
faire des vers où on calquait les vers métriques en substituant des accentuées
aux longues (dans les temps fort), et ce fut grâce à ces essais que la versification nouvelle prit conscience d'elle-même, et, se dégageant de ces imitations
serviles, finit par créer ses propre lois. (*Lettre à M. Léon Gautier* 23, qtd. in
Beare 211)

[Quantity faded away little by little in the decadent period, and its weakening made syllable-stress more and more noticeable; they got the idea of

regulating metrical lines by substituting stresses for long syllables (in the strong positions), and it was thanks to these attempts that the new versification became aware of itself and, breaking away from servile imitation, ended by creating its own rules.]

In "Deus creator omnium," perhaps exactly *because* Ambrose was observing the rules of quantitative composition, most lines lead off smoothly with two long syllables, but then break into a graceful variation of iambs and spondees that have a distinctly accentual lilt to them. It is hard to guess to what extent one is imposing retrospectively something like the rhythm in Yeats's "The Song of Wandering Angus," a poem that, as it happens, accommodates itself with great loveliness to a melody commonly attached to "Veni Creator Spiritus."

> I went out to the hazel wood
> Because a fire was in my head,
> And cut and peeled a hazel wand,
> And hooked a berry to a thread. . . .

Yeats deaccentualized his meter in this poem, partly by using a preponderance of monosyllabic words; also, many of the lines begin with two syllables that carry as much duration as one can muster in English, and then riffle into a series of shorts and longs. Ambrose took his metric in the other direction, allowing just enough accentualism to intrude on the iambic dipodies to lend them an air of effortless beauty.

A third way of looking at Ambrose's hymn is to consider it simply as composed of eight-syllable lines, with each syllable intended to be sung to a single note. This view, as we will see, is also helpful in that Church Latin, especially as employed in France, partook more and more of the syllabic leveling that occurred in Provençal and in the dialects of northern France.

However we scan it, poetry here was immersing itself again into music, abandoning its status as an independent art, and putting itself in the service of religious doctrine. For these earliest hymns it is not known for sure which music the words were meant to go with; if any effort was made to devise a notation to record the music, such notations did not survive. Some scholars have suggested that melodies suitable for strophic poems could have been carried in from Hebrew liturgy or from other sources in the East; Ruth Ellis Messenger argues that both Hilary and Ambrose were familiar with hymns used in Syria as part of the liturgy, where their purpose was to promote the Arian cause (which denied doctrine of the Trinity), and that orthodox Christian hymns could serve similar propagandistic purposes (1–3). Even the short hymn quoted above ends with a restatement of the orthodox view on that subject, evincing Ambrose's purpose that it be a reminder to the faithful of what the orthodox view should be. In addition to popular, Hebrew, and Syrian sources there could have been "the creation of hymns under the inspiration of strong religious feeling, somewhat the way today new phrases of text and new melodic variations spontaneously arise during the enthusiasm of a revival meeting or a folk sing" (Grout 19). There is no end to the suggestions for sources of early hymn melodies; others have mentioned Greek, Egyptian, and Byzantine models. Whatever it was, the melody ought to have been easily singable and pleasing. Certain imaginative reconstructions available in our own time betray the musicological prejudices of the arranger as to whether there were Syrian, Jewish, or Arabic influences at work in the original melodies; such performances are simply unpleasing and tedious to listen to—unlike Gregorian chants that seem to be authentically continuous with the distant past, or later medieval works for which reliable notations are available. It is hard to imagine Ambrose's congregation wailing his strophes with the same effect as a muezzin giving a prayer call.

Although the hymns were subordinate to the purposes of religion, their texts could achieve a grandeur in keeping with their subjects, especially in their later development. "Veni Creator Spiritus," which probably dates from the tenth century and which has exhilarated generation upon generation of worshipers, fits the Ambrosian metrical paradigm perfectly. "No other Latin hymn," wrote A. S. Walpole in his great edition, "except those of the daily offices, has been so frequently and widely used as this. It is the only one which has found its way, in alternative translations, into the English Prayer Book" (374).

> ⌣ / ⌣ / ⌣ / ⌣ /
> Veni creator spiritus
> ⌣ / ⌣ / ⌣ / ⌣ /
> mentes tuorum uisita
> ⌣ / ⌣ / ⌣ / ⌣ /
> imple superna gratia,
> ⌣ / ⌣ / ⌣ / ⌣ /
> quae tu creasti pectora.

The loose and lyrical translation by J. A. Aylward (in the Anglican hymnal) preserves the iambic meter:

> Creator-spirit, all-Divine,
> Come visit every soul of thine,
> And fill with thy celestial flame
> The hearts which thou thyself didst frame.

Other hymns have taken their place among the memorable documents of Western culture. Composers of funeral Masses continue to draw inspiration from Thomas of Celano's thirteenth-century *Dies Irae*, which captures in words the terror of the Day of Judgment graphically depicted in the *tympans* over doors of cathedrals and churches—at Autun, Vézélay, and hundreds of other places. The fourteenth-century *Stabat Mater* expresses verbally the devotion to Mary that showed itself in the painting, and much more beautifully, the statuary of the later Middle Ages. These two great works are akin in metrics both to Hilary and to Ambrose, being in trochaic meter (and with stresses marked to insure the proper pronunciation in the Catholic *Liber Usualis* and *Liber Antiphonarius*).

From the *Dies Irae*:

```
 /  ˘  / ˘    /   ˘  /  ˘
Tuba mirum sparget sonum        The trumpet will scatter its wondrous sound
 /  ˘  /    ˘ /  ˘/ ˘
Per sepulchra regionum,         through the graveyards,
 /  ˘  /    ˘  /  ˘   /  ˘
Coget omnes ante thronum.       will assemble everyone before the throne.
```

From the *Stabat Mater*:

```
 /  ˘  /  ˘   /  ˘/ ˘
Stabat mater dolorosa           The grieving mother stands
 /  ˘  /  ˘    /  ˘ /  ˘
Iuxta crucem lacrimosa          weeping by the cross,
 /    ˘   /  ˘  /˘/
Dum pendebat filius,            while her son hangs there,
 /˘  /˘  /   ˘  /   ˘
Cuius animam gementem,          she whose groaning spirit,
 /  ˘  /  ˘   /  ˘  /  ˘
Contristantem et dolentem,      sorrowing and lamenting,
 /  ˘   /˘  /  ˘ /
Pertransivit gladius.           a sword has pierced through and through.
```

The *Dies Irae* and *Stabat Mater*, although they seem to us to preserve a strophic form not much different from the earliest hymns, are both examples of the sequence (from Latin, *sequentia*). As with the *conductus*, the source and original meaning of this term is uncertain, but may have to do with their placement in the Mass following something else—a sort of musical interpolation. All sorts of speculation attaches to the origins of the sequence—that it was first nothing but a wordless prolongation of the Alleluia, that it was a chant to which words were eventually attached as a help to memorization of the music, and so on. My own experience of having retained, for nearly forty years, the rather complex and nonrecurrent melody of the twelfth-century sequence *Victimae paschali laudes* [Christians, to the Paschal Victim] through association with the words, convinces me that the words could serve that purpose. The verbal part of the first sequences—about the eighth to eleventh centuries—was quite irregular, and was even called the *prosa*, but later sequences employed regular rhymes and settled into repeating strophes. Later settings of the *Dies Irae* and *Stabat Mater* (by Mozart, Verdi, and others) somewhat obscure the fact that their original melodies were more akin to Gregorian chant; but the words of these later sequences make a recurrent strophic pattern. Whatever the precise source of the sequence, it was a wedding of words to music; indeed, by most accounts, it was a coaxing into existence by music of the accompanying poetic expression.

In both sequences illustrated above, the meter is still definitely trochaic (though more flexible in the latter). But in other hymns and sequences from those centuries and earlier the Latin itself was evidently undergoing a shift toward pure syllabism that would later characterize both Italian and French poetry. Sometimes it is hard to tell if there should be any accent at all—or whether there is even an attempt to reintroduce quantity. Along with this incipient syllabism came more regular and even intrusive rhyming, as in this hymn to St. Agatha, which probably dates from the ninth or tenth centuries:

‒ ᵕ ‒ ᵕ ‒ ‒ ᵕ ‒	
Martyris ecce dies Agathae	Behold—the day of Agatha the martyr,
‒ ᵕ ‒ ᵕ ‒ ‒ ᵕ ‒	
virginis emicat eximiae,	the chosen virgin, shines forth,
‒ ᵕ ᵕ ‒ ᵕ ‒ ᵕ ‒	
qua sibi Christus eam sociat,	day when Christ himself married her
‒ ᵕ ᵕ ‒ ᵕ ‒ ‒ ᵕ ᵕ ‒	
et diadema duplex decorat.	and the double crown honored her.

A. S. Walpole said that this "is composed in the metre invented by Prudentius for his poem on St. Eulalia" (392), and Prudentius (348–ca. 405) certainly thought of himself as the legitimate heir of Horace, and as such faithful to the Graeco-Roman metrics. But neither quantity nor stress is as important here as the fact that we have a ten-syllable line, a clear anticipation of the decasyllabics of early Romance vernacular poetry. It was most likely sung in equal time, one note to a syllable.

David Fenwick Wilson, in *Music of the Middle Ages*, gathers hymns under the rubric of what he calls *versus*, and describes the change in this way:

The long and short syllabification of classical Latin had disappeared long before the twelfth century, and both Latin and the Latin-derived dialects of northern and southern France used syllables that were now equal in duration. Poetic attention shifted to the larger concept of line length.

In this new poetic procedure, known as the *ars ritmica*, syllables are all equal in length and are arranged into lines of equal or varying numbers of syllables. Poetic lines are determined by syllable count. The end of each line is distinctly indicated by rhyme and end-of-line accent. (139)

In fact, quantitative scansions continued to be used by those who could read the ancient classics and understand or get some feeling for their metrics. One of a group of Goliardic poems in the collection known as the Cambridge Songs, put together by an English traveler in Germany in about the year 1050, is meant to be written in sapphics:

Vestiunt silve tenera ramorun	[Young thickets wear leafy branches,
virgulta, suis onerata pomis;	heavy with fruit;
canunt de celsis sedibus palumbes	from their high perches the ring-doves
carmina cunctis.	carol their songs.]

The quantitative values of the lines do not match the classical sapphic exactly: "virgulta," for example, ought to have a short second syllable; or if that might seem to be excused because the *l* is liquid, then one can point to "sollempne" in the same position further on in the poem. But the poem is undeniably modeled on the sapphic—and the freedom with which it employs the eleven-syllable line also anticipates what would be done in French and Italian syllabic verse. That is, it seems as much a hendecasyllabic as a sapphic line.

In medieval musical (or poetic) theory, we find a clear continuation of the *metrici* versus *rhythmici* debate from ancient times. The terms change, however. Medieval *ars metrica* continues to concern itself with the quantitative feet of classical scansion (with all the authority offered by the exhaustive treatment by St. Augustine in *De Musica*). *Ars ritmica*, though, ceases to treat more general questions of musicality or expressiveness, or rather, attributes such qualities to verses composed according the syllable count rather than feet. In other words, the emphasis in *ars ritmica*—the rhythm that is considered—was what was to be found in the vernacular and in Latin to the extent that it, too, was treated more in terms of syllable count than quantity. John Stevens's exhaustive account of this duality in *Words and Music in the Middle Ages*, by quoting relevant passages from numerous writers, makes clear that *ars ritmica* concerned itself with the isosyllabic popular poetry; the earliest examples of these that still exist are Provençal troubadour songs. Stevens makes one point that is particularly important to my argument for the reimmersion of poetry into music: "To repeat, the relevance of the two rhythmical traditions, *musica ritmica* and *musica metrica*, is precisely that they are rhythmical traditions, *concerned with the phenomenon of sound in general*, and therefore with song as a unified art, not with poetry or with music alone" (421). Among the many remarkable passages that Stevens instances (416) is this from the Venerable Bede (ca. 673–735), who wrote in *De Arte Metrica*:

> videtur autem rhythmus metris esse consimilis, quae est verborum modulata composito, non metrica ratione, sed numero syllabarum ad iudicium aurium examinata, ut sunt in carmina vulgarium poetarum. et quidem rhythmus per se sine metro esse potest, metrum vero sine rhythmo esse non potest. (Qtd. in Stevens, *Words and Music* 379)

> [Rhythm seems to be exactly like meter, because it is a measured pattern of words, not according to poetic metrics, but carefully considered to satisfy the ear with the number of syllables, as are the songs of the popular poets. And indeed (syllabic) "rhythm" can exist without meter, but in truth meter cannot exist without rhythm.]

Among other things this passage provides evidence for a continuing, though unrecorded, tradition of popular songs that paralleled the church hymns, and perhaps undermines the common argument that when vernacular song reappeared it owed much to the hymn. More likely, songs continued to be composed, or invented, all through the so-called dark ages but do not survive because most literate people were in the Church and did not consider secular productions serious enough to be preserved. What seems a sudden flowering of troubadours, trouvères, and minnesingers might be in part an illusion produced by a willingness in the later Middle Ages finally to write things down in the vernacular. Troubadour poems were themselves, initially and conspicuously, compositions that originated on paper, not written records of a preexisting song—but other earlier songs may have been written down also.

Remarkable in all the citations offered by Stevens of the *metrica / ritmica* duality is a failure during that period (which Stevens points out) to recognize accent or stress as of any importance in organizing the poetry. As we have seen above, stress was in fact important. There are at least three reasons for the failure to recognize the presence of stress or accent. First, earlier metrical discussions by Hephaestion, Augustine, Boethius, and others all hewed programmatically to the various possible combinations of Greek quantitative feet, and seem more intellectual exercises in classification than empirical studies of actual poetic meters, never mentioning stress at all. Second, much classical verse was already isosyllabic; one need point only to the hendecasyllabics of Catullus, which provided a ready-made pattern that suited itself very well to

Dante's Tuscan dialect. Third, stress-pattern in poetry tended to be associated with meters that were either archaic or barbarian—in particular with Germanic languages. Those who thought about metrics, therefore, tried to resolve what was occurring in a given poem (or song) into one or another of the two more civilized possibilities. That is, they preferred to think of themselves either as preserving quantitative scansion, or else as measuring out lines by syllable count. While they were certainly aware of the concept of *ictus* and even of a beat in the poetic line, they did not think of this as being based on natural stress or accent patterns in the language.

Yet much liturgical verse throughout the Middle Ages really was arranged in accentual patterns. Although it is easy to state this as a general truth, it is not easy to lay down rules of the sort that governed classical Latin poetry—definite paradigms that (especially after the example of Horace and Virgil) were known in advance of the composition of the poem. To start with, there was the general reluctance or inability to recognize accent. Next, although Latin was an international medium of communication and although its grammar and semantics approached uniformity, pronunciation of Latin would be affected (as it is today by those who continue to study Latin) by the *lingua vulgaris* of the locale where Latin was being employed. This variance in pronunciation encouraged differing emphases—different stress patterns. One has to think only of differences between American and British pronunciation of English (LAB'ratory and laBORat'ry, for example) to see how Latin must have been spoken differently from place to place. But even after allowing for uncertainty in the specific details of accentualization of medieval Latin, one remains persuaded that the great hymns of that era are in part organized according to stress patterns. As we will see, though, it was not until the later sixteenth century that stress was recognized as the true basis of English poetry, even though it had been composed according to stress for more than a thousand years and even though *Piers Plowman* was regularly mentioned with admiration. Not until Philip Sidney rather casually recognized accent (in *An Apologie for Poetrie*, 1595) did a critic legitimize what Chaucer had already discovered two hundred and fifty years earlier: "Now, of versifying there are two sorts, the one ancient, the other modern: the ancient marked the quantity of each syllable, and according to that framed his verse; the modern observing only number (with some regard to the accent), the chief life of it standeth in that like sounding of the words which we call rime."

Despite the authority of ancient treatises in prosody, then, sacred poetry in Latin gradually abandoned quantitative patterns and became organized more in terms of syllable count and recurrent accentual stress. Another way to put it is that as the vernaculars in various parts of Christendom evolved, the pronunciation of Church Latin was affected by them and by orally preserved musical culture in the vernaculars. Because there are no known texts of secular songs from earlier centuries, discussion of such songs is necessarily speculative. From the year 1100 onward, however, increasing numbers of such texts do survive and provide a more solid basis for tracing connections between secular and sacred songs. We now turn to these.

3

The Transition to Vernacular Song

A CCENT IN Latin liturgical poetry gradually replaced quantity and eventually may have provided models for rhymed verses in English. But this occurrence of accent or stress did not much affect the principles of versification that were eventually cultivated in the vernacular languages derived from Latin.

In Chapters 8–10 of Book 1 of *De Vulgari Eloquentia*, Dante recognized three great subdivisions into which Latin had separated itself, in southern France, northern France, and elsewhere around the Mediterranean, none of which made much use of accent:

> Est igitur super quod gradimur idioma tractando tripharium, ut superius dictum est: nam alii *oc*, alii *sì*, alii vero dicunt *oil*. Et quod unum fuerit a principio confusionis (quod primus probandum est) apparet, quia convenimus in vocabulis multis, velut eloquentes doctores ostendunt: que quidem convenientia ipsi confusioni repugnat, que ruit celitus in edificatione Babel. Trilingues ergo doctores in multis conveniunt, et maxime in hoc vocabulo quod est "amor." (1.9.2–3)

> [Therefore this treatise concerns itself with a threefold set of idioms, as was stated above: for some say *oc*, some *si*, and some *oïl*. And that they were all one before the start of the confusion (as was proven earlier) is clear, because we agree on much of the vocabulary, as eloquent and learned persons demonstrate: which agreement is not in accord with the confusion which fell from heaven during the building of Babel. Scholars in all three languages therefore agree on much of the vocabulary and especially on the word *amor*.]

Although there was much irregularity of syllable-count in some of the earlier epics in these vernaculars, poetry in both Provence (*langue d'oc*) and northern French (*langue d'oïl*) soon settled into predictable syllabic meters. In both Spanish and Italian (the *si* languages) syllabic regularity was also of primary importance, although the metrics did require the placement of at least one accent in each line. Exactly why poets in the Romance languages chose to organize their poems syllabically seems an insoluble question. Were the Romance vernaculars spoken in a more evenly modulated fashion (with less stress-pressure on certain syllables) than Latin had been? Were the poets taking as models those lines in ancient Latin which, in addition to being organized by quantity, were isosyllabic? This last is a very real possibility—particularly when we see W. H. Auden doing the same thing in this century, in English poems, using alcaics and sapphics as if they were syllabic meters.

There are other questions as well. What was the effect of music on the metrics? Were the poems meant to be sung one syllable to the note, as in Latin hymns and plainsong? All the early shorter poems in the Romance vernaculars, and many of the longer ones, were meant for music. That in itself must have influenced the metrics: one cannot sing a poem to musical measures, or design a poem to be sung, without its being affected by the music. There is also the problem of the degree to which the lyrics in, say, early troubadour poetry were rhythmically expressive in addition to, or in spite of, their strict syllabic structure. In explaining the term *vers*, for example, David Fenwick Wilson employs the word "rhythmic" to designate syllabically structured poetry: "*Vers* (Latin *versus*) was the name given by the first troubadours to their poems. It is an early name for a courtly poem in rhymed, rhythmic poetry designed to be sung" (170). Frank M. Chambers announces early in *An Introduction to Old Provençal Versification*, "I shall proceed on the assumption that for Old Provençal (and for French through the classical period), the numerical count of syllables, once established as a pattern, was intended to be rigorously exact" (9). These two statements may seem to be at odds with one another ("rhythmic" not being equivalent to "exact count of syllables"), but really they are not. First, the older meaning of "rhythm" set it against "metrics" or "verse" (in which quantitative values prevailed), so that "rhythmic" can very well apply to lines of poetry composed of equal numbers of syllables. But even if we allow a looser and more modern meaning of "rhythmic" to suggest changes of emphasis rather than equality of syllables, the two statements do not necessarily contradict one another. Anyone who has heard the most classically correct Alexandrines declaimed at the *Comédie Française* knows that the delivery is more rhythmical, in a contemporary sense, than one might be led to believe from classroom instruction in the United States that calls for the rattling off of six syllables at a time; the entire Alexandrine often really sounds more like a series of four anapests than a pair of six-syllable hemistichs.

Another issue to be addressed at this point is the origin of rhyme, which gradually became important in the organization of the hymn and was indispensable in the *vers* and the *canso*, the *pastorela* and the *alba*, of Provençal, as well as in almost all other Romance forms. By the time of the English Renaissance we find Philip Sidney referring to rhyme as, even in English, "the chief life" of verse. Here we are in even more problematic territory: "An accurate and synoptic history of rhyme does not presently exist and would be a daunting task." So T. V. F. Brogan informs us in the article on rhyme in *The New Princeton Encyclopedia of Poetry and Poetics*. Yet perhaps a few points may be made that will be helpful in explaining why, for example, nearly all poetry in English prior to this century (with the obvious exception of blank verse) used rhyme as part of its organization despite the handicap it places on a poet using a rhyme-poor language, as English is.

In the languages that affected English poetry, the first important appearance of rhyme was in Latin hymns, as well as in obscene and blasphemous Goliardic poetry in which hymns were burlesqued. In an inflected language the problem is not so much how to achieve rhyme as how to avoid it; in classical Latin poetry, rhyme's obviousness makes it useful for comic effect—as in Horace's well-known "Parturient montes, nascetur ridiculus mus." [Mountains will be in labor and a ridiculous mouse will be born.] The rhyming echo of the last syllable of "ridiculus" in the one-syllable "mus," which comes immediately after several polysyllabic words, makes a phonetic joke, a sudden diminution imitative of the image by diminution of sound. (The classicist Tom Cole pointed out to me many years ago a similar effect in Ovid's "vulnificus sus" [wound-inflicting pig], where the word "sus" seems to curl on the end of the line like a pig's tail.) In Christian hymns, rhyme was employed seriously and ceased to seem a distracting or vulgar nuisance. English poets have for centuries excused rhyme by calling it an aid to memorization; no doubt it served that purpose in the hymns. The rhyming pattern might also have suggested a sense of mystical correspondences between things, and at least lent the stanzas a sense of closure.

Some have speculated that the accentual character of medieval Latin encouraged rhyming. William Beare, commenting on the work of W. B. Sedgwick in his essay "The Origin of Rhyme" (1924), argues:

> Sedgwick's main point is sound: as long as stress was ignored in verse, modern rhyme, which depends on it, was obviously impossible; it is the recurrence of stress, not of verse-ictus, which is needed for rhyme. When accent began to count in Greek poetry [early in the Christian era], there was no rule that it was not to conflict with the ictus. The Greek accent was of no use for rhyming purposes. (255)

But Beare questions some aspects of Sedgwick's argument:

> Thus for Sedgwick the real beginnings of rhyme as we understand it, harmonizing with stress-accent as supporting the rhythm of the verse, are to be found in about the tenth century. And this is the conclusion of a scholar who

believes that stress-accent played a part in classical Latin verse from earliest times. Much of his argument might be turned to show that accent played no such part in Latin verse until the Middle Ages. He finds that the interaction of music and verse produced rhyme. This is a view which may well be right; but manifestly it puts the origin of rhythmic verse, as we understand the term, many centuries later than the end of the ancient world. (256)

At this point, Beare has confused matters by discussing simultaneously issues that may not be connected, or not connected in ways that he assumes. First, he agrees with Sedgwick that rhyme is impossible in poetry that ignores stress. But according to Reuven Tsur,

> [t]his is utterly irreconcilable with what happens in Mediaeval Hebrew poetry in Spain. The Qassida, adapted from Arabic poetry, is a verse form that is determined by two elements. There is an indefinite number of verse lines the metre of which is quantitative. And there is the "equi-rhyme", or "mono-rhyme": two, or ten, or one hundred, or five hundred lines may rhyme on the same group of sounds. Stress has no task in the prosodic organisation of this kind of verse. Poets have no problem in rhyming even a word like "SEfer" (with the stress on the penultimate syllable) with, e.g., "sapPER" (with the stress on the last syllable). [E-mail posting 13 May 1998 on versification@sizcoll.u-shizuoka-ken.ac.jp]

Also, as we have just been noting, stress or accent is greatly diminished in the Romance languages, especially in French, where rhyme is ubiquitous. It is true that there remains in French a degree of stress or accent on the last syllable of a polysyllabic word, and this may have something to do with the functioning of rhyme in French. In the Italian hendecasyllabic line, the final word carries more stress than the others, and this also coincides with the rhyme. But to state categorically that rhyme cannot exist without stress is at best to say something that needs careful qualification.

Second, Beare argues that Sedgwick is wrong in his view that rhyme originated in the tenth century and that this occurred because "stress accent" had become recognized as a way of organizing a line of poetry. Beare points out that Sedgwick had argued for the presence of accent in Latin poetry. The implication of what Beare says is that rhyme could have appeared long before the tenth century, because "stress accent" was already present in Latin. I remain unconvinced that such an argument even needs to be made.

Third, Beare admits that Sedgwick's view that "the interaction of music and verse produced rhyme" may be correct. When one considers the rhyming stanzas of Ambrose's hymns, one is disposed to agree with this. But for just that reason Beare's contention that "manifestly it puts the origin of rhythmic verse, as we understand the term, many centuries later than the ancient world," seems odd. Suddenly the focus shifts from the question of the origins of rhyme to "rhythmic verse." This is quite another issue. Truly rhythmic Latin verse (syllabically structured and free from classical rules of quantity) only gradually took hold in the centuries after the end of the Roman empire (ca. A.D. 500– 1000). Sedgwick's argument on that point, then, may well be reasonable. Also, although rhyme certainly appeared in both sacred and secular poetry before the tenth century, it sometimes seems as much a decorative addition as a structural essential: rhyme schemes may vary from stanza to stanza, and some- times rhyme may be completely dropped for a line or two. What one had in that period was a quantitative measure that was evolving toward a syllabic or accentual-syllabic measure punctuated by rhyme.

Not only is rhyme not impossible in quantitative meters; it was *avoided* because the plethora of similar word endings in Greek and Latin made it so commonplace that it would have seemed tiresome. Rhyme was associated with rhetoric rather than poetry, being used as means of emphasizing parallel or iterative constructions. Perhaps it might be useful to compare rhyme in classical meters to alliteration in accentual-syllabic English poetry; as we will see, Spenser and Shakespeare (among many others) employed alliteration in narrative poetry to enrich the texture, but did not make regular patterns with it. It is true that Romance languages, especially Italian, retained many more such endings than we have in modern English, and rhymes appear abundantly, at times excessively, in the poetry of those languages; this might seem to be an argument that mere availability of rhyme words does not render rhyme vulgar and pedestrian in and of itself. But the rhyming terminations in the vernacu- lars were quite different from those of classical Latin; the multisyllabic conju- gated terminations in Latin ("-orum" or "-orandum") could easily lead to ridiculous-sounding combinations. Polysyllabic rhyme in English is seldom used for serious purposes—a few poems by Hardy being among the excep- tions; Byron deliberately cultivated silly pairings in *Don Juan*, rhyming "sub- limity" with "dimity," for example, and "intellectual" with "hen-pecked you all."

Rhymes aplenty appear in medieval Latin beginning with early hymns and increasing in frequency. Sometimes they are tasteful, unobtrusive, and subor- dinated to the other elements of the song; sometimes they seem ostentatious, excessively ingenious, distracting, and unconsciously silly; and often—espe- cially in Goliardic poetry—they take on a Gilbert and Sullivan whimsy, or reach for bawdy incongruities like those we hear in the obscene limericks that are preserved in the oral subcultures of our own times, an example of such blasphemous indecency being,

> There once was a Bishop of Birmingham [pronounced in the British way]
> Who seduced young girls while confirming 'em;
> While they knelt on the hassock
> He lifted his cassock
> And slipped his episcopal . . . [etc.].

In surviving manuscripts of Goliardic poetry there is evidence of monkish censorship that has removed the most outrageously indecent examples. But there remain songs that celebrate fleshly indulgence and impiety, and that in some cases are parodies of church hymns. They all were intended to be sung, usually as part of a Feast of Fools or other bawdy entertainment; a twentieth-century analogue might be the songs of Tom Lehrer. The few musical notations that survive are impossible to interpret, but sometimes the very fact that a song is a blasphemous parody suggests that it could be sung to the melody of a hymn or sequence. (Various speculative renderings of music appropriate to the words have been offered by modern composers; however inauthentic it may be, one cannot help enjoying Carl Orff's *Carmina Burana*, as well as some of René Clemencic's versions.)

One of the most extraordinary rhyming satires to have survived is Walter of Châtillon's (ca. 1135–1180) invective against the neglect of those who are truly literate. Here the effect of the rhymes is to sharpen the sarcastic edge of his statement. Each stanza is built on a striking quotation from the classics—a hexameter or pentameter from Ovid, Persius, Horace, Juvenal, Lucan, Claudian, or Cato—which appears as the last line of that stanza. Preceding this quantitative line, though, are three others that rhyme with it. These are in a thirteen-syllable rhythmic pattern known as the "Goliardic line" that Walter may have been the first to use. The lines have a singsong swing, rather like the "poulter's measure" of the English Renaissance, and make a brilliant contrast to the terminal classical line. Probably the closest thing to Walter in English is the poetry of Swift, with his occasional macaronics. The density of irony makes it quite hard to translate Walter's poem, even literally:

> Missus sum in vineam   circa horam nonam,
> suam quisque nititur   vendere personam;
> ergo quia cursitant   omnes ad coronam:
> semper ego auditor tantum,   nunquamne reponam?
>
> rithmis dum lascivio,   versus dum propino,
> rodit forsan aliquis   dente me canino,
> quia nec afflatus sum   pneumate divino
> neque labra prolui   fonte caballino.

Translated, the lines read: "I was sent into the vineyard [i.e., went to work writing poetry] about the ninth hour [i.e., 3 p.m., perhaps meaning he started a little late, and perhaps suggesting that he is being crucified], everyone was trying to sell himself [i.e., promote his image]; therefore because they all are running back and forth after the laurels, am I always [supposed to be] so much the listener, and never put anything in [i.e., Am I just supposed to be part of the audience? This is the very first line of Juvenal's first satire.]. While I fool around with rhymes, while I drink a toast to [real] poetry [here we see a reflection of Walter's awareness of the syllabic/quantity differences in the vernacularizing of Latin], maybe someone bites me with his dog's tooth, because I am not puffed up with the divine afflatus, nor have I washed my lip in the muse's horse-trough."

The last line comes from the Prologue of the satires of Persius, and is a learned joke even in the original. Hippocrene is the fountain of the Muses on Mount Helicon, which came into existence when Pegasus left a hoofprint. Walter appropriates Persius's own "cavalier" reference; perhaps one might translate it "the nag's watering-hole."

The *Carmina Burana* are named for the monastery in the small town south of Munich where the book lay tucked away for nearly six hundred years, from the thirteenth to the early nineteenth century. A good example is "In taberna quando sumus," part of which imitates a hymn by Thomas Aquinas, and which begins,

> In taberna quando sumus,
> non curamus quid sit humus,
> sed ad ludum properamus,
> cui semper insudamus;
> quid agatur in taberna,
> ubi nummus est pincerna,
> hoc est opus ut queratur
> sic quid loquar, audiatur.

> [When we are in the tavern we don't care about this dust and ashes
>   business, but we get started gambling and we always work up a
>   sweat at it; what goes on in the tavern, where cash is the name of
>   the game, it's worth learning about—listen and I'll tell you.]

All this is very distant from classical Latin, where rhyme was used, if at all, either for incidental humor or for effects that were more akin to the art of rhetoric than to the art of poetry. William Beare, writing about the later Roman Empire, does speak of "those half-educated versifiers of Africa" who

wrote acrostics as well as using rhyme (245), but these were outlandish exceptions. When, however, predictable quantitative scansions disappeared in the
vernaculars, when Latin inflectional endings had atrophied so as not to call
attention to themselves, and when the languages had become more analytic,
using sentence structure in place of inflectional grammar, the way was left
open for the use of rhyme that would be both functional and less obtrusive. To
say this is to offer a modification of James Anderson Winn's statement: "Indeed, it may have been precisely the availability of rhymes in the vernacular
that most induced these poets to choose it as a medium; the flexibility of the
vernacular languages for poets seeking to develop ever more intricate forms
was a clear advantage over Latin" (*Eloquence* 79). In fact, Latin has plenty of
rhymes; but to use them as a means of organizing a poem might have something of the effect of using prepositions in English to construct a stanza,
producing a perfect absurdity. Every Latin noun and adjective came complete
with eight or ten endings, and every verb with thirty or forty, which could
have been used to rhyme with thousands of other nouns, adjectives, or verbs—
not to speak of the derivatives: participles, gerunds, and gerundives. The
problem in Latin was, as we have seen, not a shortage of rhymes but a super-
abundance. In the vernaculars there were still many more similar endings than
there are in English, but because their grammatical function was much diminished they could serve more as a quiet echo to one another—provided they
were not used to excess, as they were in some of the *chansons de geste*. Also, if
ease of rhyming is an inducement to rhyming, one might ask, why did poets
writing in English think of rhyme as an essential part of much poetry from
Chaucer's time to (in some quarters) the present, since rhymes are much
harder to come by in English?

One of the arguments used to explain the use of rhyme in Romance
languages is that it provides a punctuation for the syllabically measured lines,
giving them a unity, or drawing attention to their integrity. Frank M. Chambers suggests, "It should be remembered, however, that rime in English has
never played the predominant role that it did in troubadour verse; in English,
the stress accent of the words is sufficient of itself to generate a rhythm, while
in Provençal, as in French, it was apparently weaker and (in the opinion of
poets) needed the support of an accurate counting of syllables and a clear
system of rimes in order to produce recognizable verses" (45).

Whatever its sources and function, however, there is no question whatever
of the importance of rhyme in the constructing of stanza forms of almost
impossible intricacy and variety. One of the conventions of troubadour poetry
was that every poem (or song) was to be formally unique—though the truth is
that one finds many poems in identical stanza forms. Individual stanzas in the

same song were usually the same, being designed to go with a particular melody that was repeated with each stanza. An exception to this was the *descort*, where the rule was that each stanza was to be different from one another; that meant, presumably, that the melody changed as well—though none of the scores for *descorts* have survived. Somewhat similar to the *descort* was the lyrical (as opposed to the narrative or discursive) *lai* of northern France; here the stanzas were similar but a changing melody wove its way through the poem, with some repetition but without the predictability of stanzaic tunes.

Here is an example of a song that employs a regular *abbacddc* rhyme scheme, composed by one of a number of women troubadours, the "Countess of Dia," around 1160. There is no satisfactory agreement as to her exact identity, other than that she must have been the wife of a Provençal nobleman of some standing. James J. Wilhelm called her "one of the few poetesses between Sappho and, say, Emily Dickinson who sang in measures that are comparable with the best work of the men of her day" (133). Probably it would be proper to call this song a *planh*, or complaint. Most such poems are about bereavements. But Joifre de Foixà, a late-thirteenth-century grammarian, said that the *planh* should concern itself with "a theme of love or sadness" (Shapiro 129), and allowed much leeway in the number of stanzas. That description fits this poem.

Estat ai en greu cossirier	I've had a lot of misery
per un cavallier qu'ai agut,	for a knight who once belonged to me,
e vuoil sia totz temps saubut	and I want it known for evermore
cum ieu l'ai amat a sobrier;	how I loved him excessively;
ara vei qu'ieu sui trahida	that I betrayed him hurts me sore
car ieu non li donei m'amor,	for I never once returned his love—
don ai estat en gran error	my worst mistake! I miss him—dressed,
en lieig e quand sui vestida.	or naked in my lonely bed.
Ben volria mon cavallier	I want my knight so badly now
tener un ser in mos bratz nut,	to fold him in my naked arms
qu'el s'en tengra per ereubut	and make him weak with ecstasy,
sol qu'a lui fezes cosseillier;	pillowed on softness of my breasts;
car plus m'en sui abellida	I'd cherish him, I'm sure far more
no fetz Floris de Blachaflor:	than Floris did his Blancheflor:
ieu l'autrei mon cor e m'amor,	I'd offer him my love, my life,
mon sen, mos huoills e ma vida.	my heart, my eyes, my everything.
Bels amics avinens e bos,	Sweet friend, so charming, kind and true,
cora.us tenrai en mon poder?	when will I hold you in my power?

e que jagues ab vos un ser	If I could spend one night with you
e qu'ie.us des un bais amoros;	measuring kisses hour by hour!
sapchatz, gran talan n'auria	You know—I would pay quite a price
qu'ie.us tengues en luoc del marit,	to have you in my husband's place—
ab so que ma'aguessetz plevit	but only if you'd swear to do
de far tot so qu'ieu volria.	exactly what I want you to.

I have now begun to speak of the troubadour songs without distinguishing between the words and the music. The total fusion of the two is exactly the point made by John Stevens in *Words and Music in the Middle Ages*, where he illustrates—using arguments and examples of perpetual freshness and interest—this unity. Here is one example:

> The relationship between poem and melody is to be close, physical, and (I think we may infer) equal. As Ewald Jammers has written, the task of the music is "to create form in common with the text" (*mit dem Text gemeinsam Form zu schaffen*). The enterprise is a joint one, and we should beware of any interpretation which exalts one art over the other. We must allow neither the dominance of the poem over the melody nor the opposite, the dominance of the melody over the poem. (498)

If we accept Stevens's arguments (which I find entirely convincing), we must recognize that by the end of the Middle Ages *musica*, which had already been for Augustine, Boethius, and numerous other early writers a joint discussion of poetry and music, had once again achieved the homogeneity of Greek *mousike*. We can go even further. A great many of the songs were meant to accompany particular dances, good examples being the *balada* and *dansa* of the troubadours, and the *rondeau* and *carole* of later medieval French poetry. No one doubts this. Nitze and Dargan's *History of French Literature* puts it this way:

> As the epic was set to music and chanted, so also there were in twelfth-century France songs of personal or "lyric" inspiration. An essential feature of these songs is that originally they were written as accompaniments to the dance (*la carole*), so that "the leader would sing the successive lines while the rest of the dancers all joined in the refrain." Of this custom our modern May-dances, with the crowning of the May Queen, are a survival. (30)

Chaucer's translation of the *Roman de la Rose* is often cited for its account of such a dance; the following passage comes from the opening section, originally composed in French by Guillaume de Loris:

> A lady karoled hem that hyght°   was called
> Gladnes, the blysful and the lyght.
> Wel coude she synge and lustely,

Non half so wel and semely°,	elegantly
Hir voyce ful cleare was and ful swete.	
She was not rude ne unmete°	unharmonious
But couthe ynough of such doying	understood enough of such skills
As longeth° unto karolyng,	belongs
For she was wont° in every place	accustomed
To singing fyrst folk to solace°,	please
For syngyng moste she gave hir to;	
No crafte had she so lefe° do.	would rather do
Tho mightest thou karolles sene	then you might see *caroles*
And folke daunce and mery bene,	
And make many a fayr tourning	
Upon the grene gras springing.	
Ther mightest thou se these flutours,	
Mynstrales, and eke joglours,	
That wel to synge dyd her payne.	who tried hard to sing well
Some songe songes of Lorayne,	
For in Lorayne her notes be	
Ful swetter° than in this countre.	much sweeter

(745–68)

Among other things we see here reference to the *jongleur*; it is usually assumed that, especially in Provence, the actual performance of the songs was turned over to a *juglar*, or professional minstrel.

The concept of a unified performance combining melody, words, and dance had never completely died out, even during the Roman Empire, and commentaries on ancient and early medieval writers kept this essentially Greek combination of the Muses alive as an ideal on up to the Renaissance (see Stevens, *Words and Music* 381–83). Even in the Church, at times, restrained kinds of dancing—perhaps more like a processional in a ring than anything else—were introduced into the ceremonies. The secularization of song naturally encouraged the recombination of the three, since many of the occasions at which the songs would be performed—either as entertainment or as competition—were not only secular and sometimes informal, but were times of celebration or recreation at which dancing would be expected. There seems no reason to think that there was anything theoretical or programmatic about the impulse that led to these performances, but neither was there any notion that music, poetry, and dance should be kept separate. Only when the original vigor of the troubadours, trouvères, and minnesingers had spent itself was there even an effort to formally classify the various combinations—the reassembling of what I have irreverently called the Muses' chorus line—that had occurred.

Among the conventions developed by the troubadours was the *pastourelle*, extremely varied in form but almost comically repetitive in content. It nearly always had the poet singing in the guise of a young nobleman who had come across a shepherdess out in the countryside, and who tried unsuccessfully to seduce her—somewhat as if Christopher Marlowe's "Passionate Shepherd to His Nymph" were to be combined with Sir Walter Raleigh's "Nymph's Reply to the Shepherd." The following *pastourelle* is by a trouvère and is written in Old French; the author was Jean de Brienne, a French nobleman who served as king of Jerusalem from 1210 to 1225, and then as emperor-regent of Constantinople from 1231 to 1237.

Par dessoz l'ombre d'un bois	Among the shadows of a wood
Trovai pastore a mon chois;	I found a lovely shepherdess,
Contre iver ert bien garnie	Her flaxen hair hid in a hood
La tosete o les crins blois.	Against the winter's bitterness.
Quant la vi senz compaignie,	And when I saw her all alone
Mon chemin lais, vers lis vois. Aé!	I turned aside and went toward her. Aie!
La tose n'ot compaignon	She had no company at all
Fors son chien et son baston;	Except her dog and shepherd-crook,
Por le froit en sa chapete	Wrapped from the cold within her cape
Se tapist lez un buisson;	And sitting there behind a bush,
En sa fleüte regrete	Piping away a plaintive tune
Garinet et Robeçon. Aé!	Of Garinet and Robichon. Aie!
Quant la vi, sotainement	No sooner did I see her than
Vers li tor et si descent;	Quickly dismounting from my horse,
Si li dis: "Pastore amie,	I said to her, "Dear shepherdess,
De bon cuer a vos me rent:	With all the goodness in my heart
Faisons de fueille cortine,	I give myself to you; let's make
S'amerons mignotement." Aé!	A leafy bower and make sweet love!" Aie!
"Sire, traiez vos en la,	"Sir, kindly go back where you came.
Car tel plait oï je ja.	I have already heard the same
Ne sui pas abandonee	Too many times. I do not give
A chascun qui dit: 'Vien ça.'	Myself when someone says 'Come here.'
Ja por vo sele doree	Your golden saddle will not get
Garinez riens n'i perdra." Aé!	From me what I owe Garinet." Aie!
"Pastourele, si t'est bel,	"Dear shepherdess, if you'll be nice,
Dame seras d'un chastel.	I'll set you up in a chateau.
Desfuble chape grisete,	Cast off that old gray cape, put on

S'afuble cest vair mantel;
Si sembleras la rosete
Qui s'espanist de novel." Aé!

This ermine coat. You seem to me
Much like some sweet neglected rose
That dies of its own loveliness." Aie!

"Sire, ci a grant covent;
Mais mout est fole qui prent
D'ome estrange en tel maniere

"That's quite an offer, sir, you make;
But what a fool I'd be to take
From some strange man in some strange way,

Mantel vair ne garniment,
Se ne li fait sa proiere
Et ses bons ne li consent." Aé!

Ermine or any finery,
If what it means is, I must do
Whatever you may ask me to." Aie!

"Pastourele, en moie foi,
Por ce que bele te voi,
Cointe dame, noble et fiere,
Se tu vueus, ferai de toi.
Laisse l'amor garçoniere,
Si te tien del tot a moi." Aé!

"Sweet shepherdess, I swear I'll make—
Because you are so beautiful—
A noble, proud, and elegant
Lady of you if you wish.
Leave love to teenage boys, and give
Yourself entirely up to me." Aie!

"Sire, or pais, je vos en pri:
N'ai pas le cuer si failli;
Que j'aim mieuz povre desserte
Soz la fueille o mon ami
Que dame en chambre coverte,
Si n'ait on cure de mi." Aé!

"Give me some peace, sir, if you please:
My heart's not won that easily;
I only love what's there for me
Under the leaves with my sweetheart—
More than lady's fancy room
Where there's no one to care for me." Aie!

The action, dialogue, and outcome of the *pastourelle* were so predictable that originality could be achieved only by some new combination of melody and graceful language; compared to poetry of later centuries, the text is of limited interest apart from its place in the total performance. Of great importance, however, in distinguishing the works of these artists from whatever may have preceded them in the way of secular songs is that there was a written text and that in most cases it can be attributed to a particular author. Earlier hymns and sequences, too, can often be attributed to a particular writer. Individual written authorship may be the key to resolving differences of opinion as to whether or to what extent the troubadour/trouvère/minnesinger songs grew out of Church singing, and to what extent they were refinements of preexisting popular modes. According to James J. Wilhelm, "The French scholar Gaston Paris, for one, suggested that the entire troubadour tradition was an outgrowth of a secular instinct that is manifested in some popular songs and dances which have survived simply because they were written down" (16). The very ambiguity of this statement (for which Paris is not responsible) is useful: it seems to say that the songs are the same as other popular songs *that were not written down*, much as one might say that there must have been many fifteenth-century English ballads of which we know nothing because we do have some that were written down. But the songs of all these Romance poet-composers either originated on paper or were committed to paper soon after composition; it is not a question of their recording something that had been current for years. The survival of the songs, then, has much to do with their being productions by individual authors who worked out their intricately varied patterns in writing, not orally.

Because of its literary origins, troubadour poetry has much more in common with the courtly poetry of the early English Renaissance than it does with British popular songs and ballads. Both were largely invented by leisured nobility, both consist in large part of love poems written in stanzas that are calculatedly regular, both were often composed by young persons with musical talent, and both can be assigned to individual authors. There is a linear connection of the two through the influence of Italian poetry on English poets. The relationship of troubadour songs to whatever may have existed as popular oral literature before the twelfth century could well be analogous to the relationship of the songs and sonnets of Wyatt and Surrey to popular and orally transmitted English songs. That is, Wyatt, Surrey, and others wrote to some extent in a native tradition, but found in their Italian models a source of refinement for their English meters and subjects; the troubadours may have found in the highly developed melodic/textual literature of the Church something similar. Also, in each case, the impulse was to produce a carefully articulated rhyming text to be performed in conjunction with a melody, a text that from the start was written down so that it could be performed by anyone who could read. Yet the outcome was very different, at least in the case of Provençal poetry—the English poem emerging from its musico-literary context as a freestanding entity and the other simply ceasing.

Provençal poetry never had the opportunity to develop on its own. The explanation for its disappearance is simple and horrifying, and may be found by reading the history of the Albigensian Crusade. The most promising civilization in the world, in the year 1200, was simply exterminated by a series of massacres surpassing in some respects the savagery of our twentieth-century holocausts. The Church identified all the inhabitants of the region as heretics and licensed their wholesale slaughter. It remained for the more fortunate poets of northern France and other relatively stable parts of Europe to build forward from the models first brought into existence in the *Occitan*, the *Langue d'oc* region.

One minor issue (minor for our purposes) that bears on the relations of poetry to music in the Middle Ages needs to be disposed of; it is something of a red herring in the discussion of these relations. This is the subject of the "rhythmic modes" in medieval music. One must immediately distinguish rhythmic modes from Greek harmonic modes, which were various scales to which music could be composed on the kithera, whereas rhythmic modes had to do with tempo, not pitch. Questions arise as to what extent musicians of the Middle Ages understood anything about the Greek harmonic modes; whether medieval music, including popular music, employed any of these and, if so, which ones they were; and what was the nature of other modes that were the basis of melodies used by writers of vernacular songs. All these are beyond the somewhat narrow focus of the present study, but the rhythmic modes are at least tangentially significant. Simply put, the invention of the rhythmic modes consisted of taking the scansions of classical quantitative verse, probably as preserved in Augustine's *De Musica*, and applying them to classify or explain various possible temporal rhythms in music. During the thirteenth and fourteenth centuries several writers on music attempted to employ the most basic poetic feet (iamb, trochee, spondee, dactyl, and anapest—adding also the tribrach, of three shorts) as a way of notating or explaining temporal variations. Mixed in with this commonsensical appropriation of ancient metrics was a certain amount of religious mysticism, for example the idea that each of the feet could really be reduced to three units, making each a tiny epitome of the Trinity. In order to trinitize all the feet, however, rests had to be introduced, the spondee in particular posing a theological difficulty. The modern locus classicus on rhythmic modalism is William G. Waite's *The Rhythm of Twelfth-Century Polyphony* and the medieval authority most often cited is Walter Odington's *De speculatione musici* (ca. 1300). Use of quantitative metrical symbols, or at least the names of the poetic feet, to describe musical rhythms is often associated with the thirteenth-century school of composers centered at Notre Dame de Paris. Aside from the fact that those who used the rhythmic modes did recognize the possibility of a link between poetry and music, however, the modes do not seem to have been very important in achieving the synthesis of the two. But such a line of musical theory may have had some value in providing reassurance that the two arts were not intrinsically separate, and also may have nudged musicians in the direction of inventing a notation that would accommodate temporal values as well as pitches.

In Chapter 5 I will resume the account of how, as the Renaissance began in Italy and spread northward, various poetries disentangled themselves from their alliances with music, whether sacred or secular, breaking free from a thousand-year-old synthesis. Before moving ahead, though, we must take a step backward. In addition to the lyrics of the Middle Ages there existed in many European languages a vigorous oral literature of other genres that were also closely allied to music. These works grew out of warrior cultures, from semibarbaric to feudal, that bear some comparison to the culture around the Aegean in the centuries before Homer. The form that many of them take is a consequence of their being transcriptions of highly sophisticated verbal/musical performances; the poetry that came out of these has not endured as has that which owed its existence to songs and hymns, but this survey would be incomplete if it did not take into account the epic poetry of the Middle Ages.

4

Oral-Formulaic Beginnings

BURIED IN THE LAST SENTENCE of the previous chapter is the unstated assumption that the oral-formulaic explanation of origins of authentic epic poetry (as opposed to epics that are *literary* and the original work of a single author) is essentially correct. This theory, first advanced by Milman Parry, elaborated and developed by Albert B. Lord in his *Singer of Tales*, and applied to early English poetry by Francis P. Magoun, Jr., and his students, is one of the triumphs of twentieth-century literary, linguistic, and philological scholarship. Boldly imaginative in its beginnings, rooted in direct observation of oral poetry in situ and in progress, undergirded with detailed scholarly apparatus, it has nonetheless been attacked by scholars who have had little to offer in its place—somewhat as the plate-tectonic explanation of global physiography used to be regarded as "speculative" by a shrinking minority of geologists.

References to Homer in the first chapter of this book were intended only to establish the fact that, as with all other Greek poetry, the *Iliad* and the *Odyssey* originated as the verbal part of a musical (in the broader sense) performance, and were performed to the accompaniment of some sort of music, the exact nature of which cannot be known. What can be known—by analogy with living traditions (which Parry found in Yugoslavia and Magoun in Finland), and by careful study of the patterns of recurrent phrases, or formulas, in the texts—is something about how the verbal part of the performance came into existence. The theory may be summarized as follows:

1. Authentic, or oral, epics, as they have been handed down to us, are transcriptions of a highly sophisticated oral performance; they are not scripts or texts written down in advance of performance by the performer.
2. The epics as we have them are the culmination of a long tradition of oral poem-making, but are not the results of simultaneous group authorship. That is, the version that we have is the version of a single oral poet of a story or collection of stories that had been performed earlier, perhaps for hundreds of years.
3. The text is not a transcription of something memorized word for word

or line by line by the performer. Rather, it is a record of how an accomplished performer put the poem together on one occasion.

4. The performer had a talent for, and long training in, the acquisition and delivery of a large stock of metrical formulas. A superficial reading of Homer makes us aware of some of these; close statistical study shows that as much as 90 percent of Homer consists of these ready-made phrases from which lines were pieced together on the spot.

5. The oral epic, then, was a mixture of memorized recitation and improvisation, whereby an established story line was followed using a very large vocabulary of metrically suitable phrases with which the performer's memory was stocked.

This theory, originally propounded by a classicist to explain Homer, has proved readily applicable to epics in other languages, providing a satisfactory account of the origins not only of *Beowulf*, but even to a slight degree the French *chansons de geste*—though it also appears that the French epics were designed to facilitate memorization unit by unit, and were not improvised. In every case the oral epic proves, upon close examination, to consist of a tissue of identifiable formulas. To say this is not to suggest that there is anything monotonous about the final result; indeed, there is so much variety that the essential nature of the oral epic escaped attention until Parry's studies. The formulaic character was simply overlooked.

The elegant simplicity of the oral-formulaic theory provides groundwork for my own attempt at drawing together in a single treatment the numerous instances of longer poems that were originally quasi-musical performances. There is, first of all, the example of Virgil's taking Homer's hexameters and making them into a template for Latin—creating thereby a poetry full of subtle effects that are indebted to a musical model but are themselves quite independent of music. Something similar occurred in English when the four-beat alliterating line of *Beowulf*, the rhythm of which is easy to imagine in terms of its musical accompaniment, became the model for numerous Middle English alliterative romances. The same meter carried forward as well into religious writings (of which *Piers Plowman* is the apex) that were meant as much for the eye as for the ear. No Virgil of alliterative meter ever appeared to offer a refined redaction of *Beowulf*, although in *Gawain and the Green Knight* we have an incomparable masterpiece in which the Old English musical tradition includes in the "bob and wheel" pattern the Anglo-Norman syllabics that eclipsed and replaced it. Many narrative poems of northern France are developments out of the *chansons de geste*, the oral-formulaic qualities of which have been noted, and which were sung (more likely memorized than performed extempore) by minstrels.

All these lengthier productions seem not only to deal with feats of valor in war or in travel, but they all grow out of times and circumstances when the prevailing ethic was fiercely martial. This warrior ethic shows itself in a lack of sentimentality that some readers find simply brutal when they first encounter it—such as the horrifying exactness with which the passage of a spear through a warrior's kidney is described in the *Iliad*, the anatomical detail describing the shreds of flesh hanging from Grendel's wrenched-out arm, or the equine vivisection of Ganelon in the *Chanson de Roland*. The ethic of such poems suggests that they might have been invented and performed under difficult circumstances—during pauses and truces or during brief periods of peace following a local victory. Oral poems, capable of being sung without the aid of a written script (without even light to see by), accompanied by rudimentary music from an easily transported kithera or lyre, were the only extended form of literature possible amid disordered and desperate circumstances of constant fighting or readiness to fight. And the oral-formulaic theory remains by far the best way of understanding how such poems came into existence. The disordered conditions and emphasis on personal heroism in Serbia and Macedonia actually fostered the heroic recitations discovered by Parry.

Of course a considerable body of literary alliterative poetry exists in Old as well as in Middle English—that is, poetry in which an author (sometimes identifiable) working with writing implements employed the older meters— and this fact is sometimes used as an argument that *Beowulf*, say, was only an early example of such literacy. A sensitive reader, however, easily notes the difference between the half-improvised performance of the epic and the richer alliteration of the work by lettered poets, not to speak of ingenuities such as rhyme and acrostics. Subjective arguments, though, are hardly necessary, given the abundance of examples that Magoun and others have adduced to establish the oral character of *Beowulf.* Yet there remains the curious proclivity of some scholars to work backward, from compositions that were indubitably literary, in order to discredit the claim that what we see as the written text of *Beowulf* is a transcription of an oral performance. The argument is that since formulaic expressions occur in these later works—sometimes even in translations from Latin—and since the later works were certainly written, not oral, compositions, then *Beowulf* too must be the work of a scribal poet. A similar line of thought might take the design of early automobiles (which were clearly modeled at first on carriages) and, working backwards, insist that there never were such things as horse-drawn vehicles—only motorless automobiles that happened to be attached to horses. To try to make *Beowulf* into a literary epic is a literal *hysteron proteron*. The oral-formulaic theory is the only one that adequately explains how lengthy narrative poems, originating as accounts of fighting and adventure in earlier centuries and performed as songs agreeable to a warrior culture, could have reached the degree of sophistication that they possessed when they were finally written down. As no firsthand report exists about the recording of *Beowulf,* one might imagine that the person who wrote it down was also a performer of the poem. There is of course the temptation to believe that nothing as sophisticated as *Beowulf* could ever have been performed, that it has to be the work of a scribal poet imitating and improving upon the orally delivered versions of the story. But attacks on the theory, and especially attacks on Magoun's application of it to *Beowulf,* sometimes seem motivated less by a disinterested desire to establish how the poem came into existence than by academic politics, and perhaps also by a feeling that anyone as profoundly learned in philology as Magoun (who taught himself Finnish, a non-Indo-European language, at the age of fifty in order to pursue his investigations) ought not to display imaginative insight into poetry.

Happily, there exist treatments of *Beowulf* that refine and extend the original perceptions of Parry, Lord, and Magoun without introducing hostile or querulous objections; the best of these is *Beowulf: The Poem and Its Tradition,* by John D. Niles (1983). Niles, acting on some suggestions by Donald K. Fry, insists on the oral-formulaic origin of the poem but modifies the concept of the formula, abandoning the notion that it was fixed. Instead, building on Lord's work, he speaks of a grammar of prosodic units from which the *scop* could build the poem:

> To an overwhelming extent, this method did not consist of parroting fixed phrases or formulaic tags but of varying verse-length phrases belonging to a vast interlocking network of formulaic systems. In this way the poet could easily generate new verses on the model of old ones as the need arose. It is the set of abstract verse-making patterns used by the *Beowulf* poet, rather than a body of fixed phrases, that constitutes his true formulaic repertory. (129)

Niles also carefully documents an argument that not only was the poem dictated orally for transcription, but that such transcriptions by literate amanuenses were commonplace (34–37). His chief example is the account by Bede of Caedmon's performance of biblical paraphrases; these had to be written down by others because Caedmon was illiterate. Niles does admit that texts composed in alliterative meter by literate persons using writing materials were certainly possible, but concludes that "when we turn to *Beowulf* we find none of these signs of clerical authorship" (37).

Even those who wished to discredit the oral-formulaic theory would be likely to admit that what we have on paper is only the verbal part of a performance that was also musical, though there are notable exceptions even here, as one sees in the arguments of Kemp Malone (see, for example, Baugh et al. 23). Internal and external evidence connected with the poem points to this. Albert Lord always uses the words "singer" and "song" in *The Singer of Tales*, while the theory's most conscientious critic, Ann Chalmers Watts, entitled her book *The Lyre and the Harp* and likewise speaks consistently of the singer and the song. At one point in the middle of *Beowulf* a minstrel entertains the warriors with a heroic song about Beowulf himself, celebrating the initial victory over Grendel—and this song then merges insensibly with the actual narrative. (At the same time, it should be safe to take for granted that nonmusical forms of alliterative poetry have emerged from these musical contexts; almost no one thinks of the author of *Piers Plowman* as carrying a lute in place of a pilgrim's staff or shepherd's crook.)

Although it does not pretend to be literally faithful, Ezra Pound's version of "The Seafarer" captures well the spirit and tone of Old English poetry; Tennyson's "Battle of Brunanburh" seems a little stiff in comparison, but at least it observed the metrical conventions. The most common unit is a pair of half-lines, each containing two stressed syllables, resulting in a sort of 4/4 musical rhythm. (To say this is not, of course, to insist on perfect isochronic regularity.) The two half-lines are bound together by alliterating sounds, most often consonants; certain consonantal combinations (*sc* sounded *sh*, for example) require identical combinations to alliterate, and there is also the convention that any open vowel at the start of a word can alliterate with any other open-voweled syllable. Once I was brought up short in a discussion of alliterative meter when I stated that the *third* stress in each line determined the alliterative pattern; "How," a student asked, "can something that comes later determine something that comes before?" This was a fair question, requiring that the explanation be restated: in the course of oral performance the *scop*, or singer, had to come up with a word in the third stress position that alliteratively echoed one or both of the stressed syllables in the preceding half-line. The result is that the first stressed position of the second half-line always alliterates with at least one stressed syllable in the first half-line. Here are some lines from the beginning of *Beowulf* with the stresses marked; even judging with the eye it is easy to perceive the alliterating pattern:

       /   /   /   /
   Oft Scyld Scefing   sceapena preatum,
   /   /   /   /
   monegum mægpum   meodsetla ofteah,
   /   /   /   /
   egsode eorlas,   syððan ærest weard
   (4–6)

[Often Scyld Scefing took away the mead-benches of companies of
the enemy, of many foes, terrified the warrior lords, from the time
that first . . .]

These lines are especially rich in alliteration, perhaps because they come from
a carefully prepared opening; in much of the poem only one of the stressed
syllables in the first half-line matches up with the alliterating syllable in the
second half-line.

Efforts to account for the metrical patterning of Old English poetry initially
went astray because of the common practice since the Renaissance of trying to
explain all poetry using foot-scansion methods applicable to Latin verse. Similar scansions are still commonplace in "introductions to prosody"—often being
presented in textbooks either as "natural" or as absolute poetic conventions,
with the consequence that the reader may not be aware of their historical
provenance. Because of the long acceptance of these scansions in German,
English, and other languages, poets had by the nineteenth century acquired an
almost unselfconscious command of lines constructed in accentual iambs,
trochees, anapests, and even dactyls. Therefore the first attempts, in the nineteenth century, to make systematic sense of Anglo-Saxon poetry divided up
and classified the lines in terms of the "feet" from which they are supposedly
constructed. Foot-scansion has an almost pathological hold on many who go
in for prosodic theorizing, whether they consider themselves in favor of it
or against it. Two of the classics in treating Anglo-Saxon poetry from this
perspective were *Altergermanische Metrik* (1893) by E. Sievers and *Deutsche Vers-
geschichte* (1925) by A. Heusler. The Sievers system, in particular, was established for decades, with its elaborate classification into A, B, C, D, and E lines—
according to the feet that they contained—which was the basis of the system.
Suffice it to say that the system works well as a set of pigeonholes into which to
stick individual lines and is useful for purposes of statistical surveys. It is no help
at all, however, in understanding how the poetry was originally sung. For this
we turn to J. C. Pope's *The Rhythm of Beowulf* (1942). Pope's work has been
much debated and partly rebutted, both as a whole and in detail, but there is no
denying the importance of his fundamental perception that the poem might
well be viewed as a musical performance and that its rhythm can to some extent
be explained musically. Others fear a recrudescence of notational overspecification such as is complained of in discussions of musical scansions by Sydney
Lanier and Harriet Monroe, and also may wish to question many of Pope's
interpretations of particular lines, where he uses musical notation. But, like the
explanation of the verse itself by oral-formulaic theory, the explanation of the
rhythm of the poetry as a set of quasimusical units is striking and persuasive.

This explanation also makes it easier to read the poetry aloud, and encourages imaginative reconstructions of the original music. (To say this is not to endorse the random drum-banging that accompanies the recording of Pound reading his "Seafarer" with an affected Scotch-Irish accent.) Pope's notation has been much refined and improved by others, especially by F. H. Whitman (see scansion in Appendix to *A Comparative Study of Old English Meter*).

> Gewhorton ða Wedra leode
> hleo on hoe, se wæs heah ond brad,
> weg-liðendum wide gesyne,
> on betimbredon on tyn dagum
> beadu-rofes becn; bronda lafe
> wealle bewhorton, swa hyt weorðlicost
> fore-snotre men findan mihton.
> Hi on beorg dydon beg ond siglu,
> eall swylce hyrsta, swylce on horde ær
> niðhedige men genumon hæfdon;
> forleton eorla gestreon, eorðan healdan,
> gold on greote, þær hit nu gen lifað
> eldum swa unnyt, swa hit æror wæs.
>
> (3156–68)

> [Then the Geat people   gathered and built
> high on the headland   a huge funeral mound,
> easily seen   by seafarers journeying—
> in ten days they built   a barrow for the warrior
> a beacon for the bold   the battle-famous one;
> around all the ashes   they erected a wall
> excellently designed   as if architects had planned it.
> Rings and precious jewels   they placed in the barrow
> adornments of the sort   that evil-minded men
> had taken away   when the treasure-hoard was raided;
> they resigned to the earth   the riches of the nobles;
> useless in the ground   the gold lies to this day
> buried and useless   as ever before.]

Everyone who becomes familiar with *Beowulf* in the original, including those who do not accept oral-formulaic theory, comes away from it convinced that it must be the sole fortunate survivor of a considerable body of sophisticated heroic poetry. Beginning with the Norman Conquest, deliberate and accidental destruction of monastic libraries—and any other collections that might have existed—occurred continuously, with episodic intensifications such as the usurpations of Henry VIII. The Conquest itself made much of England into a French-speaking country; an occupying power always assumes that its culture is superior to the loser's, and the best that the heritage of the losing side can expect is benevolent neglect. The development of Old English literature, especially alliterative poetry, simply ceased with William's victory at Hastings—though more as a consequence of the disruptions of several years of "pacification" than from an active effort to suppress it. With a new aristocracy that was entirely French-speaking, and with all the important positions in the Church likewise filled with Norman prelates, there was little at the end of the eleventh century to encourage an author working in the old language and the old meters. Texts of the old poems remained available as models in monastery libraries, but the social and political structure that could have encouraged actual performance of the poems no longer existed. Yet in an utterly different way from the emergence of Latin poetry from Greek *mousike*, a body of written literature, the alliterative part of which became free of musical connections, did eventually establish itself in England—a vernacular movement that culminated in *Sir Gawain and the Green Knight*.

The earliest post-Conquest example of alliterative meter, now employed entirely as a literary medium, is impressive: 16,120 lines of what has come to be called *Brut*, the work of a priest named Layamon, or Lawman, who undertook to retell in English verse the Arthurian stories already written up in the French *Roman de Brut* (ca. 1155) by the Anglo-Norman poet Wace. Wace had in turn versified Geoffrey of Monmouth's mythological history of England, composed in Latin. Layamon's labors, then, were in some sense a repatriation of British materials into a meter modeled on Old English. But he either did not understand the principles of alliterative verse or chose not to abide by them; although his rhythms are faithful to Old English prosody, his use of alliteration is somewhat random, and he also employs some rhyme. Yet the effect is thoroughly English; surveys of the vocabulary in *Brut* find an unusually small stock of French words. And the work itself is extremely important both as a link with the old heroic tradition and as a source for future writers who wished to work from Arthurian materials. The language of the poem is much closer to that of fourteenth-century alliterative poetry than it is to *Beowulf*; anyone who can read *Piers Plowman* with ease will not find Layamon much more difficult.

The ultimate triumph of accentual-syllabic prosody obscures for many readers the fact that loosely accentual alliterative meter is the most authentically English prosody that has ever existed—authentically German and Scandinavian as well. The problem was that the sophistication of poetry modeled on French verse made this meter seem, to English-speaking readers, somewhat uncivilized. As much as we owe to Chaucer, it was Chaucer's example more than anything else that hastened the abandonment of purely accentual meters, which in the end became stigmatized as suitable solely for farce or popular songs. Urbane and cosmopolitan, Chaucer set an example and left behind a corpus of such size, range, and variety as to eclipse all possible rivals. Outside of London—especially to the north and west of the city—the alliterative revival of the fourteenth century brought into existence poems equal to Chaucer's in beauty and sophistication, though no single poet could begin to equal the Londoner's achievement.

It remains to be explained why the alliterative revival occurred; perhaps the disappearance of French political power over England and a restored sense of national identity encouraged it. Working with writing materials but borrowing their meter from a thousand-year-old musical tradition, these poets found themselves completely at home in the four-beat Old English line, and unlike Layamon cultivated alliteration not only as a structural method but also as ornamentation and embellishment. Something similar might have occurred in Greece had the culture not remained so completely oral and mnemonic; that is, one might imagine poets drawing inspiration from Homer in subsequent centuries, but refining and adorning his prosody through the meditation and revision made possible with writing. The English alliterative revival was a scribal phenomenon, made possible and encouraged by a society well endowed with copyists.

The ornamentation—almost, one might say, artificiality—of later alliterative poetry shows itself most obviously in the richness of alliteration in comparison with *Beowulf*. Sometimes, in a display of vulgar ingenuity, a poet will continue with the same alliterating sound for six lines or more; three alliterations per line are the norm, and four or even more are common. The following passage is from the alliterative *Morte Arthure*; it is easy to note a fairly high percentage of words derived from French (*chamber, arms, palace, presence*), but the vocabulary is more identifiably Germanic than Chaucer's:

> Nowe he takez hys leve   (and lengez no langere)
> At lordez, at lege-men   þat leves hym beyhynden.
> And seyne þat worthilyche wy   went unto chambyre
> For to comfurthe þe qwene   þat in care lenges;
> Waynour waykly   wepande hym kyssiz,
> Talkez to hym tenderly   with teres y-newe:
> 'I may wery the wye   thatt this werre movede,
> That warnes me wyrchippe   of my wedde lorde;
> All my lykynge of lyfe   owt of lande wendez,
> And I in langour am left,   leve 3e, for evere!
> Why ne myghte I, dere lufe,   dye in 3our armes,

Are I þis destnye of dule sulde drye my myne one?'
'Grefe þe noghte, Gaynour, fore Goddes lufe of hewen,
Ne gruche noghte me ganggynge: it sall to gude turne.
Thy wonrydez and thy wepynge woundez myn herte,
I may noghte wit of þis woo, for all þis werlde ryche;
I have made a kepare, a knyghte of thyn awen,
Overlyng of Ynglande undyre thyselven,
And that es sir Mordrede þat þow has mekyll praysede,
Sall be thy dictour, my dere, to doo whatt thy lykes.'
Thane he takes hys leve at ladys in chambyre,
Kysside them kyndlyche and to Christe beteches,
And then cho swounes full swythe, whe⟨n⟩ he his swerde aschede,
Sweyes in a swounyng, swelte as cho walde.
He pressed to his palfray in presance of lordes,
Prekys of the palez with hys prys knightes,
With a reall rowte of þe rounde table,
Soughte towarde Sandwyche: cho sees hym no more!

(693–720)

[Now he takes his leave and lingers no longer
With his lords, with his liege-men whom he leaves behind.
Straightway the worthy warrior went to the bedroom
To comfort the queen in her careworn suffering;
Grieving quietly, Guinevere greets him with kisses,
Talks to him tenderly with tears that spring freshly:
"How I curse that creature who caused this conflict,
That robs me of the regard of my rightful husband;
Everything I enjoy utterly vanishes,
And I remain here in misery for evermore—believe me!
Dear love, why did not I die in your arms,
Sooner than to suffer in sorrow all alone?"
"For the love of God, Guinevere, do not grieve so bitterly,
Nor begrudge my going: good things will come of it.
Your woeful weeping wounds me in my heart,
Sooner than see such sorrow, I would give anything;
I have arranged for a caretaker, among your own knights,
A governor of England, only second after you,
And that is Sir Mordred —much have you praised him—
You may command him to carry out your wishes."
Then he takes his leave of the ladies in the bedchamber,
Kisses them courteously and commends them to Christ,
And then she faints dead away when he asks for his sword,

Wavering and falling   as if she wanted to die.
He leaps onto his palfrey   in the presence of his lords,
Gallops off from the palace   with his gallant knights,
With the regal assembly   of the round table,
Sets off for the seaport: she sees him no more!]

The argument that what we see in the *Morte Arthure* is the evolution of an oral and musical form into a written one is a little speculative inasmuch as we do not know whether the *Morte Arthure* was read aloud, and if so, whether with music or not. It is hard to imagine that alliterative masterpiece, *Piers Plowman*, accompanied by music, although the author does not seem hostile to honest entertainers, noting these among others in the "fair field full of folk" of his dream vision:

And summe murphes to maken,   as munstrals cunne
And get gold wiþ her gle,   giltles, I trowe.

[And some provide entertainment, as minstrels know how to do, and
    make money with their singing—innocently, I believe.]

But the poem is so sober, moralistic, and didactic that it has far more the aspect of a sermon than a song. At least one scholar, John Murray Gibbon, has contended that the poem was, or at least could be, chanted to melodies that accompanied the Psalms; others consider this unlikely. But even Gibbon is willing to hedge a little:

Though he satirized his own profession of singing priest, he was saturated with the music by which he gained his livelihood.

The musical quality of *Piers Plowman* has been obscured by modernized versions which should be taken only as a bridge to the original. One of these versions, issued with the imprimatur of two learned scholars, one a Professor of Poetry, excuses its translation of *Piers Plowman* into prose on the ground that "the poet was not a great artist in metre." Of course, if poetry is to be confined to the straitjacket of symmetrical rhyme, this may be so. But there are some who think that King David, who did not rhyme, was a better artist in metre than Nahum Tate.

One must also remember that the English of all classes in Langland's day were familiar with this church music—the nobles heard it daily in their private chapels, the lesser folk in the churches which were their common meeting-place. They learned this music in their childhood, for, as Cardinal Gasquet points out in his *Parish Life in Medieval England*, in these days "every little boy either sang or served about the altar in church." These were tunes that did not need to be set down in notes—they were better known even than the ballad tunes which the later printers merely named on the broadsides.

While Langland wrote his visions with the psalter tunes running in his head, his verses may indeed have been recited rather than chanted by those who quoted or read them in the written copies, just as the lyrics written by Robert Burns to definite melodies have still their independent charm for the mere reader. It may be also that Langland framed his verses as much to an inner as to a sounded music. (11–12)

Most miraculous among major works of the later Middle Ages is *Sir Gawain and the Green Knight*, which borrows from the Latin and French syllabic meters even as it brings to new perfection the Old English heritage. About forty other examples exist in English and Scots poetry in which stanzas containing fifteen to thirty alliterative lines are punctuated with a syllabic "bob and wheel." The bob consists of two or three introductory syllables; the wheel in *Gawain* is a stanza of hexasyllabic lines rhyming *abab*. To many readers it seems as if the alliterative part must have been delivered as a sort of recitative, with the singer breaking into a recurrent melody in the wheel, the bob serving as a sort of transition or cue note:

'In god fayth', quop Gawayn,   'gayn hit mepynkkez,
Þaʒ I be not now he   pat ʒe of speken;
To reche to such reverence   as ʒe reherce here
I am wyʒe unworpy,   I wot wel myselven;
Bi God, I were glad,   and yow god poʒt,
At saʒe oper at servyce,   pat I sette myʒt
To pe plesaunce of your prys;   hit were a pure joye.'
'In god fayth, Sir Gawayn,'   quop pe gay lady,
'pe prys and pe prowess   pat plesez al oper,
If I hit lakked, oper set at lyʒt,   hit were littel daynté;
Bot hir ar ladyes innoʒe   pat lever wer nowpe
Haf pe, hende, in hor holde,   as I pe habbe here,
To daly with derely   your daynté wordez,
Kever hem comfort,   and colen her carez,
pen much of pe garysoun   oper golde pat pay haven.
Bot I louve pat ilk lorde   pat pe lyfte haldez,
I haf hit holly in my honde   pat al desyres,
       purʒe grace.'
       Scho made hym so gret chere,
       pat watz so fayr of face;
       pe knyʒt with speches skere,
       A⟨n⟩swared to uche cace.

(1241–62)

["In good faith," said Gawaine,   "You grant me a favor
Even if I am not he,   the one whom you speak of;

To be rated with such respect   as you rehearse here
I am an unworthy warrior   as I well know myself;
By God! I'd be glad   if I made a good impression,
In word or in deed,   I'd do my very best
To obtain your good opinion;   it would be pure pleasure!"
"Good gracious! Sir Gawaine,"   said the gay lady,
"Your honor and bravery   that everyone values,
To find fault, or undervalue,   would be failure of courtesy;
But there's a raft-full of ladies   who'd rather right now
Have you, honey,   here in hand like me,
To palaver and flirt   with your polite talk,
Make themselves comfortable,   cool off those urges,
Than much of the jewelry   or money that they own!
But praise the Lord in Heaven   I have what I want,
It's all in my hand,   what everyone wants,
      my gracious!"
    She put on quite an act
    With such a pretty face;
    Modest and matter-of-fact
    The Knight kept things in place.]

This is not the place to provide a plot summary of *Gawain* or to comment upon the complexity of its theme and its symbolism; no existing work of comparable length is as perfectly unified as this, or has such intricate crafts-manship that displays itself without leaving an impression of artificiality. Rather than being a poetry that evolves away from music, as Chaucer's is, *Gawain* is an ultimate fusion of two musico-poetic traditions—the Old English and the Church/troubadour song. Gaston Paris considered it the finest work in English of the entire Middle Ages.

The Norman Conquest can be blamed for the extinction of Old English poetry, but how do we account for the total disappearance of alliterative meter after such successes as we have just touched on? We already have the one-word answer: Chaucer. The only recognition that he offered the old tradition was to make his Parson claim incompetence in it:

But trusteth wel, I am a southren man.
I kan nat geeste 'rum, ram, ruf,' by lettre,
Ne, God wot, rym holde I but litel bettre.

For all his earthiness, Chaucer was firmly allied with those classes most of whose members were as at home in French as in English, looking to the south of England and back across the Channel for cultural values. Unfortunately for the poets north and west of London, alliterative meter was connected with dialects and vocabularies that seemed increasingly rural and provincial, out of the mainstream of European affairs, not cosmopolitan. Persons speaking with north or northwest accents may have had difficulty finding employment in learned occupations unless they improved their pronunciation—somewhat as a young American scholar was once advised to lose his Alabama accent if he wished to be tenured at Columbia University. Chaucer, on the other hand, provided numerous models of works that drew on the Latin classics, on French, and most promising of all for his future reputation, on Italian literature, and he wrote in the dialect spoken around London and at court. Alliterative verse, then, fell victim to continuing invasion—a poetic imperialism emanating from the continent, which began as an effort to emulate Chaucer's French-based metric and continued in the sixteenth century as an attempt to endow English with virtues belonging to Italian and ultimately to Latin.

Except for such songs and popular ballads as survive, fifteenth-century English poetry is a wasteland of stumbling half-syllabic meters, enlivened only by John Skelton's staccato monorhymes. Partly this was the result of a continuing evolution of spoken English. A particular problem was the final *e*, which is sometimes pronounced in Chaucer and sometimes not, and which was all that remained of Old English declension endings; as routine pronunciation of the *e* dropped away, Chaucer's metrics made less and less sense and became harder and harder to imitate. Only when the spoken language began to stabilize again, with the help of conservative linguistic forces such as printed texts and more widespread formal education, did it become possible for a new generation of poets to reinvent accentual-syllabic meters—and that did not occur until the 1500s, as we will see in a subsequent chapter.

Possibly because of its ancient association with battle poetry, alliteration became synonymous with noise and violence, and when used in this way produced effects that easily bridged the gap between the sublime and the ridiculous. Chaucer resorted to alliteration for this purpose in describing the tournament in "The Knight's Tale":

> Ther shyveren shafts upon the sheeldes thikke;
> He feeleth thurgh the herte-spoon the prikke;
> Up spryngen speres twenty foote on highte;
> Out goon the swerdes as the silver brighte;
> The helmes they tohewen and toshrede;
> Out brest the blood with sterne stremes rede;
> With mighty maces the bones they tobreste;
> He thurghe the thikkeste of the throng gan threste;
> Ther stomblen steedes strong, and doun gooth al . . .

(2605–13)

An even better example, right out of the alliterative tradition even as it was being abandoned forever, is "Swart-Smeked Smithes" from about 1450. Here the alliteration descends to a lively buffoonery, which communicates very well the speaker's exasperation at being disturbed by the proximity of a blacksmith's shop:

> Swarte smekyd smeþes smateryd wyth smoke,
> dryue me to deth wyth den of here dyntes!
> Swech noys on nyghtes ne herd men neuer:
> What knauene cry, & clateryng of knockes!
> þe cammede kongons cryen after "col! col!"
> & blowen here bellewys þat al here brayn brestes.
> "huf, puf!" sayth þat on. "haf, paf!" þat oþer.
> þei spyttyn & spraulyn & spellyn many spelles,
> þei gnauen & gnacchen, þei gronys togydere,
> and holden hem hote wyth here hard hamers.

(Robbins 106)

> [Smoke-blacked smiths, begrimed with smoke
> drive me to death with the din of their strokes!
> Such noise no one ever heard at night before:
> What hollering of helpers, and hammering of blows!
> The pugnosed thugs keep yelling, "Coal! Coal!"
> and blow at the bellows till their brains pop out.
> "Huff, puff!" says one of them—"Haff, paff," says another.
> They spit and sprawl about and spin out all these yarns,
> they grate their teeth and gripe and grumble at each other,
> and overheat themselves by pounding with their hammers.]

Spenser employed alliteration in describing the violence of combat, though with somewhat less abandon than in the passages just quoted; the dragon of Sin, stabbed in the armpit by the Redcrosse Knight, lets out a terrific roar, like "raging seas"

> When wintry storme his wrathful wreck does threat,
> The rolling billows beat the ragged shore.

> The steely head stuck fast still in his flesh,
> Till with his cruel claws he snatcht the wood,
> And quite asunder broke. Forth flowed fresh
> A gushing river of black goarie blood,
> That drowned all the land on which he stood;
> The stream therof would drive a water-mill.
> Trebly augmented was his furious mood

With bitter sense of his deep rooted ill,
That flames of fire he threw forth from his large nosethrill.

(*Faerie Queene* 1.2.22)

The ultimate epitaph of alliteration as a metrical device may have been written by Shakespeare in *A Midsummer Night's Dream*, in the summary of the
action for the "Pyramus and Thisbe" episode. Peter Quince, as "Prologue,"
delivers the lines that describe the suicide of Pyramus:

Whereat, with blade, with bloody blameful blade,
He bravely broach'd his boiling bloody breast. . . .

In his early poem "The Rape of Lucrece," Shakespeare had used alliteration as
additional ornamentation to the already elaborate rhyme royal:

Her pity-pleading eyes are sadly fixed
In the remorseless wrinkles of his face.
Her modest eloquence with sighs is mixed,
Which to her oratory adds more grace.
She puts the period often from his place,
    And midst the sentence so her accent breaks
    That twice she doth begin ere once she speaks.

(561–67)

Since the close of the Middle Ages, only scattered tours de force of alliterative meter can be found, and most of those belong to the twentieth century.
Coleridge revived the rhythm (though not the alliteration) to some extent in
"Christabel," Hopkins revived alliteration in the context of his sprung rhythm
(but did not use Old English meters), and Hardy used very loose accentual
meters (without ever attempting an alliterative structure). The meter itself
seems unlikely ever again to be widely employed; only when it can be adapted
and submerged can it function unobtrusively, as it does in some poems by
Auden ("Oh where are you going said reader to rider? / That valley is fatal
where furnaces burn.") and especially in Eliot's *Murder in the Cathedral*, as well
as sections of *Four Quartets*. Alliterative meter per se sounds strange and affected, and seems inappropriate when employed with the clipped polysyllabic
vocabulary, borrowed from Latin and Greek as well as French, with which
English has been loaded in the intervening centuries. Enough alliterative verse
survives for us to understand it far better than anyone will ever understand
Latin Saturnians, but just as that meter was exterminated by an overlay of
Greek quantitative patterns, so the gnarls and whorls of alliterative meter were
smoothed over by a veneer of syllabics, borrowed mainly from French. Possi-

bly the fact that alliterative meter originated as oral recitation and resists confinement to a page, to be scanned by the eye, went against it in the long run; more predictable line lengths and the stitching of rhyme seemed more suitable for printed poetry. Whether the printing press had anything to do with it or not, alliterative poetry, to its ultimate disadvantage, never did completely disentangle itself from its oral and musical origins.

In the debate over the oral-formulaic origins of *Beowulf* and other Old English poems, it is at least fairly clear what is being argued over; but the subject of Old French *chanson de geste* is so beset with controversy of all sorts that it is hard to articulate a coherent point of view. Were the poems aggregations of *cantilènes*—hypothetical poetic accounts of battles between Christians and Muslims, or between rival feudal lords—originally composed at the time of these conflicts (ca. 800–1000)? Or were they more coherent from the start, originating from an oral tradition beginning in the eleventh century and celebrating heroic deeds of times long past? Were they chanted in a more or less monotonous recitative, were they sung to elaborate melodies comparable to Church chanting, or were they performed in some manner in between these two possibilities? Were they composed orally or were they written down? Do they employ oral formulas? Did the same *trouvères* who carried the troubadour impulse into northern France also sing the *gestes*? Or were these the property of a particular class of entertainers? Or were the composers monks who invented metrical tales about deeds of valor connected with localities along the routes of the great medieval pilgrimages? In particular, did the *Chanson de Roland* originate as entertainment for those on their way to the shrine of San Juan de Compostella? Did songs that celebrate the earlier exploits of a hero come first, or were they invented after his renown had been established by a dramatic account of his death in battle? Are the melodies for which notations survive, from the thirteenth century, records of how the *gestes* were sung, or are they later inventions? Is there any connection between the *chansons de geste* and the narratives of the lives of saints dating from the same period? Was the *lai* a natural evolution from, or refinement of, the *chanson de geste*? Were the *chansons de geste* accompanied by musical instruments? Answers pro or con to any of these questions do not involve any commitment one way or the other on the other questions; this inconsistency facilitates disagreement and discourages consensus.

The facts are that about a hundred such songs survive, ranging in length from about 1,000 to 20,000 lines, in manuscripts dating from about 1150 to 1400, and that they are most commonly composed in lines of ten syllables, sometimes of eight or twelve. Those in ten or twelve syllables fall into passages, or *laisses*, of perhaps ten to forty lines, that are held together by assonance, rhythm, or half-rhyme, sometimes in one sweep of monorhyme and sometimes with an unpredictable pattern involving two or three different sounds at the end of the line. Eight-syllable *chansons* were composed in rhyming couplets and may have been intended more for reading than for singing. There is wide agreement, however, that most *chansons de geste* were meant for some musical performance. A poem by the Anglo-French Wace, mentioned above as the author of *Le Roman de Brut*, is one of several that claim that the *Chanson de Roland* was sung by the victorious Normans as they marched into battle at Hastings. Many other references to their musical character survive—not least the simple fact that everyone calls them *chansons, songs*.

Jean Rychner, in his authoritative study that is also eminently readable and even diverting, *La Chanson de Geste*, is quite definite on this point:

> Cet art épique était, certes, un art de diseur, un art dramatique, le joueur "jouait" sa chanson, comme un acteur son rôle. Mais cet art était aussi musical, puisqu'enfin les chansons de geste sont des chansons, chantées avec accompagnement de vielle. (17)

> [This epic art was, certainly, an art of the teller, a dramatic art, the player *played* his song, as an actor would his role. But this art was also musical, since in the end the *chansons de geste* are songs, sung with a *vielle* accompaniment.]

The *vielle* was a form of lute, used by the Provençal singers, which was not bowed, but the strings of which vibrated when touched by a rosin-coated wheel turned with a crank; some strings were fingered to produce a melody, while one provided a sort of bass drone. The surviving example of such a melody belongs to a parody of the serious epic, the *Jeu de Robin et Marion*. But as Rychner argues, parodies always replicate essential features of what they mock, and therefore the score for this poem must also represent something used to accompany an actual *chanson de geste*. He also insists: "Mais établissons d'abord le fait: nos chansons étaient chantées par des jongleurs" (10). [But let's establish one fact right away: our songs were sung by *jongleurs*.] And he adduces much proof for his position.

All the poetic lines employed by later French poets, after poetry had emerged as an independent art form, originated as the verbal part of a song. Furthermore, the aural habits inculcated by these early songs established not only isosyllabism as the basis of French poetry but also the presumption that most poetry would be in *vers pairs*—that is, in lines containing an even number of syllables. It is true that the exception, the *vers impairs*, which was revived in the nineteenth century as a precursor to free verse, can also be found. But the predominant pattern was lines of eight, ten, and twelve syllables—not five, seven, nine, or eleven.

The metrical structure of these lines is more complex than counting the syllables will discover. All ten- and twelve-syllable lines were broken by a distinct caesura. Taking its very name from the metrical romances involving Alexander, the twelve-syllable ("Alexandrine") always broke into two half-lines, or hemistichs, from its earliest use. The ten-syllable line usually had a caesura after the fourth syllable, but occasionally after the sixth. All these breaks preserve the distribution of even numbers of syllables—the *vers pairs* pattern. The lines ended with a syllable—the assonantal or rhyming syllable—that carries more emphasis than any other; this makes both ten- and twelve-syllable lines akin to Dante's hendecasyllabic. Because an extra feminine syllable was often allowed just before the caesura, the ten-syllable line often really did have eleven syllables. A lesser degree of emphasis was also placed on the last syllable before the caesura (except for the feminine ending just mentioned). The regularity with which contemporary spoken French emphasizes the terminal syllables of polysyllabic words is a reflection of this long-established phonetic tendency toward terminal emphasis. Beyond these habits, which one hesitates to call *rules* because they were uncodified and observed with a good deal of latitude, other prosodic customs can be discerned, involving elision, hiatus, and enjambment (which *never* occurs in the *chansons de geste*).

Here is an example of a short *laisse* from the *Chanson de Roland*; at this point Roland is refusing to summon Charlemagne back from the pass in the Pyrenees, although Oliver has seen the great band of Saracens approaching and begs Roland to blow his horn, the olifant, as a signal:

> "Cumpainz Rollant, sunez vostre olifan,
>   Si l'orrat Carles, ki est as porz passant.
>   Je vos plevis, ja returnerunt Franc.
> —Ne placet Deu," ço li respunt Rollant,
>   "Que ço seit dit nul hume vivant,
>   Ne pur paien, que ja seie cornant!
>   Ja n'en avrunt reproece mi parent.
>   Quant jo serai en la bataille grant
>   E jo ferrai e mil colps e. VII. cenz,
>   De Durendal verrez lacer sanglant.
>   Franceis sunt bon, si ferrunt vassalment;
>   Ja cil d'Espagne n'avrunt de mort guarant."
>
> (1070–81)

The language of the poem seems in some ways as close to Latin as to modern French, with the absence of articles for many nouns, and the identifiable endings of the Latin conjugations still in place. But the rhythm is thoroughly modern without any hint of Latin quantity surviving. The four-syllable initial segment of each line is often definite enough to be marked by a comma; it is easy to tune one's ear to the recurrent one-two-three-FOUR, one-two-three-four-five-SIX of the meter, and easy to imagine it fitted to some insistent melodic line, with a rest at the caesura evening out the rhythm. The following translation aims at preserving that pattern:

> "Roland, my friend, a blast from Olifant!
> Charles will hear it, the pass is not distant,
> The French, I swear, be back in an instant."
> "God forbid that!" Thus answered him Roland,
> "That it be said, by one living human,
> I blew my horn, because of a pagan!
> Never will I bring shame to a parent.
> When in the midst of great battles I'm found
> I'll strike such blows, strike more than a thousand,
> See bloody steel, Durendal in my hand.
> Frenchmen are brave, and show themselves valiant;
> As for Spaniards, I have their death warrant."

Studies of the *chansons de geste* have attempted to establish the existence of a formulaic vocabulary comparable to that found by Parry and Lord in Homer and by Magoun in *Beowulf*. But one may be skeptical about claims of oral composition, noting the rather severe limitations placed on a singer who is subject to the restrictions of as many successive rhymes and assonance as such composition requires. We may remember that the truncated declensions and conjugations of Latin provided the Romance languages with a huge legacy of similar-sounding terminations, and a singer need not have ranged as far as we might at first think in order to come up with the rhymes. It would be as easy as to construct twenty successive lines in English with an *-ing* sound, adding a convenient participle or gerund at the end of every line. In the end, though, one wonders if the result of such ad-lib rhyming could possibly be anything that one would wish to write down; one is left with the suspicion that these heroic songs were composed with writing materials and use rhyme as an aid to memory. Although rhymes may be abundant, the different *laisses* employ many different sounds, and this—together with the syllabic limitations of the line— would require an impossible mental agility; the memorization of individual *laisses*, however, would be greatly facilitated by the rhymes, which would help the singer to recall the exact words that had been used in a previous performance of the song. There would be room for variation between different performers of the same song, but not the sort of half-improvisation that one imagines occurring in *Beowulf.* Whatever the conditions of composition, though, no one disputes the fact that they were sung.

From the tenth century on—and from even earlier times if one accepts various theories about the dating of *Beowulf* or the origins of the *chansons de geste*—there developed in England and on the European continent a vast poetic literature nearly all of which was involved to some degree with music. This could be, as we have seen in earlier chapters, both sacred and profane—and in some cases both at once. We could be speaking of very long works or very short ones, from a 20,000-line *geste* to a four-line popular song such as

> Westron wind, when will thou blow?
> The small rain down can rain.
> Christ, that my love were in my arms
> And I in my bed again.

Authorship could be accretive and oral, or individual and highly wrought; themes could be extremely conventional and repetitive or unique to the individual poem. The song-writer might expect to perform the work herself—or might employ a *jongleur* or *munstral*, in the words of *Piers Plowman*. The song might be the result of the perilously refined courtly society of Provence, or a rude backland province on the Scottish border or in the eastern baronies of Germany. The subject could be the refinements of courtly love flirtations, or the anatomically horrifying details of wounds in combat. But in every case the words went not *to*, but *with*, music, and music with the words.

5

Nature and Artifice

Et est a scavoir que nous avons deux musiques, dont l'une est
artificiele et l'autre est naturele.

—Eustache Deschamps

The emancipation from musical accompaniment made possible
Dante's verse.

—F. T. Prince

To argue that Dante, in his poetry, distanced himself from music
may at first seem radically misguided. *The Divine Comedy*, after all, does
include numerous references to music; as one reads it one is constantly aware
of music as a metaphor for the harmonious disposition of the soul, as an
analogy of the hierarchical arrangement of the cosmos, as a source for or
expression of the soul's aspirations toward eternal beatitude.

But not at first. There is no music in hell—only groans, sighs, shrieks, curses,
animal growls, hissing of snakes, and other kinds of random clamor, including
meaningless blats and trumpetings. Climbing away from the cacophonies of
the *Inferno*, however, Dante arrives on the shore of Purgatory and immediately
is ushered into a realm where harmony, or at least melody, reflects the gradual
accommodation of the soul, stage by stage, to the divine ordinances. In Canto
2, on his first morning, a "swift vessel" arrives with a hundred shades who chant
in unison Psalm 114, the *In exitu Israel*, rejoicing in their escape from this world
and from eternal bondage as if from Egyptian exile. Only a few lines further on,
Dante encounters his friend Pietro Casella, who sings to him one of Dante's
own canzones, "Amor, che nella mente mi ragiona" [Love, which speaks in my
thoughts], "which he then began so sweetly that I can still hear that sweetness."

That Dante set great store by this song is evident in his having devoted the
entirety of Book 3 of the *Convivio* to an exposition of its theme, ideas, and
imagery. He explicates the ninety-line poem phrase by phrase, making connections with or introducing parallels from the Bible, theology, Plato, Aris-

totle, the *Aeneid*, Pythagoras, Avicenna, the *Thebaid*, and much else. His explications of this and another canzone, "Voi, che 'ntendendo il terzo ciel movete" [You who through understanding move the third heaven], prepare the way for *The Divine Comedy* by exploring and making explicit what he felt to have been implied in the passionate love-poetry of his youth. In Book 2 of the *Convivio* he explains the levels of allegory (literal, allegorical, anagogical, and moral) that poetry is capable of, while in Book 3 he works his way toward the resolution of various ethical and philosophical problems, via the poem. In assigning it to his composer-friend for performance immediately upon his entrance to Purgatory, Dante is asserting his own power, both as poet and thinker, to continue—eventually beyond the guidance of Virgil—into regions never explored by poetry; he is also preparing himself for purgation of the fleshly elements that went into the original compositions. Is it too much to argue that in leaving behind the purely erotic songs of the troubadours, in transmuting earthly music into a harmony of the spirit, Dante's canzone bridges the way for the soul as it ascends from this world to the next? "Pipe to the spirit ditties of no tone," wrote a much later poet in another language, and Dante's likewise is supersensual and ineffable.

In Canto 7 Dante is conducted into a fold in the mountain of Purgatory where a group of souls sit on the flowery sward singing the post-evensong *Salve Regina*, and after sunset he listens to the singing of one of the hymns ascribed to Ambrose, *Te lucis ante terminum*. As he enters Purgatory proper on the next day, the harsh sound of the door's hinges, reminiscent of the discord he will leave behind, gives way to the singing of another Ambrosian hymn, the *Te Deum laudamus*, the effect of which he compares to a choir accompanied by an organ, which sometimes obscures the words and sometimes allows them to be heard clearly.

As he rises through Paradise his experience of music becomes more abstracted, more instrumental, befitting the ever-increasing ineffability of the experience. In Canto 14 he sees the cross of Mars, composed of the souls of the warriors of God; these flit in and out and up and down the cross itself, like motes in a beam of sunlight, singing a hymn of which he cannot quite catch the words; he compares the aural effect to that of stringed instruments of which the listener can perceive a general harmony without being able to hear the individual notes. In the *Convivio*, Dante discussed the appropriateness of the Heaven of Mars to music; some of this seems a little far-fetched, but it does convey the musical-numerological frame of mind:

E lo cielo di Marte si può comprare a la Musica per due proprietadi: l'una si è la sua più bella relazione, ché, annumerando li cieli mobili, da qualunque si comincia o da l'infimo o dal sommo, esso cielo di Marte è lo quinto, esso è lo mezzo di tutti . . .

[L]a Musica, la quale è tutta relativa, sì come si vede ne le parole armonizzate e ne li canti, de' quali tanto più dolce armonia resulta, quanto più la relazione è bella; la quale in essa scienza massimamente è bella, perché massimamente in essa s'intende. Ancora: la Musica trae a sé li spiriti umani, che quasi sono principalmente vapori del cuore, sì che quasi cessano da ogni operazione; si è l'anima intera, quando l'ode, e la virtù di tutti quasi corre a lo spirito sensibile, che riceve lo suono. (2.13.20–24)

[And the Heaven of Mars can be compared to Music in two respects: the first is its most beautiful relationship since, numbering the moving heavens, whether we begin at the top or the bottom, this Heaven of Mars is the fifth, this is in the middle of all of them . . .

[W]ith Music everything is a matter of relations, as appears in harmonious speech and in songs, inasmuch as the sweeter the resulting harmony, the more beautiful the relationship; which is of greatest beauty in this science because it is concerned with exactly that. In addition: Music attracts the spirits of a human being to itself, which are mainly the spirits of the blood, so that they almost cease to function; and it is the inner soul, when it listens, and the strength of all the spirits collect into the sensitive spirit, which receives the sound.]

Here Dante is asserting that in a living human being the "animal spirits," which hover like vapors in the bloodstream and are controlled by the heart, are collected and sublimated into something higher by the power of music.

In the heaven of Jupiter that follows, in Canto 18, the letter *M* transforms itself into the likeness of an eagle, accompanied by a similar sort of music. (The *M* appears as the last letter of "QUI JUDICATIS TERRAM," "ye who judge the earth," the opening phrase of *The Book of Wisdom*. The letter stands for *Monarchia*, or government.) In Canto 20 several semimusical effects are described, and the canto ends with a musical metaphor, comparing the responsiveness of the listeners to the tact with which an instrumentalist accompanies a singer. The crowning and subsequent ascent of the Blessed Virgin in Canto 23 is accompanied by a display in which visual effects, a lyre-like music, and a hymn blend and exchange effects with one another in an ecstasy of pure aesthetic intuition.

The numerology of the poem also has much in common with medieval musical theory—the terza rima, for example, being suggestive of the Trinity, reminiscent of efforts of the Notre Dame de Paris school of composers to resolve all musical measures into threefold units. All these are commonplaces in discussion of *The Divine Comedy*—the division into three major units, the first two composed of thirty-three cantos each, and the last of thirty-four, bringing it to a perfected length of one hundred, for example. The seven deadly sins provide only the loosest general framework for hell; the disordering effects of sinfulness lead to many anomalies and gradations that destroy its symmetry and confuse its classifications. For the upward-bound souls in Purgatory, however, the structure and progression are most orderly, with sub-groupings of the three irascible sins (pride, envy, anger) at the bottom, the three concupiscible sins (avarice, gluttony, lust) at the top, and, in between, sloth. Other additions bring the levels there up to the perfect ten. This is not the place to lay out at length the Christian Pythagoreanism of Dante's scheme; but we should at least mention these numbers and ratios because of their importance in even so down-to-earth a poet as Chaucer, and because such ingenuities are partly responsible for the fact that poetry and music in so many respects went their separate ways in the fourteenth century. That is, both music and poetry began to cultivate, in separate ways, complexities that were unique to each art and that could not be mutually duplicated. This development tended to give each art its own identity and to separate it from the other.

Despite the impression of musical texture and structure, no one imagines *The Divine Comedy* as intended literally as part of a musical performance. Over the centuries many passages, and whole cantos, have been set to music, and the poem has provided inspiration for purely instrumental works. Such music as the poem has, though, is what we shall see Deschamps calling "natural" music; Dante has taken the echoes, assonances, onomatopoeia, and associations of all sorts and constructed out of them a new art which, whatever it may owe to musical ideas or to musical inspiration, is independent of music per se. Considering it from a purely theoretical point of view, one might imagine that a person who was himself a musician, and who was familiar with innumerable poems—sacred and secular—that did demand musical performance, as Dante was, might have aimed at a fusion of two arts that include temporal dimensions. There are at least three reasons why he did not. First, what he had to say was so elevated, so complex, so full of cross-references to persons, places, books, other poems, theology, astronomy, history, and human psychology, that a melodic setting of the poem could only have been a distraction, even if it were a recitative-like chanting, the only possible accompaniment for a work of such length. Second, there are innumerable moments or scenes with great visual and dramatic impact, in which the imagination of the reader is expected to be fully engaged in a sympathetic re-creation of what the poet had envisioned. The reader must be free to pause as long as is necessary, or as long as it is pleasing to do so, in order to experience such scenes or images; one would not wish to be hurried ahead by the demands of a musical structure. Third, and perhaps most important for his original conception of the *Comedy* as a purely verbal construction, Dante had before him the example not only of Virgil but of all Latin poetry, almost none of which was intended for music. This last consideration, perhaps, most completely accounts for his weaning himself from the fount of medieval song. Indeed, one way of distinguishing the beginnings of the Renaissance, as it moved northward across Europe from country to country and from language to language, is to point to the separation of poetry from music, sometimes in emulation of Latin verse.

Dante was, in his other writings, an immediate heir to the legacy of the troubadours; we know how often he paid tribute to the Provençal poets in his own work. He had been in the habit of thinking of poetry as song and only as song. Even when describing a form, the canzone, which neither he nor any other Italian poet seems to have believed in need of a specially composed melody, he talks about it in terms of music; the word itself is simply the Italian version of *canso* or *chanson*. And yet, as W. Thomas Marrocco says, "No thirteenth- or fourteenth-century musical settings of Dante's canzoni (or canzoni of other poets of the fourteenth century) have come down to us, whereas hundreds of madrigals, rispetti, cacce, ballate, and laude of the same period have been preserved" (709). Marrocco also argues persuasively that since Dante was the greatest poet of his time, any settings would surely have been preserved; there are examples of Italian madrigals from the same time, settings for which are found in several different manuscripts. James Haar thinks that there were settings, but that this does not strengthen a case that Dante wrote for music, however much he may have enjoyed hearing his poems clothed (*rivestita*) in music, as Boccaccio put it. Haar writes:

> Some of Dante's poetry was given musical setting during his lifetime, but these settings have not survived; and he did not write *poesia per musica* of the sort used by musicians of the trecento. Both Boccaccio and Petrarch did; and though composers turned only rarely to their poetry during the fourteenth century, it is in their lifetime that a remarkable body of music, much of it surviving in large manuscript collections and a number of isolated fragments, was written and performed. (1)

The crux of this issue in Dante's own writings occurs in Chapter 8 of the second part of *De Vulgari Eloquentia*: "Praeterea disserendum est, utrum cantio dicatur fabricatio verborum armonizatorum, vel ipsa modulatio; ad quod dicimus, quod nunquam modulatio dicitur cantio, sed sonus, vel tonus, vel nota, vel melos." [Next to be discussed is, whether the composition of harmonizing words is called *cantio*, or the word-harmony itself; to which we say, that never is the word-harmony called *cantio*, but the sound, or the tone, or the note, or the melody.] Or so I would translate it; Marianne Shapiro renders it, "Next we must discuss whether we apply the word *canzone* to the setting of words to harmonies or to the metric form itself." This version implies quite a different explanation of Dante's meaning. It puzzles me considerably, though, that Shapiro chooses to translate "modulatio" as "metric form," but then goes on to translate the same word as "music" in the next phrase: "To which I reply that music is never called *cantio* . . ." (81). The source of this difference may be the original use of "modulatio" by Quintilian to mean "rhythmical measure." Perhaps in translating it as "music" Shapiro was merely slipping into the common metaphorical use of the word. Dante then continues his argument:

> For no flute-player, or organist, or player of the lyre calls his melody a cantio, unless to some extent it has been combined with a *canzone*; but composers of music for words call their works *canzoni*. And we also call such words on paper canzoni, when no one sings them; and therefore a canzone appears to be nothing else than the finished action of writing down words to be set to music.

Then, as if the issue were not already becoming sufficiently confused, Dante broadens the definition of "canzone" to include many other forms inherited from the troubadours, including not only those for which many musical settings survive, but dances and possibly even hymns. How are we to explain the fact that at least for Italian *canzoni* no scores survive? In his book, *Dante e la Musica*, Arnaldo Bonaventura provides the score for a poem of that type (8)— but the poem is in French. Also, what are we to make of the performance in Purgatory of Dante's poem by his friend, Pietro Casella da Pistoia? Marrocco's answer to the first of these questions seems to me sufficiently convincing: "The canzone in the Italian trecento was dedicated to such lofty and serious subjects, that the addition of a musical accompaniment would serve to distract the listener rather than to heighten the poetic message" (712). Dante evidently liked the *idea* of the poems as musical performances, but the realization of such a synaesthetic and intellectual experience would have to await the afterlife; it was an ideal to be aspired to rather than a practical possibility. The *musical* canzone was rather like the Beatrice of Dante's imagination—not the real young woman who walked the streets of Florence. This may be the explanation if the canzone was meant only to suggest a musical form; but given Dante's emphasis on the stanza as essential to the canzone, there is also the possibility that many preexisting melodies could be adapted to the individual stanzas, and therefore no score needed to be invented especially for a given canzone, the choice of melody being left up to the performer. The most authoritative statement on this question may be that of Patrick Boyde, who wrote the "Note on Dante's Metric and Versification" in the edition *Dante's Lyric Poetry*, which he edited with Kenelm Foster:

> In the Italian tradition, however, where the earliest surviving canzoni date from *c.* 1230, the poet did not compose the melody for his lyric, and ordinarily the canzone was not set to music at all—this being a fact which had important consequences for the development of the genre in Italy. Nevertheless, although the Italian canzone was not set, it still had to be 'settable': *omnis stantia a quandam odam recipiendam armonizata est* (DVE II.x.2). Thus, although it was a 'literary' and not a 'lyric' poem, its form was still determined by musical conventions. (xliv–xlv)

Therefore, to revert to my oft-repeated theme, *The Divine Comedy*, via the canzone, *did emerge from music*, from a musical concept of poetry, and ultimately from the actuality of the troubadour and Italian vernacular songs. Dante made much of the importance and function of the stanzas, the little rooms or stopping places, of the canzone; as he said, ignorance of the stanza meant ignorance of the canzone. In *The Divine Comedy* the stanza is dissolved in the more fluid and stichic groupings of the terza rima, and the entire canzone, or canto, becomes the stanza of the epic, the units into which it is subdivided. A verbal music that constantly carries with it hints of actual melody replaces the literal singing; Dante's guide was Virgil, and as Dante himself pointed out, when Virgil announces with the word "cano" that he is *singing* arms and the man, in the *Aeneid*'s first line, he means something other than melody.

Following Dante's inimitable achievement there were only two ways to go. The one took Petrarch back to Latin and to quantitative hexameters, in which he composed most of his poetry. Petrarch also turned back to the troubadour models and to the canzone, which had grown out of those models. The other direction led Boccaccio into his narrative and epic poems written in terza rima and ottava rima, and ultimately into prose fiction—into a more colloquial and informal literary art. And Boccaccio in turn became the most important example for Chaucer.

Before we take up Chaucer, however, we must turn back to the literature of France, because it was in imitation of thirteenth- and fourteenth-century French poetry that Chaucer served his apprenticeship as a poet. The French poetry that most directly affected Chaucer was itself emergent from a musical context. The manner in which this emergence occurred was to some degree comparable to the transition to purely verbal epic and narrative in Italian literature. In the French poetry of the twelfth century, however, the genre that bridged the gap between the singing of the *chansons de geste* (and the trouvère lyrics as well) and the later romances and narratives in octosyllabic or deca-syllabic rhyming couplets was the *lai*. The *lai* was, as John Fox puts it, "in effect, a miniature romance relating a single sentimental adventure, lacking the sustained effort, the *conjointure*, needed in a romance of several thousand lines" (168). These middle-length poems were performed by *jongleurs* and most had to do with the *matière de Bretagne*, the Celtic Arthurian romances. As Jean Rychner says in his edition of the *lais* of Marie de France:

> A l'époque de Marie, des jongleurs originaires de Bretagne armoricaine chantaient, en s'accompagnant de la rote ou de la harpe, des chansons qu'ils nommaient des *lais* et que le public appelait bretons à cause surtout de l'origine de ceux qui les chantaient. Nous ne savons pour ainsi dire rien de certain sur ces chansons, dont l'existence cependant, abondamment attestée, ne saurait faire de doute. (qtd. in Fox 168)

> [During the period when Marie lived, some jongleurs who came from westernmost Brittany, accompanying themselves on a fiddle or harp, would sing songs that they called *lais* and which the public called Breton, above all because of the origin of those who sang them. We do not know anything definite about these songs, the existence of which is, however, abundantly attested to and is beyond doubt.]

But though the origin of the *lai* was oral and musical, those of Marie of France were composed on paper and read, not sung, aloud. This is clear from a con-temporary reference to their popularity with the nobility, who "lire le funt" [had them read] (see Fox 171). The "music" of the rhyming couplets was suffi-cient—or, to put it another way, it is very hard to imagine any sort of actual music that would be suitable for a lengthy composition in couplets, whether French or English; try to imagine a setting for *Hudibras*, or for "To His Coy Mistress." We do not know what the original oral Breton lays were like, but we may imagine that they had more in common with some ballad form or that they employed assonantal units, such the *laisses* of the *chansons de geste*.

We may view Marie's *lai* as a sufficient but not as a necessary cause of the numerous poems that followed in the thirteenth and fourteenth centuries, in which oral performance, if any was expected, would involve reading and not singing. There existed already examples of longer literary *chansons de geste* composed in octosyllabic couplets, though it may well have been the *lai* that popularized the recitation of a shorter, and more finished, narrative—ulti-mately providing a model for certain of Chaucer's *Canterbury Tales*. Another extramusical use of verse was the rhymed dialogue of twelfth- and thirteenth-century vernacular drama, such as the *Mystère d'Adam* and *Courtois d'Arras*, both in octosyllabics. In the fourteenth century, however, the presumption still was that anything modeled on the troubadour/trouvère forms was intended as a song; we shall now examine the more complex problem of how forms such as the sonnet, the ballade, and the virelay achieved independence as verbal artifacts.

The bifurcation of melody and words was the inevitable consequence of the increasing sophistication with which both were employed in their respective art forms. A great deal of the responsibility for the independence of both media, in French poetry and in Chaucer, belongs to one person: Guillaume de Machaut (1300?–1377). The consensus of musicologists is that Machaut was the greatest composer of his century, and the abundance and intricacy of his poetic works are enough to place his name among the most important poets; he is, for example, credited with introducing the strict ballade form, the virelay (which Machaut called the *chanson balladée*), and the rondeau. In the introduction to *Le Jugement du roy de Behaigne* and *Remede de Fortune*, Wimsatt and Kibler state flatly: "Machaut is the most important French poet and musical composer of the fourteenth century" (3).

Machaut, it is clear, was fascinated—obsessed, almost—with embedding the maximum amount of complexity in his works, to the point that his constructions have as much in common with cryptography as with art. Much of this is imperceptible to the listener, whether of music or poetry or both simultaneously. As late as 1970 James Wimsatt uncovered an acrostic in one of his poems that had escaped notice for centuries; gimmicks and tricks abound in his music. But let those speak who have competence to do so, as does Donald Jay Grout:

> Machaut's *rondeaux* have a highly sophisticated musical content, and one of them is an often cited example of ingenuity. Its enigmatic tenor text—"Ma fin est mon commencement et mon commencement ma fin" ("My end is my beginning and my beginning my end")—means that the melody of the tenor is that of the topmost voice sung backward; the melody of the contratenor also illustrates the text, because its second half is the reverse of its first half. (123)

James Anderson Winn's brilliant discussion (*Eloquence* 103–21) of these parallel traits in his music and poetry seems unlikely to be surpassed for authoritativeness in both areas simultaneously; Winn concludes, "A more balanced account of Machaut will have to see him as at once the heir of the trouvères, with their similarly conventional claims of sentiment and their similarly intricate poetic forms, and the heir of the early polyphonists, with their mystical reverence for number and their literary fondness for troping" (121). It could easily be argued that the music and the poetry succeed *in spite of* such numerological and alphabetic contraptions, and that these gimmicks are without real significance to the arts in which they are embedded—as if we were suddenly to decipher some personal message concealed for centuries amid the text of *Hamlet*, or discover that a Mozart symphony was constructed according to a differential equation. To repeat: such experiments as Machaut made did tend to emphasize the separateness of word and notated melody and to lever apart the synthesis he had inherited from Church music and from the troubadours. Machaut himself, and poets who came after him, continued to write words that were, or could be, set to music, but to do so was to involve oneself in an increasingly self-conscious set of pastimes. Wimsatt and Kibler point (5 n) to the fact that two ballades that Deschamps wrote on the death of Machaut were themselves set to music, perhaps as a special tribute to their subject's dual achievements. This occurred despite the fact that—as we shall see—Deschamps argued for the separation of the two arts.

Most of what Machaut wrote as poetry had no connection with music at all, being derivative from the *Roman de la Rose* and the non-musical *lais*. His octasyllabics in these works, especially in *Le Jugement du roy de Behaigne*, provided both the model and some of the actual substance for Chaucer's early work, most notably *The Book of the Duchess*. Also, of the 420 shorter poems he wrote, only about a third were provided with settings. Since the ideal of earlier composers was to provide each poem with a unique setting, this percentage may indicate an assumption that poetry could begin to stand on its own, or at least a certain indifference to what had hitherto been assumed as essential. And where scores are available, my impression, at least, is that the music offers us a display of virtuosity which soars like Shelley's skylark somewhat out of sight of the reiterated professions of adoration or laments of indifference of the beloved that are conveyed by the words. Musicologists are a good deal more confident of the authenticity of contemporary performances of Machaut than of those of earlier composers, and we may be safe in assuming that what we hear in a modern performance is close to what was intended (closer, especially, than earlier music performed so as to bring out a supposed Arabic influence). And what we hear, it seems to me, is an art poised to break away completely not only from the word, but from the human voice itself; the human voice in Machaut's music is employed much like an instrument. Conversely, in the poetry, we see a verbal construct still limited by a familiar array of love themes and romantic allegory, and still borrowing its form analogically from music, but ready to lend itself to a new range of subjects and a new complexity and seriousness. Not that his poetry achieved this extended range; his shorter poems, however skillfully executed they may be, are for the most part interminable litanies of the commonplaces of courtly love. A good example is the ballade "Dame de qui toute ma joie vient," which appears as lines 3013–36 of the *Remede de Fortune*. The situation at this point in the *Remede* is of minimal complexity (as is the entire poem, two-thirds of which is written in rhyming couplets meant for reading aloud). A lover tells how he fell in love and became embarrassed when his lady-love discovered a song he had written for her. He complains at length against Fortune. A lady named Esperance (hope) appears and spends about a thousand lines cheering the lover up. In an improved state of mind, he sings the following ballade:

Dame de qui toute ma joie vient,	Lady, who brings me all my joys
Je ne vous puis trop amer, ne cherir,	I cannot cherish you nor love
N'assés loer, si com il apartient,	Sufficiently, nor can I praise,
Servir, doubter, honnourer, n'obeïr;	Obey, respect, honor, nor serve;
Car la gracïeus Espoir,	For Hope that lends its grace
Douce dame, que j'ay de vous veoir,	That I, sweet lady, see your face,
Me fait .c. foys plus de bien et de joye	Brings me a hundred times the joys
Qu'en cent mil ans desservir ne porroie.	Than could a thousand centuries.
Cilz douls Espoirs en vie me soustient	Sweet Hope it is keeps me alive
Et me norrist en amoureus desir,	And feeds my amorous desire,
Et dedens moy met tout ce qui couvient	Gives me whatever I might crave
Pour conforter mon cuer et resjoïr;	As comfort to ward off despair,
N'il ne s'en part main ne soir,	With me from dawn to dusk,
Ainçoys me fait doucement recevoir	So that it is my easy task
Plus des douls beins qu'Amours as siens envoie	To take more sweets that love conveys
Qu'en .c. mil ans desservir ne porroie.	Than could a thousand centuries.
Et quant Espoir qui en mon cuer se tient	As since that Hope fixed in my heart
Fait dedens moy si grant joie venir	Fills me with such great joyousness
Lointeins de vous, ma dame, s'il avient	While we are yet so far apart,
Que vo beauté voie que moult desir,	Could I but see that beauteous face,
Ma joye, si com j'espoir,	No one would ever guess,
Ymaginer, penser, ne concevoir	Imagine or conceive such bliss
Ne porroit nuls, car trop plus en aroie	Bestowing more of happiness
Qu'en cent mil ans desservir ne porroie.	Than could a thousand centuries.

The music to which Machaut set this poem is far more complex than one might imagine from the text. Wimsatt and Kibler reproduce as Miniature 24 (Appendix II) an illuminated score from a manuscript in France's Bibliothèque Nationale, which they believe to have been executed under Machaut's supervision between 1350 and 1356. In a modern performance directed by Christopher Page, the polyphony embroiders itself elaborately around the simple and repetitive message conveyed by the words; the words are hardly more than an occasion for melody. Yet the musical passage (the song just quoted), embedded as it is amid so much dilatory narrative and dialogue, was meant as an essential part of the total performance, almost like an isolated aria amidst an enormous amount of recitative.

At least one of Machaut's ballades exhibits an intricacy—an almost gratuitous ingenuity—reminiscent of the concealed schemes in his music. As if the ballade form were not already sufficiently confining—the seven-line version permitting only three rhyme sounds arranged in identical patterns for all three stanzas—in this poem he adds a requirement that the first word of each line pick up the rhyme word of the previous line. This practice is called, variously, *rime fratrisée, entrelacée, enchainée,* or *annexée*—or, in English, "chain rhyme." It is comparable to anadiplosis in rhetoric. This poem appears as "Balade LXV" in the Chichmaref edition of Machaut's *Poésies Lyriques* (78–79).

Douce dame, vo maniere jolie
Lie en amours mon cuer et mon desir
Desiramment, si que, sans tricherie,
Chiérie adès en serés, sans partir.
Partir vaut miex que d'autre souvenir
Venir peüst en moy, que en ardure

Durement vif et humblement l'endure.

Dure à moy seul, de tous biens assevie
Vie d'onneur plaisant à maintenir
Tenir m'estuet du tout en vo bailliet
Liement, et, pour joie desservir,
Servir vous vueil et mes maus conjoïr.
Joïr n'espoir, helas! et sans laidure
Durement vif et humblement l'endure.

Dur espoir ay, puis qu'Amours ne m'aïe.
Aïe à vous me convient requerir;
Querir ne l'os, pour ce qu'á m'anemie
Mie ne doy ma dolour descouvrir.
Couvrir en moy l'aim mieu jusqu'au morir.
Morir me plaist, et, combien que me dure,
Durement vif et humblement l'endure.

Sweet lady, how your lovely way
Waylays my heart and my desire,
Desirous, without trickery,
Cherishing you for evermore.
More yet: if I must leave you here,
Here then remains my heart's true ardor.
Arduous, humble life—none harder!

Hard and lonely, lovely lady!
Laden with honor's weightless care
Caring only that I obey,
Obedient in your service dear,
Dear even for the pains I bear,
Bear up, to hopeless love a martyr—
Arduous, humble life—none harder!

Hard hope I have, if Love deny me.
Deny me not what I require;
Require, though, lest my enemy
My plans might learn, I do not dare.
Dire though it be, I may not share,
Not share till death comes as reward for
Arduous, humble life—none harder!

Only forty-one of Machaut's numerous ballades are *ballades notées* ("set to music"), and it therefore seems probable that he wrote poems for recitation as well as for singing. But it remained for his friend and admirer Eustache Deschamps (1346?–1407?)—one might almost call him Machaut's stepson, since he was raised by the elder poet—to enunciate the distinction clearly and to insist explicitly that poetry had a music of its own that could hold it together independently of melody. Deschamps composed an enormous number of ballades—1,017, to be exact—but wrote no music for any of them or for any other of his poems. He appears to have intended early on to pry poetry loose from its musical context, and in a treatise that he composed late in his life (1392?), *L'Art de Dictier*, he laid out his arguments for having done so.

This work is almost equal in importance to Dante's *De Vulgari Eloquentia* in defining the direction that poetry would henceforth take in European literature. To say this is not, of course, to elevate Deschamps to the level of a great critic; his is a prominence of uniqueness rather than excellence. Putting the two treatises together, however, the one at the beginning of the fourteenth century and the other at the end, gives us a Janus of poetics: Dante, looking mostly back to the classics and composing, in Latin, his argument for the use of the *vernacular*, and Deschamps insisting on something rather like Romantic inspiration as a source for poetry (in which the question of which language to use is moot). Dante reverences the Catholic tradition, while in Deschamps there appear hints of the Reformation spirit, or at least the sturdy intellectual independence of a Galileo and the humane worldliness of a Montaigne. For our purposes the contrasting attitudes toward music are even more interesting. In discussing the canzone, Dante persists in using the terminology of music, as if he were consciously reverencing the troubadour origins of all the shorter poetic forms. In using that terminology, Dante also recognizes what vernacular poetry may have owed to the musical liturgy of the Church. Deschamps, as we have seen, explicitly sets music apart from poetry. Here are some relevant passages from *L'Art de Dictier*, the first of which appears when Deschamps takes up music, which he calls, "la derreniere science ainsis comme la medicine des vij ars" [the last science, as it were the medicine of the seven arts]:

> Et est a scavoir que nous avons deux musiques, dont l'une est artificiele de son art et l'autre est naturele.
>
> L'artificielle est celle dont dessus est faicte mencion; et est appellee artificiele de son art, car par ses vj notes, qui sont appellees us, re, my, fa, sol, la, l'en puet aprandre a chanter, acorder, doubler, quintoier, tiercoier, tenir, deschanter, par figure de notes, par clefs et par lignes, le plus rude homme du monde. (60)

[We should know that we have two kinds of music, one artificial and the other natural.

The artificial is that already mentioned above; and it is called artificial because it uses art, since with its six notes, which are called *us, re, mi, fa, sol, la*, one can teach the most ignorant person in the world to sing, to harmonize, to sing in octaves, fifths, thirds, to sing tenor, to descant, by using notes, clefs, and lines.]

This facile scorn of the technical side of music was reiterated some five hundred years later in Ford Madox Ford's view that any English schoolboy can compose not only metrical verse, but verses in Latin quantities—the easiest thing in the world. Nineteenth- and twentieth-century vers-librists carried metrics a second remove away from music, paradoxically asserting (as Ezra Pound did) that poetry must be composed "according to the musical phrase." But let us hear more of Deschamps's manifesto:

L'autre musique est appellee naturele pour ce qu'elle ne puet estre aprinse a nul, se son propre couraige naturelment ne s'i applique, et est une musique de bouche en proferant paroules metrifiees, aucunefoiz en laiz, autrefoiz en balades, autrefois en rondeaulx. . . . Et ja soit ce que ceste musique naturele se face de volunte amoureuse a la louenge des dames, et en autres manieres, selon les materes et le sentement de ceuls qui en cest musique s'appliquent, et que les faiseurs d'icelle ne saichent pas communement la musique artificiele ne donner chant par art de notes a ce qu'ilz font, toutesvoies est appellee musique ceste science naturele pour ce que les diz et chancons par eulx faiz ou les livres metrifiez se lisent de bouche, et proferent par voix non pas chantable, tant que les douces paroles ainsis faictes et recordees par voiz plaisant aux escoutans qui les oyent, si que au puy d'amours anciennement et encores acoustumez en pluseurs villes et citez des pais et royaumes du monde. (62–64)

[The other music is called natural because it cannot be taught to anyone unless he has a natural aptitude for it, and it is a music of the mouth which issues in measured language, sometimes in *lais*, sometimes in ballades, sometimes in rondeaus. . . . And albeit that this natural music grows out of the amorous wish to praise women, and in other ways, according to the subjects and the feelings of those who set themselves to compose this music, and though the composers of the latter ordinarily do not understand artificial music, nor how to provide a melody using musical notation, at all events this natural knowledge is called music because one reads aloud these *dits* and *chansons* that they invent, or these versified books, not in a singing voice, although the sweet words are composed and recited by a voice that is pleasing to the listeners who hear them, as in old times it was at the fountain of

love as even now it is the custom in several towns and cities of the countries
and kingdoms of the world.]

Though he is careful always to insist on the "propre et naturel mouvement" of
the poet, Deschamps then proceeds to set out the rules for various kinds of
poetry which simultaneously reclaim ancient "enthusiasm" or inspiration and
anticipate the concept of individual artistic genius, which had its roots in the
humanistic spirit evinced by Deschamps.

Although, as Milton and others were to repeat much later, Deschamps
speaks of music and poetry as "wedded," he means to point out that poetry
may now go its own way. Those who continue to yearn for a reconciliation
sometimes accuse him of trying to cover up his own musical incompetence
(see James Wimsatt 133). That his remarks about melody are rather dismissive
may be partly excused as a polemic necessity—a need to detach his own verbal
art from the authority of Augustine and Boethius, from the *musica* of classical
scansions, so that the natural emphases and rhythms of the vernacular may
assert themselves. Deschamps may also have perceived what was to be much
more evident in following centuries, that instrumental and polyphonic vocal
music were acquiring an authority and independence of their own, and he
may have wished to claim the same independence for his own art.

A single example can hardly begin to illustrate the range of subjects treated
in the poetry of Deschamps, but perhaps this ballade, a miniature beast fable,
may suggest how far the poet has moved us along the road toward the ordinary
speech and lore of the people, and away from the liturgical and aristocratic
formulas of worship, whether the object of devotion was a saint or a beautiful
woman. With Deschamps, as in much written by his friend, Geoffrey Chaucer, we enter into a literary third estate, into a middle or even a low style.
Deschamps's detractors, indeed, have long viewed him as something of a hack.

BALLADE LVIII

Je treuve qu' entre les souris
Ot un merveilleus parlement
Contre les chas leurs ennemis
A veoir maniere comment
Elles vesquissent seurement
Sanz demourer en tel debat;
L'une dist lors en arguant:
"Qui pendra la sonnette au chat?"

Ciz consaus fu conclus et pris;

A parliament of mice, they say,
Assembled, glorious to behold,
Considering how to do away
With cats, their enemies of old,
How cats might finally be controlled
To put an end to the ancient spat;
A logical mouse at once made bold:
"Which of us will bell the cat?"

The question seemed resolved:
  straightway

Lors se partent communement.   They took their leave, greatly consoled.
Une souris du plat païs   But a flatland mouse that came that way
Les encontre, et va demandant   Wanted to chat, and buttonholed
Qu'on a fait. Lors vont respondant   Each one: "What's up?" The plans unfold:

Que leur ennemi seront mat,   With a bell to tell where he was at
Sonnette avront au cou pendant: They'd have the foe in a stranglehold:
"Qui pendra la sonnette au chat?   "Which of us will bell the cat?"

—C'est le plus fort," dit un rat gris.   —Ay, there's the rub," said a rat in gray.
Elle demande saigement   The mouse, with wisdom manifold,
Par qui sera cis fais fournis.   Kept asking who would save the day.
Il n'i ot point d'executant,   The response to this was rather cold;
Lors s'en va chascun excusant: They all backed off, not overbold:
S'en va leur besoigne de plat.   Their enterprise, of course, fell flat.
Bien fut dit, mais, au demourant,   Big talk, but then when all is told,
Qui pendra la sonnette au chat?   Which of us will bell the cat?

Envoi

Prince, on conseille bien souvent,   Prince, advice comes thousandfold,
Mais on peut dire, com le rat,   But one might say, like that gray rat,
Du conseil qui sa fin ne prent: Of counsels no one dares uphold:
"Qui pendra la sonnette au chat?"   "Which of us will bell the cat?"

Whatever analogies one may discover between Chaucer's structural and thematic patterns and those of music, and however many references—often highly appreciative—one may find in his works, all the "melody" in Chaucer is what Deschamps called *musique naturele*—rhythm and other aural effects belonging to language itself, and capable of being mastered only by a born poet (according to Deschamps). No doubt much remains to be done to demonstrate Chaucer's multifold euphoniousness—the immediate appeal to the ear that made him the "deare mayster" to emulate for the next two centuries. For my purposes, however, it is sufficient to point out that, by schooling himself in the *lais* and longer poems in octasyllabic and decasyllabic couplets of his French precursors and contemporaries, with some additions from what he learned from Boccaccio, Chaucer was able to naturalize in English poetry meters that had already separated themselves from music in the original languages and to use them to elicit lovely effects from his native speech. It will not do to overstate Chaucer's debt to Deschamps, which was probably minimal; he already had the works of Ovid and Virgil, which he knew well, to supply him with examples of a poetry whose aesthetic effect was purely verbal.

A few exceptions might be mentioned. Although most of the handful of ballades that Chaucer left do not seem to call for musical accompaniment, "To Rosemounde" is, as John H. Fisher says, "of a sort that can be sung to Machaut's music" (670). It thus deserves our attention, particularly since it renders directly into English the better qualities of the French ballades:

Madame, ye ben of alle beaute shryne	
As fer as cerceled is the mapemounde°,	map of the world
For as the cristall glorious ye shyne,	
An lyke ruby ben your chekes rounde.	
Therewyth ye ben so mery and so	
jocounde°	joyous
That at a revell whan that I se you dance,	
It is an oynement unto my wounde,	
Thogh ye to me ne do no daliaunce.	though you won't flirt with me
For thogh I wepe of teres ful a tyne°,	tub
Yet may that wo myn herte nat confounde.	
Your semy voys, that ye so small out	your thin little voice that you
twyne,	spin out
Maketh my thoght in joy and blys	
habounde°.	abound
So curtaysly I go, with love bounde,	
That to myself I sey, in my penaunce,	
"Suffyseth me° to love you Rosemounde,	it is enough for me
Thogh ye to me ne do no daliaunce."	
Nas never pyk walwed in galauntyne	there was never a pike floating
	in wine sauce
As I in love am walwed and iwounde,	
For which ful ofte I of myself devyne°	guess
That I am trewe Tristam the secounde.	
My love may not refreyde nor affounde°;	cool off or diminish
I brenne° ay in an amorouse plesaunce.	burn
Do what you lyst; I wyl your thral° be	prisoner
founde,	
Though ye to me ne do no daliaunce.	

TREGENTIL.   CHAUCER

Musical as this may be, it already shows signs of that colloquial liveliness and even something approaching Metaphysical wit that called more for a speaking voice than a singing one. The image of poached fish, too, is a burlesque of high-flown romantic metaphors, and would draw too much attention to itself for a song lyric. Or so one might say; in fact more ludicrous things than this occur in many a country-and-western song of today. But that remark in itself betrays my view that at least some of Chaucer's lyrics were not suitable for the high romantic musical art of the earlier Middle Ages—or, to put it another way, are poems in their own right.

Other examples of singable ballades and roundels may be found among Chaucer's short poems and introduced into some longer ones, such as the song of the birds at the end of the *Parliament of Fowls*. The "Tale of Sir Thopas" was a burlesque of metrical romance for which there probably did exist a melody, the repetition of which rapidly became excruciatingly tedious: "Namoore of this, for Goddes dignitee," interrupts the Host. Sections of *Troilus and Criseyde,* the stanza form of which is derivative of the ballade, could certainly be sung; as he approaches the conclusion of that poem Chaucer sends the book off with an *envoi* in which he begs, among other things, that

> So preye I God that noon myswryte the,
> Ne the mysmetre for defaute of tonge.
> And red wherso the be, or elles songe,
> That thou be understonde, God I beseche.
> (1795–98)

Chaucer had in mind the "mismetering" that might occur on account of the use of a dialect other than that spoken in London, but the "defaute of tonge" that occurred, and which obscured his achievement in prosody, was a consequence of general changes in the language over the next two hundred years, especially the complete dropping of the final *e,* that remnant of Anglo-Saxon inflection. Whether he actually thought someone might sing *Troilus* is hard to decide; that possibility might be merely a consequence of the need of a rhyme at that point in the stanza.

As we have already noted, what Chaucer achieved single-handedly in metrics was comparable to the labors of several generations of Latin poets: he took the metric of a foreign language and employed it as an overlay for a language of quite different character. That is, he took Romance syllable-counting, which had in turn grown out of later medieval Latin poetics, and attempted to write poetry in English according to that principle. Reading *The Book of the Duchess* and *The House of Fame* one cannot help feeling the struggle of the author to make his couplets sound natural—and the strain shows in the grasping after rhyme words, which came so much more easily to his models, together with the sometimes graceless inversions of word order and the use of words and phrases that are no more than convenient filler. As he expanded into the ten-syllable line, Chaucer sensed that what required management was stress placement, not syllable-count, and, as he gained facility in this, his diction became simultaneously more natural and more economical. By "sensed" I mean as an artist, not as a theoretician; even after the rediscovery in the sixteenth century of what has come to be called the accentual-syllabic compromise, it was some decades before poets understood how the poetic line functioned—they could do it but they could not describe it.

At the time that Chaucer accomplished this synthesis it was not even clear that the future of literature in England belonged to the English language; as B. J. Whiting used to joke, Chaucer's contemporary, John Gower, wanted to be on the safe side no matter which way "the linguistic cat might jump," and therefore wrote works in French, English, and Latin. Chaucer's wholehearted commitment to the one transformed English metrics forever. Paradoxically, his syllabic basis helped to put the older alliterative meters out of business and made accentual songs and ballads seem crude and rough, even as his devotion to the vernacular assured its dignity as a literary medium. After Chaucer, at least until this century, such reinvigoration of poetry from music as has occurred mostly has had to come form those songs and ballads, with occasional help from a residual legacy of the troubadours, such as the Italian madrigal, and from hymns, chiefly Protestant in origin. For most purposes of poetry, music had become more a distraction than a complement, except for the occasional interlude, tour de force, or decorative flourish. Music itself was in any case ready to set off on in search of its own constructive principles. In later centuries Italian opera could serve as inspiration for Whitman, and Beethoven's later quartets could suggest organizational strategies (as well as moods) to T. S. Eliot, but unselfconscious fusion of the two arts, where either takes itself with Arnoldian "high seriousness," has been increasingly rare since the later Middle Ages.

6

The English Renaissance

A s we have just seen, Italian poetry began to break away from music in the thirteenth century and French poetry in the fourteenth; in the year 1500, however, popular English ballads and songs still preserved a centuries-old marriage of word and melody. No serious arguments against this view can be raised; enough records of their words survive, along with a number of melodic notations of varying usefulness. Also, there are earlier references to such songs that presuppose a familiarity with them—as when Chaucer has his Pardoner sing "Com hider, love, to me," evidently the first line of a popular song. But there remains much puzzlement over their origins, the problem being that both words and melody were invented and preserved orally and that references to and written records of them are scattered, accidental, and fragmentary. The earthiness and distinctly English qualities of their subjects and meters lead some scholars to deny that they can have owed anything to, say, the poetry of the trouvères—and yet one finds among them stanzas that seem much like the French songs of the twelfth and thirteenth centuries. Many songs are conspicuously concerned with things of this world, especially with sexual love, and one finds disparaging remarks about them in Church writings; yet the whole corpus covers a continuous spectrum that ranges from frank sensuality to religious lyrics not much different from the ancient Latin hymns.

John Stevens summarizes the situation in the fifteenth century in this way:

> What happened in the meantime to popular song? The answer is, very little. There was no revolution here. Music was still invented, though rarely written down, for the singing of poems; poems were still made to the patterns of existing tunes. An account of words-and-music in popular song at the turn of the fifteenth century need do little more than show how rich and ramifying these processes could be. Unfortunately, even this is not an easy task. For obvious reasons the surviving remains of early Tudor popular songs are tantalizingly small. (*Music and Poetry* 44)

The circumstances of composition of the songs are more problematic than those of *Beowulf* or the Homeric epics; even the word "popular" is not a clear-cut designation, some scholars interpreting it to mean songs composed *by* the common people and others *for* the people. There are also the issues of individual, incremental, and group authorship, and whether word or melody came first. My suspicion, based on my own memorization in college of a fairly extensive collection of songs that one never sees written down, is that the medieval songs could have come into existence in all sorts of different ways. Some from the fifteenth century and earlier—lyrics rather than ballads—were parodies or imitations of hymns; some were English versions of continental songs; some had features in common with Goliardic poetry; some were invented for a particular occasion; some were new settings to music of older words, or vice-versa. There must have been different versions of the same song or ballad in currency at the same time, just as today some persons singing "The Wreck of the Old Ninety-Seven" will have the locomotive crossing "White Oak Mountain" while for others it is "that wide old mountain," and some will quote the orders as "you must put her in center on time" while others say "Spencer." This variation occurs despite a definitive written text, and is a tribute to the combined appeal of a lively tune, grimly vivid details ("scalded to death by the steam"), and pathos. Mark W. Booth points out in *The Experience of Song* that lines and even stanzas in older orally preserved songs could be added, dropped, or rearranged without damage, but that such variation ceases as song evolves into poetry:

> A glance at the variant forms of one of the more common ballads in Child's collection shows gross differences in length between versions of a song that is still clearly the same song. These examples testify to a fluidity in many kinds of song text that baffles much of the structural analysis applied in our time to poems.
>
> This is not to say that songs are shapeless. We will see that song texts can sometimes be parsed into elaborate patterns, particularly when they are the "texts" of preliterate song. The structures ordering songs are not, however, the subtle psychological dramas of lyric poetry. The reader of Donne's "Canonization" or Keats's "Ode to a Nightingale" is carried through intellectual and emotional process. (25)

To summarize what seems generally accepted about medieval and early Renaissance songs and ballads: almost all of them were sung aloud and were kept alive orally; singing—and often dancing—was essential. Refrains, which very often include nonsense words, allow the singing voice, and sometimes instrumental accompaniment as well, to assert its full claims. Few serious poems *not* for music are interrupted by "Down-a-down-hey-down-a-down" or "Lullay, lullay," and even simple iterative refrains tend to become displeasing without music. Whatever their origin, these songs were popular in the sense that they were known by a great many people of all social levels, and the absence of literacy or musical training presented no obstacle to their acquisition. As I have already pointed out, probably a lot of secular lyrics were never written down. Because of the antipathy of some of the clergy toward love songs, it may seem surprising that they survive in numbers roughly equal to those on religious subjects. When we remember that the Church could be ambivalent about the value of *any* music, and when we recall how it purged itself of many of its own vocal compositions, it becomes clear that a popular lyric about Mary or Christ, however devoutly intended, might not have been much more welcome to some ecclesiastics than a love ditty was. Nevertheless, secular songs probably outnumbered religious ones, and were less likely to have been written down by a cleric.

In A.D. 1500, although Chaucer was still available and read in numerous manuscripts, the most vital poetic culture of England was oral, and it was musical. The poetry of the early English Renaissance emerged from that culture, owing much less to foreign, specifically Italian, models than many scholars used to believe. Anyone who imagines that Wordsworth made radical innovations should read the pre-Romantics and pay special attention to the writings of William Whitehead, who was poet laureate when Wordsworth was a boy; he or she will find fully developed much of what is often taken to be Wordsworth's unique manner. Similarly, those who think that Thomas Wyatt returned from Italy bringing with him the New English Poetry of the 1500s should study the English songs preserved in manuscripts from 1450 through 1500; they will find much more of Wyatt there.

Take, for example, the following song, the manuscript of which dates from about 1500 and which was probably composed somewhat earlier:

[REFRAIN]
For wele or woo I wyll not fle
To love that hart that lovyth me.

That hart my hart hath in suche grace
   That of too hartes one hart make we;
That hart hath brought my hart in case
   To love that hart that lovyth me.

For one that lyke unto that hart
   Never was nor ys nor never shall be,
Nor never lyke cavse sette this apart
   To love that hart that lovyth me.

Which cause gyveth cause to me and myn
    To serve that hart of suferente,
And styll to syng this later lyne,
    To love that hart that lovyth me.

Whatever I say, whatever I syng,
    Whatever I do, that hart shall se
That I shall serue wyth hart lovyng
    That lovyng hart that lovyth me.

This knot thus knyt who shall vntwyne,
    Syns we that knyt it do agre
To lose nor slyp, but both enclyne
    To love that hart that lovyth me?

Farewell, of hartes that hart most fyne,
    Farewell, dere hart, hartly to the,
And kepe this hart of myne for thyne
    As hart for hart for lovyng me.

(slightly regularized from Greene No. 444)

This sounds rather like "Forget Not Yet," "My Lute Awake," and various other songs by Wyatt.

It may be well here to raise the issue of whether Wyatt intended such poems for musical accompaniment. John Stevens thought not:

> Was Wyatt a musician? Courtly education would certainly have laid some stress on practical music. But, in fact, outside the text of his lyrics, there is no evidence whatsoever that he had musical ability, as singer, lutenist or composer. It is likely that Wyatt was put through the mill (he was taught to joust efficiently) and learnt to sing a little and strum upon the lute. But, if he had been proficient and taken great pleasure in music, surely some contemporary would have mentioned the fact. (*Music and Poetry* 133)

C. S. Lewis, among many others, was more willing to take Wyatt at his word, believing that when Wyatt says "sing" he means it literally; Lewis quotes from a lyric and comments:

> This was not intended to be read. It has little meaning until it is sung in a room with many ladies present. The whole scene comes before us. The poet did not write for those who would sit down to *The Poetical Works of Wyatt*. We are having a little music after supper. In that atmosphere all the confessional or autobiographical tone of the songs falls away; and all the cumulative effect too. The song is still passionate: but the passion is distanced and generalized by being sung. (230)

I am inclined to favor Lewis over Stevens here, despite Stevens's politely expressed difference of opinion: "But if we are invited to see the settings as a *musical* evening, then we are, I think, being misled" (*Music and Poetry* 150). It does not much matter whether Wyatt was a composer or a musician or not; he heard many a song, and as I know from my own experience, it is possible to call up numerous melodies from memory without possessing any gift for performance or composition. And one may write verse for music without being very musically accomplished oneself. I see a fairly good modern analogy— though a comic one—to Wyatt's use of music in X. J. Kennedy's "In a Prominent Bar in Secaucus One Day." Kennedy took the folk melody "Sweet Betsy from Pike" as his model, but the lyrics of his own poem are more sophisticated than those of his source. As with the canzone in Dante's time, Wyatt's and Kennedy's poems may be recited in the absence of music, but they are written so that they *could* be sung; I feel safe in saying this even though I know nothing of either Wyatt's or Kennedy's musical talents. Stevens's argument is, however, useful in that it pays attention to the self-sufficiency of many of Wyatt's lyrics, which are poems in their own right. Lewis's statement that "this was not intended to be read" does not hold for poems such as "Forget Not Yet"—or at least should be qualified by adding that it can be read with pleasure by the solitary reader. It is worth laboring this point because an account of exactly what happened to poetry in England between 1530 and 1560, and its relations to music, is essential for my entire argument.

The problem in finding close parallels in Wyatt to the fifteenth-century poem quoted above is one of theme, not form. Wyatt was so persistently disappointed in love that his sweetly embittered lyrics seldom resemble in tone the many expressions of devotion or happiness in love that one finds earlier, where, even when the lover is miserable, the cause is often some impersonal circumstance, such as his own forced departure, and not the fault of the lady. Wyatt seems infected by a somewhat puritanical suspicion that the real purpose of earthly amorousness is to teach us its transitoriness, and because that is where his heart lies all his best poems celebrate the unkindness of the loved one. A poem of resigned commitment, such as follows, still betrays a pained edginess but otherwise seems a little flat; I quote it, however, because it resembles closely various fifteenth-century lyrics, including the one printed above.

[REFRAIN]
As power and wit will me assist,
My will shall will even as ye list.

For as ye list my will is bent
In everything to be content,

To serve in love till life be spent;
So you reward my love thus meant,
  Even as ye list.

To feign or fable is not my mind,
Nor to refuse such as I find,
But as a lamb of humble kind
Or bird in cage, to be assign'd
  Even as ye list.

When all the flock is come and gone,
Mine eye and heart, agreeth in one,
Hath chosen you, only, alone,
To be my joy, or else my moan.
  Even as ye list.

Joy if pity appear in place,
Moan if disdain do show his face,
Yet crave I not as in this case,
But as ye lead to follow the trace
  Even as ye list.

Some in words much love can feign,
And some for words give words again:
Thus words for words in words remain.
And yet at last words do obtain
  Even as ye list.

To crave in words I will eschew,
And love in deed I will ensue;
It is my mind both whole and true,
And for my truth I pray you rue
  Even as ye list.

Dear heart, I bid your heart farewell,
With better heart than tongue can tell;
Yet take this tale, as true as gospel,
Ye may my life save or expel
  Even as ye list.

The flatness of the poetry in this piece seems to require a musical accompaniment to give it more interest. Would Wyatt have supplied a refrain if he did not imagine it could be sung?

  What really pulled Wyatt away from the musical spirit that animates his best lyrics was his effort at introducing a longer poetic line. Even here he was not completely indebted to continental models (or to Chaucer), since one may find pentameters—some of them more skillful than Wyatt's—among fifteenth-century lyric poetry. The following, whose author is uncertain, dates from about 1448 and begins as a tribute to Chaucer:

> My hert ys set and all myn hole entent
> To serve this flour in my most humble wyse
> As faythfully as can be thought or ment
> Wyth out feyning or slouthe in my servyse
> ffor wytt the wele yt ys a paradyse   for you know well, it is a
>   paradise
>
> To se this flour when yt bygyn to sprede
> Wyth colours fressh ennewyd° white and rede.   renewed

(Hammond 200)

Few others among Chaucer's followers could handle the pentameter with anything approaching the competence seen here. For the most part, the history of English prosody in the sixteenth century begins with a tentative and stumbling rediscovery of how to use this meter. Most examples earlier than that betray what Eleanor Prescott Hammond called "the codeless weakness of such degeneracy and the obstinately uncomprehending codes of Lydgate and Hoccleve" (22). And Wyatt's own time brought forth examples of incompetency much beyond any infelicities found in Wyatt himself; the uncompromising Hammond says of Henry Lord Morley (1476–1556), "A mere glance over Morley's work will show the inadequacy of his imagination and the poverty of his ear. His rhythmic peculiarities are not the conscious licenses of the competent poet nor the struggles of a strong and gifted spirit with language; they are the deaf stupidities of the complacently ignorant versifier" (384).

Although Wyatt's best-known venture into pentameter ("They Flee from Me") is in Chaucerian rime royal, his emulation of the Italian poetry encountered in his travels is mainly responsible for his experiments with the longer line. We have his translations from Petrarch, in which he sometimes seems interested in approximating hendecasyllabics, counting his lines out to eleven syllables; his terza rima; and his sonnets. There was also the entire corpus of French poetry of the previous two centuries, much of it in decasyllabics, to serve as an example. As it had for Chaucer, this overlay from the Romance languages made it possible for English poetry to emerge from its musical context as completely as Italian and French themselves already had. The pentameter was cultivated for various reasons—because it did seem more civilized, because it did closely approximate lines that English poets were trying to translate from French and Italian, and because it even offered a medium that fell short of the classical hexameter by only a few syllables; it was also quite close in length to other ancient lines—hendecasyllabics, for example. But the pentameter is not a natural measure in English for a ballad, a popular lyric, a courtly *invention*, or a hymn; to use it is often to separate the poem from a musical context. Whether it was sung or not, the following stanza from Wyatt's lyric "My Lute Awake!" belongs to another world.

> My lute awake! perform the last
> Labor that thou and I shall waste,
> And end that I have now begun:
> And when this song is sung and past,
> My lute be still, for I have done.

It is closer to the complaints of the troubadours than the opening of his best-known pentameter poem:

> They flee from me that sometime did me seek,
> With naked foot stalking in my chamber.

In the latter poem we have more of the *musique naturele* identified by Deschamps and practiced by his friend Chaucer. That briefer measures than the pentameter prove more suitable for songs is immediately evident when we think of how Shakespeare lapses into tetrameters or trimeters—from blank verse or rhyming pentameters—whenever a song is called for. To repeat, then: what occurred with the reinvention of the pentameter in England in the sixteenth century was roughly comparable to the liberation of Latin verse from possible musical connections by the imposition of a foreign metrical system (Greek meters). It was also a recapitulation, or rediscovery, or revival, of Chaucer's achievement in inventing a poetry freed from music. Or, to put it more positively, the awareness that the sounds and rhythms of words themselves were capable of artistic arrangement was satisfying in itself.

Pentameter encouraged the composition of poetry for its own sake, but poems in meters and stanzas that remained the same as, or close to, the older song patterns also attained independence. Individual authorship and circulation for a cultivated audience, first in manuscript and later in printed copies, encouraged attention to effects of rhetoric, inventiveness in imagery, more careful development of the conceit, and use of irony, verbal effects, and shifts in tone that had nothing to do with melody. Leisurely composition on paper permitted a choice of words whose sounds were more cleverly adjusted to one another than in the earlier ballads and songs. Poems began to be conceived as poems. Enterprising publishers began to offer poems in printed form without any attempt at including musical scores, further widening their separation from music. Typography in the sixteenth century became increasingly ingenious and also encouraged freedom from music—somewhat as, in our own century, typography has encouraged freedom from meter itself. We must remind ourselves of the novelty, in the 1500s, of a poem's being widely available as a written text. Analogies are treacherous, but the invention of moveable type was, for poetry, somewhat like the invention of the recording equipment for music in the twentieth century. Even as it made possible the preservation and reproduction of older kinds of poetry, printing encouraged a display of verbal sophistication possible only on the page, somewhat as recording techniques make possible overlays and distortions that cannot be produced in live performances.

The achievement of the great poets of the English Renaissance only confirmed the separation of poetry from music, which was in most respects complete by 1550. The most convenient example is Philip Sidney, who wrote poems for music, but whom we remember as a poet for "Leave me o love, which reachest but to dust," which, though technically a sonnet and therefore a song form, calls for no musical accompaniment. Although composers did set some of the sonnets in *Astrophel and Stella*, it was not Sidney's purpose in those to invent song lyrics; included also, however, are songs, whose tone, style, and structure are completely different from the sonnets and which cry out for musical settings; here are the opening stanzas of the "Fourth Song":

> Only joy, now here you are,
> Fit to hear and ease my care,
> Let my whispering voice obtain.
> Sweet reward for sharpest pain;
> Take me to thee, and thee to me.
> No, no, no, no, my dear, let be.
>
> Night hath clos'd all in her cloak,
> Twinkling stars love-thoughts provoke,
> Danger hence good care doth keep,
> Jealousy itself doth sleep;
> Take me to thee, and thee to me.
> No, no, no, no, my dear, let be.
>
> Better place no wit can find
> Cupid's yoke to loose or bind;
> These sweet flowers on fine bed, too,
> Us in their best language woo;
> Take me to thee, and thee to me.
> No, no, no, no, my dear, let be.

Louise Schleiner, in *The Living Lyre in English Verse*, applies the Russian formalist tripartite subdivision of speech, song, and declamatory verse to poetry of the English Renaissance (4–14). She points out many features that contrast in the songs and sonnets of *Astrophel and Stella*—that, for example, the songs are rhythmically smooth, end-stopped, and use conventional and simple language, while the sonnets use relatively rough meters, strong enjambment, and unconventional diction and imagery.

It would be easy, though perhaps pointless, to cite one example after another from the poetry of Spenser, Daniel, Drayton, Southwell, Raleigh, and Marlowe, as well as Sidney, that trace the steps, both forward and backward, by which a pure verbal art evolved out of the musical context. Any number of poems by Donne or Marvell, Crashaw or Vaughan, might be chosen to illustrate how completely some varieties of poetry in England had severed musical connections. Cavalier poetry, with its neater stanzas that often fitted song meters such as common measure and long measure, continued to give a distinct impression of singability; but the argumentative and rhetorical manner of some Metaphysical poems, and the extravagant and ingenious figures of speech—together, often, with a certain logical complexity—made solitary reading a requirement for their comprehension. Many Metaphysical poems also captivate the reader with the lively tones of a speaking voice, but their verbal content would usually overwhelm any melody, and that verbal content, unlike much of what we find in Milton, appeals as much (or more) to the analytical intelligence and the visual imagination as it does to the ear. In Milton we can enjoy the sounds of language itself, as well as the emotive associations of certain proper names and literary echoes and allusions.

The process by which English poets in the later sixteenth century began to build upon the foundations laid by Wyatt and Surrey resulted in a three-story structure. First came Wyatt's experiments in pentameter, where the authenticity of personal statement and liveliness of metaphor more than compensate for the tentative metric. (As I have said, this uncertainty resulted partly from a failure to realize that English poetry could not be effectively organized by syllable count as French and in some respects Latin poetry had been.) The next stage was the recognition that regularity of accent could provide a template for poems in English. This regularizing was implicit in Tottel's revisions of Wyatt (and possibly others, including Surrey), and appears explicitly in Gascoigne's theorizing, which affects his own practice, especially in *The Steele Glass*. Finally—the top story of my metaphor—as poets learned to master and take for granted the iambic rhythm, they were able to introduce expressive variations of rhetoric as well as normal speech, and the natural quantities and emphases present in English, so as to play against the assumed metrics. Poetic "music" in English was thus reborn, rapidly evolving from the chamber music of Sidney to the organ blasts of Marlowe and Shakespeare's full orchestrations. That evolution, as we all know, continued in various ways through most of the seventeenth century until it was reined in by neoclassical restraints.

John Thompson, in *The Founding of English Metre*, long ago traced in detail the earlier steps in this progression. Here he is speaking of "They Flee from Me" and its subsequent revision—and then looking ahead to the manneristic license of a subsequent generation of poets in the seventeenth century that went beyond even Shakespeare:

> It seems that if Wyatt himself had any thought here of an iambic metrical pattern, he was willing to give it up for the effect of the phrases. Whoever made the revision was prepared to give up the effect of the phrases for the sake of the pattern. Donne gave up neither; his phrases demand the living voice and at the same time the line can be reconciled to the metrical pattern, not in speech, it is true, but in that counterpoint of speech and metrical pattern which today we usually recognize and value. The effects of Wyatt's line and of Donne's, then, are similar, but in structural principles the lines are at opposite poles. (16)

Speaking of the regularizing that intervened between Wyatt and Sidney, he says that

> they got what they wanted, a steady progression of alternate stresses which tends always to cause the stress-patterns of speech and the patterns of metre to become one. But when the patterns become one, the words lack a real intonation and so lack the best part of that indication of feeling which is tone. Gascoigne changes this. He does not say that there *should* be alternate weak and strong stresses in a pentameter line, presented by the words; he says there *are* alternate weak and strong stresses in a line, whether the speech fits or not. It was a profound change, even if it was largely only the conscious recognition of a principle that sometimes operated in verse whether the poets liked it or not. Gascoigne did not quite realize what could be done with it, and in his verse as a rule it takes him only as far as this:
>
> > When I recorde within my musing mynde.
>
> Another change in the understanding of the line had to take place, allowing both the metrical pattern and the pattern of speech to function, before lines like this were standard practice:
>
> > When to the sessions of sweet silent thought.
>
> (69–70)

Edward Doughtie puts it in a slightly different way:

Two crucial changes in the concept and practice of English verse took place in the sixteenth century. The first change consisted of ordering the stresses in the line into a regular pattern of alternating stressed and unstressed syllables. This change occurred between the time Sir Thomas Wyatt, in the 1530s, wrote such lines as "There was never file half so well filed," and before 1557, when the compiler of Tottel's Miscellany changed these lines, as in "Was never file yet half so well yfiled" (Rollins, 1928, 1: 33, 2: 161). The second change occurred in the 1570s and 1580s when poets like Sidney learned to internalize the abstract pattern of regular stresses and play off against it the rhythms of speech or incantation. This second change resulted in the fluid and flexible line that sustained English verse for the next three centuries. (31)

George Herbert's "Church Monuments" provides an example that may illustrate how far we have come when we compare the poetry of 1630 with that of a century earlier. Herbert's "music" is usually less spectacular than Donne's, but is often more complex. Although "Church Monuments" is sometimes printed as if it were composed in a single sweep of twenty-four lines, it divides easily into four six-line stanzas rhyming *abcabc*, reflecting a strophic repetition inherited from music; but the argument is continuous, with enjambments not only between lines but also between the quasi-stanzaic units, and this alone makes it unsuitable for any recurrent melody. For the most part, the meter—a quietly variegated pentameter—simply urges the poem along, remaining in the background, as music itself was required to do in monodic recitative, but modulating so as to support the sense. Most important in the poem is Herbert's message of reconciliation of the body with its inevitable dissolution, but next after that are the overlapping and parallel metaphors with which he conveys this idea. Before we consider the prosody of "Church Monuments," it will be well to state the argument of the poem and to explicate its tropes—especially since the literal meaning of the poem is often misunderstood—only then turning to consider the function of the meter.

CHURCH MONUMENTS

While that my soul repairs to her devotion,
Here I entomb my flesh, that it betimes
May take acquaintance of this heap of dust,
To which the blast of Death's incessant motion,
Fed with the exhalation of our crimes,
Drives all at last. Therefore I gladly trust

My body to this school, that it may learn
To spell his elements, and find his birth

Written in dusty heraldry and lines
Which dissolution sure doth best discern,
Comparing dust with dust and earth with earth.
These laugh at jet and marble, put for signs,

To sever the good fellowship of dust,
And spoil the meeting. What shall point out them
When they shall bow and kneel and fall down flat
To kiss those heaps which now they have in trust?
Dear flesh, while I do pray, learn here thy stem
And true descent, that, when thou shalt grow fat

And wanton in thy cravings, thou mayst know
That flesh is but the glass which holds the dust
That measures all our time, which also shall
Be crumbled into dust. Mark here below
How tame these ashes are, how free from lust,
That thou mayst fit thyself against thy fall.

The scene is probably the interior of a church or chapel; if we must be more particular, St. Andrew's Church of Herbert's own parish, across the street from the former rectory in Bemerton, will certainly do. While he says his prayers, while his soul turns herself toward God, in his imagination Herbert commits his flesh to the earth beneath. Readers who know that some of the dead at Bemerton, including Herbert himself, repose beneath the floor of the church, have imagined that Herbert means the earth under the floor. The reference to toppling grave markers further on, however, makes it clear that he means the ground outside (and at Bemerton, in fact, there are tombstones). In any case, he is mortifying the flesh in his imagination, introducing it to its lowly origins and destiny, "betimes," good and early, well in advance of actual death.

"To which the blast of death's incessant motion" introduces the first of several multilevel metaphors. "Blast" means "wind"—as in Milton's "not a blast was from his dungeon stray'd" and Watts's "shelter from the stormy blast." But what constitutes this wind of death? "Fed with the exhalation of our crimes" suggests that the wind gathers into itself all the confessions of sin, all the corruption of the human spirit. Without pushing the metaphor toward the macabre for its own sake, we may recognize a more ghastly significance. "Exhalations" at that time was applied to the escape of bursts of gas from the earth that were ignited in the upper atmosphere as they approached the invisible sphere of fire —indeed, meteors (or comets) were explained in this way, as when Henry IV rebuked Worcester, telling him to "be no more an exhaled meteor." The destiny of the body is to heave with invasions of worms, to swell and burst with putrefaction, releasing "exhalations." And of course there is the sense that sin itself carries the stench of corruption. There may be a suggestion of Ecclesiastes—"The wind goeth toward the south, and turneth about unto the north; it whirleth about continually, and wind again returneth according to his circuits" (1.6). The ultimate result is that flesh becomes a "heap of dust."

The second stanza introduces the metaphor of the school, where the body may "spell his elements." There seems little value in commenting on Herbert's gendering of soul and body as feminine and masculine; since they are to be reunited in perfected form at the Last Judgment, it seems no more than a metaphor of their essential marriage, though he does not use or imply this in any figure of speech. The school metaphor, though complex, is not hard to explain. The "elements" are the ABCs, the basics, elementary education. They are also the four elements that suffer continual transformation in sublunary nature. His body is learning, in this school, just what it is composed of, and is in addition learning to read the elemental facts of its life, the simple message conveyed by the names and dates on a tombstone ("find his birth / Written in dusty heraldry and lines"). "Heraldry" reminds us that family coats of arms and other emblems often appear on gravestones, and anticipates the discounting of these pretentious "signs." The word "lines" suggests lines of descent—but also lines of writing, even of poetry or Scripture as well as family names and connections. All these may occur as "lines" carved in a tombstone.

The next line ("Which dissolution sure doth best discern") can be read either of two ways, both of which dovetail with other meanings. The meaning can be construed as, "Which best perceives inevitable decay," or as "Which inevitable decay sees most clearly." The antecedent of "which" is "body"; the sense is that the body understands its sure mortality best by comparing itself with the dust and earth already in the graves. The dust and earth make merry with the pretensions of the living, the markers carved from expensive stone, that would continue distinctions of class and family beyond the grave, as if one heap of dust could keep separate from another. "What shall point out them?" Who will set up tombstones for the tombstones, when they finally topple over? One might pause from explication to note the sweet-tempered language—"spoil the meeting," "kiss those heaps," "dear flesh."

The rest of the poem hardly needs comment. "Stem" is biblical—but also suggests a growth out of the soil. We are not even the rod and the stem of Jesse; our true descent is from the earth itself. "Stem and true descent" also lead into the next trope, where the flesh is likened to an hourglass, a container of dust that sifts away our mortal hours, a soundless descent of particles. "Which also shall be crumbled into dust" may be just a little ambiguous; it means that the body, the container of life, will disintegrate, but the phrase also seems in apposition with "time," suggesting that time itself is part of the transitory universe. "Fit thyself against thy fall" can mean "prepare for death," but also "resist temptation." Also, "here below" carries the sense of "while still alive" and "here in the earth below you." All these ambiguities are controlled—one might say, orchestrated.

It could be argued that the main function of the meter and all other prosodic details is to present the subject as quietly and transparently as possible, without drawing attention to themselves. The first two lines repeat much the same rhythm, each leading off with a reversed foot that, combined with the following iamb, makes a choriamb (/ ★ ★ /):

```
  /     ★  ★ /  ★ /  ★  /  ★ /  ★
While that my soul repairs to her devotion,
  /     ★  ★ /   ★ /   ★  /  ★/
Here I entomb my flesh, that it betimes. . . .
```

In these two lines there is little alliteration, assonance, or internal rhyme; there are more differences than likenesses of sounds. All this makes the opening very quiet. The third line, though, leads off with four long syllables, three of which are long *a*'s, and two of which are closed with a hard *c* sound: "May take acquaintance of this heap of dust." The sudden emphasis adds force to "betimes" of the previous line and to the "heap of dust" that follows.

```
  ★   /   ★  /  ★  /   ★ /  ★  /   (★)
To which the blast of Death's incessant motion,
```

not only allows very heavy stresses, and long syllables, to fall on the *ictus* (in the English sense) of the line, but adds to each a similar consonant sound (*ch, s, sh*). "Fed with the exhalation of our crimes" returns to the rhythm of lines one and two—receding from the intensity just achieved, and preparing for the stop after "Drives all at last" (/ / / /—or possibly, / / ★ /), in which all four syllables are long and at least three are stressed. "Last" rhymes with "blast," closing the statement in the same position within the line. After a sweep of four lines, two of which are strongly enjambed, the arrested rhythm is most striking. The picking-up in midline that follows adds emphasis to "gladly"; the enjambment with the following stanza removes emphasis from "trust" ("trust / My body to this school") so that we do not readily anticipate the recurrence—both in midline and as a rhyme—of "dust." That last word occurs fully six times—twice in the last stanza—and once more as "dusty." Herbert deliberately inserted it as often as possible.

The second stanza, like the first, opens with two lines of nearly identical rhythm—in this case, perfect iambic pentameter with a pause after the sixth syllable. It is hard to characterize the effect of alliteration and sibilance in "Which dissolution sure doth best discern." The sounds strongly anticipate the word "dust"; "doth best" contains all the sounds of "dust." One does not wish to push interpretation too far, but perhaps the sibilance means to echo the soundless sifting of the particles of dust. The rhetoric of "Comparing dust with dust, and earth with earth," certainly jars with the preceding line. The tempo picks up across the next stanzaic boundary. A pyrrhic occurs in the second position of the pentameter line, and such a substitution always carries a line rapidly forward:

> ★ / ★ ★ / / ★ / ★ /
> To sever the good fellowship of dust,
> ★ / ★ / ★ / / / / /
> And spoil the meeting. What shall point out them . . . ?

The sudden arrest in midline that follows certainly suggests the "spoiled meeting" that would result if expensive markers could separate the dead from one another. A note of kindly exasperation informs the five emphatic syllables of "what shall point out them," and the following two lines telescope the dilapidations of decades into twenty more monosyllables, an emphasis that continues to the end of the stanza, showing that, Pope to the contrary, ten low words that creep in one line need not necessarily be dull. The first four lines of the last stanza reenact the earlier effect of a sweep followed by a sudden arrest in the middle of the line to suggest the ultimate closure of death: "Be crumbled into dust." The repetition of "dust" literally reiterates what has just been said, following "also shall." This is the real conclusion of Herbert's statement; the remainder is a peroration and restatement.

It would never have occurred to me to try singing "Church Monuments" if I had not discussed it in the context of this book. I have now tried it and it will not do. Perhaps the first melody that occurred to me was not a happy inspiration (it was Campion's, composed for the six-line stanzas of "My Sweetest Lesbia"). But no musical setting is likely to coexist peacefully with a poem whose enjambments carry it to its conclusion like a through-composed madrigal, but whose structure is nevertheless strophic. Actual melody could only submerge the articulations of vowels and consonants, could only distract from the majesty and power of the language. In a more subdued way than what we will see Milton doing, Herbert has woven the vowels and consonants into an audible texture of sound that requires no—indeed cannot admit any—admixture of music. The damage might not be as serious as it could be to a work composed in a language that employs pitch as a semantic variable (as in

Chinese), but the poem could only lose dignity. "The Gettysburg Address" delivered to an accompaniment of bagpipes would be more dissonant and pointless, but not by much. In Paul Valéry's much-quoted analogy, adding music would be like viewing a painting illuminated by a stained-glass window. "Church Monuments" is a self-sufficient work of art; here, if anywhere, we hear the triumph of *musique naturele*.

7

Arranged Marriages

OTHER DEVELOPMENTS in English metrics, besides those just sketched out, assisted the continuing self-definition of English prosody during the Renaissance. The chapter following this will illustrate at some length how—for all his devotion to music itself—Milton kept his verbal art entirely separate from its "twin sister," partly by pushing accentual-syllabic meter, the rediscovery of which was barely a century old, to the verge of free verse in *Paradise Lost* and beyond that limit in *Samson Agonistes* (as well as in some earlier poems). Much earlier, experiments in adapting classical meters to English, which might have seemed a promising way to rejoin poetry to music, had had the paradoxically opposite effect. In a different way, the transformation of the madrigal (which began as a musical performance) into a literary genre also ended by helping to emancipate poetry.

The attempt at imposing quantitative scansions on English has often been dismissed as a "foolish campaign for the use of classical meters" (Rollins and Baker 625), but is nevertheless important in the history of English prosody. The incoming tide of the Renaissance had already spread classicizing currents through the literatures of other countries. An increasingly broad acquaintance with the classics, and especially the revival of Greek studies, suggested to scholars and some poets that the English vernacular might be further refined by recasting poetry in modern languages into classical scansions. In the end, the isosyllabic nature of French and the accentual rhythms of German and English defeated Renaissance quantitative prosodists. (Ancient Latin, as we have seen, had just enough incipient quantity to make Greek meters possible.) No one argues that such quantitizing projects were very successful, and it is easy to point out the absurdities of certain examples. Yet the concept encouraged by such attempts—that words could be regulated according to a set metrical scheme—did encourage the cultivation of poetry as an independent art. For English poets, the threat of dactylic hexameters or the *iambicum trimetrum* (a twelve-syllable line) was sufficient to scare the music out of poetry— literal music, that is, not rhythm or euphony. In other words, the foredoomed attempt at writing English poems in classical meters ultimately tended to separate English verse from musical settings by drawing attention to the intrinsic rhythm of the language. And the separation from music made way for a more genuine native prosody. As Edward Doughtie perceptively and convincingly puts it, "In other poems from the *Arcadia*, Sidney engaged in experiments that may have helped him realize the possibilities of separating the metrical pattern from the words, namely writing English verse in classical quantitative meters" (84). Doughtie then quotes John Thompson as saying that "it was the exercise in classical metres that brought in a new idea of the relation of metrical pattern and language, and consequently a new idea of poetry. In these experiments, Sidney and Spenser must have learned to recognize the possibility that these two elements of verse [metrics and language] could be joined without losing their separate identities" (Thompson 147). And, one might add, the joining of metrical pattern and language gave poetry a form of its own and a referential scheme against which the natural emphases of the language could play, allowing language itself to acquire a range of effects that could no longer be accommodated to music. The Renaissance poets who crafted the accentual-syllabic meter may not at first have realized what they were doing, but classical metrics encouraged them toward the invention of that meter.

Derek Attridge's *Well-Weighed Syllables: Elizabethan Verse in Classical Meters* treats the quantitative movement in English poetry with great acuity and thoroughness, bringing out, among much else, how what is sometimes thought of as a British aberration was in fact widespread. Attridge mentions not only the French experimenters (in what some called "vers mesurés à l'antique") and the sixteenth-century German writers in quantitative meters, but he also traces the movement's beginnings in Italy and its remoter proliferation in Russia, the Netherlands, Spain, and elsewhere (125–26). Attridge explains the appeal of ancient metrics.

> [T]he mention of Pythagoras hints at the importance of metre within the tradition of numerological thought, whose influence on Renaissance literature has been brought out in several recent works. . . . Quantitative metre, with its theory of exact proportions of duration, its attention to every letter, and its careful and testable patterning, obviously accords with these ideas much more than accentual verse, particularly as it was understood in the sixteenth century. (115)

Attridge cites authorities in support of the view that English prosodists believed that parts of the Bible were written in quantitative meters (119), and argues that this lent authority to efforts at importing the meter into English.

Readings in the original texts of sixteenth-century prosodic theory give one a lively sense of the urgency with which poets sought to establish rigorous principles for metrical composition. One often discovers them doggedly going against the grain of spoken English and blundering, at times, into conclusions that we may view with the smugness of those who have four hundred more years of poetic experience to learn from. There was, for example, William Webbe's idea that *Piers Plowman* "observed the quantity of our verse without the curiosity of Ryme" (32, somewhat modernized). Webbe also tried to demonstrate how to write sapphics by redoing Spenser's April eclogue from *The Shepherd's Calendar* in the ancient stanza form. Spenser had written:

> Ye daynte Nymphs, that in this blessed Brooke
>   doe bathe your brest,
> Forsake your watry bowres, and hether looke,
>   at my request:
> And eke you Virgins that on Parnasse dwell,
> Whence floweth Helicon, the learned well,
>   Helpe me to blaze
>   Her worthy praise
> Which in her sexe doth all excell.
>
> Of fayre Elisa be your siluer song,
>   that blessed wight:
> The flowre of Virgins, may shee florish long,
>   In princely plight.
> For shee is Syrinx daughter without spotte,
> Which Pan the shepheards God of her begot:
>   So sprong her grace
>   Of heauenly race,
> No mortall blemishe may her blotte.

Webbe, after printing the scansion of the sapphic, gives us this version, casting each stanza into two sapphic units:

> O ye Nymphes most fine who resort to this brooke,
> For to bathe there your pretty breasts at all times:
> Leaue the watrish bowres, hyther and to me come
>   at my request nowe.
>
> And ye Virgins trymme who resort to Parnass,
> Whence the learned well Helicon beginneth:
> Helpe to blase her worthy deserts, that all els
>   mounteth aboue farre.
>
> Nowe the siluer songes of Eliza sing yee,
> Princely wight whose peere not among the virgins

Can be found: that long she may remaine among vs.
                            now let vs all pray.

For Syrinx daughter she is, of her begotten
Of the great God Pan, thus of heauen aryseth,
All her extent race: any mortall harde happe
                            cannot aproche her.

(82, somewhat modernized)

The singsong quality of Spenser's opening makes Webbe's version seem almost as good a poem as the original. The ingenuity, as well as the ingenuousness, of his undertaking is amusing, even if not entirely successful.

Other important documents in the controversy over quantity include the letters between Spenser and Gabriel Harvey; additional passages from Sidney's *Defense*; the strictures of earlier grammarians and critics, such as Ascham's *Scholemaster* and Gosson's *School of Abuse*; and Gascoigne's *Certain Notes of Instruction*. It is sufficient for our purposes to note that the entire debate resulted in a consideration of poetry as an art completely separated from music. Although the quantitative method did not stick, the application of various Renaissance versions of ancient rules had at least something of the same effect as it had had for the Roman poets: it encouraged poets to cultivate poetry as a self-sufficient art form.

The sacred name of music continued to be invoked to justify what poets were doing, reinforced by a dawning awareness of what *mousike* had meant to the Greeks. Also, much of the music theory bequeathed to the Renaissance by the Middle Ages referred back to Augustine and Boethius; and we have seen how the Notre Dame school of composers and others had employed the classical poetic feet to notate and to explain musical rhythms. Even as poetry set off on its own, those who talked about poetry could not refrain from using musical analogies or from reconnecting poetry, in its origins, with music—as they still do. In *An Apologie for Poetrie* Sidney links music with poetry, and both with a state of divine inspiration, intending thereby to claim the greatest dignity for his art:

And may not I presume a little further, to shew the reasonableness of this worde Vates? And say that the holy Davids are a divine Poem? If I doo, I shall not do it without the testimonie of great learned men, both auncient and moderne: but even the name Psalmes will speake for mee, which being interpreted, is nothing but songes. Then that it is fully written in meeter, as all learned Hebricians agree, although the rules be not yet fully found. Lastly and principally, his handeling his prophecy, which is meerely poetical. For what els is the awaking his musicall instruments?

And further on, Sidney seems willing to forget that there has been any separation at all:

> Nowe therein of all Sciences, (I speak still of humane, and according to the humane conceits) is our Poet the Monarch. For he dooth not only show the way, but giveth so sweete a prospect into the way, as will intice any man to enter into it. Nay, he dooth as if your journey should lye through a fayre Vineyard, at the first give you a cluster of Grapes: that full of that taste, you may long to passe further. He beginneth not with obscure definitions, which must blur the margent with interpretations, and load the memory with doubtfulnesse: but hee commeth to you with words sent in delightfull proportion, either accompanied with, or prepared for the well inchaunting skill of Musick.

As he neared the conclusion of his essay, Sidney enunciated his much-quoted distinction between ancient and modern meters, making clear his awareness of the essential genius of English rhythm. Here he also hints at the sufficiency of a purely verbal meter, but in so doing cannot forbear reverting to the idea of music ("striketh a certain music to the ear"), and goes on to claim that the English language is also eminently suitable for music despite its lack of a quantitative basis:

> Now, of versifying there are two sorts, the one Auncient, the other Moderne: the Auncient marked the quantitie of each silable, and according to that, framed his verse: the Moderne, observing onely number, (with some regarde of the accent,) the chiefe life of it, standeth in that lyke sounding of the words, which we call Ryme. Whether of these be the most excellent, would beare many speeches. The Auncient, (no doubt) more fit for Musick, both words and tune observing quantity, and more fit lively to expresse divers passions, by the low and lofty sounde of the well-weyed silable. The latter likewise, with hys Ryme, striketh a certaine musick to the eare: and in fine, sith it dooth delight, though by another way, it obtaines the same purpose: there beeing in eyther sweetness and wanting in neither majestic. Truely the English, before any other vulgar language I know, is fit for both sorts.

Neil Rudenstine summarizes well Sidney's relation to music:

> If he had ideas, however, about reviving the classical fusion of poetry and music, he failed to work them out in detail or put them into practice. He seems not to have known enough about musical composition himself, and he apparently developed no close working relationship with the skilled musicians to whom he had access. Instead, he gradually reconciled himself to English prosody and concentrated his energy on discovering a means of developing the "music" of poetry itself. He makes it clear on several occa-

sions that he responded strongly to the melodic and expressive powers of verse, apart from its relationship to music. (158–59)

George Gascoigne intended that all his advice on the composition of verse pertain to a purely verbal art; all his practical counsels concern themselves with syllable counts, pronunciation, rimes, and stanza forms. He does not speak of the music of poetry or use music as a metaphor for what poetry might achieve. One passing reference makes clear how completely settled the divorce of the arts was for Gascoigne: "There are also certain pauses or rests in a verse which may be called ceasures, whereof I would be loth to stand long, since it is in the discretion of the writer and they have been first devised, as should seem, by the musicians." He devotes the rest of this sentence and one brief additional statement to offering some rudimentary rules for caesuras. "The first and most necessary point that I ever found meet to be considered in making of a delectable poem is this, to ground it upon some fine invention." Poetry is to be an art of the intellect, not the senses, "shewing the quick capacity of a writer." Poetry is to be more like rhetoric—but rhetoric regularized into matching periods. Timothy Steele argued in *Missing Measures* that one determinant in the movement toward free verse in the twentieth century was the emulation of scientific prose, which wrenched poetry away from meter; the separation of poetry from music in the English Renaissance might be seen as a precursive step in that direction, with the additional impetus of the conceit or as Gascoigne puts it, "invention," which became in the hands of the Metaphysical poets not just "fine" but at times impossibly intricate.

William Webbe, writing in *A Discourse of English Poetry* (1586), imagined that the separation of poetry from music had occurred in ancient Greece and that rhetoric had originated simultaneously:

[T]hey that were most pregnant in wytt, and indued with great gyfts of wyesdome and knowledge in Musicke aboue the rest did vse commonly to make goodly verses, measured according to the sweetest notes of Musicke, containing the prayse of some noble vertue, or of immortalitie, or of some such thing of greatest estimation: which vnto them seemed, so heauenly and ioyous a thing, that, thinking such men to be inspyrde with some diuine instinct from heauen, they called them *Vates*. So when other among them of the finest wits and aptest capacities beganne in imitation of them to frame ditties of lighter matters, and tuning them to the stroake of some of the pleasantest kind of Musicke, then began there to grow a distinction and great diuersity betweene makers and makers. Whereby (I take it) beganne thys difference: that they which handled in the audience of the people, graue and necessary matters, were called wise men or eloquent men, which they meant by *Vates*: and the rest which sange of loue matters, or other lighter deuises alluring vnto pleasure and delight, were called Poetae, or makers. Thus it appeareth, both Eloquence and Poetrie to haue had their beginning and originall from there exercises, beeing framed in such sweete measure of sentences and pleasant harmonie called Ρίθμος, which is an apt composition of wordes or clauses, drawing as it were by force ye hearers eares euen whether soeuer it lysteth: that Plato affirmeth therein to be contained λοητεία an inchauntment, as it were to perswade them anie thing whether they would or no. And heerehence is sayde, that men were first withdrawne from a wylde and sauadge kinde of life, to ciuillity and gentlenes and ye right knowledge of humanity by the force of this measurable or tunable speaking. (22)

Webbe's seriousness of purpose went beyond his exhortations to poets to foreswear "barbarous" meters and rimes in favor of classical quantity; he had misgivings about the fine conceits and devices as well:

[A]s the number of Poets increased, they styll inclyned thys way rather then the other, so that most of them had speciall regarde, to the pleasantnesse of theyr fine conceytes, whereby they might drawe mens mindes into admiration of theyr inuentions, more then they had to the profitte or commoditye that the Readers shoulde reape by their works. And thus as I suppose came it to passe among them, that for the most part of them, they would not write one worke contayning some serious matter: but for the same they wold likewise powre foorth as much of some wanton or laciuious inuention. (27)

This had occurred in ancient times, but for more recent developments in poetry Webbe felt even greater contempt. He could only view the native oral traditions, complete with music, as a reversion to a barbarism that had preceded classical civilization. Listening to Webbe, we hear the familiar accents of the neoclassicist, a breed that we have still with us in the late twentieth century:

If I let passe the vncountable rabble of ryming Ballet makers and compylers of sencelesse sonets, who be most busy, to stuffe euery stall full of grosse deuises and vnlearned Pamphlets: I trust I shall with the best sort be held excused. Nor though many such can frame an Alehouse song of five or sixe score verses, hobbling vppon some tune of a Northen lygge, or Robyn hoode, or La lubber etc. And perhappes obserue iust number of sillables, eyght in one line, sixe in an other, and there withall an A to make a iercke in the ende: yet if these might be accounted Poets (as it is sayde some of them make meanes to be promoted to ye Lawrell) surely we shall shortly haue whole swarmes of Poets. (36–37)

Webbe is in line with Roger Ascham who, toward the end of *The Scholemaster* (ca. 1568), had scolded English poets:

They wished, as Virgil and Horace were not wedded to follow the faults of former fathers (a shrewd marriage in greater matters) but by right imitation of the perfit Grecians had brought poetry to perfitness also in the Latin tongue, that we Englishmen likewise would acknowledge and understand rightfully our rude, beggarly riming, brought first into Italy by Goths and Huns whan all good verses and all good learning, too, were destroy'd by them, and after carried into France and Germany, and at last received into England by men of excellent wit, indeed, but of small learning and less judgment in that behalf.

But now, when men know the difference and have the examples both of the best and of the worst, surely to follow rather the Goths in riming than the Greeks in true versifying were even to eat ackorns with swine when we may freely eat wheat bread emonges men. Indeed, Chaucer, Thomas Norton of Bristow, my Lord of Surrey, Master Wyatt, Thomas Phaer, and other gentlemen, in translating Ovid, Palingenius, and Seneca, have gone as far to their great praise as the copy they followed could carry them; but if such good wits and forward diligence had been directed to follow the best examples, and not have been carried by time and custom to content themselves with that barbarous and rude riming. . . .

Here we see the neoclassical usage of "Goth" as a term of abuse, as it was to remain until rehabilitated by the Romantic medieval revival. Webbe picked up this particular passage and summarized it approvingly, speaking of the "brutish poetry" for which the "Huns and Gothians" were responsible.

The quantitative movement found affirmation in *The Arcadian Rhetoric* of Abraham Fraunce (1588) just at the time when English poetry was well launched into the accentual-syllabic norm. Here we also see the notion of poetry as a more regularized form of rhetoric. Chapter 13, "Of Verse and Rime," reads in its entirety:

The figure of words consisteth either in the just dimension and measuring of sounds or words, or else in the pleasant repetition of the same. This dimension or measuring is either belonging to poets or used of orators. Poetical dimension is that which is bound to the continual observation of prescript spaces. Poetical dimension maketh either rime or verse. [Here we see the continuation of the *rhythmici* versus *metrici* debate, "meter" being assumed to be quantitative and "rhythm" reserved for Romance-type syllabism.] Rime containeth a certain number of syllables ending alike.
Sir P Sid:
My heart, my hand, my hand hath given my heart;
The giver given from gifts shall never part.

Chapter 14 begins:

> Verse or meter is a poetical dimension comprehending certain feet settled in certain places. A foot is a dimension of certain syllables with a strict observation of distinct time or quantity. A foot is either of two syllables or three, and both of them either simple or compound.

The relentless construction of dichotomies betrays Fraunce's work as a piece of Ramist logic; indeed, much of it is translated directly from a disciple of Ramus, Talaeus. The codifying is not as bloodless, however, as it might seem from this description and these examples; Fraunce included many poems in his work and seems genuinely to have enjoyed poetry. Attridge quotes with qualified approval some of Fraunce's own quantitative verse, concluding, "The movement produced little verse as good as this—which is, of course, more a censure of the movement than a commendation of Fraunce" (*Well-Weighed Syllables* 194). His theorizing and his practice did as much as anyone's to confirm the separation of poetry from music, partly by the approximation of poetry to rhetoric.

George Puttenham's *The Art of English Poesy*, published in 1589, makes a graceful critical transition from obsessive quantitizing to an acceptance of the real nature of the English language and the poetry written therein. Derek Attridge, having provided examples and arguments, concludes:

> In fact, Puttenham says some perceptive things about accentual metre while talking about it as if it were quantitative, for the Latin terminology gives him a framework and a vocabulary to discuss metrical patterns that he lacked when he was discussing native metre on its own terms. . . . But as far as English quantity is concerned, his main contribution was to insist that it should be based on the phonetic properties of the language, and to show that this meant that stress, as the most prominent feature in native English rhythms, would have to be taken into account. It is another step away from the conception of metre that sprang out of the training in Latin prosody, and a further advance towards an adequate account of the real metrical potential of the English language. (219)

Puttenham makes his contribution toward the establishment of poetry as an independent art by recognizing its earlier associations with music but insisting that language has a mellifluousness of its own:

> Vtterance also and language is giuen by nature to man for perswasion of others, and aide of them selues, I meane the first abilite to speake. For speech it selfe is artificial and made by man, and the more pleasing it is, the more it preuaileth to such purpose as it is intended for: but speech by meeter is a kind of vtterance, more cleanly couched and more delicate to the eare then prose is, because it is more currant and flipper vpon the tongue, and withal tunable

and melodious, as a kind of Musicke, and therfore may be tearmed a musicall speech or vtterance, which cannot but please the hearer very well. (8)

He mentions poetry in connection with rhetoric, but sees it as more a precursor than a companion:

> The vtterance in prose is not of so great efficacies because not only it is dayly vsed, and by that occasion the eare is ouerglutted with it, but is also not so voluble and flipper vpon the tong, being wide and lose, and nothing numerous, nor contriued into measures, and founded with so gallant and harmonical accents, nor in fine alowed that figuratiue conueyance, nor so great licence in choice of words and phrases as meeter is. So as the Poets were also from the beginning the best perswaders and their eloquence the first Rethoricke of the world. (8)

Although Puttenham sees poetry not as a refined form of rhetoric but rather as a precursor to it, the linking of the two, as always, tends to displace poetry from actual musical melody. Puttenham heaps other honors upon poetry, making it the source of almost every other sort of learning as well, calling poets among many other things the "first Astronomers and Philosophists and Metaphisicks" (9). Indeed, in his view, poetry preceded music: "[T]herefore were they the first Philosophers Ethick, & the first artificial Musicians of the world" (9). Here we see him positively reversing the arguments of Deschamps, making *musique naturele* a forerunner of *musique artificiele*. In fact, a common neoclassical concern, shared by Ben Jonson, was that the art of poetry have something artificial to it. For Puttenham the problem was not so much, as it had been for Deschamps, to insist on the "natural music" of language to distinguish poetry from music as it was to assert some claim on behalf of poetry that it had attained an artificiality of its own.

Puttenham, in exalting the status of poetry as the *fons et origo* of other branches of art and learning, did not aim at detracting from those other disciplines. There is perhaps some inconsistency in emphasis at different points in his treatise (he seems to have gone on inserting additions and revisions as it was being printed, having worked over it for a decade or so). This inconsistency shows itself when, at one point, he cites music as superior to poetry and a model for it:

> Of all which we leaue to speake, returning to our poeticall proportion, which holdeth of the Musical, because as we sayd before Poesie is a skill to speake & write harmonically: and verses or rime be a kind of Musicall Utterance, by reason of a certaine congruitie in sounds pleasing the eare, though not perchance so exquisitely as the harmonicall concents of the artificial Musicke, consisting in strained tunes, as is the vocall Musicke, or

that of melodious instruments, as Lutes, Harpes, Regals, Records and such like. (64–65)

Puttenham is so confident of the separateness of the two arts, and so enamored of the effects possible in music, that he seems at some points to anticipate by three centuries Walter Pater's dictum that all art aspires to the condition of music. In this passage he speaks of how the best poetry may "counterfeit harmonical tunes."

> This proportion consisteth in placing of euery verse in a staffe or ditty by such reasonable distaunces, as may best serue the eare for delight, and also to shew the Poets art and variety of Musick, and the proportion is double. One by marshalling the meetres, and limiting their distaunces hauing regard to the rime or concorde how they go and returne: another by placing euery verse, hauing a regard to his measure and quantitie onely, and not to his concorde as to set one short meetre to three long, or foure short and two long, or a short measure and a long, or of diuers/lengthes with relation one to another, which maner of Situation, euen without respect of the rime, doth alter the nature of the Poesie, and make it either lighter or grauer, or more merry, or mournfull, and many wayes passionate to the eare and hart of the hearer, deeming for this point that our maker by his measures and concordes of sundry proportions doth counterfeit the harmonicall tunes of the vocall and instrumentall Musickes. (84)

In the end, however, the good neoclassicist in Puttenham prevails; the artifice, however lovely, serves a didactic or at least an edifying purpose. Following the passage just quoted he mentions the Greek musical modes as an analogy for the various effects that may be achieved by poetic meters and forms, and by implication assigns to poetic *music* the informing power recognized in the ancient modes by Plato and Aristotle. In Chapter 19 Puttenham represents the poet again as "the most auncient Orator," able "to pleade, or to praise, or to aduise," but with the advantage over the speaker to whose "figures rhetoricall" the poet alone can add "a certaine sweet and melodious manner of speech."

> For the eare is properly but an instrument of conueyance for the minde, to apprehend the sence by the sound. And our speech is made melodious or harmonicall, not onely by strayned tunes, as those of Musick, but also by choise of smoothe words: and thus, or thus, marshalling them in their come-liest construction and order, and as well by sometimes sparing, sometimes spending them more or less liberally, and carrying or transporting of them farther off or neerer, setting them with sundry relations, and variable formes, in the ministery and vse of words, doe breede no little alteration in man. For to say truely, what els is man but his minde? (197)

The evolution of poetic meter in England continued over the decades from 1550 to the end of the century with minimal indebtedness to any literary theorists—as it usually does—and the evolution took it ever farther away from music. Chapter 9 will examine some increasingly self-conscious efforts of composers and poets—mainly composers—to bring the two arts back together. But with one exception, the madrigal—a consideration of which will conclude this chapter—there seems little else to say except that from 1570 onward the huge corpus of Renaissance poetry evolved according to its own prosody as poets learned to write with grace and verve in the accentual-syllabic meters, predominantly in pentameter. Thousands of plays were composed in blank verse—with interpolated songs, dances, ballads, ditties, jingles, and so on, which owed much to rhetoric and only a little to music. By the early seventeenth century stanzaic poems, their strophes modeled on songs and often enough called by that name, were commonly composed with a complexity of imagery, dramatic situation, rhetoric, and logic that would make the expectation of a melody ludicrous. To take an extreme example, one might just possibly imagine singing Donne's "Song," which begins "Go and catch a falling star"—for which in fact an anonymous melody is known (see Kime 87–99)—but what about "The Canonization"? F. R. Leavis is not as accurate as one could wish when he implied that Donne's stanza form always recalled music, but his perception of Donne is fundamentally sound:

> In an age when music is for all classes an important part of daily life, when poets are, along with so large a proportion of their fellow-countrymen, musicians and write their lyrics to be sung, Donne uses in complete dissociation from music a stanza-form that proclaims the union of poetry and music. The dissociation is positive; utterance, movement and intonation are those of the talking voice. (Keast 32)

In most poems Donne seems deliberately unsingable—to the point that neoclassic metricists from Ben Jonson to Yvor Winters have found him hard to read; in Jonson's view, he should have been hanged for not keeping his meter. Yet the sudden halts and reversals, the wrenchings and jerkings, are all possible within the much-extended accentual-syllabic prosody he employs and which one can enjoy when one is accustomed to the gait, described by Coleridge as riding "With Donne, whose muse on dromedary trots."

The availability of printed texts of poems, beginning with Tottel's *Miscellany* in 1556, did much to confirm the rift between music and poetry. Tottel's own revisions, especially of Wyatt (most of all in his notorious regularizing of "They Flee from Me"), encouraged the idea of a poetic meter that had to be consistent and self-sufficient. Irregularities that in the past might have been glided over as part of a musical performance had to be brought into the pattern. The concept of a printed poem that might be studied in private, as we have already noted, also encouraged poets toward a meditative manner and complexity of thought, and encouraged more careful revision. Edward Doughtie points to some of these factors and adds yet others, connecting developments in poetry with larger intellectual and theological currents:

> The content of many of these poems also makes them difficult to set to music. In the sonnet of the late sixteenth century, English poets like Sidney, but especially Shakespeare, were developing a lyric verse not for social performance but for brooding over in private. The fruits of printing, literacy, Protestant private scripture-reading, Counter-Reformation meditation, and other silent, solitary literary pursuits, as well as more traditional rhetoric and possibly Ramist logic, were poems like Shakespeare's Sonnet 124 and Donne's "The Canonization" (cf. Booth, 1981, 94−96). Multiple or shifting meanings, subtle arguments, logical development through stanzas instead of parallel reiteration—these qualities of the new poetry are not compatible with the aurally comprehensible verse that is most natural for song. (159)

Elise Bickford Jorgens recognizes the same sorts of problems:

> One of these features was the personal character of metaphysical verse. Where the Elizabethan song lyricist wrote of idealized or universal situations, the metaphysical poet was far more likely to write about personal experience. The persona often seems to assume the voice of the poet himself, and a completely different tone results from the poet's attitude toward his subject. Since musical setting lends abstraction or distance from direct statement, it was difficult for a composer to adopt an appropriate stance toward poetry of this kind. At best, he was compelled to seek a way for singer and persona to be identified. . . .
>
> Strophic setting is similarly discouraged by the thematic structure of much metaphysical poetry. The stanzas of the Elizabethan song poem often were parallel statements, with little or no narrative continuity from one stanza to the next and without appreciable change in tone, so that the same musical interpretation would be appropriate for all stanzas and musical structure would reinforce poetic structure. Metaphysical poetry, on the other hand, is more likely to have a dialectical or narrative structure, so that even where stanzas correspond to logical divisions in the development of the theme, to sing succeeding stanzas to the same music as the first is in a sense a contradiction to the poetic structure. (14−15)

Because the focus of this study is on the repeated separation of poetry from music, or its origination in combination with music, the discussion will break off here with an expansive gesture toward the riches of poetry in the accentual-syllabic prosody that is still quite alive, though still under attack, at the end of the twentieth century. Although music is often invoked as a critical term in discussions of such poetry—whether one is speaking of Herrick or Housman, Donne or Dickinson—the word is always metaphorical and inexact, much like "flow," "harmony," or "resonance." "Music" can be a useful, if subjective, descriptor when the poet's purpose is to invent lovely combinations of words that are evocative of vague thoughts and feelings, as in certain poems by Poe, Longfellow, Swinburne, Morris, and even Tennyson and Yeats, but it is a mistake if this Baconian idol leads us to imagine, as it too often does, that there is anything literally musical in the prosody. Even when musical notation seems useful as a way of identifying rhythmic effects in a poem, the employment of notes and rests is merely a borrowing, analogous to the macron-breve notation from ancient times that reflected the origins of Latin meter in Greek song. Accentual-syllabic metrics have long since evolved into a freestanding referential system. Some contemporary neoformalist poets even resist the idea that such a metrics could ever have had anything to do with music, feeling that such an admission would open the way to subversive influences. The influences to be resisted range from Walter Pater to the Violent Femmes. Extremists in the other direction, such as Projectivists and "Language" poets, reject accentual-syllabics in part for the same reason—for a supposed lack of musical interest. This New Formalist/Language Poetry duality distracts some academic scholars from attending to the best poetry of our times, directing their attention away from Seamus Heaney, for example, and toward a figure like Jackson MacLow.

It is hardly startling to maintain that by 1600 there existed a central prosodic tradition in which the best poetry in English over the next four hundred years was to be written. In this century much good free verse still belongs to this tradition, at least in the sense that free verse works contrapuntally against that tradition. Over the same sweep of time, however, new English and American prosodies that have effected major readjustments of the accentual-syllabic base have continued to emerge from musical contexts. The first of these contexts, the madrigal, flourished simultaneously with many of the developments discussed earlier in this chapter.

In concluding with a consideration of the madrigal I am deliberately scanting other musical-poetic developments that might be viewed as having affected English poetry. Two of these are the air, especially as it is exemplified in the collections of John Dowland and Thomas Morley (both published in 1597), and sacred music, such as William Byrd's Catholic masses. These belong far more to the history of music than to poetry, the musical interest being very great and the poetic minimal. Numerous airs were new settings for older poems and, like the madrigal, intended mainly for the diversion of the performers themselves. The persistence of a musical context for poetry, such as the air provided not only into the later Renaissance but, with interruptions, right on through the eighteenth century, lent a songlike authenticity to poems modeled on such works. That is, from the time of Wyatt to the present, poets have felt free to write poems they call *songs*, *ballads*—even *tunes* or *melodies*—the structure and effect of which are reminiscent of music. But the decisive break from song or air had occurred well before 1597. The break from the madrigal, however, occurred a little later because of its history as an import from Italy and France, and led to different results.

It seems appropriate that the etymology of "madrigal" remains uncertain; those who worry about it seem to lean toward "mother tongue." But the word's meaning in both music and poetry is very flexible. We are concerned here with the sixteenth-century madrigal, a song imported into England from Italy, which became the model for free-form poetry of the later sixteenth and early seventeenth centuries. There had been songs in the fourteenth century that the Italians called *madrigali*, but these consisted of one to four stanzas and a closing couplet. The sixteenth-century madrigal was invented as a way of accommodating words to the increasingly sophisticated music composed in Italy. The form was left indefinite; lines could vary in length to fit musical phrases and be repeated as often as necessary so that, although the poem itself might be only seven to twelve lines long, it could serve a piece of music of much greater length.

But even in its irregularity the Italian madrigal was meant to be serious poetry; this was less often true of the English madrigal, perhaps because the responsibility for its initial cultivation lay almost completely with composers, not poets. We should not be misled by the fact that in the *Old Arcadia* Sidney included poems which he called "madrigalls." Sidney announces in his narrative that these are sung, but he does not provide music for them. Furthermore, Sidney's intention was not to innovate by making use of the free-form characteristics of later English madrigals; in fact, he used the identical form for more than one poem in the *Arcadia*. The first truly English madrigals were pieces of Italian music provided with English words and phrases that came rather readily to hand and that showed no particular ingeniousness as poetry. Joseph Kerman says:

> Like the "New Poetry" of Sidney and Watson, the madrigal was a sudden
> growth for which immediate models had been available for decades, extend-
> ing a current that on the Continent had already passed its prime. The time

for it was ripe in England only in the 1570's and 1580's, and allowing for certain anomalies in the music-publishing business, it is obviously to this time that the origin of the English madrigal belongs. With it comes a preoccupation with Italianate *poesia per musica* which parallels the genuine literary Italianization of the same time, typified by the sonnet sequences of the 1590's. But unlike the Italian madrigal, the English was never a literary movement; it was imported by musicians, and the important poets of the day are not found in close contact with the madrigalists or the madrigal, nor were their poems much used for madrigal setting, as was the rule with Italian music. (248)

Bruce Pattison, in considering the change in relationship of text and music from the Italian madrigal to the English, says of the English, "The text may mean little, but it nearly always sounds natural and attractive when sung. Take the text away, and musical interest will remain" (99). The same cannot be said with much confidence for the text, in which there would often remain, without the music, little more than a superficial prettiness. "The suspicion that the majority of ordinary madrigals really did put the music before the poetry led ultimately to a reaction against counterpoint in the very literary circles that had encouraged the madrigal," says Pattison, who nevertheless is willing to allow that a "good deal of its attractiveness it really owed to its poetry" (99–100). To that one could add, "because the poetry did not interfere with the music." As others have recognized (Jorgens 77), madrigals were intended more for the pleasure of the performers than for an audience. The text, therefore, need not be particularly interesting or even comprehensible to a listener. This makes it easy to parody madrigal lyrics; one might repeat phrases such as, "I fixed my car up; I changed the oil; I bought new spark plugs; I set the timing," et cetera. An actual sixteenth-century madrigal by J. Wilbye runs like this:

> Adieu, Adieu, Adieu, sweet Amaryllis,
>   [repeated twelve times by four voices]
> For since to part, to part your will is,
> O heavy tiding
> Here is, here is for me no abiding.
> Yet once again, again, yet once again ere that I part with you
> Yet once again, again, ere that I part with you,
> Amaryllis, Amaryllis, sweet,
> Adieu, Adieu, Adieu, sweet Amaryllis,
> Amaryllis sweet, Adieu, Adieu.
>
> (http://www.englishcentre.fi/mpoy/cw_files/cw030.pdf)

Participants in madrigal singing can give themselves over to impassioned musical interpretation of simple phrases; the words are to a great degree something to keep the singing voice occupied.

Purely in terms of the music the word "madrigal" in English encompasses a wide range of possibilities. It might be written for anywhere from three to six voices, and later madrigals could involve much larger ensembles. There might or might not be instrumental accompaniment. The music might be homophonic, with a topmost melody and underlying harmony, or polyphonic with interweaving melodic lines. The one consistent difference between the madrigal and the songs that Wyatt's poems were modeled on, and that continued to be composed by others, was that it was "through-composed"—that is, the melody did not repeat itself, making it perhaps a distant descendant of Gregorian chant and related to the motet, even as the strophic song was a great-grandchild of the hymn. Beyond this description it seems best not to go, for several reasons. First, there exist several well-written and authoritative treatments of the madrigal from the point of view of its music as well as its words (see Doughtie, Pattison, Haar, Kerman, Boyd, and Roche). Second, the musical madrigal is best experienced as music, and numerous recordings are available as well as concerts by madrigal societies; best of all, one should join a madrigal group.

We will now abandon the musical madrigal in favor of its unmusical progeny, the literary madrigal, which first appeared in the 1590s. Musical performance was no more expected for the literary madrigal than for Shakespeare's sonnets. This is the first example in English poetry of a mode that arose from an instinctive rebellion against the constrictions of formal verse, and an instance of the same spirit that in this century has led to a wholesale rejection by many poets of the accentual-syllabic tradition. The best way to illustrate this rebellion is to quote a madrigal by John Mundy that Thomas Morley included in the collection *The Triumphs of Oriana* (1601) and that Rollins and Baker reprinted in *The Renaissance in England*:

> Lightly she whipped o'er the dales,
>   Making the woods proud with her presence;
> Gently she trod the flow'rs, and they as gently kiss'd her tender feet.
> The birds in their best language bade her welcome,
>   Being proud that Oriana heard their song;
> The clove-foot satyrs, singing, made music to the fauns a-dancing,
> And both together with an emphasis sang Oriana's praises
> Whilst the ajoining woods with melody did entertain their sweet harmony.
> Then sang the shepherds and nymphs of Diana,
>   "Long live fair Oriana!"
>
> (Rollins and Baker 265)

The freedom of this piece and others like it, which one can ascribe to the exigencies of the music, suggested to poets of the later sixteenth century an escape from the confines of regular metrics and especially from the rigors of the sonnet form—be it Italian, English, Spenserian, or any other variant. An exhaustive search of manuscripts might turn up earlier candidates, but I have nominated Barnabe Barnes as the first English poet who, using the madrigal as an excuse, invented a kind of free verse. In the midst of his sonnet sequence *Parthenophile and Parthenope*, so entitled in infelicitous emulation of Sidney, Barnes interpolated many literary madrigals. "Madrigal 25," though not as free as Hilton's poem, does employ lines of unpredictable length and an irregular rhyme pattern, including one unrhymed line:

> Whiles these two wrathfull goddesses did rage,
> > The little god of might,
> (Such as might fitter seeme with craynes to fight,
> Then with his bow to vanquish goddes, and kinges)
> > In a cherry-tree sate smiling;
> And lightly wauing with his motley winges,
> Fayre winges, in bewtie boyes, and gyrles beguiling,
> And cherry garlandes with his hands compiling
> > Laughing, he leaped light
> Vnto the Nymph, to try which way best might
> Her cheare, and with a cherry braunche her bobbed:
> > But her soft louely lippes
> The cherryes, of their ruddie rubye robbed:
> > Eftsoones he to his quiuer skippes,
> And bringes those bottles whence his mother sippes
> > Her nectar of delight,
> Which in her bosome clamed place by right.

(63–64)

Where Sidney, in the songs interpolated into *Astrophel and Stella*, looked back to the courtly lyric of the earlier sixteenth century, Barnes anticipates the expanded literary madrigals of the early seventeenth. The looseness of this kind of poem is quite comparable to the Italian *versi liberi* of Leopardi in the early nineteenth century and the vers libres of Laforgue and others among the French Symbolists. It could even be argued that it is not much different in rhyme and meter from some of T. S. Eliot's short poems. Enjoying the authority of their more serious Italian precursors, literary madrigals encouraged experimentation with longer irregular poems, such as William Drummond's "Phoebus, Arise" and some of Milton's earlier work. This free-form tendency reached a culmination in "Lycidas" where a demusicalized madrigal base expanded into a "monody"—a word that, as we shall see, suggested a recitative-like manner in which music was completely subordinate to text. "Lycidas" gathered into Milton's unfurling sails a good deal of the developing anti-stanzaic afflatus, much as *Paradise Lost* took the wind out of experiments in blank verse for some time after its composition. Fortunately for those who wished to open themselves to metrical experimentation, along came Abraham Cowley, whose fame in the seventeenth century exceeded Milton's, whose *Pindariques* authorized enthusiastic wildness, and whose modest abilities as a poet made him not intimidating as a model. Though in my own view William Carlos Williams was a far more interesting poet than Cowley, Williams's example has served somewhat the same purpose in this century for those seeking greater metrical freedom.

As in other ways, it was Milton who preempted many of the freedoms encouraged first by the Italianate forms and then by the supposed emulation of Pindar. If, as T. S. Eliot argued, *Paradise Lost* erected a "Chinese wall" across the seventeenth century, *Samson Agonistes* brought down the pillars of Renaissance prosody so that little was left for the eighteenth century but cautious masonry and fastidious landscape gardening. Not until English poetry was invigorated by renewed contact with songs and ballads in the later eighteenth century did metrics move forward into new territory. To say this is not to dismiss the accomplishments, mostly in the closed heroic couplet, of Dryden, Pope, and their precursors and successors, nor is it to view Samuel Johnson's poems as nothing more than versified rhetoric. Although the Augustan Age was in large part a retreat from the ebullience and adventure of the Renaissance (and also from the irrationalities of seventeenth-century conflict), the refinement of its metrics is real and the ability to savor the closed heroic couplet is a good test of poetic sensitivity. At the same time, English poetry of the Restoration and eighteenth century from time to time included attempts at close cooperation with music, if not a complete rejoining with it. But we cannot pass on to these without first coming to terms with Milton.

8

"God-gifted Organ Voice of England"

To argue that by the beginning of the seventeenth century the main currents of English poetry had long since diverged from their musical sources is not to argue that combinations and rapprochements could no longer be found. In many of these we must take words and music together if we are to enjoy the total effect of either. Campion's "My Sweetest Lesbia" and "I Care Not for These Ladies" recline insipidly on the page without their accompaniment of lute and voice, and some of Shakespeare's loveliest songs decline into jingles: "It was a lover and his lass / That o'er the green corn fields did pass, / With a hey and a ho, / And a hey nonny no." Many Cavalier songs, even a few Metaphysical ditties, could be and were set to music. Herrick tempted a number of composers, among whom were both William and Henry Lawes (see Jorgens 34–35, 156). In 1969 Mary W. Kime collected and discussed a dozen settings for eight of Donne's poems. It is not surprising that these included "The Baite," since that poem was just one more contribution to the Marlowe/Raleigh "Passionate Shepherd" debate and easily singable. That "An Hymne to God the Father" was set by both John Hilton II and Pelham Humphrey is initially startling because we hear Donne's distinctively passionate voice in melodramatic declaration of his guilt, but reexamination of the poem shows that the line of thought and the imagery are less challenging than, for example, "The Ecstasy," and easier to follow as a vocal performance.

The vogue for metrical psalms, collections of which had already been included in numerous editions of the Book of Common Prayer, continued as one of the few forms of music acceptable to most Puritans. Milton composed such translations; his earliest, "Psalm 106," exhibits a flatness that makes it an obedient companion when conjugated to music:

> Let us with a gladsome mind
> Praise the Lord, for he is kind,
>> For his mercies aye endure,
>> Ever faithful, ever sure.

Let us blaze his Name abroad,
For of gods he is the God;
    For, *&c.*

O let us his praises tell,
That doth the wrathful tyrants quell.
    For, *&c.*

(1–11)

Some of his later translations, especially those of Psalms 3 and 4, were in a much freer form and are themselves prime examples of real poetry emerging from a musical context.

PSALM 3

When he fled from Absalom.
Lord, how many are my foes!
    How many those
That in arms against me rise!
    Many are they
That of my life distrustfully thus say,
"No help for him in God there lies."
But thou, Lord, art my shield, my glory,
    Thee through my story
Th'exalter of my head I count,
    Aloud I cried
Unto Jehovah, he full soon replied
And heard me from his holy mount.
I lay and slept, I wak'd again,
    For my sustain
Was the Lord. Of many millions
    The populous rout
I fear not though encamping round about
They pitch against me their Pavilions.
Rise Lord, save me my God, for thou
    Hast smote ere now
On the cheek-bone all my foes,
    Of men abhorr'd
Hast broke the teeth. This help was from the Lord;
Thy blessing on thy people flows.

These two examples epitomize much about Milton and music. The first is close to early sixteenth-century hymns and songs—another instance of a Protestant metrical psalter; the second is monostrophic, free, and similar to the choruses of *Samson Agonistes* (though not, to be sure, nearly as interesting as poetry). The version of Psalm 3 may give the illusion of greater musicality, but in fact it is at a double remove from music. It goes beyond strophic independence such as that attained by the stanzaic poems of Donne and Herbert, Herrick and Lovelace, for which musical accompaniment is superfluous or, at best, a decorative addition. In his version of Psalm 3 Milton achieves a kind of free verse, the precursors for which were the literary madrigals and the successors to which were the pseudo-Pindaric odes, none of which employed a predictable metric.

Milton often gives an impression of musicality, to the point that T. S. Eliot found it impossible to discuss his verse without speaking (in "The Music of Poetry") of music: "The late Shakespeare is occupied with the other task of the poet—that of experimenting to see how elaborate, how complicated, the music could be made. . . . Of those whose exploration took them in this one direction only, Milton is the greatest master" (*On Poetry and Poets* 29). As I will tacitly admit in making a comparison with Haydn, expressive variants in poetic meter and form in the opening movements of "L'Allegro" and "Il Penseroso" certainly do parallel musical effects and may well be inspired by music. But they have moved away from music and resist recombination with it; to set either of that pair of poems to music results in a performance that diminishes the prosodic charm of the unaccompanied text. To attempt an analysis of them by treating them literally as music might reveal or explain some things about them but would end by falsifying or obscuring others.

While Milton pursued his independent course, others continued to cultivate the older combinations of verse and music. Later in the century, operas imitated from Italian productions already popular in England, began to be composed and these required librettos. Popular songs, broadsides, hymns, and other varieties of profane and sacred music persisted despite Puritan strictures and crescent neoclassicism. But, as we have repeatedly noticed, poetry had gone its own way as an independent art. Even though *A Midsummer Night's Dream* and *The Tempest* exhibit masque-like qualities, Shakespeare's entire corpus keeps music completely subordinate to plot and structure; often it is no more than a part of a transitory spectacle. To say this is not to question Shakespeare's knowledge of music, which was extensive, or the multitude of musical references in his work; a glance at the entries in a concordance to Shakespeare under "music" turns up numerous metaphors, comparisons, and expressions of emotion that employ the word figuratively—and many literal uses as well. But in "Shakespeare and Music," Edward J. Dent, after tracing in great detail the place of music and musical instruments in Elizabethan culture, as well as throughout Shakespeare's plays, ends by insisting that music was at all times subordinate to larger dramatic purposes, that "for all his knowledge of music and sensitiveness to the theatrical value of music, [he] never adopts the principles of opera" (Granville-Barker and Harrison 159). Dent adds, "From the operatic point of view music is the normal language in which human intercourse is carried on; Shakespeare, however, except perhaps in the case of Ariel, and the fairies in *A Midsummer Night's Dream*, gets no nearer to this principle than the adoption of poetry as a normal language. Music is for him always something extraneous, as it is in ordinary daily life" (160).

The more ambitious attempts at reproducing in Renaissance drama the effects of Greek tragedy, complete with choruses that were sung, had also largely disappeared by the end of the sixteenth century, having never taken hold at all in England to the extent that they had in Italy and France (see G. L. Finney 221–27). Partly this failure was a consequence of following Senecan rules and models rather than Greek originals. Even when English drama had directly emulated ancient tragedy there had been no real approximation to *mousike*; there was no effort to include choral odes that were set to music. Sackville and Norton's *Gorbuduc* (1561) employed a chorus of "four ancient and sage men of Britain" to comment upon the action at the end of each act of the play, and the chorus did express itself in strophes, in contrast to the mechanically stichic blank verse of the dialogue. Also, each act began with a dumb show, and the authors included instructions for musical accompaniments to these interludes. But, however flattering it may have been to a learned audience to find themselves in the presence of a recognizably Senecan revival, the effect was stilted, academic, and self-conscious. In later plays the chorus was, often enough, a single character, as in *Doctor Faustus*, or even a pair of characters with separate speeches, such as the Ghost of Andrea and Revenge at the start of *The Spanish Tragedy*. The single-figure chorus resembles more the commentator or interpreter in the old morality plays, such as the Doctor in *Everyman*. Seventeenth-century French drama, though more self-consciously classical than anything ever written in England, especially in its obedience to the "three unities," did not retain even remnants of the chorus in the tragedies of Corneille or Racine.

As we have seen, music pursued an independent career. By the seventeenth century, madrigal singing in Italy had combined with narrative and dance in masque-like productions from which opera was born, and words tended to be subservient to melody. Continual innovations in instrumentation and technique made possible compositions whose intrinsic interest estranged them from any verbal text. The written parts of madrigals, as we know, often made little sense. The composer Henry Lawes, whom Milton venerated for his appreciation of good poetry, contrived a practical joke on some madrigal singers by giving them a text that consisted of nothing but titles of a set of Italian songs, and few took any notice.

It would appear, then, that in identifying the occasions on which poetry emerged from music one might glide to the end of the eighteenth century when, once again, varieties of poetry appeared that had only recently broken from a musical context or were partly still immersed therein. Along the way one would note the quasimusical pretensions of the *Pindarique* ode, some of which were set to music; to other poems written to be performed as oratorios or composed so as to invite musical accompaniment of some sort; to continued successes in hymnody, including adaptations of classical scansions; and to song-writing of other sorts that never died out. Also, it would be well to give examples of exactly how various seventeenth- and eighteenth-century prosodies—whether Metaphysical or Cavalier, Cowleyesque or Popeian—continued the emancipations of the previous centuries. The really formidable obstructions to such cheerful forward progress, though, are the poetical works of Milton—or rather not the works themselves so much as the misinterpretations of Milton's prosodic achievement in relation to music.

Milton's poetry, even more than Sidney's or Spenser's, is an independent artistic medium, yet it is often discussed as if it had achieved some sort of fusion with music, instead of growing out of and away from it. Readers who are intensely responsive to Milton's verbal effects, and who also love music, often wish to explain those effects in terms of what they instinctively consider a higher form of art than poetry. Even if they have consciously freed themselves from Paterian heresy they cannot help but feel that in Milton they hear something that transcends ordinary poetry. They are perfectly correct in those feelings, but incorrect if they attribute what they hear to anything emulated or aspired to in vocal or instrumental music. Milton did carry prosody so far ahead that in some ways he has never been surpassed—somewhat as Beethoven preempted a good deal of the musical future in his later works. But to see Milton's achievement as a reintegration with music is a retrograde view; in speaking of his "music" we must be careful to understand it metaphorically, as we should in speaking of "Lycidas," say, as *mannerist* or *baroque.* We must not allow the exhilaration (if we feel it) toward the conclusion of "Lycidas," or the magnificence of the opening lines of Book 3 of *Paradise Lost,* to become confused with similar feelings aroused by a concerto grosso of Corelli or an organ concerto by Handel (or, to keep the chronology more relevant, a Monteverdi Gloria), to the point that we call Milton, literally, *musical.* In similar fashion we may speak of the "architecture" of *Paradise Lost* as long as we do not go on to claim that Milton is adopting, literally, principles learned from Palladio or Inigo Jones.

Another important reason for confusion is that Milton's knowledge of and devotion to music were profound (see Spaeth 12–27; 56–80), and the way that he speaks of music does make it sound as if he values it above all other arts. He tends constantly to slip into musical terminology. Sometimes he revised poems so as to remove musical jargon that was so familiar to him that he fell into it as a natural mode of expression; words such as *concent* or *descant* might remain but in "At a Solemn Music" he changed "chromatik jarres" to "ill sounding," and then omitted the line entirely. In the same poem "Mixe your choise chords" became "wed your divine sounds" (see Langdon 48). Milton's father was a professional musician and the son inherited a love and proficiency that kept him singing hymns and playing the organ into his old age. The presumption is too often, then, that the poet often had in mind a piece of music or a musical strategy, or was emulating music, when he composed in verse. Also, Milton repeatedly evoked the ecstasy with which, *in heaven*, one might expect to hear a perfect blend of voice and music, word and instrument. Some of those who admire Milton are willing to allow him to have achieved on earth what he himself considered possible only to our perfected, restored, and resurrected bodies and souls in heaven. Such admirers feel that a poet inspired by music as Milton, as learned and proficient in it as he was, must have incorporated music itself literally into his poetry—or at least that he brought his prosody *closer* to music than that of his precursors (see Hardison 22). My argument will be that he did just the opposite, and that his achievement is all the greater for it.

In the same way that he was concerned to purify Platonism of its connections with erotic love poetry, Milton saw poetry itself as aspiring away from the more sensual art form—even as he admitted poetry to be "simple, sensual, and passionate" and "less subtle and fine" than the highest form of rhetoric (in "Of Education"). As we will see, his concept of the "music" to be heard in heaven was supremely intellectual, beyond speech itself and far beyond earthly melodies. Gretchen Finney explains it thus:

> Music produced by man, however, does not reflect divine origins. Beauty, as in orthodox Neoplatonic tradition, comes from light, not proportion. It shines not in music, but in the face of God's earthly image, man himself, and this "grace" alone inspires love in man that leads back to God. It is love of man for woman (governed always by Reason), not love for music, "By which to heav'nly Love thou maist ascend." Love is music of a higher order than audible sound, "Harmonie to behold in wedded pair / More grateful then harmonious sound to the eare." (171)

Returning to his comments in "Of Education," we should note that Milton finds poetry rooted in principles that can be explained by grammar—as they had been for more than a century in William Lily's standard text, which included a chapter on prosody. But he insisted that poetry must transcend such scansions, which were themselves considered as "musical," having been pre-served as such in Augustine's *De Musica*, and by Boethius as well. Milton wrote, "I mean not the prosody of a verse, which they could not but have hit on before among the rudiments of grammar; but that sublime art which in Aristotle's *Poetics*, in Horace, and the Italian commentaries of Castelvetro, Tasso, Mazzoni, and others, teaches what the laws are." Milton's inspiration often did come from music, but his aspirations always carried him toward the realm of the "unexpressive."

Few readers of Milton would care to argue that many of his references to song or singing are anything more than conventions inherited from the clas-sics. "Who would not sing for Lycidas? he knew / Himself to sing, and build the lofty rhyme" (10–11). This is almost a direct translation of "Neget quis Carmina Gallo," (Who would deny Gallus a song?) from Virgil's third *Eclogue*, and was itself so thoroughly part of pastoral conventions by the time Milton used it that Henry King, the subject of "Lycidas," need not even have been a poet himself, let alone skilled in musical composition. And even in the imme-diate context, it hardly sounds as if Milton meant that King employed musical notation to "build the lofty rhyme." It will not do to slip into the error, with which one querulous critic was taxed, of being contentious about things over which no one contends. But it is worth remembering that most of the time when Milton says "sing," and always when he says "I sing," he means poetry and not music.

Since much of what can be elicited from passages scattered throughout Milton's works regarding his views of music may be found in condensed form in "At a Solemn Music" (1633–34), we will use this poem as an introductory example and then revert to a chronologically ordered discussion.

> Blest pair of *Sirens*, pledges of Heav'n's joy,
> Sphere-born harmonious sisters, Voice and Verse,
> Wed your divine sounds, and mixt power employ
> Dead things with inbreath'd sense able to pierce,
> And to our high-rais'd fantasy present
> That undisturbed Song of pure concent,
> Aye sung before the sapphire-color'd throne
> To him that sits thereon,
> With Saintly shout and solemn Jubilee,
> Where the bright Seraphim in burning row
> Their loud uplifted Angel-trumpets blow,
> And the Cherubic host in thousand choirs

Touch their immortal Harps of golden wires,
With those just Spirits that wear victorious Palms,
Hymns devout and holy Psalms
Singing everlastingly;
That we on Earth with undiscording voice
May rightly answer that melodious noise;
As once we did, till disproportion'd sin
Jarr'd against nature's chime, and with harsh din
Broke the fair music that all creatures made
To their great Lord, whose love their motion sway'd
In perfect Diapason, whilst they stood
In first obedience and their state of good.
O may we soon again renew that Song,
And keep in tune with Heav'n, till God ere long
To his celestial consort us unite,
To live with him, and sing in endless morn of light.

In this poem Milton represents the union of music and poetry as a prelapsarian ideal, attainable now only in heaven. One wonders just what to make of his calling them "Sirens." At best, they are "pledges of Heaven's joy," tokens of bliss to come in another life. But they are "Sphere-born harmonious sisters"—that is, they seem to belong to the created universe rather than to heaven itself. And the Muses themselves remain independent of one another—"sisters"—although Milton calls on them to "wed" their "divine sounds" and employ their separate powers in producing for mortal listeners some simulacrum of divine harmony, which will help raise us above our earthly limitations so as to answer "with undiscording voice." The tenor of the whole poem is intensely Platonic, as in the idea that Voice and Verse are temporary visitants from the quintessential spheres above.

Although he removed some of them in revision, Milton happily harmonizes the multiple meanings of terms that he has borrowed from music. "Concent" carries the same senses that it did for Campion when he wrote (in "Rose-Cheek'd Laura"), "From consent divinely framed"—the literal meaning being what we call "harmony," and for which another common word was "agree." To this Milton adds a suggestion of the perfect obedience and reconciliation possible in heaven. The entry for "diapason" in the OED includes a quotation by Robert Burton from *The Anatomy of Melancholy*: "A true correspondence, perfect amity, a diapason of vows and wishes." For Milton similarly the most perfect musical interval, the octave, is a metaphor of perfect *concord* (a word that he does not use here). "Jarr'd" and "chime" have both technical and metaphorical meanings; "consort" could mean simply "choir," but it also

carries the sense of a marriage made in heaven, or rather, a union that transcends anything possible on earth. This he referred to again toward the end of
"Lycidas" as "the unexpressive nuptial Song" (176)—the marriage hymn too
ethereal for human voice or imagination. "Voice and Verse" resemble a pair of
vestals devoted to the service of God ("pledged"), whose sisterly agreement
shall be further purified in the ineffable harmony of word, voice, and instrument before the throne of God. Milton, naturally, says much more than this,
and says it much better, in his poem, but it is worth pointing out some of the
resonances that we may catch only after repeated readings of the poem.

In form, "At a Solemn Music" is an expanded madrigal and therefore, for its
time, a variety of free verse. The rhythmic norm is iambic pentameter, but line
lengths and placement of rimes are as irregular as in the *versi liberi* of Leopardi in
the early nineteenth century or the vers libre of Laforgue later on (as well as in
some shorter poems of Arnold and Eliot). Milton counterpoints the natural
rhetorical emphasis of each phrase against the implied norm with greater freedom and flexibility than most English poets that came before him and many
that came after; his chief precursor in this manner is William Drummond who,
like Milton, learned much from his reading of Italian poetry, especially the canzone, which permitted liberties not possible in strictly strophic compositions.

The ebullient lyrical freedom of "At a Solemn Music," together with the
musical references and metaphors, misleads some readers into imagining that
here we have actual music. But this is not true. We have words, but no melody.
In fact, the monostrophic unity of the poem even tends to defeat a musical
interpretation or arrangement; it is an example of what Milton, in other
contexts, called *apolelymenon* (in the introductions to *Samson Agonistes* and to
"Ad Joannem Rousium"). Even when Milton observed a set form he could
not help taking liberties with it; the Miltonic sonnet licentiously merges
octave and sestet of the Italian form, and the enjambments of *Paradise Lost* for
some readers, including Samuel Johnson, compromise the integrity of the
individual line. At the time that Milton composed the poem, musicians were
only beginning to employ increasingly predictable rhythms, intervals, harmonies, and temperings that made possible musical structures of greater interest
and complexity; Milton's progress was in precisely the opposite direction,
away from strophic predictability, from rhyme, and in the end from regular
meter itself. "At a Solemn Music" may give the illusion of musicality and
certainly celebrates the promise of a restored "consort" in heaven, but as a
work of poetic art it represents a further step, beyond Sidney, Spenser, and
even Donne, and a further departure from music.

Analysis of sound patterns in "At a Solemn Music" reveals how much closer
it is to rhetoric than to music. In 1630, for reasons just given, music was

enjoying a rapid evolution toward structural complexity. The rhythms of Milton's poem, though, *disrupt* the iambic pentameter (while assuming it as a norm)—and the pentameter itself was already amusical, in comparison with tetrameters or trimeters. Milton commonly breaks the pentameter in the openings of his poems, either by introducing a pause or by enjambment or both; seldom is the first line end-stopped. The first pause often follows a salutation, as it does here:

> Blest pair of *Sirens*, pledges of Heav'n's joy,
> Sphere-born harmonious sisters, Voice and Verse,
> Wed your divine sounds, and mixt power employ. . . .

The second line precisely reverses the rhythm of the first, the patterns expressed in feet being 2 : 3 / 3 : 2. The meaning parallels this, the significant words being "pair . . . pledges" / "sisters, Voice and Verse" and the sequence in terms of numerical exactness being definite : indefinite / indefinite : definite. Rhetorically and rhythmically this pairing reinforces the concept of the separation of the two arts—complementary and parallel but not identical. Line three is perfectly divided by the caesura into five-syllable halves, exemplifying the separation that prevents music and poetry from being perfectly "wed" or "mixed" yet sufficiently close to remind us of such a possibility in heaven. The Platonic ascent into auditory paradise is thenceforth swift, hastened by the verse that for the next thirteen lines soars uninterrupted by a single interior pause and only by momentary breaks at line endings, more than half of the lines being completely enjambed. In meaning we move from inert matter to "high-raised phantasy" and thence to the throne of God in the space of four lines. The incomplete lines ("To him that sits thereon" and "Singing everlastingly") suggest the ineffable and immeasurable power and glory, the eternity of God's presence. "Singing everlastingly" is so far removed from its companion in rhyme ("jubilee") as to defeat any sense of closure at its occurrence. It might as well have been unrhymed, as are many lines in "Lycidas." At this point the poem has opened up, perhaps not enough to have provided Charles Olson the *lebensraum* he claimed in the divagations of *Maximus*, but much beyond previous English prosody. One feels inadequate, even pretentiously condescending, speaking of Milton's superb tact as a prosodist, but his instinct (or art) is perfect when, following "Singing everlastingly," he offers us a closed couplet, suggesting thereby the earthly limitations we must transcend if we are to approximate anything like the bliss above. The first internal breaks since line 3 occur in lines 19 and 20, before and after "Jarred against nature's chime," and the rhythm of that phrase is itself imitative, as is "and with harsh din," a cacophony of displaced stresses. "Broke" in the next line repeats the effect of "Jarr'd." Man's fallen state contrasts, rhythmically, with the prelapsarian, perfectly iambic line, "In perfect Diapason, whilst they stood."

The poem abounds in minor instances of accommodation of sound to meaning, and rhythm to rhetoric. A good example is

★ / / /   / / ★ /
And to our high-rais'd fantasy,

where the iamb (or possibly, pyrrhic) followed by two spondees elevates the line to a higher plateau. "O may we soon again renew that Song" *renews* the sound of "soon" in the word "Song," with a good approximation of the "oo" sound in the second syllable of "renew" as well, so that the word echoes the vowels of "we soon." As Pope showed us in *An Essay on Criticism*, although an Alexandrine need not necessarily give an impression of slowness, it may well suggest temporal duration; the last line, "To live with him, and sing in endless morn of light," makes an expansive gesture by its contrast with all other lines in the poem.

Other readers might wish to discover other patterns and effects in the poem, and their readings, though different, would supplement one another in proving that Milton's range and variety and the complexity of his aural effects go beyond those of any other English poet—even Tennyson, whom W. H. Auden credited with having "the best ear, perhaps, of all the great English poets." Tennyson's versatility and technical facility sometimes draw attention to themselves, but—as in much else from the Victorian era—gratuitous display and ornamentation are part of his art. Milton's art is always at the service of his subject, even when his choice of subject involves an immense degree of presumption. His poetry is the poetry of convinced personal statement, of the righteous and self-assured Protestant conscience; his strength is as the strength of ten because his heart is pure—too strong and pure, at times, for some readers who find his inner light insufferable. But if we judge a poet purely by what Yeats called the "articulation of sweet sounds," we must set Milton above all others, at least in English. These sweet sounds, however, are not actual music. Milton did not carry poetry toward a devoutly desired consummation with music; instead, he did much to make possible a final decree of divorce from it.

In 1629, four years before "At a Solemn Music," Milton used musical terms in *On the Morning of Christ's Nativity* to register his exhilaration at the prospect of heavenly bliss. In the central stanzas of this ode we encounter his belief that the perfect blending of voice and instrument, of note and word, can only have been heard at the moment of creation and will only recur after the Last Judgment, and that although the pure in heart may catch faint resonances of the music of the spheres, even such harmony as this falls short of what is to be expected in heaven. To human ears that ultimate sound is, again, "unexpressive," inexpressible. When the heavens open to the shepherds at the birth of Christ, the promise of some future reconciliation stirs the human souls of the shepherds and the whole of sublunary nature; Milton himself evidently heard the distant strains with sufficient clarity to draw poetic inspiration from them.

9
When such music sweet
Their hearts and ears did greet,
  As never was by mortal finger strook,
Divinely-warbled voice
Answering the stringed noise,
  As all their souls in blissful rapture took:
The Air such pleasure loath to lose,
With thousand echoes still prolongs each heav'nly close.

10
Nature that heard such sound
Beneath the hollow round
  Of *Cynthia's* seat, the Airy region thrilling,
Now was almost won
To think her part was done,
  And that her reign had here its last fulfilling;
She knew such harmony alone
Could hold all Heaven and Earth in happier union.

11
At last surrounds their sight
A Globe of circular light,
  That with long beams the shame-fac't night array'd;
The helmed Cherubim
And sworded Seraphim,
  Are seen in glittering ranks with wings display'd,
Harping in loud and solemn choir,
With unexpressive notes to Heav'n's new-born Heir.

12
Such Music (as 'tis said)
Before was never made,
  But when of old the sons of morning sung,
While the Creator Great
His constellations set,
  And the well-balanc't world on hinges hung,

And cast the dark foundations deep,
And bid the welt'ring waves their oozy channel keep.

13
Ring out ye crystal spheres,
Once bless our human ears
    (If ye have power to touch our senses so)
And let your silver chime
Move in melodious time;
    And let the Bass of Heav'n's deep Organ blow,
And with your ninefold harmony
Make up full consort to th'Angelic symphony.

(93–132)

In this passage we again note the numerous terms borrowed from, or applicable to, music ("warbled," "harmony," "close," "chime," "consort"), as well as Milton's familiarity with musical instruments.

    The poem is also of great interest as a giant step in the direction of his later free verse. The *Nativity Ode* remains regularly stanzaic within its two sections, yet it has already escaped from its formal model, the Spenserian stanza. In the four introductory stanzas Milton modified the nine-line *ababbcbcc* pattern into rhyme royal (*ababbcc*), but retained the Alexandrine for the last line; in the "Hymn" he further loosened the original structure, simultaneously roughening the meter of certain lines to the point that conclusive scansions are problematic. Taking the first two lines of the "Hymn" out of context ("It was the winter wild, / While the Heav'n-born child"), one could not be perfectly sure whether we have a dimeter or trimeter couplet, and even if we can agree that it is more nearly trimeter, it is not easy to decide which syllables are stressed. To be confident of the meter we must wait for more regular opening lines, such as

    ★ /   ★ / ★ /
    But peaceful was the night
    ★ / ★ / ★ /
    Wherein the Prince of light,

before we can be sure of what Milton's paradigm really was. Of course, once into the swing of the poem, one tends to make all the necessary adjustments instinctively, pronouncing the silent *e* in past participles (stringèd, helmèd) and supplying synaereses (Cynth-ya's, melod-yus), syncopes (glitt'ring, circ'lar), elision (th'Angelic), and diaeresis (uni-ón)—as well as extra beats or offbeats. The line "When such music sweet" has only five syllables, for example, and begins with a syncopation, or silent interval, that can be called an *implied offbeat*, giving it a rhythm that might be diagrammed: (★) / ★ / ★ /. To mention these things is only to hint at the complexity of Milton's counterpointing, if one may use that term as a metaphor or analogy, always remembering that what we have is a *prosodic* counterpoint that works against an implied accentual-syllabic meter, an iambic template of a3, a3, b5, c3, c3, b5, d4, d6.

Milton's "Hymn" does give the effect of a series of stanzas that *need* music for their completion; rhythmically it reads in places somewhat as the old ballads do, with a halting quality that could be remedied by accommodation to a tune. Here, though, this is not an approach toward music, but rather the illusion of a performance that is partly musical.

No such illusion could be attached to what Milton intended as a companion poem, "The Passion," which he composed for the following Easter. The best thing that can be said about "The Passion" is that Milton set it aside and did not try to finish it. One suspects that Shelley would have persisted; the poem includes passages that resemble the unfortunate parts of "Adonais." "My muse with Angels did divide to sing," he writes in the first stanza, recalling the success of the *Nativity Ode*, but introducing an unhappy bit of musical jargon: "divide" means to sing in equal or parallel parts. Among other things Milton presumptuously sets himself on an equal footing with the heavenly host. The second stanza begins with expressionless platitudes, "For now to sorrow must I tune my song, / And set my Harp to notes of saddest woe." We have reverted to *Gorboduc*-like metrics as well: mechanical pentameters. Most lines in "The Passion" are, for Milton, uncharacteristically end-stopped or paused. Although he attempts to enliven the poem with some preposterous metaphysical conceits, it never takes wing. The references to music are as copious, given its length, as in most of Milton's poems, but few readers would call the poem "musical." The failure, though, is a failure of verbal prosody—along with its other infelicities.

Turning to secular subjects in 1631, Milton recovered his liveliness—most appropriately in "L'Allegro." Given his fundamental seriousness and extreme sense of moral propriety, we are justified in interpreting the poem, however delightful we may find it, as a pleasing fiction, a pose, a literary performance, an exercise. In "L'Allegro" he did allow himself to sport with Amaryllis in the shade; the imagined luncheon that Corydon and Thyrsis share with Phillis and Thestillis is a fanciful interlude. As we near the end of the poem we need not place too weighty an interpretation on the equally fanciful wedding of poetry and music, any more than we should imagine Shakespeare, in the line "Warble his native Wood-notes wild," to have had much in common with a thrush or redbreast. Perfect accommodation of melody and words is no more than a pastoral fantasy:

Then to the well-trod stage anon,
If *Jonson's* learned Sock be on,
Or sweetest *Shakespeare*, fancy's child,
Warble his native Wood-notes wild.
And ever against eating Cares,
Lap me in soft *Lydian* Airs,
Married to immortal verse,
Such as the meeting soul may pierce
In notes, with many a winding bout
Of linked sweetness long drawn out,
With wanton heed, and giddy cunning,
The melting voice through mazes running;
Untwisting all the chains that tie
The hidden soul of harmony.

(131–44)

Indeed, in allowing "*Lydian*" airs, Milton has flown directly in the face of his most important mentor among the pagans, Plato, who disallowed this mode as effeminate and enervating. Of the prosody of "L'Allegro," though, we might say as Dryden did of Chaucer, "Here is God's plenty." Many studies already exist, and many others might be made, without beginning to exhaust the range of particular effects. The basic rhythm cannot even be identified using conventional terminology. Is it trochaic or is it iambic? Are the exceptional lines headless or anacrustic, hypermetric or catalectic? *Are* there any exceptional lines? Are not all of them exceptional?

Even as he loosens the meter toward unpredictability, Milton knits his lines up in other ways. Alliteration (sometimes called "initial rhyme") occurs in at least eight of the fourteen quoted lines, in the same positions that it would have appeared in Old English. Where there is no alliteration one may find internal near-rhyme or assonance—all this a surplus addition to the regular end-rhymes, but not a surplusage, never intrusive. I had never noticed the alliteration until I began to looking for objective evidence to support a general impression of aural riches.

Milton's opening is perfectly designed to introduce this ambiguous, lively, supple tetrameter that he invests with a freedom never achieved before or since, employing to start with lines that alternately fall short of and exceed that measure:

Hence loathed Melancholy
    Of *Cerberus* and blackest midnight born,
In *Stygian* Cave forlorn
    'Mongst horrid shapes, and shrieks, and sights unholy,

Find out some uncouth cell,
   Where brooding darkness spreads his jealous wings,
And the night-Raven sings;
   There under *Ebon* shades, and low-brow'd Rocks,
As ragged as thy Locks,
   In dark *Cimmerian* desert ever dwell.
But come thou Goddess fair and free,
In Heav'n yclep'd *Euphrosyne*,
And by men, heart-easing Mirth,
Whom lovely *Venus* at a birth
With two sisters Graces more
To ivy crowned *Bacchus* bore.

(1–16)

Few poems in English open with a more brilliant display of prosody; Milton surpassed himself later with "Lycidas," but except for "Kubla Khan" it is hard to think of other worthy competitors. The poet Donald Davidson, confronting the general problem of writing well, made a comparison that can be applied to Milton's capacity for orchestrating many effects at once; Davidson recalled

> the condition of crisis described by Julius Caesar when, on a famous summer evening in France, over two thousand years ago, he was attacked by the Nervii. Part of Caesar's army, protected by a cavalry screen, was pitching camp; and part, encumbered by the baggage train, was crossing a river. The Nervii, Caesar says, broke and tore up his cavalry screen and hit his legions at three points simultaneously. And then, Caesar tersely remarks, he had to do everything at once—*omnia uno tempore agenda*. And what he had to do all at once was the more difficult because lack of time and the onrush of the enemy were something of an obstacle to the performance of military duties. (v)

Milton, the great general of the language, has it doing everything simultaneously; armchair poetic strategists are hard put to account for how it all works together. Yet we may make a few points. To start with, the dragging out of the pentameter, in catalogues of what were to become conventions of Gothic horror, alternates with abrupt imperative trimeters—a metrical pattern that, were it sustained, would be unbearably tedious—as if the slow introductory measures of a Haydn symphony were to persist for the entire movement. This uncertainty of rhythm—the trimeter being too spritely and the pentameter constantly dragging it down—is the ideal platform from which to launch the unpredictably stressed tetrameters that make up the body of the poem. Even in the first six tetrameters, just quoted, two are headless (or, if one prefers, catalectic and trochaic): "And by men heart-easing mirth" and "With two sisters Graces more." Because "and" and "with" both carry stress only with difficulty, the irregularity of the lines is even more striking, the natural stress patterns being ★ ★ / / / ★ / and ★ / / ★ / ★ /. Throughout the poem a four-beat rhythm hovers over the lines, rarely scanning as regularly as in "To ivy crowned *Bacchus* bore." For this calculated uncertainty the ten lines of the opening provide the perfect preparation.

After arguing the appropriateness of this opening to the mood and subject of "L'Allegro," one might well be embarrassed at having to explain how the same can be said for "Il Penseroso," since the form is exactly the same. Even the rhetoric is parallel, with trimeters in lines 1 and 5 that are imperative dismissals. But the introduction to "Il Penseroso" is less of a catalog, less an accretion of details that agglomerate into a single impression, and more a series of parallel images and phrases that appeal to judgment rather than to the concrete imagination—"deluding joys," "toys," "fancies fond," "gaudy shapes"—with only one imaginable detail: "gay motes that people the Sunbeams." Therefore, when combined with the rhetoric, the prosody produces the opposite effect from "L'Allegro"; when the tetrameters appear they suggest that we have settled into a sober and predictable frame of mind, following the irregular expostulations of the first ten lines:

> But hail thou Goddess, sage and holy,
> Hail divinest Melancholy,
> Whose Saintly visage is too bright
> To hit the Sense of human sight;
> And therefore to our weaker view,
> O'erlaid with black, staid Wisdom's hue.
>
> (11–16)

As before, the meter shifts between trochaic and iambic, but rhythmically the introductory pairs of lines are both identical and metrically regular: a pair of perfect trochaic tetrameters followed by two pairs of iambic tetrameters. Lines in the same position in "L'Allegro" are much less regular, giving an impression of speeding the pace rather than retarding it. The meter in the body of both poems is in fact much the same, a flexible vehicle for many purposes; it will not do to labor its accommodations with pedantic ingenuity. And yet, of the first fifty tetrameters of "Il Penseroso," about sixteen couplets are consistently either iambic or trochaic, while such consistency occurs in only about ten for "L'Allegro." Irregularity adds to the spritely feel of the latter.

"Il Penseroso" ends with passages mostly in regular iambic tetrameter, including one in which Milton pays tribute to the power of music:

But let my due feet never fail
To walk the studious Cloister's pale,
And love the high embowed Roof,
With antic Pillars massy proof,
And storied Windows richly dight,
Casting a dim religious light.
There let the pealing Organ blow
To the full voic'd Choir below,
In Service high and Anthems clear,
As may with sweetness, through mine ear,
Dissolve me into ecstasies,
And bring all Heav'n before mine eyes.

(155–66)

Although they have been set to music, few readers think of these companion poems as intended for that purpose. Their continuous tetrameters (after the openings) exhibit both rhythmic constancy and variability that musical progressions are not compatible with, and ingenious musical embroidery that aims at imitating the substance of the poem can do nothing but distract the listener from the words.

Milton's masques are another matter. Although references to *Comus* sometimes give the impression that singing and dancing were continuous throughout its performance, in essence it is a series of speeches in blank verse, enlivened with a certain amount of song and spectacle. *Arcades* strikes more of a balance between poetry and music, and a third of its central declamation deals explicitly with music. In this he returns to the Platonic cosmology suggested by "At a Solemn Music." But even the music of the spheres, perhaps because tainted with Catholic doctrine, seems to Milton to belong more to the pagan than the Christian world; even the quintessence was part of fallen nature. In *Arcades* the Genius of the Wood, a nature deity, can hear this music that controls the created universe and keeps it in order:

But else in deep of night, when drowsiness
Hath lockt up mortal sense, then listen I
To the celestial *Sirens'* harmony,
That sit upon the nine infolded Spheres
And sing to those that hold the vital shears
And turn the Adamantine spindle round,
On which the fate of gods and men is wound.
Such sweet compulsion doth in music lie,
To lull the daughters of *Necessity*,
And keep unsteady Nature to her law,

And the low world in measur'd motion draw
After the heavenly tune, which none can hear
Of human mold with gross unpurged ear;
And yet such music worthiest were to blaze
The peerless height of her immortal praise,
Whose luster leads us, and for her most fit,
If my inferior hand or voice could hit
Inimitable sounds.

(61–78)

This speech, in rhyming couplets, occupies fifty-eight lines, or about half of the masque; the other half consists of three madrigal-like songs. This is as close as Milton ever came to an actual blend of verse and music in a single production, except for his translations of the Psalms and a few songs; the intellectual content of the central section, however, sets it distinctly apart from music and tends in the direction of the rhetorically constructed Augustan closed couplet. Even the songs of *Arcades* are best seen as independent poems for which Henry Lawes provided melodies (now lost).

In *Comus* the connection between poetry and music is even weaker. About 750 lines of the total 1,020 are blank verse, and therefore resistant not only to melody but even to delivery as recitative. In productions that tended toward opera, recitative became a link between songs; in *Comus* not only does blank verse predominate but the intellectual content is much more complex and elevated than the *Arcades*. Indeed, it is common to see *Comus* as a sort of disquisition on Platonism (as well as a celebration of the virtue of chastity). Milton admired Henry Lawes, the composer with whom he worked in writing *Comus*, because of the way that he made his music subordinate to poetry, and in 1646 praised him for doing so, in "Sonnet XIII":

To My Friend, Mr. Henry Lawes, On His Airs

Harry, whose tuneful and well measur'd Song
   First taught our English Music how to span
   Words with just note and accent, not to scan
   With *Midas'* Ears, committing short and long,
Thy worth and skill exempts thee from the throng,
   With praise enough for Envy to look wan;
   To after age thou shalt be writ the man
   That with smooth air couldst humor best our tongue.
Thou honor'st Verse, and Verse must lend her wing
   To honor thee, the Priest of *Phoebus'* Choir
   That tun'st their happiest lines in Hymn, or Story.

> *Dante* shall give Fame leave to set thee higher
> Than his *Casella*, whom he woo'd to sing,
> Met in the milder shades of Purgatory.

(February 9, 1646)

We might recall at this point that Dante, like Milton, reserved the perfect fusion of voice and music for the souls in heaven, and compelled himself to wait until he had entered Purgatory before allowing himself to hear a musical performance of his own canzone. Lawes purchased Milton's admiration at the expense of his own fame; Bruce Pattison explains:

> One cannot help reflecting that poets liked Lawes because his music has insufficient intrinsic interest to distract attention from their verse. He is at his best when he forgets to be declamatory and composes graceful little tunes in triple time that recall Campion. But his art is very miniature, and there was no future for music along his lines. Instrumental composers were busy creating a technique that owed nothing to poetry, and it was their achievements that opened a new realm for music and laid the foundations for the art of Bach and Handel. (198)

Madrigal composers and singers had long since begun to ignore text in favor of the musical performance; looking at developments in poetry, Gretchen Finney saw the power of prosody as subversive of music in England:

> The seriousness and intensity of the Italians [the composers] were lacking. Devotion to an aesthetic was replaced by imitation of superficial characteristics.
>
> Yet their [the English composers'] music demonstrates the same subordination to poetry. Madrigal parts could be, and were, played satisfactorily on instruments, without the words. Musical settings for recitative or monody, however, are of little interest apart from words, while words, on the other hand, have slight need of music. One feels no lack because Lawes's setting of Milton's "Arcades" is lost; the songs of *Comus* have as much charm in reading as in singing. It is revealing, comments a present-day musicologist, "that the only tangible result of masques and 'operas' performed during the Commonwealth was literary and not musical." [Finney supplies a footnote: "Lang, *Music in Western Civilization*, pp. 414, 410."] Even English instrumental music, so impressive at the turn of the century, lost its distinction, a loss that may be ascribed, at least in part, to the general trend toward emphasis on the written word. (136)

"Lycidas" requires the greatest care of all of Milton's poems in discerning its relationship to music. "In this Monody the Author bewails a learned Friend," wrote Milton in the introductory comment. The Thrall and Hibbard *Hand-*

book to Literature tersely defines "monody" as "a dirge or lament in which a single mourner expresses individual grief, e.g. Arnold's *Thyrsis, A Monody.*" Arnold took his title in imitation of Milton, apparently without appreciating Milton's understanding of the word, as Arnold's elegy is composed of Keatsian ode stanzas. "Monody" is a musical, not a poetic, term; one finds it explained in histories of music and defined in musical dictionaries, but not in reference books such as *The Oxford Companion to English Literature.* That Milton used it to describe his poem, however, no more makes "Lycidas" literally a monody than Eliot's "Prufrock" is literally a love song, or his *Four Quartets* literally chamber music.

To call the poem a monody was in some sense to make a declaration of its superiority to instrumental or vocal music. The sixteenth-century Italian performance known as the *monodia* was a reaction against the increasing sophistication of polyphonic music, especially against the showier kinds of madrigal polyphony. It was a form of musical Puritanism, to start with an elimination of ornament. The idea was to imitate, from Greek tragedies, not the strophic choruses but rather the declamations of individual actors, and to provide a simple accompaniment to these that would support the sense of the declamation. Donald Jay Grout says:

> Real monody aimed at a quite different kind of melody and, moreover, distinguished clearly between solo and accompaniment. Strict fidelity to the supposed Greek models would doubtless have required that the accompaniment be abolished altogether; although it was not abolished, it was minimized to the utmost, reduced in fact to a few simple chords. These provided an almost impalpable background for the solo voice, which declaimed in free rhythm, following the natural accent and flow of the words; the melodic line was thus halfway between speech and song. (306)

The result was much like operatic recitative, except that the music (much of which is lost) must have been more sensitive to the specific nuances of meaning and feeling, and more interesting to listen to. In any case, the intention was to assist in interpreting or evoking emotions connected with the text, rather than fusing the two in a rhythmic structure. Elise Bickford Jorgens compared what the Italians did with what was going on in France at the same time:

> The monodic style of writing for the voice, which swept Italy around the turn of the seventeenth century, had its roots—like those of musique mesurée in France—in the humanists' desire to return to the ancient conception of lyric in which music and poetry were interdependent, if not virtually inseparable. The ultimate goal was the re-creation of the storied effects, by making music subservient to text. But whereas the French approach to the re-

creation of this ideal union of music and text was to fuse the rhythm and meter of the two, thus making music an extension of the verse structure, the Italian approach was much more concerned with the projection of the "affetti" or the emotions of the text through its narrative structure and ultimately with the dramatic possibilities of such a union. (176)

By a sort of back-formation, the monody eventually evolved into real opera as arias of greater complexity were added to restore the musical interest; but initially the form was an effort at rescuing poetry from musical domination, an effort that owed much to Italian Renaissance Platonism.

Gretchen Finney in "A Musical Background for Lycidas" (195–219) tries to identify a particular work or works that Milton might have been influenced by and might have used as a musical model. She ends by focusing on four proto-operas that treated the story of Orpheus, arguing, "This is the story of Orpheus, too, poet and prophet, who, forsaken, was destroyed and cast into the sea, a singer, mourned by all nature" (210). She distinguishes "choral" passages and "recitative" passages in preparation for identifying parallels with the operas, saving discussion of monody for the conclusion as a way of clinching the musical parallels.

Finney's analysis is sensitive to the aural effects of the poem and valuable in drawing attention to them. Also, the discussion of music history is intrinsically interesting, and one finds it easy to believe that Milton knew and admired the music that she believes he did. The best explanation may be that in calling it a monody Milton meant to announce that he was preparing to deliver a non-strophic poetic speech in which he intended to permit himself freedoms that would allow a maximum display of his poetic powers, touching "the tender stops of various quills." This literary use of the word "monody" makes it a metaphor of freedom from strophic, and even from regular stichic, organization, just as the musical monody gave poetry its freedom from melody and especially from polyphony. Once again, therefore, we see him not only moving away from music but breaking with established English versification.

"Lycidas" does, however, retain not only iambic meter but also, except for a few lines, rhyme. Milton had silently dispensed with the latter on earlier occasions; he announced his considered apostasy from rhyme in the introduction to *Paradise Lost*. But he returned to the vision of an ideal musical future in Book 3 of that work:

> Then Crown'd again thir golden Harps they took,
> Harps ever tun'd, that glittering by thir side
> Like Quivers hung, and with Preamble sweet
> Of charming symphony they introduce

> Their sacred Song, and waken raptures high;
> No voice exempt, no voice but well could join
> Melodious part, such concord is in Heav'n.

(365–71)

The music in heaven is an expression of devout obedience, of harmony with the will of God. It is the *fallen* angels who choose to revive ancient *mousike*, scorning (in Mammon's words) "to celebrate his throne / With warbled hymns, and to his Godhead sing / Forced hallelujahs." Some of the demons, instead, drew aside in Pandemonium,

> Retreated in a silent valley, sing
> With notes Angelical to many a Harp
> Thir own Heroic deeds and hapless fall
> By doom of Battle; and complain that Fate
> Free Virtue should enthrall to Force or Chance.
> Their Song was partial, but the harmony
> (What could it less when Spirits immortal sing?)
> Suspended Hell, and took with ravishment
> The thronging audience.

(1.546–55)

This sounds rather like Schopenhauer's theory of the function of art as having the power to "stop the wheel of Ixion." But for Milton, whose hope of Heaven prevailed over his innate romantic rebelliousness, the effort at achieving heaven on earth—or rather, in this case, in Hell—with a self-celebrating union of music and heroic poetry was no more than a suspension of the pains of eternal damnation. One hardly needs to repeat how powerfully the depiction of heroic endurance among the fallen angels, of resistance to what they see as God's tyranny, has appealed to many romantic souls, from Blake and Shelley to Bertrand Russell. That the demons find surcease even momentarily is a sign of Milton's Protestant belief in psychic self-sufficiency. That this suspension occurs in Hell and cannot last points to the ultimate insufficiency of human efforts, unaided by God's grace, at achieving happiness, and betrays a Puritan (and Platonic) distrust of delights of the senses against those of reason. Milton himself was prepared to entrust his justification of the ways of God to man to a heroic poetry that pursues its own ends in the absence of actual music, though in hope of a transcendent celestial harmony; he had as his grand examples Virgil and Dante, both of whose epics, as we have seen, had worked free from musical models and contexts.

Yet if one is prepared to see Milton as divinely inspired, and to accept that he literally incorporated into himself the ineffable intellectual music of Heaven (with something resembling a Protestant inversion of the mystery of transubstantiation), then one may argue that *Paradise Lost* is in fact a musical production. This is one way to explain O. B. Hardison's comments on Milton in *Prosody and Purpose in the English Renaissance*—a work to which, because of its enormous erudition, sensitivity to poetic effects, and fundamental soundness in most respects, one is reluctant to take exception. I do not myself believe that Milton was divinely inspired, at least not in the direct way that Milton imagined, though I do not think that he could have written *Paradise Lost* without believing himself to have been accorded a specially elected role. Perhaps it is appropriate for the scholar and critic to take Milton, as Hardison does, on his own terms. Yet even in saying that, I must add an additional reservation about the paragraphs that I am about to quote; it seems to me that they allow Milton more of a measure of the Romantic genius than he wished to claim for himself. Presumption there may be in great measure in Milton, but one does not find the egotism, the presumption of self-creation, that one associates with, in its best form, Goethe. But let us hear Hardison, whom I quote at some length, partly because he mentions T. S. Eliot, to whom I also wish to refer in connection with Milton:

> As a radical Protestant dependent on the guidance of the Holy Spirit and as a poet familiar with the doctrine of inspiration, he knew that he could only succeed if assisted by a heavenly Muse. His Muse is an aspect of the Holy Spirit and a symbol of the constitutive aspect of poetry, the fact that poetry in some sense makes itself. The Muse takes Milton to the pit of hell, where he finds "darkness visible," and to the pinnacle of heaven, where he encounters an unimaginable brightness—"bright effluence of bright essence increate." She visits him in nightly dreams, filling his mind with her music, so that his "numbers" seem "voluntary" and flow "unpremeditated" while he sleeps. The music is "natural" in the sense intended by Eustache Deschamps in *L'Art de dictier.*
>
> Whatever Milton's references to the Muse might mean to a psychoanalyst or to a theologian, they have a very specific meaning in relation to the history of poetry. Milton has heard the music of epic. He commands the Muse to sing, and *Paradise Lost* is the song that follows. Its facade of images is sustained by—in a way, it crystallizes out of—the music, which is instinctive, coming from beyond him like the song of a bird. In his blindness, he is like a nightingale that "Sings darkling, and in shadiest Covert hid / Tunes her nocturnal note." Like Orpheus, the archetypal musician-poet, he is "Taught by the heav'nly Muse to venture down / The dark descent, and up to reascend." Also, like Orpheus, he has "fall'n on evil dayes." The threat

appears in the poem as a threat to its music, and he prays the Muse to "drive far off the barbarous dissonance" of those unsympathetic to his art.

Eliot was not primarily interested in the relations between music and poetry or, for that matter, in Milton. He was distressed by the banalities that passed for poetry in the early twentieth century, and he traced them to imitations of Milton by poets who understood only Milton's surface techniques. He believed that if poetry was once again to have a living relation to culture, Milton's influence had to be opposed, and other poets—especially Donne and the Jacobean dramatists, who aimed in their poetry at the tonalities of everyday speech—had to be set up in Milton's place. (259–60)

Hardison's reference to Deschamps is apposite and penetrating. But when Hardison speaks of "the constitutive aspect of poetry, the fact that in some sense poetry makes itself," he seems to be writing from the point of view of someone who has (among other things) accepted the Coleridgean concept of the poetic imagination. In his preface he writes, "The musical aspect of prosody is often associated with the ability of poetry to be constitutive—that is, to make objective otherwise unimaginable realities rather than simply to imitate what is" (xii). Hardison espouses the concept of the secondary imagination, the creative power of the poet, while my own view of the source of poetry is more naturalistic and evolutionary.

Leaving aside the ultimate theological or philosophical grounds of my differences with Hardison, Milton's achievement was that of a poet who carried the artistry of the *sound* of language further than any poet ever has in English. Hardison, prompted in part by his awareness of Milton's fondness for and abilities in music, and in part by his acceptance of Milton's own view of himself as a divinely inspired poet, sees *Paradise Lost* as pervaded with *musical* effects; I see it as full of *verbal* harmonies, effects of human speech, however remote from ordinary language. I hear echoes, syncopations, arrests, abrupt reversals, undulations, euphonies, cacophonies, towering culminations, modulations, irresistible rushes, quiet interludes, harsh dissonances, and mellifluous resolutions—the ultimate in the "natural music" of language, but having not much more in common with actual music than Renaissance sculpture does with architecture, or than music does with either. "Oh mighty-mouthed inventor of harmonies," wrote Tennyson truly of Milton. But verbal harmonies, not musical ones. Hardison's perception of how much Milton owed to Italian poetry is invaluable—especially since the Italian canzone and madrigal encouraged a looseness and freedom in poetic expression. Also, in the actual discussion of Milton's verse (258–76) it becomes clear that Hardison often uses "music" as a metaphor of the range of audible effects found in *Paradise Lost*. These effects are described with a sensitivity and thoroughness that leaves nothing to be desired—but they are not literally musical. Milton owed more to other human poets—Hebrew, Greek, Latin, Italian, and French, as well as English—than to the ineffable melodies of the Holy Spirit. Those who wish to preserve for Milton the reality of divine inspiration, however, might well argue that the Holy Spirit has also worked through other human poets and musicians, if not with the directness claimed by Milton.

In regard to music Milton's case is different from Dante's; *The Divine Comedy* was still close enough to the canzone that portions of it can, with some success, be set to music; the notion of singing any part of *Paradise Lost* is less promising. By Milton's time English poetry had long been emergent from music—though it is still possible, as T. S. Eliot and many others have done, to see in Milton an appreciation of verbal effects that remain analogous to music. This is what we see in Eliot's own poetry, in an even more sophisticated—which is not to say more successful—form. But we must guard carefully against any conception of Milton's poetry that would see it as merging *with* music.

Samson Agonistes is not the most frequently read of Milton's works, but its mere presence in its entirety in the *Norton Anthology of English Literature* argues not only its importance to literary historians but its continuing accessibility and interest for many common readers. As a work of literature, of poetry, *Samson* is not only emergent from music but from earlier poetry as well. Not only were the choruses not intended to be sung, but they are *apolelymena*, without regular divisions, nonstrophic. And not only are they nonstrophic; they are not written in predictable rhythms or meters. With this work we have moved almost as far from any connection with actual music as Ezra Pound did in the twentieth century with "The Return."

As a play, *Samson*'s reputation still suffers from Samuel Johnson's strictures—among which was the objection that it lacked development and had no middle—as well as from a few historical critics who wish to date it as one of Milton's earlier works and hence less mature. The force of these and other criticisms is to disqualify *Samson* as a play intended for the instruction and pleasure of a human audience. So frequently did Milton make the point, however, that he was writing primarily to obtain divine approval that it is hard to see why anyone should wonder at his failure to please mere human beings. Even when we do take into account a possible human audience we realize that what we have is a closet drama intended for the solitary reader. Furthermore, such pleasure as one takes in it must largely be due to its expressive poetic "music," to effects that Johnson was largely impervious to. Because, like Milton, Samson is blind and at the mercy of his enemies, and because Dalilah is a more complex invention than Milton's Eve, the human interest of *Samson* is greater than that of *Paradise Lost*. But did anyone ever imagine that Milton exhibited, or even aspired to, imaginative insight into human character and motivation other than his own—or those of his enemies? How can a performable play (and Milton explicitly says that it is not) be written without such insight? A critical paper once appeared that discussed laboriously "the function of the narrator" of *Paradise Lost*, as if Milton had the sympathetic detachment of a modern novelist—as if the "narrator" could be anyone other than John Milton. The play is really a poetic dialogue in which Milton wrestles with his own adversaries, including himself, with God as his chief audience.

Much of *Samson Agonistes*, especially the choruses, is free verse. I have argued this elsewhere, perhaps more minutely than it really requires (*The Origins of Free Verse* 76–79). As a supplement to those arguments I would like to draw attention to an exercise of Milton's that I overlooked in my earlier study, which now seems to me critically important in the history of free verse in English. This is his Latin poem *Ad Joannem Rousium* ("To John Rouse"), which he wrote in 1647. This poem he composed more or less as a Pindaric ode, dividing it into three pairs of strophes and antistrophes, and concluding it with a single epode. Now of course this is not strictly Pindaric, as Ben Jonson's "To the Immortal Memory of That Noble Pair . . ." had been. The true Pindaric ode should consist of groupings of three units, triads of strophe, antistrophe, and epode, and strophe and antistrophe the same in each triad, and all of the epodes formally identical. Milton not only modified the stanza structure of the Pindaric—nine years before the appearance of Abraham Cowley's *Pindariques*—but also wilfully neglected to keep strophes and antistrophes consistent. To explain what he had done he appended an explanatory note:

> Ode tribus constat Strophis, totidemque Antistrophis, una demum epodo clausis; quas, tametsi omnes nec versuum numero, nec certis ubique colis exacte respondeant, ita tamen secuimus, commode legendi potius, quam ad antiquos concinendi modos rationem spectantes. Alioquin hoc genus rectius fortasse dici monostrophicum debuerat. Metra partim sunt κατὰ σχέσιν, partim ἀπολελυμένα.

> [The ode is made up of three strophes, and an identical number of antistrophes, closing with an epode; which, although they do not all correspond exactly to one another in the number of lines or in divisions, we have divided them for easier reading rather than in the style called for by ancient rules. Perhaps it would be more accurate to call this kind of poem monostrophic. The meters are partly regular and partly free.]

Note the appearance of the Greek *apolelymena*, "without regular pauses," as in the introduction to *Samson*. Thus, many years before the completion of *Samson* (according to some historians, at the time that he originally began work on it), Milton had taken leave of ancient authority even as he employed the ancient language. In modifying—almost discarding—the strophic pattern of the authentic Pindaric, he not only precluded any musical setting for the poem that employed repeated melodies, but introduced a flexibility that pointed toward free verse.

References to music, scarce in *Paradise Regained*, can hardly be found at all in *Samson*—though of course that is no argument that the work itself could not be constructed upon musical principles. But few seem disposed to see it as anything other than poetry—a poetic closet drama written by one individual person, Milton, for private reading by other individual persons as well as by God. Neither Pattison nor Hardison in their discussions of Renaissance music and poetry makes any mention of *Samson*; Gretchen Finney, after considering numerous possible musical connections for the play, concludes:

> When Milton wrote *Samson Agonistes*, neither the theory and practice of music nor speculation about music remained the same as when he was born. "Modes" had been replaced by "keys"; music and poetry existed as independent arts; rationalists had anatomized music and found it to be nothing but air, its purpose not to move but to entertain. The aims of the Camerata were all but forgotten. Milton himself disclaimed any need for music. But even here he revealed his feeling of kinship with the Italian humanists who, in their own way, had also depreciated old values of musical sound. (237)

The Camerata was the Florentine circle that included Vicenzo Galilei, who opposed polyphonic music as a distraction from the superior art of the spoken word, and who encouraged the monodic style of composition.

T. S. Eliot, who made up for his 1936 treatment of Milton by recommending his works, especially *Samson*, in a 1947 paper as a model for future poets, continued to speak of "the music of verse." Eliot's usage, though, was metaphorical; his intention was to encourage poets to cultivate some organizational strategy and to make use of the tones and rhythms of the spoken language. And entire crop of 1950s formalists misunderstood this advice, settling down to their villanelles and rhymes royal, their sonnets and their terza rimas, and failing to notice that what Eliot endorsed was the expressive freedom of *Samson*. The current New Formalism continues and exaggerates that retrograde development, while at the same time even more poets ignore the rest of Eliot's advice, that "a monotony of unscannable verse fatigues the attention even more quickly than a monotony of exact feet" (*On Poetry and Poets* 183). Eliot was still harking to the earliest Imagist and Poundian pronouncements about substituting the musical phrase for the rhythm of the metronome.

For our present purposes we may conclude by observing that, especially in *Samson Agonistes*, Milton had carried poetry so far away from music, and so far ahead in the cultivation of effects possible to language itself, that the response of the next three or four generations of English poets was to withdraw into cautiously modulated syllabism—or, worse, to depart into a frenzied extravagance of pretended feeling. Not until Amy Lowell, Ezra Pound, and (in the end) T. S. Eliot began to look for free-verse precursors, and found one in Milton, did his most radical departures from earlier metrics begin to be understood for what they were. In the eighteenth century, only certain of what are now called pre-Romantics, by taking Milton's blank verse and even his diction and applying it to homelier, more earthly subjects, profited directly from his example. Milton continues to offer lessons that few poets, especially since the Romantic period, have cared to take advantage of. In a sense, then, he still belongs to the future.

9

"Can Empty Sounds Such Joys Impart!"

FOR THE MOST PART, the Augustan Age only confirmed the separation of the "twin sisters." Yet relations between poetry and music in England from the Restoration until well into the eighteenth century were richer and more complex than in any comparable period before or since, as studies in both disciplines amply document. The two most important transdisciplinary books treat these relations at length. John Hollander's ninety-page concluding chapter in *The Untuning of the Sky* and a central chapter nearly as long in James Anderson Winn's *Unsuspected Eloquence* cover in detail topics such as the efforts of English poets, Dryden in particular, to make English opera a distinctively literary genre; the annual production from 1683 onward of songs and odes for St. Cecilia's day; the jealousy and insensitivity toward music, especially toward Italian opera, by all the chief literary figures of the day; the numerous poems about music, or which make references to music; and the treatises that discussed the relationship between the two.

It was impossible to be a cultivated English citizen, especially in London, during this period without hearing a great deal about music whether one cared for it or not. England produced its first, and some say its last, great native-born composer in Henry Purcell (1659–1695). One need only mention Handel's forty-seven years of residence (from 1712 to 1759) should there be any doubt as to the country's hospitality toward the latest in musical sophistication. Satire directed against music and musicians only proves how secure their presence was. Swift's "A Cantata" (the humor of which is as much at expense of poets as it is of composers) is excruciatingly funny, but poets went on composing in this form and finding composers to set their work to music. One now obscure early eighteenth-century poet, James Miller, protested in sexist terms the effeminization of English music by importation of foreign genres and instruments; in *Harlequin-Horace; or, The Art of Modern Poetry* (1731), he complained that "In Days of Old, when Englishmen were—*Men*, / Their Musick, like themselves, was grave and plain," but that now,

> Since *Masquerades* and *Op'ras* made their Entry,
> And *Heydegger* reign'd *Guardian* of our Gentry;

A hundred various Instruments combine,
And foreign *Songsters* in the Concert join:
The *Gallick Horn*, whose winding Tube in vain
Pretends to emulate the *Trumpet's* Strain;
The *shrill-ton'd Fiddle*, and the *warbling Flute*,
The *grave Bassoon, deep Base*, and *tinkling Lute*,
The *jingling Spinnet*, and the *full-mouth'd Drum*,
A *Roman Capon*, and *Venetian Strum*,
All league, melodious Nonsense to dispense,
And give us *Sound*, and *Show*, instead of *Sense*.

(# 132 in *The Oxford Book of Eighteenth Century
Verse*, ed. David Nichol Smith, Oxford: Clarendon, 1926. [Hereafter cited as OBECV–1926])

John Gay's *The Beggar's Opera* was meant as a travesty of Italian opera. It found
an eager segment of the public that was tired of the foreign phenomenon. But
when the Royal Academy of Music sponsored operas by Handel, a rival organization was formed to keep Italian opera in business. Even before this split,
though, in 1725, John Byrom had made fun of the developing competition:

Some say, compar'd to Bononcini
That Mynheer *Handel's* but a Ninny;
Others aver, that he to *Handel*
Is scarcely fit to hold a *Candle*.
Strange all this Difference should be
'Twixt Tweedle-*dum* and Tweedle-*dee*!

(# 144 OBECV–1926)

It would be easy to multiply examples of poems for or about music and
critical discussions of the relations between the two. Bertrand H. Bronson
provides hundreds of references in "Some Aspects of Music and Literature in
the Eighteenth Century," introducing his treatment as follows:

Whichever way we turn, while we trace the cultural topography of eighteenth-century England,—its ideological or artistic hills and vales and water-
courses, we are within sound of music. Are we following the antiquarian and
historical impulse? There are for evidence the Three Choirs Festivals, begun
in 1724 (and still continuing); the Academy of Ancient Music, established
1725/26; the Madrigal Society, formed about 1741; the Ancient Concerts,
founded in 1776. There are the two ambitious and important Histories of
Music, by Hawkins and Burney. There are the ample compendia of earlier
cathedral music, anthems and motets, gathered by Greene and Boyce and
Arnold. Are we observing the powerful and strengthening interest in the

earlier poetry? With it go the abundant fresh settings of Elizabethan and seventeenth-century lyrics. There is the Shakespearean revival, of which Arne's and Boyce's settings and incidental pieces are only the most successful musical manifestation among many attractive things. And still more impressively there stretches the long line of varied and magnificent settings by Handel of great English texts: the Bible, Milton, and Dryden foremost among them. (23)

Yet, despite these instances of cooperation and mutual inspiration, for the most part the eighteenth century confirmed that the sister arts had taken separate roads. Music set off on its own more confidently; the best composers hardly seemed to notice the reservations of poets or philosophers about the legitimacy of their autonomous and increasingly instrumental art, with its own principles of construction. Constant refinements in the manufacturing of instruments and in the techniques of eliciting tones from them encouraged, as in the past, the self-sufficiency of music. A vast body of poetry as well consolidated and exploited, though without much advancing, the independence earned by English Renaissance poets. The cultivation of the heroic couplet— excellent models for which had existed for almost a century in poets as different in other respects as Jonson and Donne, Chapman and Waller—was in some sense a retreat from the frontiers reached by Milton. Yet few would disagree that great Augustan poets made the limitations of rhyme ("bondage," as Milton called it) into a distinctive medium. To this day the neoclassical closed couplet resists imitation, and is even difficult to parody because of its polish and glitter. Poets who imitated Milton's freedom mostly ruined their own poems, but a toned-down Miltonic licentiousness together with a somewhat simplified vocabulary made an accommodative and flexible blank verse that suited itself to pre-Wordsworthian nature poetry, as we will see in an example by William Whitehead. Rhymed or not, eighteenth-century poems in regular pentameters, even when about music, almost never suggest the need for musical accompaniment or imply companionship with music. Pope's catalogue of desirable and undesirable effects in *An Essay on Criticism* mentions music and uses the word "tuneful" (scornfully), but all the examples of poetic effects that Pope offers have to do with qualities of sound to be found in words. Samuel Johnson felt that Pope had gone too far even in this, paying too much attention to audible effects. (This and further references to Johnson's opinions may easily be found in any edition of his *Lives of the English Poets* and in extracts therefrom in various anthologies, unless otherwise noted.)

Yet if the eighteenth century was not remarkable for poetries emerging from music, it did prepare the way for such. In this, strangely enough, it resembled the Middle Ages. Because song meters were seldom taken seriously as a medium for high Augustan poetry, the eighteenth century was a period of unselfconscious fusing of music and verse: in hymns, the cultivation of which had been delayed and discouraged first by the Reformation and even more severely by the Puritan era, and in songs for plays or for independent performance. This development occurred rather more naturally than in Campion's case, where a doctrinaire belief in the identity of musical and poetic measures and scansions enforced the union. In the eighteenth century the existence of "official" poetry in heroic couplets allowed hymns and songs to go their own way, making possible a new emergence of poetry with Burns, especially Blake (who made up his own now-lost melodies), and others to some extent. The sophistication of serious music and, to a lesser degree, serious poetry allowed the minor genres of both to prosper together, whereas in the Middle Ages lack of sophistication had produced the same effect.

Sometime during 1673 a visit took place the consequences of which epitomize what happened to most English poetry during the following hundred years. John Dryden went to see John Milton, partly with the object of getting Milton's permission to "tag" *Paradise Lost*—that is, to produce a rewritten version in rhyming couplets (Freedman 99–100). Dryden's hope was to provide a libretto for an opera, the spectacular staging of which would attract large audiences (see Winn 262–65). As it turned out, his grandiose aspirations guaranteed that the opera would never be produced; the stage directions at the opening require among other things that "from the Heavens (which are opened) fall the rebellious Angels wheeling in the Air, and seeming transfix'd with Thunderbolts: The bottom of the Stage being open'd, receives the Angels, who fall out of sight. Tunes of Victory are Play'd, and an Hymn sung" (12.98). That is by no means the end of the directions, which aimed at reproducing the conclusion of the War in Heaven, complete with appropriate music ("a Tune of Horrour and Lamentation"). Toward the end of the opera the producer is advised, "*The Scene shifts, and discovers deaths of several sorts. A battle at land and a Naval fight*" (12: 143). Forty-six lines further we find, "*Here a Heaven descends, full of Angels and blessed Spirits, with soft Music, a Song and Chorus*" (12: 145). Dryden does not supply words for the song and chorus.

Dryden's "opera," which was more like a cosmological masque, offered even fewer opportunities to a musical composer than did Milton's *Comus*; with the exception of three or four very brief songs, and a few shortened lines, the entire work is in heroic couplets. How such a thing could be set to music escapes me entirely; the regularity of the "tags" would defeat a recitative as surely as it would prevent anything like an aria. Perhaps Dryden expected the composer simply to add musical embellishments, and the producer to add elaborate mechanical contraptions, to what was essentially a neoclassical drama. The whole thing ended as a closet performance; Dryden claimed that he sold hundreds of copies of *The State of Innocence*.

Dryden's project, however unsuccessful, pointed toward two important lines of development in Augustan poetic form. First was the effort to re-regularize, smooth, and restore rhyme to English heroic meter—in this instance, by replacing Miltonic blank verse with couplets. (Rewriting of Shakespeare subjected him to "correction" as well.) Next came the interest in exploring new combinations that would make poetry part of some grander multimedia spectacle, which would at the same time reestablish the preeminence of the poetic author over more sophisticated and imposing musical techniques. Had Dryden himself supplied all the songs that seem called for by the text of *The State of Innocence* we could add a third category, the song. (None of the older varieties of vocal music, including the ballad, ever died out completely. Thus one can point to a continuity of traditions from the Middle Ages to the present, somewhat as one can discover an actual, if tenuous, continuity of Gothic architecture from the Middle Ages to the nineteenth century.)

More important for Dryden, however, was the fad for the *Pindarique* that Cowley popularized. "In Dryden's day," wrote George Sherburn, "a song was less valued as poetry than was 'the greater lyric,' by which term was meant the Cowleyan Pindaric, a rimed poem of irregular verses arranged in strophes of no fixed structure. In this form the cult of irregularity, sublimity, and enthusiasm was to express itself for many a year" (Baugh et al. 730). In most Pindarics we see poets vainly trying to pull out the stops of human emotions, employing uneven and unpredictable verses in the hope of rousing in the reader a sense of enthusiasm that, unhappily, was mostly lacking in the poets themselves. As we will see, Dryden was much affected by the fad, or chose to exploit it; but while Dryden found it expedient to acknowledge the still-famous Cowley's precedence, he improved on Cowley to the point that he hardly seems to owe anything to him. One way of looking at the genre of the *Pindarique* which, like much twentieth-century free verse, was more popular with its practitioners than with readers, is to see it as a poetic grab for musical power. George Saintsbury's distaste for the results is amusing; he refused to print any of these in his massive history of prosody and said that they "almost immediately 'made a school'; that they produced, during the last half of the seventeenth century and much of the eighteenth, some of the very worst verse (poetically, not always prosodically) to be found in the English language" (2: 340). The exhilaration felt by poets who wrote these irregular poems may have been comparable to what music evoked for them, but exclamatory irregularity did not usually succeed in communicating this afflatus. The *Pindarique* at times was companionable to music, possibly even inspirational to composers, but it cannot be pointed to as a form that in any vital way *emerged* from music.

For the most part the trend established by Cowley, and treated with such roughness a century later by Samuel Johnson, served only to authorize a metrical licentiousness that aimed, in passages of erratic frenzy, at arousing the excitement supposedly felt by those who heard Pindar's odes sung on public occasions in ancient times. It aimed at *mousike* without the music. To say this might seem to contend that the *Pindarique* was the perfect example of poetry emerging from music—but in fact, in its wild irregularity, it aspired to produce the effect of music without really cultivating the resources of language itself. Most *Pindariques* make terribly boring reading.

In pursuit of the first goal—of "tagging" the pentameter—Dryden was most successful. His management of heroic couplets (not in his makeover of Milton, but in "Mac Flecknoe," "Absolom and Achitophel," and elsewhere) perfected the vehicle for the new poetry of rhetoric, of satire, of quasi-philosophical argumentation, and even for a landscape poetry (as in Pope's "Windsor Forest") that had more in common with the gardens of Versailles than with those of England. Modulation, balance, and compression, together with an impression of direct plain speech (curiously, given the couplet's studied artificiality), signaled a retreat from Milton's prosodic and linguistic grandiloquence. In the jargon of today's book reviewer, poets became less willing to "take risks" and instead set a premium on polish, neatness, conciseness, and correctness. Or so it often seems. In fact the compression of the Augustan closed couplet releases more energy than some realize—conspicuously more than the grandiose afflatus of *Pindariques*. To judge from the numbers of entries in dictionaries of quotations, Pope remains eight times as interesting as Cowley after nearly three centuries.

For most readers the Augustan high poetic style marks an even more definite step away from music than does Milton—indeed, some would see it as a toning down of Milton's "music." For Samuel Johnson it meant the perfection of English poetry; Boswell remembered hearing him say, "Sir, a thousand years may elapse before there shall appear another man with a power of versification equal to that of Pope" (Boswell 936). For Johnson the divorce from music was entire, and entirely desirable, and we still see it that way. Today, when we read that Pope "lisped in numbers, for the numbers came" we think only of poetry, not music. No one imagines that he means anything other than regular numbers of syllables, or feet. As with the original invention of the pentameter line, the Augustan heroic couplet was to some degree—especially in the attention paid to exact count of syllables—modeled on French practice, and this imitation of a foreign meter encouraged, as it always does, a view of poetry as a purely verbal art. That is, a rationalized prosody, or one that is imitative of prosody in another language, aims at finding rules that apply to words independently of music, even when the rules may be in some ways also applicable to music. Close textual critics are fond of analyzing the careful displacements of the caesura within the poetic line, and of distinguishing various kinds of parallels and balances, contrasts and antitheses, all of which are obviously rhetorical effects. To point to other effects, such as imitative sounds or rhythms, to assonances, or to reflective sound patterns within a line or a couplet, shows little that is actually akin to music. The delicate internal "music" of the closed heroic couplet comes close to being a metaphor of a metaphor, such is its refinement.

Although to some, right-brain/left-brain analysis may be suspect, the idea that eighteenth-century poetry appeals to the left hemisphere of the brain, where language is organized, while music is a right-brain phenomenon, seems reasonable enough. Poetry that develops in linear fashion rather than recurrently or incrementally (as in songs), especially when that almost stichic progression is combined with ingenuity either in imagery or argument, encourages a nonmusical use of language, whether it is the progression of interwoven Metaphysical conceits, or an expository or narrative passage in one of Pope's poems. Such developments also carry poetry in the direction of rhetoric and even of prose; the structure of many paragraphs in Johnson's *Rambler* pieces much resembles what we find versified in his "Vanity of Human Wishes." And Dryden did more than anyone else to set English poetry on this nonmusical track.

Dryden became more cooperative in later joint ventures with Purcell, but Dryden's initial view put him directly in line with the musical humanists of the Florentine Camerata: the poet was to be the dominant partner when his work was produced in company with music. By the end of the seventeenth century Italian operas had mostly ceased to treat poetic text as anything more than an excuse for connecting a series of arias; an opera was recognized as, first and foremost, a musical event. As such, most opera lies beyond the purposes of my discussion, though it might be argued that certain Romantic literary genres, such as those represented by Byron's *Manfred* and Shelley's *Prometheus Unbound* (not to speak of Goethe's *Faust*), have much of the operatic in them. But because Dryden is remembered for writings that proved sympathetic to musicians, though not exactly emergent from music, we may look briefly at one of his operatic enterprises.

Among the other inconsistencies in Dryden was his ambition to mount a musical spectacle while at the same time retaining the authority of the poet; it was as if he hoped to dignify his verse as the composers of monody had done, simultaneously trying to attract a large paying public with an extravaganza. In the preface to *Albion and Albanius* (1685) he testily asserts his prerogatives as the poet:

> The same reasons which depress thought in an *Opera*, have a Stronger effect upon the Words; especiallly in our Language: for there is no maintaining the Purity of *English* in short measures, where the Rhyme returns so quick, and is so often Female, or double Rhyme, which is not natural to our Tongue, because it consists too much of Monosyllables, and those too, most commonly clogg'd with Consonants: for which reason I am often forc'd to Coyn new Words, revive some that are Antiquated, and botch others: as if I had not serv'd out my time in Poetry, but was bound 'Prentice to some doggrel Rhymer, who makes Songs to Tunes, and sings them for a livelyhood. 'Tis true, I have not been often put to this drudgery; but where I have, the Words will sufficiently show, that I was then a Slave to the composition, which I will never be again: 'Tis my part to Invent, and the Musicians to Humour that Invention. I may be counsell'd, and will always follow my Friends advice, where I find it reasonable; but will never part with the Power of the Militia. (15: 10)

Though perhaps it is only the magnitude of the undertaking that makes the opera seem more outlandish than scenes called for in earlier English masques, *Albion and Albanius* is one of the strangest projects ever undertaken by a major poet. One imagines it being conceived in Pope's Cave of Spleen in *The Rape of the Lock* and delivered at the Smithfield Fair. Dryden apparently hoped to emulate the elaborate sets, costumes, and machinery that were common in Italian opera, especially at the opera house in Venice. As James Anderson Winn explains (*Dryden* 416), although the opening date and accompanying publicity were carefully calculated, high prices set for tickets, and an expensive libretto prepared, the entire project failed because after six performances the abortive "invasion" by the Duke of Monmouth caused something like martial law to be imposed in London. The theaters were closed, and the company that produced *Albion and Albanius* lost thousands of pounds, much of it spent on elaborate props and machinery.

A single stage direction toward the end of the first scene tells much about the nature of this undertaking: "Iris appears on a very large *Machine*" (15: 27). An accompanying sketch for the "*Machine*" identifies it as "The Celestial Phenomenon Seen at Calais by Captain Christopher Gunman." What Gunman saw, to judge from the design, must have been the early morning sun flanked by two "sun-dogs," and surrounded by intersecting haloes of light. Such atmospheric effects, caused by refraction of light by ice-crystals in cirrus clouds, are fairly common, but the combination must have caused a stir at the time. Marble pedestals, gold statues, and elaborate costumes are liberally called for. Scene 1 includes a stage direction, "*The Clouds divide, and* Juno *appears in a Machine drawn by Peacocks; while a symphony is playing, it moves gently forward, and as it descends, it opens, and discovers the Tail of the Peacock, which is so Large that it almost fills the opening of the Stage between Scene and Scene*" (26). Not many lines further on in Act 2, directions begin with, "*The Scene is a Poetical Hell. The Change is Total . . .*" (30).

I quote from the stage directions because they are more interesting than the poetry. In the preface Dryden explains that his models are Italian "Dramatique Musical Entertainment," arguing that he has followed the best examples as others have in other genres. Of particular interest is this analogy: "Thus *Pindar*, the Author of those Odes, (which are so admirably restor'd by Mr. *Cowley* in our Language,) ought for ever to be the Standard of them; and we are bound according to the practice of *Horace* and Mr. *Cowley*, to Copy him" (15: 4). Unless Dryden is simply humoring a common prejudice in favor of Cowley, as well he may be, he seems to believe that Cowley's Pindarics resembled the real thing, and that Horace's odes were similar to Pindar's. One hesitates to judge Dryden to be either this ignorant or this dishonest; perhaps the entire enterprise to which these remarks are added was so absurd that Dryden did not much care what he said. More relevant to my own purposes, though, is the evidence here and elsewhere that in the 1680s Dryden, as much as anyone else, was attracted to the freewheeling possibilities opened to poetry by supposed imitation of Pindar and to music by Italian opera. The lyrics and speeches in *Albion and Albanius* are free verse that goes beyond even what Cowley allowed himself. If to say this seems to be taking liberties with the chief progenitor of Augustan neoclassicism, one may turn to George Sherburn's comments on other writings dating from the same time: "The meters are very apt and nimble, Dryden being curiously expert in triple rhythms. His 'Sea Fight' in *Amboyna* approaches roughly the rhythms of free verse" (Baugh et al. 730). Winn notes much the same thing:

> Despite Dryden's later grumpy comments about the "drudgery" of writing in the various lyric meters used in *Albion and Albanius*, which entail very short lines and force an uncomfortable simplification and compression, the freedom and flexibility of the Pindaric measures in which he wrote some of his most impressive poetry from 1685 on may owe something to this exercise. (*Dryden* 394)

In other respects *Albion and Albanius* defines the relationship of Dryden's music to poetry at that time. Most who have studied the opera conclude that, as with Lawes and Milton, the music is obsequiously subservient to the poetry; others simply call it dull. But Winn argues that the music, provided by the French composer Louis Grabu, deserves to be revived:

> Though scoffing at Grabu's music has been a commonplace in accounts of this collaboration, the last musicologist to give careful study to the score, which appeared in a sumptuously printed folio in 1687, gives Grabu credit for "respond[ing] instantly to the changing moods of the verse, while retaining an elegant homogeneity." (394)

In the opera's preface Dryden makes a claim that might seem odd to anyone who is not already aware of the expectations of the Italian Camerata and Milton's concept of monody: "The recitative part of the *Opera* requires a more masculine Beauty of expression and sound: the other, which (for want of a proper English Word) I must call *The Songish Part*, must abound in the softness and variety of Numbers: its principal Intention, being to please the Hearing, rather than to gratify the understanding" (15: 4). The monodic style, as we have seen, grew out of the insistence that music subordinate itself completely to poetry, the latter being thought the more rational art form; and out of this in turn grew operatic recitative. Then, as a back-formation to add musical interest, arias were added ("*The Songish Part*"). These Dryden felt to be even more constricting to the poet. All parts of *Albion and Albanius* show Dryden allowing himself every sort of prosodic liberty; even the "songish parts" are more like madrigals; nowhere in the opera do we find two successive identical stanzas, but rather brief through-composed passages such as the following:

TWO NYMPHS AND TRITON SING.

Sports and Pleasures shall attend you
  Through all the Watry Plains.
   Where *Nepture* Reigns:
Venus ready to defend you,
  And her Nymphs to ease your Pains.
   No storm shall offend you,
    Passing the Main;
Nor Billow threat in vain,
  So Sacred a Train,
Till the Gods that defend you,
  Restore you again.

(2.3.164–74)

The recitative, though metered and rhymed, is much more irregular. To judge from what Dryden says in the preface, he was quite pleased with Grabu's capitulation to "the Power of Militia."

Enjoying the self-indulgence that his dominance allowed him, he found it pleasing enough in *Albion and Albanius* to continue in the *Pindarique* manner that he had poked fun at some years earlier in "The Medall":

> Almighty Crowd, thou shorten'st all dispute;
> Pow'r is thy Essence; Wit thy Attribute!
> Nor Faith nor Reason make thee at a stay,
> Thou leapst o'er all eternal truths, in thy *Pindarique* way!
>
> (91–94)

The fashion for writing odes to music coincided closely with the cult of Pindarism, and faded along with it, as poets gradually accepted the truth that Pindar had never written in the manner, or at least not in the form, attributed to him. Pindarism is responsible for some of the worst poetry ever written in English; to pay any attention to it is, as I have learned to my sorrow, to be accused of having a "gusto for the bad." Even among its contemporaries the fad for loose, expressive, supposedly "musical" writing fell from favor. Samuel Johnson's disdain for both music and Pindarism reflected and affected this disillusionment. Writing of John Hughes in *Lives of the English Poets*, Johnson said, "In 1703 his ode on Music was performed at Stationer's Hall; and he wrote afterwards six cantatas, which were set to music by the greatest master of that time [Johann Christoph Pepusch, 1667–1752], and seemed intended to oppose or exclude the Italian opera, an exotic and irrational entertainment, which has been always combatted, and always has prevailed."

Among the few pseudo-Pindaric productions that attained enduring merit as poetry we may count Dryden's "To the Pious Memory of the Accomplished Young Lady, Mrs. Anne Killigrew." As their stylistic innovations did more than two hundred years later for H. D. and Pound, Dryden's new manner left him freer to enrich his lines with frequent though unobtrusive alliteration, and with vowel progressions that may remind us of Milton and that anticipate Keats—a pervasive euphoniousness which, even if a shade disingenuous and calculated, conveys genuine emotion. Notice in the second line below the internal slant rhyme of "last" with "blest"; the triple alliteration of "palms," "plucked," and "paradise" in the third line; the transformation of "rise" to "rich" from the fourth to the fifth line; and additional alliterations in succeeding lines. These are among the more obvious patterns; the rhythm assists the sense in ways that please the ear and resist analysis.

Thou youngest virgin-daughter of the skies,
Made in the last promotion of the blest;
Whose palms, now plucked from paradise,
In spreading branches more sublimely rise,
Rich with immortal green above the rest:
Whether, adopted to some neighbouring star,
Thou rollest above us, in thy wandering race,
Or, in procession fixed and regular,
Moved with the heavens' majestic pace. . . .

(1–9)

This *Pindarique* freedom allowed Dryden to compose in great sweeps, as free as Milton ever was and with a more convincing diction than that of "Lycidas." Dryden is so much better than Cowley that one even hesitates to acknowledge the latter as a precursor; to compare Cowley's constructions to this poem is like comparing an arrangement of dried flowers to a garland of leafy branches.

The two poems that Dryden composed in the Pindaric manner explicitly for music—"A Song for St. Cecelia's Day, 1687" and "Alexander's Feast" (1697)—are not so much exercises in merging poetry with music as they are witty invitations to composers to accommodate music to the words. It is amusing to listen to Handel's setting (1739) for the former, especially when we get to "The double double double beat / Of the thundring DRUM" and "Sharp VIOLINS proclaim / Their jealous Pangs and Desperation, / Fury, frantick Indignation." In *Unsuspected Eloquence* James Winn discusses at length the original setting by Giovanni Baptista Draghi, pointing out not only the "locally imitative" effects essayed by Draghi, but also structural imitations that Dryden concealed within the poem (218–28). Dryden put himself to a lot of trouble to construct the poem according to what he believed to be musical principles; Winn concludes that he did this "only to have music itself bury that virtuoso achievement under well-intended but structurally destructive local imitation" (228).

That "Alexander's Feast" appears in every anthology of English Literature and in many general anthologies of poetry attests to its appeal as a poem, unencumbered with musical interpretation. Its operatic manner puts off some readers who simply find it silly; others who enjoy it agree that it is just as well that no more than one such poem exists. Paradoxically, this poem that purports to celebrate the power of music illustrates how easily poetry can do without music; Dryden, too wise or too conscious of his status as a poet to aim seriously at a reintegration of the arts, gives us only the illusion of doing so; he is a brilliant technician with a temperament utterly different from, but skills almost equal to, Tennyson. This is not to say that in "Alexander's Feast" Dryden hopes, as Cowley and others evidently did, to stir up in the reader emotions not felt by the poet. Rather he manipulates language and invites the reader to connive with him and to enjoy the verbal spectacle, somewhat as did Vachel Lindsay hundreds of years later with "The Congo." (Douglas Bush is said to have set the following examination topic at Harvard: "Resolved: Dryden is the John Philip Sousa of the English ode.")

In honoring St. Cecilia, Dryden capped a tradition that was already under way. In 1683 Purcell had composed *Laudate Ceciliam* and *Welcome to all the Pleasures*, which also honored the saint, with words by Christopher Fishburn. John Oldham's poem for the celebration of 1684 was set by John Blow, who composed four additional odes to St. Cecilia. Nahum Tate, who did the libretto for Purcell's *Dido and Aeneas*, produced an ode for the next year; Hollander finds Tate's ode seriously wanting in value (*Untuning* 396–97), and Tucker Brooke said of his libretto that it "has no value apart from what the composer gave it in his rare music" (Baugh et al. 751).

The success that Dryden's two pieces for music achieved in his own lifetime roused emulative hopes in numerous other poets, and such aspirations could only have been revived when in the 1730s Handel gave both of them new settings (the "Ode" has been set numerous times in the twentieth century as well). Others before and after Dryden also tried their hands at honoring the patron saint of music. In addition to the poets that I will mention, Hollander lists Thomas D'Urfey, Thomas Shadwell, Theophilus Parsons, and Christopher Smart as authors of St. Cecilia odes. William Congreve's "Hymn to Harmony, In Honour of St. Cecilia's Day" (1691), with music by John Eccles, was followed in 1692 when Purcell wrote music to go with Nicholas Brady's *Hail Bright Cecilia*; Grout speaks of this as the "magnificent *Ode for St. Cecilia's Day* composed in 1692," and adds that "these works were the direct ancestors of Handel's English oratorios" (359). In 1693 Thomas Yalden gave the world "An Ode for St. Cecilia's Day." Joseph Addison in 1694 wrote "A Song for St. Cecilia's Day, At Oxford," and again in 1699 "An Ode for St. Cecilia's Day" that was set to music by Daniel Purcell. Edmund Smith, characterized by Johnson as "one of those lucky writers, who have, without much labour, attained high reputation," offered to the public at Oxford in 1707 an "Ode in Praise of Music," which was set by Charles King.

In 1708, at the age of twenty, Pope wrote his "Ode for Music on St. Cecilia's Day," a seven-strophe *Pindarique*; having kept it only five years instead of the Horatian nine, he published it in 1713. William K. Wimsatt, Jr., found the results not pleasing: "The *Ode to Music*, Pope's attempt 'to boldly follow Pindar's pathless way,' is one of his least impressive performances" (*Pope* xxi).

One might argue that Pope's poem fails because it makes at least as close an approach to free verse as many another *Pindarique*, thereby implying that— what is obvious—the real metier of the eighteenth century was to compose with discipline and restraint. I overlooked this "Ode to Music" when tracing the beginnings of free verse, but some of the lines are more consciously disruptive of regular meter than anything Cowley wrote:

> Hark! the numbers soft and clear,
> Gently steal upon the ear;
> Now louder and yet louder rise
> And fill with spreading sounds the skies;
> Exulting in triumph now swell the bold notes,
> In broken air, trembling, the wild music floats.
>
> (12–17)

To a twentieth-century ear these lines may sound hopelessly trammeled with iambics and rhymes, but the "wild music" of the last two lines disrupts them so that they do not scan regularly, even using anapests:

> ★ / ★ ★ / ★ / / ★ / /
> Exulting in triumph now swell the bold notes,
>
> ★ / ★ / / ★ ★ / / ★ /
> In broken air, trembling, the wild music floats.

The lines are tetrameters but the feet, should we wish to name them, would nearly exhaust the vocabulary for two- and three-syllable units. They are willfully irregular, at least as poetry; possibly they could be understood as a 6/8 musical pattern. In any case, it is all too clear that Pope wished to offer his poem for setting to music; indeed, it is slavishly similar to Dryden's St. Cecilia's Day poem in that respect.

In 1718, the last year of his life, Nicholas Rowe published several odes that end with choruses and include other evidence that musical performance was intended, such as this stanza in "Ode to Peace":

> Awake the golden lyre,
> Ye Heliconian choir;
> Swell every note still higher,
> And melody inspire
> At heaven and Earth's desire.
>
> (French 2: 438)

Thomas Warton's "Ode for Music," performed at Oxford in 1751, is composed in the secular cantata style brought in from Italy. Pseudo-Pindaric odes to music also continued to be written, including William Mason's, performed in 1749 to music by William Boyce. Around 1760 John Cunningham published "An Irregular Ode on Music," the title of which reflects a reluctant awareness that Pindar never wrote in this fashion. Cunningham's response to music resembles that of Boswell, who tried unsuccessfully to communicate his enthusiasm to the musically insensitive Johnson. Boswell told Johnson in 1777 that music "affected me to such a degree, as often to agitate my nerves painfully, producing in my mind alternate sensations of pathetick dejection, so that I was ready to shed tears; and of daring resolution, so that I was inclined to rush into the thickest part of the battle. 'Sir (said he) I should never hear it, if it made me such a fool'" (Boswell 745). Cunningham's poem would be a strong contender in a contest for the most exclamation points in a single stanza:

> Now wild with fierce desire,
>   My breast is all on fire!
> In soften'd raptures, now, I die!
> Can empty sound such joys impart!
> Can music thus transport the heart,
>   With melting ecstasy!
> O art divine! exalted blessing!
> Each celestial charm expressing!
>   Kindest gift the gods bestow!
>   Sweetest good that mortals know!
>
> (French 6: 173)

Set against this we might consider Joseph Warton's "Ode: To Music," which consists of six staid couplets of trochaic tetrameters and which asks "why thy powers employ / Only for the sons of joy?" thereby implying that music has more sober purposes.

Although poets from Addison to Swift and from Pope to Johnson responded with hostility to Italian opera, the genre sometimes inspired emulation. One might simply offer a translation—but in doing that it was hardly possible to lay claim to the credit of having authored an original work. Or one could work the native English masque into something more extravagant, as Dryden did. A third possibility, also essayed by Dryden, was collaboration with a native composer of distinction (Purcell) on an original work. Two other musico-poetic genres, neither of which came to much in the end, were the so-called monody and the poetic cantata.

From time to time on into the eighteenth century a poet might offer an irregularly stichic poem; these "monodies," though they owed much to "Lycidas" as a model, were really monostrophic *Pindariques*. They could also be compared to the recitative segments of operas; as so many other similar productions did, they looked back toward the musical humanism—that speculative attempt to revive some version of a speech from Greek tragedy—of the Renaissance. Examples include John Langhorne's "A Monody, Inscribed to My Worthy Friend John Scott, Esq." (1769), which opens with a Pope-like salute, "Friend of my genius! on whose natal hour" (French 6: 515), but which oscillates between Alexandrines and trimeters, blending agreeably every poetic fashion of the previous hundred years and meandering gently to a quiet conclusion. In 1777 Thomas Warton published "Monody, Written Near Stratford Upon Avon" (only three lines of which depart from straight iambic pentameter), in which he describes a sudden transformation much like that experienced by the Knight in Keats's "La Belle Dame Sans Merci." Gazing at the meadows surrounding the stream, which seem as lovely as in Arnold's description in "Thyrsis," the poet sees the possibilities of horror that lie beyond:

> Sudden thy beauties, Avon, all are fled,
> As at the waving of some magic wand;
> An holy trance my charmed spirit wings,
> And awful shapes of warriors and of kings
> People the busy mead,
> Like spectres swarming to the wizard's hall.

(French 7: 509)

Another possibility was to cultivate something more "songish." John Hughes (1677–1720), whom Johnson admitted to be "considerably skilled" in music, was largely responsible for popularizing the secular cantata in England. That form, a sort of mini-opera, had appeared in Italy in 1630 and became especially popular late in the century during a papal prohibition on opera performances. In some ways the cantata was an elaboration of the madrigal. "Toward the middle of the century *cantata* came to mean a composition usually for solo voice with continuo accompaniment, in several sections which often intermingled recitatives and arias, on a lyrical or sometimes quasi-dramatic text" (Grout 320). Hughes adapted it in exactly this way:

CANTATA VI.

THE COQUET

RECITATIVE.

> AIRY Cloe, proud and young,
>> The fairest tyrant of the plain,
>> Laugh'd at her adoring swain.
> He sadly sigh'd—she gayly sung,
>> And wanton, thus reproach'd his pain.

AIR.

Leave me, silly shepherd, go,
You only tell me what I know,
    You view a thousand charms in me;
Then cease thy prayers, I'll kinder grow,
    When I can view such charms in thee.
Leave me, silly shepherd, go,
You only tell me what I know,
    You view a thousand charms in me.

RECITATIVE.

Amyntor, fir'd by this disdain,
Curs'd the proud fair, and broke his chain;
    He rav'd, and at the scorner swore,
    And vow'd he'd be love's fool no more—
But Cloe smil'd, and thus she call'd him back again.

AIR.

Shepherd, this I've done to prove thee,
Now thou art a man, I love thee:
    And without a blush resign.
But ungrateful is the passion,
And destroys our inclination,
    When, like slaves, our lovers whine.
Shepherd, this I've done to prove thee,
Now thou art a man, I love thee,
    And without a blush resign.

(French 2: 588)

Hughes also wrote pieces for two voices in a form called the *serenata* that Handel had made use of while in Italy. John Gay provided most of the libretto for a similar production, *Acis and Galatea*, to which Hughes also contributed, which was performed to Handel's music in 1718. Hughes also wrote a slightly longer work with several singers, which he called *A Pastoral Masque*; these, together with the cantatas, mostly date from the decade 1702–1712. For the cantatas he supplied a preface that is of much interest, though seldom quoted or referred to, in which he ruminates:

Since, therefore, the English language, though inferior in smoothness, has been found not incapable of harmony, nothing would perhaps be wanting towards introducing the most elegant style of music, in a nation which has given such generous encouragements to it, if our best poets would sometimes assist this design, and make it their diversion to improve a sort of verse, in regular measures, purposely fitted for music, and which, of all the modern kinds, seems to be the only one that can now properly be called lyrics.

It cannot but be observed on this occasion, that since poetry and music are so nearly allied, it is a misfortune that those who excel in one are often perfect strangers to the other. If, therefore, a better correspondence were settled between the two sister arts, they would probably contribute to each other's improvement. The expressions of harmony, cadence, and a good ear, which are said to be so necessary in poetry, being all borrowed from music, show at least, if they signify any thing, that it would be no improper help for a poet to understand more than the metaphorical sense of them. And on the other hand, a composer can never judge where to lay the accent of his music, who does not know, or is not made sensible, where the words have the greatest beauty and force. (French 2: 586)

Hughes goes on to offer an explanation of recitative, arguing that it "is founded on that variety of accent which pleases in the pronunciation of a good orator, with as little deviation from it as possible." Most remarkable is his claim that in recitative the tones of the voice "make a sort of natural music," so that the words fall into "musical cadences." However it may have happened, Hughes has echoed Deschamps's *musique naturele* from three hundred years earlier and has anticipated the wording of the Imagist manifesto of two hundred years later ("compose in the rhythm of the musical phrase"). Also, in the longer passage quoted above, he has continued to promote the notion of the "sister arts."

Despite his clear perceptions, persuasive arguments, and useful examples, Hughes could, in the end, only revert to the old nostalgia for a golden age of *mousike*; nothing he could say could prevent the most sophisticated poetry and music from pursuing separate careers. Yet Hughes was well known and much admired in his own time; Johnson credits him with having persuaded Addison to complete and produce his tragedy *Cato*. If Swift and Johnson had not both considered music a frivolous waste of time, Hughes might have been valued even more highly and his reputation might have lasted longer. His pieces were set by the most important composers in England at that time: Johann Ernst Galliard (1680–1749), Pepusch, and even Handel. He was imitated by Edward Moore, who in midcentury produced *Solomon*, a *serenata* with music by William Boyce. Another imitator was William Thompson, who wrote "Beauty and Music," an ode with specifically marked airs and recitatives—a pattern that may be found in several other odes to music or to St. Cecilia. In the 1760s John Cunningham's "Love and Charity: A Cantata" appeared in a form shaped exactly according to Hughes's example. (Of course, some cantatas were probably modeled directly on Italian examples.)

The most genuine fusion of music and poetry in the eighteenth century, it turns out, was in those forms least favored by the standards of high neoclassicism: the song, the ballad, and especially the hymn. There seems little need to rehearse the history and further exemplify the growing interest in the remnants of older English poetry that culminated in the publication of Thomas Percy's *Reliques of Ancient English Poetry* in 1765. More ballad writing went on prior to the appearance of this volume than is usually recognized; also, Percy included some contemporary ballads in his collection. An important subspecies of both the song and the ballad was that written for children and meant to be sung to familiar tunes. All through the century, too, appeared the work of Scots women and men who in their upbringing found themselves still close to what would soon become a fashionable antiquarian and Romantic trend. The specific precursors to Blake and Burns will appear in the next chapter, but we should note here the existence of a lively musical culture much like that immediately preceding the Renaissance, whose unself-conscious vitality helped make possible a second poetic renaissance, that of British Romanticism.

In the commentary that follows the texts in Volume 15 of *The Works of John Dryden* we read, "As a dramatist, Dryden had long since come to terms with music in songs that were but interludes in a play, songs often accompanied by, and being specifically written for, certain dance forms such as the zambra" (325). And as George Sherburn recognized, "Dryden was also a lyric poet of considerable ability. His comedies and *Miscellanies* are sprinkled with deftly turned witty songs in the Cavalier tradition" (Baugh et al. 729–30). In this respect Dryden was another representative of a continuous tradition of courtly song that stretched back earlier than the beginnings of the Renaissance. *The Oxford Book of Eighteenth Century Verse* consists in large part of such pieces, with space available only for excerpts from the masterpieces in heroic couplets, even "The Rape of the Lock" being represented only by isolated passages. Older songs and ballads persisted; newer ones caught on as audiences remembered them from plays, learned them from librettos, or purchased them as collections or single broadsides. Such musico-poetic culture was nearly as rich as it is today, where it is possible to be simultaneously familiar with Schubert lieder, "numbers" from musicals, songs by Burl Ives or Bill Haley, blues songs, country and western songs, arias, and various "popular" music— as well as children's songs, commercial jingles, hymns, and anthems. The ten volumes of *Minor English Poets: 1660–1780* include some 7,000 pages of poetry; much of that consists of longer poems, or translations, but short poems fill many a page, and of those, many are songs or songlike lyrics. French estimates in his Preface (1: xv–xvi) that if we add twelve major poets such as Pope and

Swift to the eighty-three minor poets in his edition, 55 percent wrote in the genre that he identifies as "song." An equal percentage composed odes of some description or other; many of these are the pseudo-Pindaric that continued as the irregular ode used by Wordsworth and Coleridge. Seventeen percent of the poets wrote ballads.

Many of these shorter "songs" were rendered brittle and artificial by poetic diction and mythological references. This is the beginning of Elijah Fenton's "To a Lady Sitting Before her Glass" (1712):

> So smooth and clear the Fountain was
> In which his Face *Narcissus* spy'd,
> When gazing in that liquid Glass,
> He for himself despair'd and dy'd:
> Nor, *Chloris*, can you safer see
> Your own Perfections here than he.

(# 115 OBECV–1926)

In 1759 Frances Macartney composed "A Prayer for Indifference" in ballad meter, making it singable to any number of tunes. Here are her opening stanzas:

> Oft I've implor'd the Gods in vain,
> And pray'd till I've been weary;
> For once I'll try my wish to gain
> Of Oberon, the fairy.
>
> Sweet airy being, wanton sprite,
> That lurk'st in woods unseen,
> And oft by Cynthia's silver light
> Tripst gaily o'er the green;
>
> If e'er thy pitying heart was mov'd,
> As ancient stories tell,
> And for th' Athenian maid, who lov'd,
> Thou sought'st a wondrous spell. . . .

(# 276 OBECV–1926)

Others were satirical or bawdy, such as Matthew Prior's "A True Maid"— although this may qualify more as an epigram than a song:

> "No, no, for my virginity,
> When I lose that," says Rose, "I'll die."
> "Behind the elms last night," cried Dick,
> "Rose, were you not extremely sick?"

(# 35 in *The New Oxford Book of Eighteenth Century Verse*, ed. Roger Lonsdale. New York: Oxford UP, 1984. Hereafter abbreviated NOBECV–1984)

We will be tracing resemblances between Blake's "songs" and earlier eigh-teenth-century poetry, but it seems unwise to claim any connection between the urbane wit of Prior's poem and "The Sick Rose," as some do (see discus-sions in Meyerstein, Anshutz, and Gleckner). Far more apposite would be a citation of David Mallet's ballad, "William and Margaret" (1723), stanzas 4 and 5:

> Her bloom was like the springing flower,
>   That sips the silver dew;
> The rose was budded in her cheek,
>   Just opening to the view.

> But love had, like the canker-worm,
>   Consum'd her early prime:
> The rose grew pale, and left her cheek;
>   She dy'd before her time.

> (# 178 OBECV–1926)

Mallet's poem also sounds remarkably like Wordsworth, especially "She Dwelt Among the Untrodden Ways," and one even wonders if Keats had it in mind when he was writing "La Belle Dame Sans Merci." According to Johnson in his brief life of Mallet, "His first production was William and Margaret; of which, though it contains nothing very striking or difficult, he has been envied the reputation." Pastoral simplicity did not appeal to Johnson. Most of Mallet's work addresses itself to sophisticated urban audiences; the popularity of "William and Margaret," which is very different from most of his other work, proves that readers early in the eighteenth century were ready for Blake and Burns, that there was a market waiting for *Lyrical Ballads*. Mallet himself appended a note to the poem:

> N. B. In a comedy of Fletcher, called the Knight of the Burning Pestle, old Merry-Thought enters repeating the following verses:

> When it was grown to dark midnight,
>   And all were fast asleep,
> In came Margaret's grimly ghost,
>   And stood at William's feet.

> This was probably the beginning of some ballad [collected eventually as Child No. 74], commonly known, at the time when that author wrote; and is all of it, I believe, that is any where to be met with. These lines, naked of ornament, and simple as they are, struck my fancy: and, bringing fresh into my mind an unhappy adventure, much talked of formerly, gave birth to the foregoing poem; which was written many years ago. (French 5: 48)

By way of contrast, Samuel Johnson's prosy and sardonic "A Short Song of Congratulation" mocks its own form as well as its subject. It concludes:

When the bonny blade carouses,
Pockets full, and spirits high,
What are acres? What are houses?
Only dirt, or wet or dry.

If the guardian or the mother
Tell the woes of wilful waste,
Scorn their counsel and their pother,
You can hang or drown at last.

(# 216 NOBECV–1984)

The eighteenth century, skeptical, urbane and cosmopolitan as it may seem in some respects, also saw the first appearance of patriotic, even nationalistic songs. Most of us who remember James Thomson for *The Seasons* are startled at being reminded that he also invented "Rule Britannia" as a song for the masque *Alfred* (1740). "God Save the King" (author unknown) appeared in 1745 in the *Gentleman's Magazine*, leading off originally as "God save Great George our King." Scottish patriotic airs anticipated Burns's stirring "Scots, wha hae wi' Wallace bled." The national anthem of the United States is likewise a good example; trailing some decades behind English fashions, as most American poetry did, "The Star Spangled Banner" is sung to the melody of a drinking song that owed its words to Ralph Tomlinson, Esq., and its music to John Stafford Smith. First sung in the Crown Anchor Tavern in the Strand circa 1780, the original leads off with this stanza:

To Anacreon in Heav'n where he sat in full glee,
A few Sons of Harmony sent a petition
That he their Inspirer and Patron would be;
When this answer arrived from the Jolly Old Grecian:
"Voice, Fiddle and Flute,
No longer be mute,
I'll lend you my name and inspire you to boot

CHORUS.
And besides I'll instruct you, like me, to entwine
The Myrtle of Venus with Bacchus's Vine."

(http://www.ccil.org:^{6502}/$_{30958}$.html)

A facility for lyric prosody never disappeared during the eighteenth century, but it remained for a revival of more authentic folk materials, such as those collected earlier in Percy's *Reliques* and elsewhere, to invest the forms with medieval glamor. Some of the resulting songs can be heard occasionally today—such as the anonymous "The Vicar of Bray" and Henry Carey's "The Ballad of Sally in our Alley," both written in common measure doubled (eight lines of alternating iambic tetrameter and trimeter). Songs from John Gay's *The Beggar's Opera* offered an alternative to Italian importations:

> Youth's the Season made for Joys,
>   Love is then our Duty,
> She alone who that employs,
>   Well deserves her Beauty.
>   Let's be gay,
>   While we may,
> Beauty's a Flower, despis'd in Decay.
>
> CHORUS.
> Youth's the Season, &c.
>
> Let us drink and sport to-day,
>   Ours is not to-morrow.
> Love with Youth flies swift away,
>   Age is nought but Sorrow.
>   Dance and sing,
>   Time's on the Wing,
> Life never knows the Return of Spring.
>
> CHORUS.
> Let us drink, &c.
>
> (# 106 OBECV–1926)

In comparison with centuries before and after, few serious poems (except hymns) in recognizable song meters were composed in the eighteenth century, and those that were seem oddities. One would like to know, for example, why Samuel Johnson chose long measure (tetrameters rhyming *abab*) for "On the Death of Dr. Robert Levett," where the meter seems at odds with the diction—that is, the tripping tetrameters hardly seem suitable for the dismal personifications in this stanza:

> In misery's darkest caverns known,
>   His useful care was ever nigh,
> Where hopeless anguish pour'd his groan,
>   And lonely want retir'd to die.
>
> (# 224 OBECV–1926)

Because Johnson was celebrating a fundamentally happy and useful life, perhaps he found it appropriate to compose in a meter reminiscent of a song, perhaps a hymn, to honor his friend. But the rhetorical structure and figures, the explicit personification, make the poem closer to prose than to music.

To mention William Cowper at this point is to range ahead of my fundamental arguments. In Cowper we see a poet who epitomizes many eighteenth-century qualities, but out of whose work emerges "The Castaway" (1799), a thoroughly romantic poem, a wrenching personal testament of his feelings at the loss of his companion of many years and at the prospect of his own death. The form is strongly reminiscent of a song, but the matter hardly seems suitable for melody (other examples include "To Mary" and "The Shrubbery: Written in a Time of Affliction"). He intensifies the personal note, which Charles Wesley and others carried into hymnody, into messages of despair; his poem is anticipatory of American confessional poets of the last few decades (Plath, Sexton, Lowell, Berryman, and in some poems, Snodgrass) who depict personal emotional pain in technically masterful meters. After nine stanzas that describe with horrifying vividness the condition of a man washed overboard in a storm, "The Castaway" concludes:

> No voice divine the storm allay'd
> No light propitious shone;
> When, snatch'd from all effectual aid,
> We perish'd, each alone:
> But I beneath a rougher sea,
> And whelm'd in deeper gulphs than he.

(# 363 OBECV–1926)

Cowper initially made himself famous with his adaptation of ballad meter, or common measure, for comic purposes, in "The Diverting History of John Gilpin" (1782). Before 1779 he was known as the author of hymns, some of them very familiar to present-day congregations, such as those beginning, "God moves in a mysterious way" and "Oh! for a closer walk with God."

In fact the eighteenth century initiated the most important era of British hymn writing both for the Church of England and for dissenting denominations. Many poets better known for other productions wrote hymns, some of which remain in standard collections. But (for reasons that would be interesting to explore) little secular poetry in Great Britain shows kinship with religious hymns until the later nineteenth century, at which time the form seemed appropriate for quasireligious expressions of doubt or skepticism such as *In Memoriam*, W. E. Henley's "Invictus," and poems by Hardy and Housman. Possibly hymn meters seemed, in the eighteenth century, too completely identified with established religion to serve for secular purposes. Whatever the reasons, the first response to hymns among British poets was not to treat them as a resource for their own poems, but to react against them by composing secular "hymns" in strophes totally unlike those of religious hymns—even in couplets or blank verse, or in some sort of irregular ode or monodic style. These did not resemble hymns that might be sung in Protestant church services; instead, one sees a kinship with the oratorio, the German cantata, and the mass.

One thinks of these unhymnlike "hymns" initially as Romantic productions, such as Coleridge's "Hymn Before Sunrise in the Vale of Chamouni":

> Hast thou a charm to stay the morning-star
> In his steep course? So long he seems to pause
> On thy bald awful head, O sovran Blanc,
> The Arve and Arveiron at thy base
> Rave ceaselessly; but thou most awful Form!
> Risest forth from thy silent sea of pines.
>
> (1–6)

Shelley's "Hymn of Pan" (1820) is, like Thomas Gray's "Hymn to Adversity" (1748), a homostrophic ode, with long stanzas conspicuously unlike most recognizable hymn meters. But as with the irregular ode, the origins of the secular hymn in a nonhymn form can be traced back to the seventeenth century and to Abraham Cowley, whose "Hymn to Light" employs regular stanzas that do not seem particularly singable, each consisting of a pentameter followed by two tetrameters and an Alexandrine, and rhyming *aabb*. The poem mingles promiscuously a few Christian references with pagan mythology, and includes scientific speculation about the nature of light; the whole is a dreadful conglomeration of poetic diction, personification, thoughtless epithets, clichés, and unconvincing similes, and not worth quoting.

Around 1712 Thomas Parnell wrote three hymns—for morning, noon, and evening—in tetrameter couplets; these nonstanzaic devotional poems are addressed to God and not to the time of day. But in the 1690s Thomas Yalden had composed "Hymn to Darkness," in which he reproduced Cowley's idiosyncratic stanza and some of Cowley's language. Samuel Johnson liked this poem well enough, calling the tenth stanza "exquisitely beautiful":

> Thou dost thy smiles impartially bestow,
>   And know'st no difference here below:
>   All things appear the same by thee,
> Though Light distinction makes, thou giv'st equality.
>
> (37–40)

In "Hymn to the Morning: In Praise of Light" Yalden expanded Cowley's form by an additional four lines per stanza, creating in effect a homostrophic ode. Johnson did not like this one, writing in his *Lives of the English Poets*: "His hymn to light is not equal to the other. He seems to think that there is an East absolute and positive where the Morning rises." John Gilbert Cooper (1723–1765) wrote a "Hymn to Health" in heroic quatrains, which ends with a prayer to Aesculapius, and about 1745 William Thompson employed Spenserian stanzas for "An Hymn to May," adding in for good measure "antiquated words"—by this time doubly antiquated—from Spenser, together with notes that remind one of Eliot's appendix to *The Waste Land*. In 1746 Mark Akenside offered the world his "Hymn to the Naiads" in Miltonic blank verse and with even more elaborate apparatus; the notes are longer than the poem. Akenside also wrote a "Hymn to Science" in jouncy tetrameters and trimeters, a poem that reflects his wide interests and his medical training. John Langhorne's "Hymn to Hope" (1761) is an imitation of "L'Allegro," employing Milton's meter, and his "Hymn to Plutus" is a satire on himself in rhyming couplets. Langhorne wrote a number of other hymns in various forms and styles; at least one, "Hymn to Eternal Providence" (an imitation of Addison), seems religious.

William Whitehead's "An Hymn to the Nymph of Bristol Spring," in blank verse, dates from 1751; from the summit upon which he sets us we may gaze backward a century to Milton and ahead a few decades to Wordsworth:

> These are thy handmaids, goddess of the fount,
> And these thy offspring. Oft have I beheld
> Their airy revels on the verdant steep
> Of Avon, clear as fancy's eye could paint.
> What time the dewy star of eve invites
> To lonely musing, by the wave-worn beach,
> Along the extended mead. Nor less intent
> Their fairy forms I view, when from the height
> Of Clifton, tow'ring mount, th' enraptur'd eye
> Beholds the cultivated prospect rise
> Hill above hill, with many a verdant bound
> Of hedge-row chequer'd. Now on painted clouds
> Sportive they roll, or down yon winding stream
> Give their light mantles to the wafting wind,
> And join the sea-green sisters of the flood.
>
> (French 7: 211)

Among the few pieces called hymns that are not meant for use in religious services, but which resemble hymns in form, is Henry Brooke's "Hymn to Beauty" from *Montezuma*; it is in long measure. John Logan's "Ossian's Hymn to the Sun" (ca. 1775) is in end-stopped heroic couplets; this formality is very odd, since the "Ossian" poems themselves are a kind of pseudobiblical prose. Logan wrote a number of serious Christian hymns and perhaps was reluctant to paganize the form. Thomas Blacklock, of about the same time, followed Langhorne's example and wrote hymns to divine love, to benevolence, and to fortitude in a variety of unhymnlike forms.

The *Poems* of Sir William Jones appeared in 1772, containing a series of hymns based on Sanskrit poetry and Indian mythology. Jones apparently wished them to be thought of as translations, but he offers a curious argument in the preface: "Were I to produce the originals themselves, it would be impossible to persuade some men, that even they were not forged for the purpose, like the pretended language of Formosa" (French 7: 625). Admired to the point of idolatry by some who knew him, and referred to reverentially in the *Oxford Companion to English Literature* as "a distinguished orientalist and jurist, [who] was judge of the high court at Calcutta from 1783 to his death," we may still suspect that if Jones was in fact working from originals, he made very free with them. "The Hymn to Durga," for example, is a perfect Pindaric ode (Pindar's true lineaments having by this time been recognized) divided into nine numbered sections, each of which contains the required triad of strophe, antistrophe, and epode. One may suspect that the influence of Pindar on Sanskrit was minimal. "The Hymn to Camdeo" is homostrophic, with ten-line stanzas in varying line lengths and rhyming in couplets, while "A Hymn to Indra" is an irregular ode, as are several others. One need look no further than Jones's work to find all the forms of the ode employed by the Romantics, illustrating yet again the truism that British Romanticism was in most ways a shift of emphases, a culmination of trends long in existence. Keats's odes and Shelley's "Ode to the West Wind" are homostrophic; Wordsworth's "Immortality Ode" is irregular, a descendant of the *Pindarique*.

Jones also added two essays to his collection, "On the Poetry of the Eastern Nations" and "On the Arts, Commonly called Imitative." The second of these is of particular interest in documenting the shift from imitative to expressive theories of art:

> It seems probable, then, that poetry was originally no more than a strong, and animated expression of the human passions, of joy and grief, love and hate, admiration and anger, sometimes pure and unmixed, sometimes variously modified and combined: for, if we observe the voice and accents of a person affected by any of the violent passions, we shall perceive something in them very nearly approaching to cadence and measure; which is remarkably the case in the language of a vehement orator, whose talent is chiefly conversant about praise or censure; and we may collect from several passages in Tully, that the fine speakers of old Greece and Rome, had a sort of rhythm in their sentences, less regular, but not less melodious, than that of the poets. (French 7: 692)

From here it seems but two quick strides would carry us past Walt Whitman and into full view of Charles Olson at the podium. Jones's comments on music are anticonstructive. He calls music "poetry, dressed to advantage" (French 7: 694), perhaps implying what he does not add, that music is "what oft was *felt*, but ne'er so well expressed." And he anticipates Coleridge's Secondary Imagination: "Thus will each artist gain his end, not by imitating the works of nature, but by assuming her power, and causing the same effect upon the imagination, which her charms produce to the senses: this must be the chief object of a poet, a musician, and a painter" (French 7: 695).

In England, then, the conventions of sacred hymnody did not for a long time supply a context for the emergence of poetry. Many poets, including several of those just mentioned, composed hymns that were meant to be used as such, in religious services. Poems called "hymns," on secular subjects, were mostly written in forms actually or supposedly borrowed from the pagan classics. I have suggested that a spirit of romantic rebelliousness accounted for this, an unwillingness to use established forms, but there may also have been a reluctance to profane the rhymes and meters associated with worship—or just a feeling that this mode had been preempted by various Protestant sects. The emergence of poetry from hymnody had to await other poets on another continent, where the singing of hymns seemed an essential part of the culture, something taken for granted in religious services and less emblematic of a break from Catholicism.

For all the interest in music in the England of the Restoration and eighteenth century, and despite the various efforts at tying poetry back in with music, or composing poems as if they could resemble musical genres, the most enduringly interesting poems from that period remain those that distanced themselves from actual music. Ballads and songs were mostly comic or satirical—or, if serious, prettified and pedantic. A good example of the latter is a stanza from William Collins's "Ode to Simplicity," the poetic effects of which belie the title:

> By all the honey'd Store
> On *Hybla*'s Thymy Shore,
> By all her Blooms, and mingled Murmurs dear,
> By Her, whose Love-lorn Woe
> In Ev'ning Musings slow
> Sooth'd sweetly sad *Electra*'s Poet's Ear!

(# 234 OBECV–1926)

The intrinsic tendencies of Augustan neoclassicism toward pomposity and artificiality dispose themselves more effectively in larger works whose dimensions seem more appropriate to such pretensions. In the course of this chapter I have referred to numerous shorter works (few of which find their way into anthologies of the period), but I have quoted almost nothing because the sad truth is that most of these poems are spoiled by poetic diction and decorative mythologizing, just as Wordsworth claimed they were. The pretense that these "songs," "ballads," "hymns," and "cantatas" had any vital connection with music could no longer be sustained; they were as distant from music as English pastoral poetry had always been from an actual countryside. But the actual countryside was still there, in the border country and Scotland even more than in England, and as we will see in the following chapters, native British melody had never lost its potential to reinvigorate the poetry. And at the same time, the vast heritage of purely verbal "music"—of Shakespeare and Milton, if not quite yet of Donne—was newly available to the poets of the nineteenth century as an inspiration, an adequate appreciation of its vigor and variety having been somewhat beyond the ken of eighteenth-century poets and their readers.

10

The Revival of the Lyric

EMBOSSED IN GOLD into the cover of a facsimile edition of *Robert Burns's Commonplace Book, 1783–1785* is a coat of arms, above which floats a scroll bearing the words "Woodnotes Wild." An entry from August 1783 tells us: "For my own part I never had the least thought or inclination of turning Poet till I had got once heartily in Love, and then Rhyme & Song were, in a manner, the spontaneous language of my heart" (3).

> Gie me ae spark o' Nature's fire,
> That's a' the learning I desire;
> Then tho' I drudge thro' dub an' mire
>   At pleugh or cart,
> My Muse, though hamely in attire,
>   May touch the heart.
>
> ("Epistle to John Lapraik, An Old Scottish
> Bard," *Poetical Works* 163)

Burns's own view of himself as the untutored, or self-tutored, genius of rural Scotland established itself immediately and has persisted ever since. In 1786, an anonymous reviewer in the *Edinburgh Magazine* commented, "The author is indeed a striking example of native genius bursting through the obscurity of poverty and the obstructions of laborious life" (qtd. in Low 64). Few poets are so easily sentimentalized as is Burns, or so easily seen as fulfilling Romantic prescriptions for poetic genius; in America, Emerson set Burns alongside Goethe and Byron—while recognizing his affinity with a "homely landscape" (see Low 435).

In a 1934 article in *Scrutiny*, John Speirs offered one of the more stringent correctives to such views, insisting that Burns was the result more of evolution than of spontaneous generation. Speirs said of his poetry, "What it is connected with is the Scottish vernacular verse which for at least two centuries precedes it and of which it is for all practical purposes the culmination" (117). Although Speirs sees Burns mainly as a satirist and his world as a world of comedy, he does recognize a musical context as essential to his work:

> Metrically, and otherwise, Burns's verse (I wish finally to suggest) is affected
> by Scottish folk-dance. It seems to me to bear something of the same kind of
> relation to the folk-dance as is borne by much Jacobean verse to Jacobean
> Stage-Play. This is certainly true of the vernacular Songs. Words, tune and
> dance are, in these, essentially one. The tunes to which Burns composed
> new, or rehandled old, words were as often as not reels and strathspeys. The
> dance affects the Songs through these tunes and . . . the rest of his verse in less
> tangible ways. (127)

"Words, tune and dance are, in these, essentially one." Is this not *mousike* alive
and well in Scotland? James Macpherson's "Ossian" poems, admiration for
which was inspired by the same nostalgic nationalism that helped bring Burns
rapidly into prominence, were not the authentic epics that many wished they
had been; but the songs that Burns admired, collected, and imitated were a
genuine folk culture matrix within which a vital poetry awaited liberation.

In terms of Burns's own poetry, one might put it somewhat the other way,
saying that it was not until he had immersed himself in the songs—tunes as
well as words—that he went over almost completely to that mode. His first
published book, *Poems Chiefly in the Scottish Dialect* (1786) comprises verse
epistles, satires, and didactic poems, with a few songs. But as Burns became
known in Edinburgh, he was drawn into an increasingly self-conscious awareness of himself as the inheritor and most recent exemplar of Scottish traditions, rather than a British poet of the eighteenth century. Once that happened, he found that the best way into the past was by way of Scottish music, a
high road that, according to Raymond Bentman, he was well prepared to take:

> Burns's knowledge of music was extensive. A few manuscripts exist that
> demonstrate his ability to use musical notation. He could play the fiddle.
> And his correspondence with song editors demonstrates a good knowledge
> of musical techniques. He did not write any of the music; the airs were all
> traditional. When he revised a traditional song, he usually kept the words
> with the melody that he had heard sung with them. But at times he assigned
> words to other traditional tunes. When he wrote an original song he as-
> signed it to some traditional air. (77)

In 1787 he heard that the printer James Johnson was putting together a
collection of songs, *The Scots Musical Museum*, and in May of that year he sent
Johnson a copy of "a Song never before known, for your collection" (*Letters*
1: 113). He went on to become deeply involved with the project, which
continued year after year, reaching five volumes before Burns's death. He
constantly supplied Johnson with new material; late in 1792 he wrote, "As to
our Musical Museum, I have better than a dozen songs by me for the fifth

volume. . . . If we cannot finish the fifth volume any other way—what would you think of Scots words to some beautiful Irish airs?" (2: 156).

Also in 1792 he received an invitation from George Thomson to contribute to *A Select Collection of Original Scotish Airs for the Voice*. Numerous letters that track the progress of this enterprise communicate his excitement; Burns, like Keats after him, could seldom refrain from spilling his feelings onto the page. Answering Thomson's inquiry, he wrote, "I shall enter into your undertaking with all the small portion of abilities I have, strained to their utmost exertion by the impulse of Enthusiasm" (2: 148). Refusing to haggle over terms, he added, "In the honest enthusiasm with which I embark in your undertaking, to talk of money, wages, fee, hire, &c. would be downright Sodomy of Soul!" (2: 149).

For Burns, this seven-year immersion in song represented a baptism in the natural sources of Scottish poetry, a joyful rediscovery of things he had known all along but which, at first distancing himself with comedy and satire, he had somewhat neglected. Though poems written in Scots dialect before Burns had not always struck the authentic note, even indulging in condescending farce that made fun of rural ignorance, important precursors had prepared the way for Burns's work. Allan Ramsay (1685–1758) not only anticipated Burns in using dialect for serious literary purposes, but also in collecting Scottish songs, issued first in 1724 as the *Tea-table Miscellany* and *The Evergreen*. (Ramsay was forty years ahead of Thomas Percy, whose *Reliques of Ancient English Poetry* [1765] is commonly cited as the beginning of Romantic interest in the rural and the medieval.) Another important collection was David Herd's *Ancient and Modern Scottish Songs, Heroic Ballads etc.* (1769; rev. 1776). Similar volumes had, in fact, appeared as early as 1706. Most important of all were the poems of Robert Ferguson, whom Burns admired enough to commission an architect, at considerable expense, to design Ferguson's burial monument. In some ways the relationship of Burns to Ferguson might be compared, in our own time, to the indebtedness of Seamus Heaney to Patrick Kavanagh. Burns saw it as his job to continue the work of these earlier poets, and to celebrate those parts of Scotland that they had overlooked:

> However I am pleased with the works of our Scotch Poets, particularly the excellent Ramsay, and the still more excellent Ferguson, yet I am hurt to see other places of Scotland, their towns, rivers, woods, haughs, &c. immortalized in such celebrated performances, whilst my dear native country, the ancient Bailieries of Carrick, Kyle, & Cunningham, famous both in ancient & modern times for a gallant, and warlike race of inhabitants; a country where civil, & particularly religious Liberty have ever found their first support, & their last asylum; a country, the birth place of many famous Philoso-

phers, Soldiers, & Statesmen, and the scene of many important events recorded in Scottish History, particularly a great many of the actions of the
GLORIOUS WALLACE, the SAVIOUR of his Country; Yet, we have never had
one Scotch Poet of any eminence, to make the fertile banks of Irvine, the romantic woodlands & sequestered scenes on Aire, and the heathy, mountain-
ous source, & winding sweep of Doon emulate Tay, Forth, Ettrick, Tweed,
&c. this is a complaint I would gladly remedy, but Alas! I am far unequal to
the task, both in native genius, & education. (*Commonplace Book* 36)

Burns brought into prominence a way of writing and a subject that had
gradually been taking possession of the popular imagination, at least in Scotland, for a century or more. In much the same way, in England, Wordsworth
was thoroughly anticipated by the blank-verse pre-Romantic poets. The process of self-identification was a matter of intense excitement for Burns, who
wrote to Thomson in 1793:

You know that my pretensions to musical taste, are merely a few of
Nature's instincts, untaught & untutored by Art.—For this reason, many
musical compositions, particularly where much of the merit lies in Counterpoint, however they may transport & ravish the ears of you, Connoisseurs,
[appear (*deleted*)] affect my simple lug no otherwise than merely as melodious Din.—On the other hand, by way of amends, I am delighted with
many little melodies, which the learned Musician despises as silly &
insipid.—I do not know whether the old Air, "Hey tutti taitie," may rank
among this number; but well I know that, with Fraser's Hautboy, it has often
filled my eyes with tears.—There is a tradition, which I have met with in
many places of Scotland, that it was Robert Bruce's March at the battle of
Bannock-burn. (*Letters* 2: 235)

That Burns looked to music for inspiration, for a revitalizing of his language,
marks an important shift in the relations of poetry to music and in the manner
in which poems were henceforth to evolve from music. In some sense this
moment distantly anticipates T. S. Eliot's taking the late quartets of Beethoven
as a model, or as a source of musical suggestions that he could carry into his
poetry. More self-conscious than Dante's, Machaut's, or Wyatt's, and less
cerebral than Campion's or Dryden's, Burns's relationship to music is nonetheless authentic. He described this in another letter to Thomson in Septem-
ber, 1793:

I do not know the air; & untill I am compleat master of a tune, in my own
singing, (such as it is) I never can compose for it.—My way is: I consider the
poetic Sentiment, correspondent to my idea of the musical expression; then
chuse my theme; begin one [verse (*deleted*)] Stanza; when that is composed,

which is generally the most difficult part of the business, I walk out, sit down now & then, look out for objects in Nature around me that are in unison or harmony with the cogitations of my fancy & workings of my bosom; humming every now & then the air with the verses I have framed: when I feel my Muse beginning to jade, I retire to the solitary fireside of my study, & there commit my effusions to paper; swinging, at intervals, on the hind-legs of my elbow-chair, by way of calling forth my own critical strictures, as my pen goes on. (*Letters* 2: 242)

The correspondence with Thomson was even more extensive than it appears from Burns's letters, for Thomson succeeded in censoring the letters after Burns's death to remove passages that reflected badly on him. He had treated Burns shabbily, often revising his language without permission, or supplying melodies other than those chosen by Burns (see note on Thomson, *Letters* 2: 484).

As best one can tell, though, Burns remained astonishingly free of rancor—more generous-spirited and gallant even than John Keats, when, with death approaching, he wrote one of his last letters to Thomson, promising additional songs and asking for five pounds because he thought himself threatened with prison (it is a relief to learn that in this case Thomson sent the money). Among the few expressions of impatience that one finds in the correspondence is in a letter of October 1794, where Burns complains, "These English songs gravel me to death.—I have not that command of the language [as (*deleted*)] that I have of my native tongue.—In fact, I think that my ideas are more barren in English than in Scotish" (2: 318). From Burns's side of the correspondence it appears that Thomson was constantly pressuring Burns to make the dialect more accessible, to which Burns acceded: "If you honor my verses by setting the air to it, I will vamp up the old Song & make it English enough to be understood" (2: 319).

That Burns was willing to compromise ought not to make him seem a linguistic "collaborator"; art is art, poetry is poetry, and a Scots dialect modified in the direction of greater intelligibility for a wider public is not an act of treason. The poetry that came out of this transformation (I am speaking of the songs) owes its existence to the musical context, but the fact is that from Burns's time to this day many of the poems have been printed and read, memorized and loved, for the words themselves—for the freshness, directness, and simplicity with which they touch on the afflictions and transports of the human spirit. Still, to read Burns is to encounter a language invigorated and informed by music, very different from the stale and mechanical contrivances that, sad to say, were all too common in English eighteenth-century verse.

To what extent do the songs stand alone as poetry? My own impression is that, delightful as it is to listen to them performed, they are at least as independent of their music as many of Wyatt's poems; the music is invigorating to the text, but not essential to the poem as a poem. Few readers of poetry feel the lack of music when they encounter "Red, Red Rose" on the page for the first time, rather than as a performance; conceived as a song, it is, first and foremost, poetry. A somewhat less familiar example might be this:

I'LL MEET THEE ON THE LEA RIG

When owre the hill the e'ening star	
Tells bughtin° time is near, my jo°,	sheep-folding sweetheart
And owsen° frae the furrow'd field	oxen
Return sae dowf° and weary O;	dull
Down by the burn°, where birken° buds	stream birch
Wi' dew are hangin clear, my jo,	
I'll meet thee on the lea-rig°,	grassy ridge
My ain kind Dearie O.	

At Midnight hour, in mirkest° glen,	darkest
I'd rove, and never be eerie O,	
If throt the glen I gaed to thee,	
My ain kind Dearie O;	
Althot the night were never sae wild	
And I were nel er sae weary O,	
I'll meet thee on the lea-rig	
My ain kind Dearie O.	

The hunter lo'es° the morning sun	loves
To rouse the mountain deer, my jo;	
At noon the fisher takes the glen	
Adown the burn to steer, my jo:	
Gie me the hour of gloamin° grey,	twilight
It maks me heart sae cheery O,	
To meet thee on the lea-rig	
My ain kind Dearie O.	

The poem takes something like a basic ballad meter, doubles it to eight-line stanzas, and adds an extra repetitive foot to the second, fourth, and sixth lines (except in the second stanza, where there are three feet, or six syllables, in the fourth line). Scansion by syllable count would work nearly as well; to say this is not to deny any accentual pattern, but rather to recognize that the iambic rhythm is extremely regular, and that one might as well apply hymn notation to it: 8.8.8.8.8.8.7.6, then 8.8.8.6.8.8.7.6, then 8.8.8.8.8.8.7.6. (Such notation is even more useful in the case of "Scots Wha Hae"; in that poem, to apply a mechanical trochaic template falsifies the rhythm, whereas notating each stanza as 6.6.6.5 works perfectly.) "I'll Meet Thee on the Lea Rig" works with a complex pattern of repetitions, most obviously with the two-line refrain that ends each stanza, but also with the curiously endearing mosaic rhymes ("weary O," "eerie O") that mark the intimate speech of the lover. The one anomalous line (12) proves, upon examination, to be a functional repetition of the refrain; the effect is not to detract from the stanza pattern but to weld the poem into a single structure. Alliteration also ties lines functionally together (note especially lines 3, 5, 9, 11, 13, and 21), though not obtrusively. To note these effects, however, is to leave much more unsaid; most of the graces of this poem are unnameable.

More than anything, what lifts these stanzas into the realm of poetry are the convincingly realized details. The first stanza localizes the poem in time and space—evening of the day, spring of the year, a hilly farm, a stream, and a grassy ridge. In the second stanza, the lover's imagination carries him through something comparable to the valley of the shadow of death—something of an exaggeration, perhaps, of what he would put himself through to meet his "ain kind Dearie O," but true to the language of the heart; true, also, to the storms that sweep across Scotland, swiftly transforming a familiar glen into a dark and ominous chasm. With the third stanza we are back into broad daylight, perfect for hunter and fisherman, but for the lover only a time to get through until the twilight trysting hour has returned. What strikes the reader is Burns's deep imaginative grasp of the scenes to which he alludes; these are lived images, not decorative poeticisms, handled with a meter and rhythm that is firm and resilient, owing much to music, but transcending that derivation.

That William Blake meant to invoke the power of music in his poems would be clear to anyone who knew no more than the titles of his companion volumes, *Songs of Innocence* and *Songs of Experience*. But whereas Burns's melodies might be heard on any street corner or at the end of any farmhouse lane, Blake's were more like those of Milton: "unexpressive," unheard by ordinary mortals. Blake, however, heard things inaudible to human hearing as well as seeing things invisible to human sight. John Thomas Smith (*Nollekins and his Times*, 1828) reported: "Much about this time, Blake wrote many other songs, to which he also composed tunes. These he would occasionally sing to his friends; and though, according to his confession, he was entirely unacquainted with the science of music, his ear was so good, that his tunes were sometimes most singularly beautiful, and were noted down by musical professors" (Bentley 457). Smith also remembered, "I have often heard him read and sing several of his poems" (26). Allen Cunningham, in *Lives of the Most Eminent*

British Painters, Sculptors, and Architects (1830), also mentioned Blake's music, but concluded that it no longer existed:

> In sketching designs, engraving plates, writing songs, and composing music, he employed his time, with his wife sitting at his side, encouraging him in all his undertakings. As he drew the figure he meditated the song which was to accompany it, and the music to which the verse was to be sung, was the offspring too of the same moment. Of his music there are no specimens—he wanted the art of noting it down—if it equalled many of his drawings, and some of his songs, we have lost melodies of real value. (Bentley 482)

It turns out, of course, that just as Blake's visionary powers were rooted in earthly experience, so was his auditory imagination; in his paintings God and Sir Isaac Newton both have Michelangelesque modeling, and it is no surprise to learn that Blake's melodies had their sublunary precursors as well. A letter from Mary Ann Linnell to her husband in October of 1825 may be cited as evidence:

> He was very fond of hearing Mrs. Linnell sing Scottish songs, and would sit by the pianoforte, tears falling from his eyes, while he listened to the Border Melody, to which the song is set, commencing—
>
> 'O Nancy's hair is yellow as gowd,
> And her een as the lift are blue.'
>
> To simple national melodies Blake was very impressionable, though not so to music of more complicated structure. He himself still sang, in a voice tremulous with age, sometimes old ballads, sometimes his own songs, to melodies of his own. (Bentley 305)

We may also imagine that, for all his disgust with conventional Christianity, Blake's auditory memory was stocked with hymns and chants, psalms and responsories—though to some degree his distaste for the churches of his day had to do with the austerity of eighteenth-century liturgies. One feels tempted to allow Blake a willing suspension of naturalistic skepticism when one reads:

> He passed from Death to an Immortal life on the 12th of August 1827 being in his 69th Year. Such was the Entertainment of the last hour of his life[.] His bursts of gladness made the room peal again. The Walls rang & resounded with the beatific Symphony. It was a prelude to the Hymns of Saints. It was an overture to the Choir of Heaven. It was a chaunt for the response of Angels.
>
> No taught hymns, no psalms got by rote from any hypocritical Sty of Cant, no sickly sanctified Buffoonery; but the pure & clear stream of divine fervour, Enlivened by firm faith & unrelenting hope. 'By the rivers he had sat down & wept[;] he had hung his Harp upon the Willow: 'for how should

he sing the Lords Song in a Strange land.' But he is now on the borders of his promise, he is tuning his strings[,] he is waking up his Lyre. He is lifting up the throat as the lark in the clouds of morn. He is rising[,] he is on the Wing, Sing ye Sons of Morning for the Vapours of Night are flown, & the dews of Darkness are passed away. (Bentley 528)

G. E. Bentley Jr., editor of the *Blake Records*, warns us about this account, which comes from Frederick Tatham's *Life of Blake* (ca. 1832), that "Tatham's vigorous but naive piety both colours his views and repeatedly leads him from his subject. Further, Tatham's facts are not uniformly reliable" (508). But the more reliable Cunningham also said, "He lay chaunting songs, and the verses and the music were both the offspring of the moment" (502). As with Milton, we may allow a miraculous intervention of the Holy Spirit, so long as we also allow the (equally miraculous) conduits through which the Spirit passed, filling Blake's imagination with melody as well as with visual images, and making us regret that along with the drawings with which he illuminated his songs, he did not leave us musical scores as well. And yet how much are we really missing? How many of us, after years of loving "The Sick Rose" and "The Tyger," have found that our experience of Blake as a poet is much intensified by acquiring copies of, for example, the lovely and inexpensive Dover Press facsimiles? Would the poems seem better than they already do if we had Blake's music? I doubt that they would.

Blake did not have much to say directly about music. A recurrent notion in his poetry is "airy music," "music in the air," or "the music of an angel's tongue." Listing the senses and their functions in the introduction to *Europe*, he assigns to the ear only this: "Thro one hears music of the spheres." Most of the time, then, Blake conceives of music as an act of the auditory imagination, or a divine communication. The right to self-contradiction, however, was as dear to Blake as to Emerson and Whitman; in *A Descriptive Catalogue*, which accompanied an exhibition of his paintings, he wrote: "Poetry, as it exists now on earth, in the various remains of ancient authors, Music as it exists in old tunes or melodies, Painting and Sculpture as it exists in the remains of Antiquity and in the works of more modern genius, is Inspiration, and cannot be surpassed; it is perfect and eternal" (*Complete Writings* 579). In the same passage he mentions Michelangelo and Raphael, the lineaments of whose work pervade his paintings, much as the "old tunes and melodies" do his poetry.

Just as Burns had his precursors among Scottish poets, Blake had his among the British. Isaac Watts not only wrote hymns and devotional poetry for adults but composed *Divine Songs for the Use of Children* (1720), the tone of which clearly anticipates Blake's "songs." A single one of these, "Against Quarreling

and Fighting," may bring to mind several poems by Blake, as well as favorite
figures of speech:

> Let Dogs delight to bark and bite,
>   For GOD hath made them so;
> Let Bears and Lions growl and fight,
>   For 'tis their Nature too.
>
> But, Children, you should never let
>   Such angry Passions rise;
> Your little Hands were never made
>   To tear each other's Eyes.
>
> Let Love thro' all your Actions run,
>   And all your Words be mild;
> Live like the blessed Virgin's Son,
>   That sweet and lovely Child.
>
> His Soul was gentle as a Lamb;
>   And as his Stature grew,
> He grew in Favour both with Man,
>   And GOD his Father too.
>
> Now, LORD of all, he reigns above,
>   And from his heav'nly Throne
> He sees what Children dwell in Love,
>   And marks them for his own.
>
> (# 37 OBECV–1926)

Colley Cibber's contribution to *The British Musical Miscellany* (1734) anticipates the humanitarianism of Blake's "Little Black Boy" and chimney sweeper
poems. Cibber's "The Blind Boy" begins:

> O say! What is that Thing called Light,
>   Which I can ne'er enjoy;
> What is the Blessing of the Sight,
>   O tell your poor Blind Boy!

It concludes:

> Then let not what I cannot have
>   My Chear of Mind destroy;
> Whilst thus I sing, I am a King,
>   Altho' a poor Blind Boy.
>
> (# 151 OBECV–1926)

Blake, whose temperament could be genuinely angelic, improved on this mode, which tended to sentimentality or faux-naivete; but the mode was there waiting for him, along with numerous other types of songs and nursery rhymes. The first chapter in Zachary Leader's *Reading Blake's Songs*, entitled "Children's Books, Education, and Vision," amply documents many other connections of this sort; Morton D. Paley in the introduction to *Twentieth Century Interpretations of Songs of Innocence and of Experience* mentions Anna Letitia Barbauld and Christopher Smart's *Hymns for the Amusement of Children*. But Blake's poems are not, of course, children's poems, any more than are Ted Hughes's in *The Earth Owl and Other Moon Creatures* of our own century. Less darkly and sardonically than Hughes (and less comically as well), Blake transformed the well-meant condescension of cautionary and inspirational children's poetry into an ironic vehicle for the instruction (and delight) of adult readers.

Most eighteenth-century orthodoxies disgusted Blake; he let loose on these in his wildly comic play, *An Island in the Moon*, which dates from about 1785. The characters in the play represent types, or actual persons, whom Blake wished to lampoon (including himself). A good example of the Ionesco-like satire is this passage from the beginning of "Chap 9.":

"I say, this evening, we'll all get drunk—I say—dash! An Anthem!
"An Anthem" said Suction.

> "Lo the Bat with Leathern wing,
> "Winking & blinking,
> "Winking & blinking,
> "Winking & blinking,
> "Like Doctor Johnson."

QUID.
" 'Oho', said Doctor Johnson
"To Scipio Africanus,
" 'If you don't own me a Philosopher,
" 'I'll kick your Roman Anus'."

SUCTION.
" 'Aha', To Doctor Johnson
"Said Scipio Africanus,
" 'Lift up my Roman Petticoat
" 'And kiss my Roman Anus'."

"And the Cellar goes down with a step." (Grand Chorus)

(*Complete Writings* 54)

Among the many objects of mockery in the play are the minor modes of eighteenth-century poetry, including the hymn. I can never read the song of the Cynic without hearing the words attaching themselves irreverently to familiar common-measure melodies; I see it as a parody of the hymn, whether Anglican or Methodist. It also reminds me of Milton's parody (invented for utterly different purposes, of course) in *Paradise Lost*, the Unholy Trinity of Satan, Sin, and Death. Blake's obscene antihymn manages simultaneously to call into question God's providence, to lampoon various useless pieties, and to satirize human pretensions that anything can be done about various evils, especially given the state of medicine at the time:

1.
"When old corruption first begun,
     "Adorn'd in yellow vest,
"He committed on flesh a whoredom
     "O, what a wicked beast!

2.
"From them a callow babe did spring,
     "And old corruption smil'd
"To think his race should never end.
     "For now he had a child.

3.
"He call'd him surgery, & fed
     "The babe with his own milk,
"For flesh & he could ne'er agree,
     "She would not let him suck.

4.
"And this he always kept in mind,
     "And form'd a crooked knife,
"And ran about with bloody hands
     "To seek his mother's life.

5.
"And as he ran to seek his mother
     "He met with a dead woman,
"He fell in love & married her,
     "A deed which is not common.

6.
"She soon grew pregnant & brought forth
     "Scurvy & spott'd fever.

"The father grin'd & skipt about,
    "And said, 'I'm made for ever!

7.
" 'For now I have procur'd these imps
    " 'I'll try experiments.'
"With that he tied poor scurvy down
    And stopt up all its vents.

8.
"And when the child began to swell,
    "He shouted out aloud,
" 'I've found the dropsy out, & soon
    'Shall do the world more good.'

9.
"He took up fever by the neck
    "And cut out all its spots
"And thro' the holes which he had made
    "He first discovered guts."

(*Complete Writings* 50–51)

Further on a songfest commences:

"Hang Italian songs! Let's have English!" said Quid. "English genius for
    ever! Here I go:

"Hail Matrimony, made of Love,
"To thy wide gates how great a drove
    "On purpose to be yok'd do come!
"Widows & maids & youths also,
"That lightly trips on beauty's toe,
    "Or sits on beauty's bum.

(56)

The song continues until interrupted by "Scopprell," who asks "How can you
have the face to make game of matrimony?"

Before the play ends, though, we see Blake verging on the serious, if often
ironic, mode of the *Songs of Innocence*, including an early version of "Holy
Thursday." These poems (and, of course, *Songs of Experience*), grow out of
musical patternings, the conventional associations of which Blake has rejected
and burlesqued. Musical in their origins, the *Songs* are resolutely iconoclastic
of the major Augustan poetic norms, especially the weightiness of the closed
heroic couplet; but neither does Blake want any truck with thoughtless (or

conventional) pieties or vapid diversions. For students of prosody, Blake's *Songs* provide a wide variety of examples—combinations of meters and line lengths that are unpredictable among themselves but which usually seem perfectly suited to their individual subjects. Form and matter seem to emerge simultaneously, realized and fused in Blake's auditory, visual, and moral imagination—a structured organicism with expressive functionality in the form. One of the best examples is "The Garden of Love":

> I went to the Garden of Love,
> And saw what I never had seen:
> A Chapel was built in the midst,
> Where I used to play on the green.
>
> And the gates of this Chapel were shut,
> And "Thou shalt not" writ over the door;
> So I turn'd to the Garden of Love
> That so many sweet flowers bore;
>
> And I saw it was filled with graves,
> And tomb-stones where flowers should be;
> And Priests in black gowns were walking their rounds,
> And binding with briars my joys and desires.

Anapestic rhythms are not necessarily always joyful in effect, and never have been; "Lord Randall," for example, which hardly qualifies as a lighthearted sally, is largely anapestic. Serious, even lugubrious, anapestic poems by Tennyson, Yeats, and others are easy to cite. But it is likewise true that—especially in the context of the eighteenth century—anapestic meter seemed somewhat flippant and irreverent in comparison with the staid isosyllabism of iambic pentameter. The opening of "The Garden of Love" in regular anapestic rhythms, then, does establish an expectation of frivolity. It is a settled habit of poets using the meter in English to open the anapestic line with a single unstressed syllable, so we may count these as regular:

> ⋆ ╱ |⋆   ⋆ ╱| ⋆ ⋆ ╱
> I went to the garden of love,
> ⋆   ╱ |⋆ ⋆╱ | ⋆ ⋆   ╱
> And saw what I never had seen:
> ⋆ ╱ |⋆   ⋆ ╱ |⋆ ⋆ ╱
> A Chapel was built in the midst,

At this point the poet tells us that something has changed, that he found something unexpected, and the blithe procession of anapests stumbles over itself:

★ ⁄ |⁄   ★   ⁄ |★   ★   ⁄   [possibly: ★ ★ ⁄ | ★ ⁄ | ★ ★ ⁄]
Where I used to play on the green.

Three of the four lines of the second stanza are metrically ambiguous. To say this is not to suggest that there is any problem in reading the poem, aloud or silently; still less that Blake is mismanaging the meter. Quite the opposite: it is functionally expressive, communicating the corruption that has overtaken the garden:

★   ★   ⁄ |★⁄   ⁄ | ★   ★ ⁄
And the gates of this Chapel were shut,
★   ⁄   ⁄ |⁄   ★   ⁄ |★   ★ ⁄
And "Thou shalt not" writ over the door;
★   ★ ⁄ | ★   ★ ⁄ |★   ★ ⁄
So I turn'd to the Garden of Love
★   ⁄   ⁄ |★ ⁄   ⁄ | ★ ⁄
That so many sweet flowers bore;

The disruptions, especially the prohibitory "Thou shalt not," are almost severe enough to destroy the line's rhythmic basis. With the last stanza, we at first seem to be returning to regular anapests (especially if we pronounce a second syllable in the word "filled"). But at this point the lines expand to tetrameters, further broken apart into dimeters by the internal rhymes. The dance has turned into the plodding gait of a penitential procession. The song has entangled itself in a metrical briar-patch. These alterations parallel and reinforce other changes in theme, imagery, and symbolism—such as the transformation of green to black, flowers to tombstones, childish spontaneity to clerical repression. All of this is the complexity of a purely verbal art, where paradoxically the liberation of the poem from literal music leaves us with an impression of constraint and penury. But this is not imitative form; indeed, the poem has transcended not only any song pattern it may have initially resembled, but has taken wide liberties with the expectations of stanzaic poetry.

As we move forward into the Romantic Era, we find an abundance of lyric poetry, but not much that seems as closely emergent from actual music as that of Burns and Blake. The intent of the poems is to give the impression of musical freshness and spontaneity—which they often do—but melodies, including the lost airs improvised by Blake, can be associated with few of them. Wordsworth does make a few references, scattered through *The Prelude* and elsewhere, to music as a rural diversion, in a marketplace or on a holiday, but for him it is only another picturesque detail of country life, not a source of poetry. When he speaks of music he often means something in nonhuman nature, such as bird songs, waterfalls, or the wind in the trees; or else he uses it as a metaphor of some inaudible moral harmony ("The still, sad music of humanity"). In Raymond Dexter Havens's landmark two-volume study of Wordsworth, *The Mind of the Poet*, no reference to music in connection with the poet can be located in 669 pages of close commentary, analysis, and indexing. As we will see in the following chapter, Coleridge, Keats, and others adapted a ballad pattern as an excuse or occasion to experiment with metrical effects not possible in blank verse, ode, or short lyric, but only for Walter Scott and Thomas Moore, among the better-known poets of the nineteenth century, can we claim an authentic musical derivation, as opposed to a conscious effort to rejoin poetry and music. At this point we may encounter the objection (which could be lodged earlier in connection with Campion and Dowland, as well as eighteenth-century song lyrics) that the Romantics did write poems to be accompanied by music. Keats, Shelley, and Byron mention music in their poems, also writing "songs," "stanzas for music," and so on, but their art is by and large a verbal art that, especially in the case of Byron, has more in common with Cavalier lyrics of the seventeenth century than with any musical context. What these poets did with the lyric was more a revolution in theme, diction, and imagery than in anything metrical. Indeed, just the idea of using a form that appeared on the page to be a song or ballad was sufficiently revolutionary.

But this is not true for Walter Scott, who immersed himself so completely in his medium when collecting and writing the pieces that make up *Minstrelsy of the Scottish Border* (1802–03) that what is folkloric and what his own composition (or that of others with whom he collaborated) cannot, in every instance, be distinguished with certainty. Scott believed that the Border ballads were the compositions of individual minstrels (hence "minstrelsy"), and he saw them in an aristocratic setting comparable to the Provençal troubadours. In the Scott household, ballads were sung, accompanied by piano or harp—a traditional domestic entertainment in aristocratic families (see Sutherland 76). It appears that Scott did not see music and text as inseparable; his earliest interest in the ballads had come through reading, not performances. But as surely as with the troubadours, Wyatt, and Burns, the close connection with a musical tradition lent a grace and power to Scott's compositions. Also, without being literally down to earth as Burns, an actual farmer, had been, Scott always seems in touch with something authentic and living, freed from the artificiality of his English predecessors even as he writes a language much closer to theirs than Burns did. Not exactly a ballad, "Proud Maisie" must be counted among the most rare and valuable of all the tinier gems of British poetry.

Proud Maisie is in the wood
    Walking so early;
Sweet Robin sits on the bush,
    Singing so rarely.

"Tell me, thou bonny bird,
    When shall I marry me?"—
"When six braw gentlemen
    Kirkward shall carry ye."

"Who makes the bridal bed,
    Birdie, say truly?"—
"The gray-headed sexton
    That delves the grave duly.

"The glow-worm o'er grave and stone
    Shall light thee steady,
The owl from the steeple sing,
    'Welcome, proud lady.' "

Unlike Burns and Scott, Thomas Moore composed lyrics that are conspicuously defective without the Irish airs he wrote them to go with. Stripped of the music, the language seems commonplace—in bondage rather than emancipated as in Burns. A comparison reveals the difference; first Burns:

Till a' the seas gang dry, my dear,
    And the rocks melt wi' the sun;
And I will luve thee still, my dear,
    While the sands o' life shall run.

Then Moore:

The harp that once through Tara's halls
    The soul of music shed,
Now hangs as mute on Tara's walls
    As if that soul were fled.—
So sleeps the pride of former days,
    So glory's thrill is o'er,
And hearts that once beat high for praise
    Now feel that pulse no more!

The facile personifications of Moore's poems have too much in common with eighteenth-century poetic diction, whereas Burns ventures boldly into a figure of speech that anticipates the cosmological vision of our own times of the ultimate end of the earth and all earthly things (whatever kinship it may also have with a biblical account as well). As a poet Moore is somewhat retrograde, though in his own way thoroughly successful and enduring, an early nine-eenth-century Bob Dylan, whose lyrics hardly stand alone as poetry.

To a very large extent the revival of the lyric, or revivification of it, had more to do with poets' willingness to commit themselves once again to metrical adventure than with music itself. To write under the inspiration of, or in emulation of, or in conjunction with, melody was only one of many ways of reclaiming for poetry much abandoned territory, of setting forth from the confines of the heroic couplet, of daring to learn from poets whom the eighteenth century, fearing them to be inimitable, had pronounced "incorrect," at least in some respects: Milton, and, in the case of Keats, Shakespeare. Somewhat as Wyatt and Surrey had turned back to Chaucer to make a new beginning, the British Romantics looked to their Renaissance predecessors, and earlier, for help in carrying their art forward, reestablishing a connection with its musical roots, but only for the purpose of moving, with renewed assurance, away from actual music.

❦ 11

A Second Renaissance

EVEN WHEN they composed pieces plainly intended to resemble songs and ballads, the British Romantics grounded themselves firmly in earlier prosody. The resources of this well-established verbal "music" were so familiar to them that they took them for granted. Though within the context of accentual-syllabic meter some changes seemed revolutionary in comparison with the Augustan closed couplet, there was more rediscovery than disruption. Romantic free verse is almost nonexistent, except for sections of Blake's prophetic books. A discussion of Romantic poetry's indebtedness to music, then, becomes largely a matter of saying repeatedly that the poets of the early nineteenth century took their art's emancipation from actual music as a given, and that their own work, for all its genuine originality, exhibits an intensification or variation of specifically poetic art. A discussion of their work as emergent from music, therefore, is virtually identical with a conventional discussion of Romantic prosody. Nevertheless, because of the renewed interest in the *idea* of poetic music, evident in both words of the very title of Wordsworth and Coleridge's collaborative enterprise, *Lyrical Ballads*, a brief survey of Romantic poetic art is useful.

How completely Wordsworth understood the separation of poetry and music, and how far he is from imagining any literal fusion of the two, is made clear in the Preface to the 1802 edition of *Lyrical Ballads*. When he writes "music," he means no more than aural effects found in spoken language; there is no suggestion whatever of actual music.

> Now the music of harmonious metrical language, the sense of difficulty overcome, and the blind association of pleasure which has been previously received from works of rhyme or metre of the same or similar construction, an indistinct perception perpetually renewed of language closely resembling that of real life, and yet, in the circumstance of metre, differing from it so widely, all these imperceptibly make up a complex feeling of delight, which is of the most important use in tempering the painful feeling, which will always be found intermingled with powerful descriptions of the deeper passions. This effect is always produced in pathetic and impassioned poetry;

while, in lighter compositions, the ease and gracefulness with which the Poet manages his numbers are themselves confessedly a principal source of the gratification of the Reader. I might perhaps include all which it is *necessary* to say upon this subject by affirming, what few persons will deny, that, of two descriptions, either of passions, manners, or characters, each of them equally well executed, the one in prose and the other in verse, the verse will be read a hundred times where the prose is read once. We see that Pope by the power of verse alone, has contrived to render the plainest common sense interesting, and even frequently to invest it with the appearance of passion. In consequence of these convictions I related in metre the Tale of GOODY BLAKE and HARRY GILL, which is one of the rudest of this collection. I wished to draw attention to the truth that the power of the human imagination is sufficient to produce such changes even in our physical nature as might almost appear miraculous. The truth is an important one; the fact (for it is a *fact*) is a valuable illustration of it. And I have the satisfaction of knowing that it has been communicated to many hundreds of people who would never have heard of it, had it not been narrated as a Ballad, and in a more impressive metre than is usual in Ballads.

Wordsworth's intention, in the ballad-meter poems that first appeared in *Lyrical Ballads* as well as in the "Lucy" poems, was, as everyone knows, to write poetry that resembled ordinary human speech, preferably that used by plainspoken persons in a rural setting. The result, however, was a species of verse that is characteristically and idiosyncratically Wordsworthian, a voice that never sang on sea or land. Simplicity of language and meter did not really suit Wordsworth; balladry was for him something to dabble in, regularizing what he called the "artless" meter of the old ballads and limiting the vocabulary to the plainest speech. Some of the poems retain a certain charm and pathos, but the narrow range of Wordsworthian pseudosimplicity in the end seems an affectation, easy to identify and often parodied. Phoebe Cary (1824–1871) viewed the affectations and pretensions of her male contemporaries with amusement; here is her version of Wordsworth, "Jacob":

> He dwelt among "apartments let,"
>   About five stories high;
> A man I thought that none would get,
>   And very few would try.
>
> A boulder, by a larger stone
>   Half hidden in the mud,
> Fair as a man when only one
>   Is in the neighborhood.

He lived unknown, and few could tell
  When Jacob was not free;
But he has got a wife,—and O!
  The difference to me!

(Hollander, *American Poetry* 2: 160–61)

But Wordsworth's greatest prosodic achievement was to take what one might call the picturesque pentameter, the toned-down Miltonic blank verse that the British poetic landscapists had been using for nearly a hundred years, and add new stops and voices to it until it could peal out from time to time in the *Prelude* in an organ-blast of Romantic sublimity. That this poetry is at a double or even triple remove from actual music makes it difficult to discuss in terms of music (despite the metaphor that I just employed) without stopping every sentence or two to explain that the relationship was by then profoundly estranged. Many examples leading up to Wordsworth can be cited; passages in the works of William Whitehead, as we have seen, could easily be misidentified as Wordsworth's, and as early as the 1720s we may find in "Winter," from James Thomson's *The Seasons*, the following:

Wide o'er the brim, with many a torrent swell'd,
And the mix'd ruin of its banks o'erspread,
At last the rous'd-up river pours along:
Resistless, roaring, dreadful, down it comes,
From the rude mountain and the mossy wild,
Tumbling through rocks abrupt, and sounding far;
Then o'er the sanded valley floating spreads,
Calm, sluggish, silent; till, again constrained
Between two meeting hills, it bursts a way,
Where rocks and woods o'erhang the turbid stream;
There, gathering triple force, rapid, and deep,
It boils, and wheels, and foams, and thunders through.
  Nature! great parent! whose unceasing hand
Rolls round the seasons of the changeful year,
How mighty, how majestic, are thy works!
With what a pleasing dread they swell the soul.

(94–109)

Thomson has, of course, considerably tempered the headlong rush of Milton's blank verse, and he has restricted himself to things visible to human sight, but the looseness makes a distinct contrast with the epigrammatic terseness introduced by Dryden and perfected by Pope in their closed couplets. Wordsworth and Coleridge, Byron and Shelley, however, felt the enthusiastic fit, the impulse of sublimity, allowing themselves to be swept along by the awful power inherent in nature, and in so doing reverted to a metrics like Milton's. The afflatus with which the Holy Spirit worked through Milton now became the vast breath of a pantheistic spirit that in its milder moments agitated gently the wind harp set in the casement, but which could also roll through all things with resistless violence and splendor. Their confidence in themselves and their vatic role restored by notions gathered from transcendental philosophy, the Romantics put on with renewed confidence the singing robes that the eighteenth century dared not assume.

The evolution from Thomson's relatively restrained descriptive passages to the full-blown sublime of the Romantics occurred in stages, which one can illustrate by quoting from William Somerville's *The Chase*:

> Once more, ye jovial train, your courage try,
> And each clean courser's speed. We scour along
> In pleasing hurry and confusion toss'd;
> Oblivion to be wish'd. The patient pack
> Hang on the scent unwearied; up they climb,
> And ardent we pursue; our labouring steeds
> We press, we gore; till once the summit gain'd,
> Painfully panting, there we breathe a while;
> Then like a foaming torrent, pouring down
> Precipitant, we smoke along the vale.

(223–32)

Mark Akenside, in *The Pleasures of the Imagination* (1744), sets up—in advance of Edmund Burke's formulations—the opposition of the sublime (Shakespeare) and the beautiful (Waller) that would become the basis of Wordsworth's "ministries" of nature; in so doing, Akenside reintroduces a heavily enjambed metric:

> Hence when lightning fires
> The arch of Heaven, and thunders rock the ground,
> When furious whirlwinds rend the howling air,
> And Ocean, groaning from his lowest bed,
> Heaves his tempestuous billows to the sky;
> Amid the mighty uproar, while below
> The nations tremble, Shakspeare looks abroad
> From some high cliff, superior, and enjoys
> The elemental war! But Waller longs
> All on the margin of some flowery stream
> To spread his careless limbs amid the cool

Of plantane shades, and to the listening deer
The tale of slighted vows and love's disdain
Resound soft-warbling all the live-long day

(3:550–63)

Shakespeare's example as well as Milton's authorized what came to be called a "gothic" irregularity, while Waller had been seen as the original model for neoclassical correctness.

A brief catalogue of the sublime may be found in Edward Young's "Night Thoughts" (1742–44):

A part how small of the terraqueous globe
Is tenanted by man! the rest a waste,
Rocks, deserts, frozen seas, and burning sands:
Wild haunts of monsters, poisons, stings, and death.
Such is earth's melancholy map! But, far
More sad! this earth is a true map of man.
So bounded are its haughty lord's delights
To woe's wide empire; where deep troubles toss,
Loud sorrows howl, envenom'd passions bite,
Ravenous calamities our vitals seize,
And threatening fate wide opens to devour.

(284–94)

Passages with metrics similar to these may be found in Whitehead, in the poems of the Wartons, and in many another more obscure poet of the mid- and late eighteenth century. Just as Waller and Denham smoothed the way for neoclassicism, these poets gradually added voices and stops that, when English poetry had need of him, Milton might once again inspire it with what Tennyson called the "God-gifted organ voice of England." As I have argued at length, Milton's "music" had actually carried British poetry further from its original union with its "twin sister" than ever before; the Romantics built upon Milton in their own handling of iambic pentameter, rediscovering that lost or abandoned vitality and extending its range even further. "Who called you forth from night and utter death, / From dark and icy caverns called you forth, / Down those precipitous, black, jaggèd rocks, /Forever shattered and the same forever?" asks Coleridge, in "Hymn Before Sunrise in the Vale of Chamouni" (1802). And he continues a few lines further on:

Ye ice-falls! Ye that from the mountain's brow
Adown enormous ravines slope amain—
Torrents, methinks, that heard a mighty voice,

And stopped at once amid their maddest plunge!
Motionless torrents! silent cataracts!
Who made you glorious as the gates of heaven
Beneath the keen full moon? Who bade the sun
Clothe you with rainbows? Who, with living flowers
Of loveliest blue, spread garlands at your feet?

(49–57)

A few years later, after the disappointment of discovering that he had, as it were, accidentally crossed the Alps without realizing it, Wordsworth recovered sufficiently to experience sublimity after all, and recorded it in one of the most powerful passages of poetry ever written in English. To judge from the 1805 version of *The Prelude* it was the memory of this experience that excited him, more than what he actually felt at the time—an example, perhaps, of commotion recollected in tranquillity.

The immeasurable height
Of woods decaying, never to be decayed,
The stationary blasts of waterfalls,
And in the narrow rent at every turn
Winds thwarting winds, bewildered and forlorn,
The torrents shooting from the clear blue sky,
The rocks that muttered close upon our ears,
Black drizzling crags that spake by the way-side
As if a voice were in them, the sick sight
And giddy prospect of the raving stream,
The unfettered clouds and region of the Heavens,
Tumult and peace, the darkness and the light—
Were all like workings of one mind, the features
Of the same face, blossoms upon one tree;
Characters of the great Apocalypse,
The types and symbols of Eternity,
Of first, and last, and midst, and without end.

(6.617–40)

Alpine scenery figures repeatedly in English Romantic poetry as a subject to be dealt with in terms that became almost predictable, using a freely enjambed pentameter. The speech that Byron assigned to Manfred on the Jungfrau (1816), "alone upon the cliffs," recalls these earlier passages, and mingles something of Edgar's imaginary description of the cliffs of Dover from *King Lear*:

And you, ye crags, upon whose extreme edge
I stand, and on the torrent's brink beneath

Behold the tall pines dwindled as to shrubs
In dizziness of distance; when a leap,
A stir, a motion, even a breath, would bring
My breast upon its rocky bosom's bed
To rest for ever—wherefore do I pause?
I feel the impulse—yet I do not plunge.

(*Manfred* 1.2.13–19)

Shelley, in "Mont Blanc" (1816), borrowed extensively not only from Coleridge's description of the valley of Chamounix, but also from "Kubla Khan," composing in the mode that had by that time become thoroughly established as the sublime. This is not blank verse, but the rhyme scheme is loose and flexible enough to offer little constraint to the onward rush of the poem:

> The race
> Of man, flies far in dread; his work and dwelling
> Vanish, like smoke before the tempest's stream,
> And their place is not known. Below, vast caves
> Shine in the rushing torrents' restless gleam,
> Which from those secret chasms in tumult welling
> Meet in the vale, and one majestic River,
> The breath and blood of distant lands, for ever
> Rolls its loud waters to the ocean waves,
> Breathes its swift vapours to the circling air.
>
> (117–26)

The point in all these examples is to show how Milton's achievement in extending the verbal "music" had been revived and extended by the Romantics.

Coleridge seems to have been more sensitive to the power of actual music and more inspired by it than Wordsworth, but it does not occur to us to think of many of his poems as written for music. He thinks of music, when he is writing in his more prosaic manner in the "conversation" poems, as Wordsworth does, metaphorically and somewhat mystically, the response of the soul to the "plastic and vast" breeze that sweeps through it as does the wind through the aeolian harp, in the poem of that name. When he writes, in his other major mode, the poems of magic and mystery, music takes on supernatural powers, whether to dispel evil forces in *Christabel*, or to conjure up his vision of the pleasure dome in "Kubla Khan" ("That with music loud and long, / I would build that dome in air, / That sunny dome, those caves of ice . . ."). Coleridge did draw inspiration from Percy's *Reliques* and from the poetry of Chatterton that was in part imitated from that source, as in "The Ballad of the Dark Ladié" or, satirically, in "The Devil's Thoughts." His most conspicuous example of medievalized balladry, of course, is "The Rime of the Ancient Mariner." Here he takes the basic ballad stanza, extends it at times to five, six, as many as nine lines; varies it with internal rhyme; even breaks it in two when it serves for dialogue. The handling of the meter is more resilient, more controlled, more adapted to the imagery and rhetoric than in authentic ballads. Coleridge raised to a higher level the kind of poetry that was added to eighteenth-century collections of ballads by contemporary writers; but his intention was to learn from and to improve upon what he found upon the page, not to aspire to a reunion with music. Where trisyllabic feet occur in the old ballad (if, indeed, it is appropriate to speak at all of feet in accounting for their rhythm), they appear often enough simply because the original authors were unable to get by without them. In "The Rime of the Ancient Mariner" such variations are more functional. Take, for example, these two stanzas:

> An orphan's curse would drag to hell
> A spirit from on high;
> But o! more horrible than that
> Is the curse in a dead man's eye!
> Seven days, seven nights, I saw that curse,
> And yet I could not die.
>
> The moving Moon went up the sky,
> And nowhere did abide:
> Softly she was going up,
> And a star or two beside.
>
> (257–66)

The extreme smoothness of "The moving Moon went up the sky, / And nowhere did abide"—a succession of seven perfectly regular iambs—surely gains in effect by the contrast it makes with the troubled meter in the preceding stanza. The calm progress of the heavens turns out to be a harbinger of the mariner's changed fortunes for the better. Although one grasps in vain for rationalizations that will completely account for the power of these and many other lines in the poem, it surely is true that the "music" that comes to the aid of the imagery and the fable is poetic. Unlike Burns and Scott, Coleridge worked only from a written text. That he was untroubled by the separation of music and poetry is evident in his essay "On the Principles of Genial Criticism Concerning the Fine Arts." He subsumes all the arts under the general heading of poetry, but sees them as divided from one another.

> Regarded from these points of view, painting and statuary call on our attention with superior claims. All the fine arts are different species of poetry. The

same spirit speaks to the mind through different senses by manifestations of itself, appropriate to each. They admit therefore of a natural division into poetry of language (poetry in the emphatic sense, because less subject to the accidents and limitations of time and space); poetry of the ear, or music; and poetry of the eye, which is again subdivided into plastic poetry, or statuary, and graphic poetry, or painting. The common essence of all consists in the excitement of emotion for the immediate purpose of pleasure through the medium of beauty; herein contra-distinguishing poetry from science, the immediate object and primary purpose of which is truth and possible utility. (*Biographia Literaria* 2: 220–21)

In "A Defence of Poetry," Shelley made extraordinary claims for his own art and for the poet, making both the origin of almost everything else of value in human life:

> But poets, or those who imagine and express this indestructible order, are not only the authors of language and of music, of the dance, and architecture, and statuary, and painting: they are the institutors of laws, and the founders of civil society, and the inventors of the arts of life, and the teachers, who draw into a certain propinquity with the beautiful and the true, that partial apprehension of the agencies of the invisible world which is called religion.

Possibly because of the inordinate power he assigned to poetry, Shelley found no difficulty in seeing it as entirely separate from music, although he repeatedly lapses into musical metaphors to account for poetry, including the most commonplace Romantic analogies:

> Poetry, in a general sense, may be defined to be "the expression of the imagination"; and poetry is connate with the origin of man. Man is an instrument over which a series of external and internal impressions are driven, like the alternations of an ever-changing wind over an Eolian lyre, which move it by their motion to ever-changing melody. But there is a principle within the human being, and perhaps within all sentient beings, which acts otherwise than in the lyre, and produces not melody alone, but harmony, by an internal adjustment of the sounds, or motions thus excited to the impressions which excite them. It is as if the lyre could accommodate its chords to the motions of that which strikes them, in a determined proportion of sound; even as the musician can accommodate his voice to the sound of the lyre.

Shelley's view of the relations of the arts in ancient times is close to our contemporary consensus:

> It was at the period here adverted to, that the drama had its birth; and however a succeeding writer may have equalled or surpassed those few great

specimens of the Athenian drama which have been preserved to us, it is indisputable that the art itself never was understood or practised according to the true philosophy of it, as at Athens. For the Athenians employed language, action, music, painting, the dance, and religious institutions, to produce a common effect in the representation of the highest idealisms of passion and of power; each division in the art was made perfect in its kind by artists of the most consummate skill, and was disciplined into a beautiful proportion and unity one towards the other.

He goes on to state complacently that music has no part in modern tragedy.

Shelley makes it very clear that whatever its ultimate purposes and claims, poetry itself is an art of words:

Language, colour, form, and religious and civil habits of action, are all the instruments and materials of poetry; they may be called poetry by that figure of speech which considers the effect as a synonyme of the cause. But poetry in a more restricted sense expresses those arrangements of language, and especially metrical language, which are created by that imperial faculty, whose throne is curtained within the invisible nature of man. And this springs from the nature itself of language, which is a more direct representation of the actions and passion of our internal being, and is susceptible of more various and delicate combinations, than colour, form, or motion, and is more plastic and obedient to the control of that faculty of which it is the creation. For language is arbitrarily produced by the imagination, and has relation to thoughts alone; but all other materials, instruments, and conditions of art have relations among each other, which limit and interpose between conception and expression.

The last sentence just quoted might serve as well as anything else yet offered as an explanation of contemporary "Language" poetry in the United States. To say that "language is arbitrarily produced by the imagination" is to arrogate to the individual artist the creative logos, the Word of God. Even more apposite to the issue of how poetry relates to music, though, is the following:

An observation of the regular mode of the recurrence of harmony in the language of poetical minds, together with its relation to music, produced metre, or a certain system of traditional forms of harmony and language. Yet it is by no means essential that a poet should accommodate his language to this traditional form, so that the harmony, which is its spirit, be observed. The practice is indeed convenient and popular, and to be preferred, especially in such composition as includes much action: but every great poet must inevitably innovate upon the example of his predecessors in the exact structure of his peculiar versification.

Shelley equates the original break from musical patterning with the much greater latitude to be allowed poets in his own day, and on into the future, to rely on their original genius to provide them with prosodies suitable for their inspired effusions.

Much of the effect of Shelley's poetry comes from its contrast with eighteenth-century modes and styles, especially the headlong rush, the pause only for exclamation, the inattention to consistency in metaphors:

> Then, from the caverns of my dreamy youth
> I sprang, as one sandalled with plumes of fire,
> And towards the lodestar of my one desire,
> I flitted, like a dizzy moth, whose flight
> Is as a dead leaf's in the owlet light,
> When it would seek in Hesper's setting sphere
> A radiant death, a fiery sepulchre,
> As if it were a lamp of earthly flame.

("Epipsychidion" 217–24)

Although the poem moves in scannable pentameters, the only way to read it is to submit oneself to the evolving process without stopping to reflect—a requirement that Charles Olson carried a step further in his expectation that we accommodate ourselves to the "breath" of the poet. Unlike Dante, who anchors his visionary experience in imagery drawn from ordinary experience, Shelley expects to be followed blindly; to visualize the words quoted above would be disastrous. Words, images, are to be entertained only momentarily, only long enough to communicate their evanescent numina, their transient associations; mainly, we are to listen to the sound of the language, to patterns such as the consonance of "flit" and "flight" in a single line; to alliterations (leaf/light, seek/setting/sphere); to cumulative sound groupings such as the "r" pattern in "A radiant death, a fiery sepulchre." There is also the sinewy and flexible rhythm, a counterpoint of bounds and pauses, the incremental lengthening of introductory phrases, "Then," "I sprang," "I flitted," "A radiant death," most of which are immediately followed by a line in which no caesura can be identified. The poem can be enjoyed only if we refuse to pause. (F. R. Leavis paused frequently in his consideration of Shelley's "Ode to the West Wind" to examine whether the images evoked show any consistency with one another, and concluded that they did not; those of us who continue to enjoy that poem may find in Leavis's strictures an explanation of its power.) Shelley, with more than Miltonic presumption, identified himself with the shaping and transforming spirit that he felt sweeping through all things and assumed it to himself as a source of power; when the sublime madness is upon him, his metrics, more violently than Milton's ever did, hurry us along with rushes and eddies. With rare exceptions, however, he retains an identifiable scansion; he writes little that can be called free verse. One might see an innocent cunning in this: he keeps the meter, but only that it may be continually disrupted. I am speaking of what I take to be Shelley at his most characteristic—the Shelley of *Prometheus Unbound*, for example. He wrote in many other ways as well; "Ozymandias," though freely enjambed, leaves us with an impression of solidity of imagery and stateliness of rhythm.

Of great interest would be a careful study that documented the relative indebtedness of the various British Romantic poets to Milton and to Shakespeare. On the whole the balance tips in the direction of Milton. Milton's prosody authorized licenses that flew in the face of neoclassic orthodoxy, and especially in the face of Doctor Johnson, for whom "Lycidas" was sheer nonsense and who quoted with approval William Locke's remark that blank verse, as in *Paradise Lost*, "seems to be verse only to the eye." Also, Milton's rebelliousness and spiritual self-sufficiency appealed to romantic temperaments, mistaking as they often did the energy with which he endows Satan as sympathy for all those oppressed by authority. One may imagine that Milton's views on divorce found favor with them too, especially with Byron and Shelley. Milton's range was more limited than Shakespeare's, his example less intimidating, more accessible, and more imitable. The only poet of that age who possessed enough courage, humility, and sensitivity to assimilate such riches as Shakespeare had to offer was John Keats. The consequence is that Keats's best poems rise solidly to elevations unattained by any of the others, despite their Alpine sublimity; Shelley's skylark might have soared as high had it not perished from oxygen deprivation after the third or fourth stanza of his poem. Keats's nightingale occupies its proper habitat.

At first, like the others, Keats was much affected by Milton:

Two years later [1818], the powerful influence of Milton suddenly lifted Keats to the high plateau on which he henceforth proceeded. The clairvoyant perception of Longinus, when he speaks of the value of great models in freeing our own aspirations and energy, is relevant to no major poet so much as to Keats. After Milton, the vigor of Dryden was to catch his imagination; and at all times from early 1818 until the end, there was the gradual, pervasive effect on him of Shakespeare. (Bate 86)

The effect was to encourage him in his unintellectual grasp of the auditory riches of his native language, and to trust the evidence of his own senses in the ways that he responded to the wealth of beauty that nature and art had to offer his impressionable mind. Wordsworth saw nature through the bifocals of

Burkean beauty and sublimity; Coleridge, laboring under the weight of literally tons of books (he read thousands), metamorphically transformed their
contents, sometimes ejecting them volcanically; Shelley's doctrinaire views
too often schematized his poetry so that he vitiated his own metaphors and,
despite Keats's good advice, he never did learn to "load his rifts with ore"; and
Byron was in all his writings a performer, dominating center stage for which
his poetry too often served as flies and backdrop. Keats responded to what he
heard, saw, felt, or read with a candor, freshness, and vigor not known since
the Renaissance—indeed in some respects never known before or since in
British poetry—and in Shakespeare he found a model whom, in the lyric
intensity and thematic unity of his mid-length narratives and odes, he eventually surpassed.

The richness of Keats's own poetic line in the great odes has never been
surpassed. At the risk of making the point with deadly insistence, however, I
must say that in achieving this, Keats set even greater distance between his art
and the art of music than had Shakespeare or Milton, so that in discussing his
poetry one tends to forget about music entirely. From time to time Keats
mentions music (as, for example, one element in the scene-painting of "The
Eve of St. Agnes"), or uses the word as a metaphor. But he seems to have had
no particular interest in it as an art; he responded to music much less than to
sculpture or painting. The only use of *music* in his letters is as a synonym for
piano, for (the instrument itself), and that occurs only casually and only a few
times. Instead, from his earliest years he responded to the "music" of English
poetry—as, for example, in his first really successful poem, inspired by reading
George Chapman's translation of Homer. The most perfect example of his art
is probably "To Autumn." A cumulation of images of abundance and fulfil-
ment in the first stanza pour forth from his horn of plenty in a wealth of
vocalic resonances, echoes, and reflections, beginning with the opening lines:
"Season of mists and mellow fruitfulness, / Close bosom-friend of the matur-
ing sun." Other more complex developments follow in "To Autumn," but
always subliminally so that they do not distract (as such things often do in
Tennyson) from the total impression offered by the poem. But "To Autumn"
is not characteristic of the Keats with his pleasure thermometer turned up to
its highest setting, if we may take such a liberty with the metaphor in one of
his letters. Although it misses the perfection of "To Autumn," his "Ode to a
Nightingale," despite one or two near disasters from which we must indul-
gently rescue its author, furnishes more examples of Keats's music, the whole
gamut, the diapason, the changes, or whatever dead metaphor we choose to
characterize his living poetry.

Recognizing that other readers will hear various lines differently from the way I hear them, I have nevertheless, in the transcription of the poem below, marked the lines as follows:

⋆ perfect or nearly perfect iambic pentameter
/ line begins with a stressed syllable
⋆/⋆ line includes a triple foot

Unmarked lines are those that include variants other than the last two above; in other words, as one should expect in most successful poems, the great majority of the lines in the poem are expressive variants on the basic meter.

ODE TO A NIGHTINGALE

1.

My heart aches, and a drowsy numbness pains
    My sense, as though of hemlock I had drunk,
Or emptied some dull opiate to the drains
    One minute past, and Lethe-wards had sunk: ⋆
'Tis not through envy of thy happy lot,
    But being too happy in thine happiness,—
        That thou, light-winged Dryad of the trees,
        In some melodious plot
    Of beechen green, and shadows numberless,   ⋆
    Singest of summer in full-throated ease.   /

2.

O for a draught of vintage! that hath been   /
    Cooled a long age in the deep-delvèd earth,   /
Tasting of Flora and the country green,   /
    Dance, and Provençal song, and sunburnt mirth!   /
O for a beaker full of the warm South,   /
    Full of the true, the blushful Hippocrene,   /
        With beaded bubbles winking at the brim,   ⋆
        And purple-stainèd mouth;
    That I might drink, and leave the world unseen,
    And with thee fade away into the forest dim: ⋆/⋆ [see also discussion]

3.

Fade far away, dissolve, and quite forget   /
    What thou among the leaves hast never known,   ⋆
The weariness, the fever, and the fret   ⋆
    Here, where men sit and hear each other groan;   /

Where palsy shakes a few, sad, last grey hairs,
    Where youth grows pale, and spectre-thin, and dies;
        Where but to think is to be full of sorrow
           And leaden-eyed despairs,
    Where Beauty cannot keep her lustrous eyes,   ★
        Or new Love pine at them beyond to-morrow.   ★

4.
Away! away! for I will fly to thee,   ★
    Not charioted by Bacchus and his pards,   /
But on the viewless wings of Poesy,   ★
    Though the dull brain perplexes and retards:
Already with thee! tender is the night,   ★
    And haply the Queen-Moon is on her throne,
        Clustered around by all her starry Fays;   /
           But here there is no light,
    Save what from heaven is with the breezes blown   /
        Through verdurous glooms and winding mossy ways.   ★ [allowing syncope]

5.
I cannot see what flowers are at my feet,   ★
    Nor what soft incense hangs upon the boughs,
But, in embalmèd darkness, guess each sweet
    Wherewith the seasonable month endows   ★
The grass, the thicket, and the fruit tree wild;
    White hawthorn, and the pastoral eglantine;   /
        Fast fading violets covered up in leaves;   /
           And mid-May's eldest child,
    The coming musk rose, full of dewy wine,   ★
        The murmurous haunt of flies on summer eves.   ★ [allowing syncope]

6.
Darkling I listen; and, for many a time   /
    I have been half in love with easeful Death,
Called him soft names in many a musèd rhyme,   /
    To take into the air my quiet breath;
Now more than ever seems it rich to die   /
    To cease upon the midnight with no pain,   ★
        While thou art pouring forth thy soul abroad   ★
           In such an ecstasy!
    Still wouldst thou sing, and I have ears in vain—
        To thy high requiem become a sod.

7.

Thou wast not born for death, immortal Bird!   ★
   No hungry generations tread thee down;   ★
The voice I hear this passing night was heard   ★
   In ancient days by emperor and clown: ★
Perhaps the self-same song that found a path
   Through the sad heart of Ruth, when, sick for home,
      She stood in tears amid the alien corn;   ★ [allowing
         The same that oft-times hath   synaeresis]
    Charmed magic casements, opening on the foam /
    Of perilous seas, in faery lands forlorn.   ★/★

8.

Forlorn! the very word is like a bell   ★
   To toll me back from thee to my sole self!
Adieu! the fancy cannot cheat so well
   As she is famed to do, deceiving elf.   ★
Adieu! adieu! thy plaintive anthem fades   ★
   Past the near meadows, over the still stream, /
    Up the hillside; and now 'tis buried deep /
      In the next valley glades:
Was it a vision, or a waking dream?   /
   Fled is that music:—Do I wake or sleep?   /

Keats wrote by ear, especially in the great odes; these he transcribed with almost Shakespearian facility, making very few revisions in comparison with, for example, his work on "The Eve of St. Agnes." In his earlier writings—especially in *Endymion*, which is mainly to be admired as a protracted preliminary exercise—Keats had trained himself to choose the words for each line of poetry so as to include, in most lines, the maximum variety of vowel sounds; in doing this, he made certain that when such sounds, or even entire words or parts of words, were repeated in proximity to one another, they would stand out. In other words, the incidence of identical or closely similar vowels is always controlled. To say this is not to suggest that such a strategy had been consciously articulated by Keats; but that is what he usually does in his best poetry. With consonants he went pretty much the other way; many lines are knitted together not necessarily by initial alliteration or complete consonance but by reflective patterning, often by internal slant rhyme, that sometimes carries through to the next line. The general texture of the poems, then, is a language enriched simultaneously by variation of sounds and by recurrence. The units of such variation and recurrence range from the individual syllable to passages that may be several lines long.

In terms of rhythm, Keats's practice is (like that of the late Shakespeare) to take the iambic pentameter completely for granted; only a small proportion of his lines need to observe the template with enough exactness to keep that context in place. In the first stanza of "Ode to a Nightingale" the second and ninth lines are regular enough to lay claim to iambic pentameter, but the second stanza immediately stretches the limits of the metric with six straight lines that invert the initial iambic foot, a declaration of expressive independence. No more than two or three lines in most stanzas seem completely regular, and sometimes it is only the penultimate line that scans regularly, until we come to the ringing declaration that opens the seventh and penultimate stanza: "Thou wast not born for death, immortal Bird!" That line displays some variation (it seems to require a stress on "not"); but it would be hard to mark the next three lines as anything other than quite regular pentameters. That evenness continues into the final stanza, but abruptly disappears; the poem concludes with a remarkable series of five lines, every one of which begins with a syllable that carries at least a partial stress, culminating with the heaviest, "Fled is that music."

To apply conventional accentual-syllabic scansion to this poem, to talk about feet and foot-substitution, is to falsify Keats's meter. As far as I know, Keats never consciously aimed at making quantity a basis of his line, nor did he know enough Latin to have experimented in quantitative meter had it occurred to him to do so. But to ignore the effect of syllable duration in a poem that begins, "My heart aches, and a drowsy numbness pains," is to miss much of the poem's beauty. With Keats, I believe, the management of quantitative effects was intuitive; had Tennyson written the line, it would have been part of some preconceived strategy. Because quantity is not a clearly definable part of English phonology (unlike stress), no rules exist to differentiate clearly between long and short syllables, though some are certainly longer than others. In English, we call a vowel long if it actually consists of two vowel sounds, or is pronounced as if it had a consonant attached to it. Long *a* and *i* are sounded, in standard pronunciation, as if they were followed by an "ee" or "i" sound, whereas long *o* is pronounced as if followed by a "w" and long *u* as if preceded by a "y." Consonants also add to duration, as in Latin poetry, though in English the rule (if it can be called that) is simply that the more consonants that surround a vowel, the longer that syllable is going to be. Stress also adds length. The first line of "Ode to a Nightingale" leads off with a long vowel, followed by a syllable that is stressed and also has three consonants surrounding it, followed by a somewhat lengthened and a short syllable, both unstressed. The opening is actually more remarkable for its stress irregularity than for quantity; a line that read, "My heart aches as I see a robin's egg" renders the quantity unnoticeable (and ruins the line in several other ways as well). Keats, however, rescues his line from incipient melodrama and reinforces the quantitative values by using words that surround each of the remaining syllables with up to five consonants, the stressed syllables being lengthened to about double, I would guess, the average duration in spoken English. Quantity may not be exactly definable but it is certainly there; most people will read a line made up of shorter syllables ("The weariness, the fever, and the fret") in less than three seconds, whereas the opening line needs close to 3.5 seconds—about 20 percent more time. This is as far as I care to go in the direction of specious objectivity on this issue; I think that most readers with good ears for poetry will accede to my general contention that the management of quantity is important in Keats.

Cautious always to avoid overingenious analysis, one might pick out various lines in which quantitative effects are especially prominent. The phrase "some dull opiate" clogs the center of its line with narcotic sluggishness. "Cooled a long age in the deep-delved earth" lengthens and deepens the sense of the line with drawn-out syllables. "Though the dull brain perplexes and retards" entangles its rhythm in tethers of ever-lengthening sounds, as well as in irregularities of rhythm. Sometimes length of syllable isolates and emphasizes: "Haply the Queen-Moon is on her throne" places that monarch in isolation in the middle of the sky, most of the other syllables surrounding her like the "starry fays" of the next line. The declaration, "Thou wast not born for death, immortal Bird!" contains only one syllable that is definitely shorter than average, and this adds to its firmness. More examples might be pointed out, but perhaps these are enough to make the point. I am aware, of course, that I am making some rather large assumptions about the nature of meter in discussing Keats this way; I do believe in the functionality of meter as something more than a pleasing context.

To discuss management of stress and quantity in the poem is only to make a beginning; much else about the patterns of sound invites explication. To explain precisely, for example, why the truncated eighth line in each stanza seems appropriate, and how it functions in each stanza, is difficult. In one way, even better than the rhyme pattern, the shorter line signals in advance the conclusion of the stanza, affords a sort of pause or prosodic punctuation. Keats does maintain the integrity of his stanzas. (Curiously, in the manuscript of the poem, they all seem run together.) Every stanza includes at least two or three enjambed lines, but the closest thing to a link between stanzas is in the third, where Keats picks up the word "fade" from the last preceding line. For all its enthusiasm, for all the exclamatory phrases and purple language, the progress of the poem is strophically decorous.

Several other effects are easy to point out. In response to a list of terms to identify, a student of mine once wrote of *onomatopoeia*, "More often found on tests than in poetry." As Keats concludes the catalog of the sweets "wherewith the seasonable month endows" the scene, a listing that must owe something to the "Musk-rose and the well-attired woodbine" of "Lycidas," he does give us an opportunity to use the term that provoked my student: "The coming musk-rose, full of dewy wine, / The murmurous haunt of flies on summer eves." The rhythm of the last stanza, with its lilting dips and ascents, certainly manages to suggest the flight of the unseen bird as it wings its way out of hearing. "Where palsy shakes a few, sad, last gray hairs" likewise seems to imitate that sad eventuality with forced and not entirely convincing pathos; one feels inclined to excuse Keats for this particular passage since he was clearly thinking of the death of Tom Keats, his brother, and the threat to himself as well from tuberculosis. At least he does not lapse into explicit self-pity as Byron sometimes did, or the Shelley of "I fall upon the thorns of life; I bleed!"

One anomaly in the ode requires commentary. The last line of the second stanza does not scan as a pentameter and makes only a problematic hexameter: "And with thee fade away into the forest dim." Editors may have stuck with this version of the line because its very uncertainty seems appropriate to the idea of losing one's identity as Keats wishes to lose his, with the help of some intoxicant. I do not think that Keats meant the line to read that way, despite the seeming usefulness of the rhythm. Some of the first recensions omitted "away," and this certainly solves the problem technically. What I do not understand is why, since Keats crossed out "the" in his manuscript, the line never appears as "And with thee fade away into forest dim." In isolation, of course, the rhythm is not very pleasing. But other lines in the poem allow trisyllabic substitution, as in "Of perilous seas, in faery lands forlorn," where once again the effect is a trailing-off, and where once again a key work is picked up and repeated to introduce the following stanza. I realize that the rhythm of what one sees in Keats's manuscript is not as smooth as what one obtains by simply removing "away," but a case can be made that it is a functional "fading" of the rhythm. More than that: it's what Keats wrote.

The greatest work of Romantic literary balladry may also be assigned to Keats: "La Belle Dame Sans Merci." Remaining within the traditional four-line pattern, and retaining the length appropriate to many authentic ballads, Keats nevertheless departed at least as far as Coleridge had from the manner and intention of his models. Indeed the very existence of any particular model is problematic. Sources have been suggested (see Bate 478n) for the memorable repeated line, "And no birds sing," and also for the depiction of a young knight who has fallen under the enchantment of an elfin lover; but the poem is in some ways as far from these and as much a work of Keats's own imagination as "The Eve of St. Agnes" is when one thinks of its similarities to *Romeo and Juliet*. I have pointed out, in Chapter 9, a precursor that Keats must have been familiar with: Thomas Warton's "Monody, Written Upon Avon," which describes a vision in which "awful shapes of warriors and kings" suddenly replace the pastoral scene. Also the ballad sometimes called "The Demon Lover" achieves something of the mood that Keats cultivates, though there is more narrative in the older poem.

LA BELLE DAME SANS MERCI
A Ballad

O what can ail thee, knight-at-arms,
    Alone and palely loitering?
The sedge has withered from the lake,
    And no birds sing.

O what can ail thee, knight-at-arms,
    So haggard and so woe-begone?
The squirrel's granary is full,
    And the harvest's done.

I see a lily on thy brow
    With anguish moist and fever dew;
And on thy cheek a fading rose
    Fast withereth too.

"I met a lady in the meads,
    Full beautiful—a faery's child,
Her hair was long, her foot was light,
    And her eyes were wild.

"I made a garland for her head,
    And bracelets too, and fragrant zone;
She looked at me as she did love,
    And made sweet moan.

"I set her on my pacing steed,
    And nothing else saw all day long,
For sideways would she lean, and sing
    A faery's song.

"She found me roots of relish sweet,
    And honey wild, and manna dew;
And sure in language strange she said
    'I love thee true!'

"She took me to her elfin grot,
    And there she wept and sighed full sore,
And there I shut her wild wild eyes
    With kisses four.

"And there she lullèd me asleep,
    And there I dreamed—ah! woe betide!
The latest dream I ever dreamed
    On the cold hill side.

"I saw pale kings, and princes too,
    Pale warriors, death-pale were they all;
Who cried—'La Belle Dame sans merci
    Hath thee in thrall!'

"I saw their starved lips in the gloam,
    With horrid warning gapèd wide,
And I awoke, and found me here,
    On the cold hill side.

"And this is why I sojourn here,
    Alone and palely loitering,
Though the sedge has withered from the lake,
    And no birds sing."

The real subject of "La Belle Dame sans Merci" (if we look for something more serious than a charming, if ominous, vignette of the supernatural) is the darker side of romantic love, where the lover commits himself or herself to another being whose nature suddenly reveals itself to be altogether different from what the lover had supposed. The loss of self-definition that results from putting oneself into the power of another transforms enchantment to horror; the object of devotion seems evil, or possessed by an evil spirit—something other than human, something that cares for the lover only as an object of selfish exploitation. Or, to put it more simply, it is about disillusionment and disappointment in romantic love. Infatuation indulged for its own sake, which under religious sanctions might be transformed into fruitful marriage, gives way instead to a horrible intuition of mortality. Also, the knight-at-arms has allowed himself to be seduced into forgetfulness of whatever other obligations he might have been under; a wretched and dishonorable death awaits him, who has forgotten his quest. That is one reason why Keats's unfortunate revision, at the suggestion of Leigh Hunt, changing the line to, "O what can ail thee, wretched wight," is never honored: it spoils the effect by announcing it in the first line of the poem. To say all this is not, of course, to suggest that Keats was writing cautionary verses, but romantic love was a favorite subject for him (though he could view it with something approaching sardonic amusement at times), and in this poem he explores it, albeit indirectly and through a fable.

The tetrameter of the first three lines of Keats's stanza, though common in ballads, is also the meter used in English poetry for spells or exorcisms (as, for example, in the concluding lines of "Kubla Khan"). Like the lady in the poem, Keats casts a spell and then dissipates it. He makes us feel the uncanniness by leading off with three regular lines in each stanza, followed by a fourth which— sometimes by simplifying the meter even further, sometimes by adding extra syllables—suggests that something has gone wrong with our expectations. Some last lines can be scanned into either two or three stresses ("And her eyes were wild" and "On the cold hill's side"). Another example of rhythmical variation to give an impression of unanticipated disorder, of the discovery of some morbid flaw, may be found in lines 38 and 48. Except for those two lines, the first three in each stanza are perfectly regular iambic tetrameters: first, where the word "death" appears for the first and only time: "Pale warriors, death pale were they all"; second, in "Though the sedge is withered from the lake," where the extra syllable emphasizes the transformation that has occurred since we first heard that line.

Some effects in the poem belong more to rhetoric than to prosody. The use of parataxis ("And . . . And . . ."), common in primitive forms of narrative and in the speech of children, suggests the bewilderment of the knight, his in- ability to make any sense of what has happened. Then there is the effect of switching from "I . . . I . . ." to "She . . . She . . ." and back again, which parallels the enchantment and disillusionment of the speaker. Absent are the devices noted above that enrich Keats's pentameter to the point of satiety; the greater simplicity of sound patterns is in keeping with the other imitations of naivete, of innocence and simplicity.

I have dwelt on Keats at greater length than other poets from this period because in his poems one finds a more complete assimilation of Shakespearian and Miltonic poetic "music" than anywhere else. Of course, other develop- ments besides those mentioned above connect British Romantic poetry with the Renaissance. The sonnet once again came into vogue—Italian, Shake- spearian, and other variants. The Spenserian stanza, employed sporadically in the eighteenth century, was the favored vehicle for important poems by many poets—conspicuous examples being Byron's *Childe Harold's Pilgrimage*, Keats's "Eve of St. Agnes," and Shelley's "Adonais." Curiously, very little can be found in this period that resembles the literary madrigal or other irregular songs. Numerous short poems by these poets were eventually set to music, but compositions of that sort belong rather to the history of music than poetry. It is true, as Edward Doughtie has remarked to me, that settings can reveal a possible reading of a poem, and this surely would be a rewarding direction for further study; but to consider that is to take up problems, such as in Schubert's *Lieder*, that are involved with actual music in a way that I am not qualified to discuss.

To account for the particular ways in which poets writing in English for the rest of the nineteenth century, whether British or American, imitated, varied, or improved upon the innovations of the Romantics would itself require an encyclopedic work. In general, we may say that Tennyson and Browning, Poe and Longfellow, exploited these innovations in ways that were more self-conscious, at times even exhibitionistic or mechanical and "poetic" in a bad sense. The age of accelerating progress in mechanical engineering encouraged, in poetry, a certain amount of gimcrackery, of experimentation with less commonly used feet and meters in various combinations and permutations, of repetition of sounds pushed to the point of deadening tintinnabulation. To say this is not to deny the power of, say, Tennyson's "Ulysses," or the miraculous illusion of actual speech in the enjambed couplets of "My Last Duchess." The Romantics reestablished direct and indirect connections with the musical origins of poetry; the Victorians exploited those connections until the time came when it seemed to many poets most profitable to abandon them altogether—or at least, as Gerard Manley Hopkins did, to wrench them loose. In America, the impulse toward implementing a poetic Declaration of Independence and, later, a prosodic Emancipation Proclamation made new poetries possible that, as always before, evolved out of music. In Britain, three courses lay open: first, complete iconoclasm; next, to continue the work of the Romantics while giving the illusion of reverting to closer connections with music; and finally, and most heroically, to recapitulate the whole process of struggling free from an authentic musical context into an independent poetics.

12

Three American Originals

Two generations after the signing of the Declaration of Independence, the United States of America was still a cultural colony of England. Among those to deplore this was, repeatedly, Emerson, who complained in "The Poet" (1844) about American artists' tame imitativeness: "Their knowledge of the fine arts is some study of rules and particulars, or some limited judgment of color or form, which is exercised for amusement or for show. It is a proof of the shallowness of the doctrine of beauty as it lies in the minds of our amateurs, that men seem to have lost the perception of the instant dependence of form upon soul." Further on he issues his call:

> I look in vain for the poet whom I describe. We do not, with sufficient plainness, or sufficient profoundness, address ourselves to life, nor dare we chaunt our own times and social circumstance. If we filled the day with bravery, we should not shrink from celebrating it. Time and nature yield us many gifts, but not yet the timely man, the new religion, the reconciler, whom all things await. Dante's praise is, that he dared to write his autobiography in colossal cipher, or into universality. We have yet had no genius in America, with tyrannous eye, which knew the value of our incomparable materials, and saw, in the barbarism and materialism of the times, another carnival of the same gods whose picture he so much admires in Homer; then in the middle age; then in Calvinism.

Whitman's almost immediate response to Emerson's exhortation initiated a division in American poetry and poetics that persists to this day: indigenous versus inherited; formality versus free verse; academic versus street poetry; "cooked" versus "raw." At this writing Language Poetry and the (already aging) New Formalism continue the split, which in some respects parallels the way that the American political structure owes much to English common law, while simultaneously embracing a vastly expanded concept of the natural rights of individual human beings that is distinctively American. Many Americans have accepted British poetry, from Chaucer (or even *Beowulf*) to Hardy and Yeats, as a large part of their heritage, a poetic Toryism. At the same time, the "roughs" (to use Whitman's term), the unenfranchised, the shaggy messiahs, the undisciplined mystics, the literary Johnny Appleseeds and Paul Bun-yans, have found audiences for their quirky or apocalyptic utterances. Milton, but more especially Keats and Tennyson, remain important points of contact or initiation, at least for more formally inclined American poets, into the resources of poetic "music" that has for hundreds of years pursued its own development at a great distance from its literally musical associations. The more authentically American kinds of poetry, however, have availed them-selves—with a certain awkward frankness not found in Horace or Ovid, Dante or the troubadours, or even in Wyatt and Burns—of musical contexts and models that had been relatively unexplored. Or perhaps the way to put it is to say that an instinct for poetic self-preservation prompted them to appropriate what seemed to their ears both familiar and vital, eschewing the cultivated and reassuring rhythms and diction of successive ages of British poetry—of Pope, Wordsworth, and Tennyson.

To illustrate what I have just said adequately would result in a fat history of American poetry. Instead of trying to cover everything, taking the time, say, to explain what Carl Sandburg's poems may have owed to his guitar playing, or how some of e. e. cummings's suggest a jazz solo, I will consider only three figures whom most will agree are distinctively American and also of first importance in American literary history.

WHITMAN

Opinions about Walt Whitman's indebtedness to music are as various as opin-ions about Whitman himself. Robert D. Faner's 249-page *Walt Whitman and Opera* makes the case with legalistic pertinacity that Whitman's experience with opera was the most important determinant of his poetry, using as his fundamental authority a sentence in an article that Faner claimed to be "con-vincingly identified as by Whitman" (vii n), which defends "Out of the Cradle Endlessly Rocking." That sentence reads, "Walt Whitman's method in the construction of his songs is strictly the method of the Italian Opera." At the opposite extreme is Roger Asselineau's statement: "If Whitman attached to form—especially at the beginning of his career—only a secondary impor-tance, his indifference to music was even greater" (239). Asselineau was con-vinced that Whitman's appeal was altogether typographical, from the page, and he succeeds in tracking down passages and phrases from Whitman's prose and poetry that appear to support such a view. Somewhere between is Gay Wilson Allen: "The flat assertion that 'Walt Whitman's method in the con-struction of his songs is strictly the method of the Italian Opera' was certainly an exaggeration. But the musical analogy was pertinent, and may still lead readers to a clearer understanding of the poem" (232–33).

What shall we say to all this? Does Whitman contradict himself? Very well, he contradicts himself, being large enough to contain multitudes of scholars and critics as well as everything else. But what are the facts?

One fact is that Whitman did love music and reveled in the many different forms it took. In the *Broadway Journal* of November 29, 1845, he wrote:

> Great is the power of Music over a people! As for us of America, we have long enough followed obedient and child-like in the track of the Old World. We have received her tenors and her buffos [buffas]; her operatic troupes and her vocalists, of all grades and complexions; listened to and applauded the songs made for a different state of society—made, perhaps, by royal genius, but made to please royal ears likewise; and it is time that such listening and receiving should cease. The subtlest spirit of a nation is expressed through its music—and the music acts reciprocally on the nation's very soul. Its effects may not be seen in a day, or a year, and yet these effects are potent invisibly. They enter into religious feelings—they tinge the manners and morals—they are active even in the choice of legislators and high magistrates. Tariffs can be varied to fit circumstances—bad laws can be obliterated and good ones formed—those enactments which relate to commerce or national policy, built up or taken away, stretched or contracted, to suit the will of the government for the time being. But no human power can thoroughly suppress the spirit which lives in national lyrics, and sounds in the favorite melodies sung by high and low. (*Poetry and Prose* 1: 104)

It sounds as if Whitman is carrying over into music Emerson's prescriptions for American poetry, which affected Whitman's views of himself as a writer. But although he here protests that "it is time such listening and receiving should cease," he himself had been and continued to be very much the listener and receiver of European music. At about the same time that he was writing the passage just quoted, he found time to share his compatriots' enthusiasm for foreign imports:

> We welcome this man [the violinist Camillo Sivori] among us;—for heavenly genius belongs to no country, and we scorn the common cant which would sneer at such genius' highest development, merely because its birthplace was in a distant land! We scorn to join in the ready cry of "humbug" at such a man as Sivori—merely because he speaks broken English, and has ascended in his profession to that "height of the great argument," for which the vulgar taste has no appreciation! (*Gathering* 355)

As much as we may wish to pause and savor a denunciation of vulgarity by Walt Whitman, we must move on a few years, to a piece in the New York

Evening Post of August 14, 1851. The cause of Whitman's transport was a performance of Donizetti's *La Favorita*:

> Have not you, in like manner, while listening to the well-played music of some band like Maretzek's [manager of the New York Opera House], felt an overwhelming desire for measureless sound—a sublime orchestra of a myriad orchestras—a colossal volume of harmony, in which the thunder might roll in its proper place; and above it, the vast, pure Tenor,—identity of the Creative Power itself—rising through the universe, until the boundless and unspeakable capacities of that mystery, the human soul, should be filled to the uttermost, and the problem of human cravingness be satisfied and destroyed? (*Poetry and Prose* 256)

Numerous other attestations to an enthusiasm for music may be garnered from Whitman's letters, essays, and poems. The indefatigable Faner assembled from the titles and text of *Leaves of Grass* a list of more than two hundred musical terms, arranged alphabetically from "accompaniment" to "wardrum" and comprising more than a thousand occurrences. Leading the list are "song" (154), "sing" (117), and "chant" (77). Faner's purpose throughout is to drum up support for the opera-as-causation theory, and he makes much of the fact that the list is heavily weighted with terms applicable to opera—including names of composers, performers, and characters. But the evidence works even better to support the general contention that Whitman loved music and habitually thought in musical terms and analogies. One need go no further than the opening lines, or even the title, of "Song of Myself" to illustrate this. Many readers are struck with the odd appropriateness of "Thee for my recitative" at the start of "To a Locomotive in Winter." For numerous other examples, easy to find, we might look at the beginning of "Passage to India":

> Singing my days.
> Singing the great achievements of the present,
> Singing the strong light works of engineers. . . .

The catalog of all sorts and conditions of men and women in section 15 of "Song of Myself" leads off with "The pure contralto sings in the organ loft," and also includes, "The conductor beats time for the band and all the performers follow him"—along with the prostitutes, the President, the pike-fisher, the patriarchs, the pilot, the paving-man, and the policemen, to name only those that begin with *p* in that enormous multitude.

How do we reconcile this enthusiasm for music and musicians with ordinary perception that the great bulk of Whitman's work is conspicuously, almost aggressively, unmusical in the poetic sense—that he distanced himself from the imported gentility of British meters, and especially from the false Tennysonian refinement of so much American poetry of his time? It may be worth remark-ing parenthetically at this point that Whitman much admired Tennyson both as a poet and as a person, setting him alongside the great names of the past (see Blodgett 122); but he thought Tennyson appropriate to England and the English. If there was going to be American music, or American poetry, he felt, it would have to be something new and different; and the way to make sure that the poetry, at least, was different was to write it so that it perpetually challenged imported prosodies. But in doing this Whitman connected himself with a line of poetic development that was in its remoter origins musical, though so distantly that to this day unsympathetic readers find in *Leaves of Grass* little more than amorphous and self-indulgent rant, unwilling to go even as far as Tenny-son did when he said of him, "Whitman is a great big something, I do not know what. But I honor him" (qtd. in Blodgett 126). The strains that really filled Whitman's ears had nothing to do with the Italian arias that filled his heart with joy, or the homely songs and ballads in which he found comfort and reassur-ance; neither the cadenzas of visiting virtuosi nor the street-corner bands of Manhattan found their way into his poetry except as subjects, or as part of his omnivorous acceptance of the riches that life had to offer. Instead, echoing down the ages, resounding by then most faintly through the readings of Scripture in and out of church, and in the quotations from Scripture in popular oratory, was something closer to the blast of the ram's horns that brought down the walls of Jericho: the impassioned cantillation of the Jewish Temple, as rendered into English by the committee of scholars who had prepared the King James Version of the Bible. With the original music, of course, Whitman could have no contact—and I am certainly not suggesting that the God of Isaac and Abraham had made his way to Camden to give Walt private music lessons. But Whitman, as others before him—Traherne, Smart, and Blake, for example—sensed the possibility of a musically inspired metric behind the biblical ca-dences, inherent in the rhetorical patterns, that could authorize a new poetics. The problem is that the actual musical context was already so remote and problematic that it could not actually enter into the poetry, and in fact served more as an excuse for writing free verse, for writing *against* the accepted conventions of English poetry.

To see just how Whitman's metrics play against the expectations of regular iambic meter, let us examine a single short poem—one of his best—"Cavalry Crossing a Ford":

> A line in long array where they wind betwixt green islands,
> They take a serpentine course, their arms flash in the sun—hark to the
> musical clank,

Behold the silvery river, in it the splashing horses loitering stop to drink,
Behold the brown-faced men, each group, each person, a picture, the
    negligent rest on the saddles,
Some emerge on the opposite bank, others are just entering the ford—while,
Scarlet and blue and snowy white,
The guidon flags flutter gayly in the wind.

Although it is pleasant to read the poem for the beauty of its phrasing and the candor of the imagery, accepting its vision as we might accept a photograph by Matthew Brady or a painting by one of the American Realists, we may also account for its effect if we consider the rhythmical progression that occurs. The basic pattern establishes itself in the first phrase:

★ / ★ / ★ /
A line in long array

For the first five lines we have phrases or groups of phrases that subdivide each line into three-stress units, and the phrase is itself subdivided by three in the fourth line ("each group, each person, a picture") as the poet's eye singles out individual soldiers. The simplicity of the initial three iambs disappears and never recurs; "where they wind betwixt green islands" could be scanned in various ways, using conventional feet, calling it either anapest-iamb-spondee, or amphibrach-iamb-spondee, but it may be best simply to observe that every three-stress group that follows introduces some new variation:

A line in long array // where they wind betwixt green islands, //
They take a serpentine course, // their arms flash in the sun— // hark to
    the musical clank, //
Behold the silvery river, // in it the splashing horses // loitering stop to
    drink, //
Behold the brown-faced men, // each group, each person, a picture, // the
    negligent rest on the saddles.

The meter used by James Dickey, a twentieth-century Southern transcendentalist, in many of his best poems is much like this, except that Dickey made a separate line of each three-stress group, as in the opening of "Cherrylog Road":

Off Highway 106
At Cherrylog Road I entered
The '34 Ford without wheels. . . .

The result, in Whitman's poem, is similar in some ways to another famous passage that begins, "Out of the cradle endlessly rocking," where he sets up a dipodic rhythm (much like the classical Adonic foot): / ★ ★ / ★, repeated twice. In that passage he then retains the Adonic (which could also be called a dactyl/trochee) for the first part of each following line, then varies the second part of the line. Though in "Cavalry Crossing a Ford" the iambic trimeter occurs only once, there is the same sense of continuous variation against an established standard. The effect is very beautiful, and equally lovely is the way that Whitman undoes and resolves what he has established. The fifth line seems to lead off like all the others:

    ★   ★ /   ★ ★ / ★ ★ /
    Some emerge on the opposite bank. . . .

Or does it? Read without the context of the established rhythm, as ordinary prose, the stress pattern might well be: / ★ / ★ ★ / ★ ★ /. The rest of the line is even more ambiguous; indeed, it is hard to read "others are just entering the ford—while" with any regular rhythm. To reduce that phrase to three stresses wrenches the natural intonation. The line that follows is unambiguously four beats, and the last line seems to "flutter" between four and six stresses. I am not arguing that the meter is imitative or expressive of what is described, but that the rhythm interweaves with the rhetoric and imagery, making us see and hear more clearly what Whitman had seen, heard, and felt. The most obvious example occurs when the red, blue, and white of the guidons makes a visual parallel with the tripartite rhythms up to that point.

Analysis of this brilliant vignette could easily be protracted. Deft touches of alliteration—both initial consonants and open vowels—spot themselves through the poem: "line in long," "behold the brown-faced men," "person, a picture," "emerge on the opposite, others are just entering." But the alliteration does not really take possession of the line until the three-beat rhythm has been completely defeated in the last line: "guidon flags flutter gaily." In the first two lines a succession of terminal nasals makes us feel the continuity (initially) of the line of march: "line," "long," "wind," "between," "green islands," "serpentine," "arms," "sun."

Where did Whitman get his poetic music from? Not from the operas that he loved, surely, although one might make the case that his deliberate prosiness, in comparison with most of his contemporaries (Poe or Whittier, for example), resembles the flatness of recitative as compared to aria. Nor is there anything in Whitman remotely like the songs and ballads of his times. His metrics fly in the face of all earlier writings known to him as poetry, with the possible exception of "Ossian." I have already answered this question, as have numerous others; we all recognize the rhythms modeled on the original Hebrew (and which the New Testament authors often reproduced in Greek), the repetitive and often responsive, loose, three- and four-beat patterns that the King James translators tried to carry into English: "Thou preparest a table before me // in the presence of mine enemies; // thou anointest my head with oil; // my cup runneth over."

The problem is that too often Whitman's license, which this biblical manner allowed, strays into licentiousness. He seduces us with a series of mellifluous cadences—and then dilates in an expanse of self-indulgent rant. That, at least, is my own experience in reading Whitman. Rapt Olsonian, even Ginsbergian, cultists will start out of their rhapsodic abandon and emerge from the Oversoul to vilify such a description of their messiah. Anglophilic formalists will sidle away lest they be enfolded in Walt's bearhug, and will refuse him even a polite handshake. Borrowing Mark Twain's quip about Wagner, however, we may say that sometimes Whitman is not as bad as he sounds. If only he were always at his best! But Emerson had excused him in advance from any doubts that whatever he did was good enough, and even more than Wordsworth he suffered the consequences of his spontaneity.

Some who are not very fond of Whitman may not wish to go so far as Yvor Winters did:

> To say that a poet is justified in employing a disintegrating form in order to express a feeling of disintegration, is merely a sophistical justification of bad poetry, akin to the Whitmanian notion that one must write loose and sprawling poetry to "express" the loose and sprawling American continent. In fact, all feeling, if one gives oneself (that is, one's form) up to it, is a way of disintegration; poetic form is by definition a means to arrest the disintegration and order the feeling; and in so far as any poetry tends toward the formless, it fails to be expressive of anything. (144)

George Santayana, who clearly felt Whitman's appeal and did not despise him, censured him in terms that even some of Whitman's admirers may be able to understand, though they will not agree: "This abundance of detail without organisation, this wealth of perception without intelligence and of imagination without taste, makes the singularity of Whitman's genius" (128).

Reverting to the question of Whitman's use of a musical tradition and of his own poetic musicality, we may say that he was much more the innovator than the accomplished artist. The tendency of Americans to reverence originality, even eccentricity, above all else—to value the "voice" of the poet for its distinctive qualities—accounts for much of Whitman's stature in American literature. "Whoso would be a man must be a nonconformist," said Emerson in "Self-Reliance." No one can deny Whitman his distinction, but as Tennyson recognized, he is more of a phenomenon than a poet. The tradition to which

he attempted to attach himself was rhetorical rather than musical. He cultivated a messianic manner that derives from the religious authority of biblical
utterance, the cadenced prose of the King James Version and not religious
chanting. In that respect Ginsberg was a more authentic poet than Whitman,
because Ginsberg was a Jew for whom the Hebrew chant was a living reality,
not a distant cultural recollection imperfectly communicated through English
translation. In cultivating his biblical-anaphoric metrics, Whitman escaped
the deadening influence of Tennyson that ruined much nineteenth-century
American poetry, but in so doing also cut himself off from earlier British resources that would fountain forth so copiously in American poetry of the next
century—in the work of Robinson, Stevens, Frost, Ransom, Tate, Roethke,
and numerous others. The "new wood"—to use Pound's phrase—that Whitman broke has yet to be carved and finished; instead, we have had squads of
incompetent ax-wielders who hack about with abandon, irresponsible Whit-
manizers who only occasionally succeed as poets. Enduring poetry will always
be an art that requires the poet to articulate sweet sounds together, as Yeats put
it, and in Whitman we find such poetry only in isolated patches.

DICKINSON

Emily Dickinson's prosody has been more completely analyzed than that of
any other poet. To say this is not to imply that there is more written about hers
than anyone else's but, because her range is more limited than any other great
poet's, coverage is more intense and complete; scholarship has been not only
thorough, but also cumulative. Nothing sensible is likely to occur to one to say
that someone else has not already said. I had thought it was my own perception, for example, that in her best poems, as in many of Hardy's, the hymn
meter—usually associated with expressions of faith and rejoicing—offers an
ironic comment on the uncompromising severity of her own outlook. But
this idea, or something like it, has been debated for thirty years or more (see
Small 41). The poems lend themselves to tabulations and classifications in
terms of their forms; despite her huge output, there are so many seeming
similarities that one student after another has been tempted into statistical
analysis or minute differentiations of scansion in an effort to identify and
quantitize the beauties of her poems as well as her quirkiness (see, for example,
Lindberg-Seyersted 127–80). A good example is the following:

Of 4,840 rhymes in Dickinson's poems, 2,006 (41.4%) are exact (of the type
see/me, 1732); 167 (3.5%) pair a vowel with a reduced version of itself
(me/immortality, 712); 80 (1.6%) are assonantal (breath/quench, 422); 731

(15.1%) are vowel (blew/sky, 354); 1,535 (31.7%) are consonantal (mean/sun, 411); 164 (3.4%) pair a consonant with a cluster containing that consonant (night/erect, 419); 23 pair a cluster with another cluster that shares one consonant with it (disclosed/blind, 761); 2 rhyme a cluster with the same cluster reversed (used/birds, 430); 84 (1.7%) rhyme one nasal consonant with another (thing/begun, 565); 20 rhyme one fricative with another (breeze/divorce, 896); 2 rhyme one voiced stop with another (sob/wood, 45); 5 rhyme one unvoiced stop with another (frock/night, 584); 21 rhyme-positions show less close approximations to exact rhyme, and cannot be considered rhyme at all (for instance, blaze/forge in 365). (Timothy Morris 30; qtd. in Small 14–15)

Thomas H. Johnson is usually credited with first describing at length something that has occurred independently to numerous readers of Dickinson: "Basically all her poems employ meters derived from English hymnology. They are usually iambic or trochaic, but occasionally dactylic. They were the metric forms familiar to her from childhood as the measures in which Watts's hymns were composed" (84). Johnson continues, supplying evidence that Watts's hymn books were in the Dickinson house and that they included advice on formal patterning of language meant for hymns. He describes many of the named hymn measures and explains how Dickinson accommodated what she had to say within these rather strict limitations, with the help of slant rhyme, assonance, and so on in place of the expected exact rhymes. Other studies point to the children's poems by Watts that I have mentioned as models for Blake, to ballads, and to various song books, including those used at schools that Dickinson attended. There is, indeed, a minor bibliographical industry founded on such investigations (see discussion and notes, Lindberg-Seyersted 129–31; Small 41–51).

From whatever source or combination of sources she drew on, the general impression of Dickinson's verse is of idiosyncratic improvisations, on familiar rhythmic patterns, that set themselves sharply apart from any grand tradition of iambic pentameter versification. This is a prosodic analogue, or rather, dimension, of her self-definition, another way of isolating herself. Earlier commentaries, such as those of Allen Tate and Yvor Winters (283–99), tended to account for this isolation in religious or intellectual terms, as a consequence of her "puritan temper" or immersion in Calvinism and rejection of it, a sense of election but an election, in the end, to nothingness, leaving her with little else than an intense intuition of her own immediate and lonely existence. Feminist treatments see her predicament as sexual and her metrics as part of her sexual self-definition, even going so far as to argue, in Annie Finch's study, that her meter is a wrenched and rejected patriarchal iambic pentameter.

Whatever the precise sources and whatever the ultimate function of her meters and forms, few readers of Dickinson are likely to reject the idea that her poems are as close to music as many I have examined so far—not as intimately entwined as troubadour poetry or of as immediate a provenance as Burns's, but perhaps as close as Wyatt's. There seems no record of her actually singing them, as Blake sang his—but who is to say that she did not? Hardly anyone even saw them on paper, and although it is nothing but speculation, it is easy to imagine that she, like the slightly more gregarious Blake, sometimes composed according to tunes that she knew or invented. What is definitely known is that as a child she loved to play the piano, and that she entertained some sort of ambition as a musician:

> That, at a certain point, she made a professional decision about music is suggested in Clara Bellinger Green's memory of her conversation with ED after Nora Green sang for her: "She told us of her early love for the piano and confided that, after hearing Rubinstein [?]—I believe it was Rubinstein— play in Boston, she had become convinced that she could never master the art and had forthwith abandoned it once and for all, giving herself up then wholly to literature." (Sewall 409 n)

A number of different accounts describe how in later years Emily, in the middle of the night, would play the piano for herself, improvising "heavenly music"—what she herself called "the old, odd tunes . . . which used to flit about your head after honest hours" (see Sewall 406–7).

> At any rate, the nocturnal sessions that John was privileged to hear are of no little significance in what they tell us about her music and the part it played in her developing poetic career. In the early days she enjoyed most of the musical opportunities of the neighborhood. She took lessons in voice and piano. She heard Jenny Lind in Northampton in 1851 ("*Herself,* and not her music," she wrote Austin, "was what we seemed to love"); in 1853, Graves took her and Vinnie to a concert by the famous Germania Serenade Band, then on a national tour (she called them "*brazen Robins*"); she spoke of a pleasant meeting of the "girls 'Musical'" at her house in April 1853 and (perhaps) of being unable to attend another some six years later.
>
> But all this time she was getting deeper and deeper into a music of a different sort. In her second letter to Higginson she wrote that "the noise in the Pool, at Noon—excels my Piano." As her practical interest in music declined, her metaphoric interest increased. In trying to capture in her poetry the "music" of nature, she put to use all she had learned about music as a child, and in college, and from the hymns she heard in church, whose metrical schemes were to become her chosen and all but exclusive form. (Sewall 407–8)

This may well remind us of Blake—Emily picking tunes out of the air that only she could hear, but which must necessarily have borne, for all their uncanny charm, some resemblance to songs and hymns of her childhood. The inner melody was the auditory equivalent of the Inner Light, but for her more tentative, uncertain, perhaps jarring at times, and fading in the end until she could not only "not see to see" but also not hear to hear. In much the same way, both rhythm and meaning trail into obscurity in many of her poems, as faith wavers, changed into an expectation of annihilation. The good news, told over and over in the hymns, gives way to an inconclusive journey.

THERE IS A LAND OF PURE DELIGHT

There is a land of pure delight,
Where saints immortal reign,
Infinite day excludes the night,
And pleasures banish pain.

There everlasting spring abides,
And never with'ring flow'rs,
Death, like a narrow sea divides
This heav'nly land from ours.

(Watts, 1709)

712

Because I could not stop for Death—
He kindly stopped for me—
The Carriage held but just Ourselves—
And Immortality.

We slowly drove—He knew no haste
And I had put away
My labor and my leisure too,
For His Civility—

We passed the School, where Children strove
At Recess—in the Ring—
We passed the Fields of Gazing Grain—
We passed the Setting Sun—

Or rather—He passed Us—
The Dews drew quivering and chill—
For only Gossamer, my Gown—
My Tippet—only Tulle—

We paused before a House that seemed
A Swelling of the Ground—
The Roof was scarcely visible—
The Cornice—in the Ground—

Since then—'tis Centuries—and yet
Feels shorter than the Day
I first surmised the Horses Heads
Were toward Eternity—

No discussion has ever succeeded in capturing the essence of this poem, though some, such as Allen Tate's, give the impression of a reader who has vividly experienced it. To explain it is constantly to approach from a direction tangential to its meaning, perhaps because the location that we aim at is itself elusively in motion. "Because I could not stop for Death": she had thought herself a traveler—one must be moving before one can stop; but in fact she was going nowhere at all, the short course that she pursued through the world suddenly shrunk to an immobile point in time by the perception of its finitude. And then Death, kind gentleman in a black waistcoat, pauses, opens the door to his carriage, and she is off again on a chronological trajectory that is so fast that it, too, is a stasis, or almost, shrinking the remainder of life into a single day so that the childhood of the morning reaches instantly to night, to the grave, with the sun arcing overhead much as a technician in a planetarium will accelerate the sweep of the stars to suggest the telescoping of eons into seconds. The poem also seems an uncanny anticipation of various metaphorical explanations of physical relativity, the shrinking of linear dimension as acceleration approaches the speed of light, for example: Death, Immortality, and a young woman together as passengers—an even more striking conjunction of antinomies than the guiltless forces of nature in Thomas Hardy's "The Subalterns." How can both Death and Immortality be companions on the same journey? The woman does not know—she only knows that she and they are together in a moment of eternal duration, a vanishing point. Both Tate and Winters remark on the inconclusiveness of the poem—Tate to praise it, Winters to fault it. To me it seems an admission of human finitude, mental as well as bodily, a statement of what it is like to intuit in the most vivid way, and every day, the certainty of death, refusing—not even recognizing—the promises of any religion. One wonders if Spinoza's dictum, that a wise person's thoughts will be a meditation on life, not death, could have been of any use to her, or his statement, interpreted in varying ways over the years, that a person who truly loves God cannot expect to be loved by God in return. All that she arrives at, however, is the perception of mortality—and this is, after all, a poem about that perception. The man in Scriptures who brought his possessed son to Jesus for a cure could pray to him, "Lord, I believe; help thou my unbelief." Emily, beginning with unbelief, could not pray at all.

The poem is full of poetic music that complements the effects of imagery and the management of emotion. The austerity of Dickinson's insight is emphasized in the first two stanzas by the choice of short and simple words of one or two syllables for the first three lines, with a concluding line that subsides into the quiet formality of a Latinate polysyllable. This pattern prepares for the last word in the poem: "Eternity." Vowel quantity plays its part: "We slowly drove, he knew no haste" combines vowels that are already long with clusters of consonants that lengthen them further. Numerous lines are enriched and tightened with alliterating pairs of words (7, 10, 11, 12, 15, 16). Internal rhymes and assonances occur only sparingly (3, 5, 11, 14); a continual variation of vowel sounds within the context of consonantal enrichment may help to imply (as it does in a more lush and obvious way in Keats's "To Autumn") the richness of this transient existence, the full maturity of the "Gazing Grain," a strangely ironic personification that is hallucinatory in its intensity.

Through all this the meter carries us with the inevitable progress of a hymn that is going to be sung through to its conclusion. Few hymns, however, are so structured as to require the singing of all the stanzas, and even those that are (such as "While Shepherds Watched Their Flocks by Night") recount stories so familiar that only parts of them may be sung. Neither do hymns often offer images or diction of striking originality, although many are intensely moving when sung; the individual stanzas tend to be restatements of a common theme, or illustrations of it using different imagery from one stanza to the next—an excellent example being Watts's "Man Frail, and God Eternal," commonly known in its hymnal version as "O God Our Help in Ages Past":

> Our God, our Help in Ages past,
> > Our Hope for Years to come,
> Our Shelter from the Stormy Blast,
> > And our eternal Home.

> Under the Shadow of thy Throne
> > Thy Saints have dwelt secure;
> Sufficient is thine Arm alone,
> > And our Defence is sure.

> Before the Hills in order stood,
> > Or Earth receiv'd her Frame,
> From everlasting Thou art God,
> > To endless Years the same.

Thy Word commands our Flesh to Dust,
    Return, ye Sons of Men:
All Nations rose from Earth at first,
    And turn to Earth again.

A thousand Ages in thy Sight
    Are like an Evening gone;
Short as the Watch that ends the Night
    Before the rising Sun.

The busy Tribes of Flesh and Blood
    With all their Lives and Cares
Are carried downwards by thy Flood,
    And lost in following Years.

Time like an ever-rolling Stream
    Bears all its Sons away;
They fly forgotten as a Dream
    Dies at the opening Day.

Like flow'ry Fields the Nations stand
    Pleas'd with the Morning-light;
The Flowers beneath the Mower's Hand
    Ly withering e'er 'tis Night.

Our God, our Help in Ages past,
    Our Hope for Years to come,
Be thou our Guard while Troubles last,
    And our eternal Home.

Far less than Burns's poems, less even than Moore's songs, can this majestic anthem interest and move us when viewed upon a silent page, except as we feel the strength of its simple piety. Nothing in the imagery or diction surprises; the metaphors are hardly realized. How do hills stand "in order" and just what is earth's "frame"? One image succeeds another; none are connected or much developed (as poetic images). Take away the music and the life goes out of it.

Consider the opposite situation: Emily Dickinson's poem with music added to it. In fact, it occurs to every generation of students to amuse one another by singing her poems to some common tune, most often, perhaps, "The Yellow Rose of Texas." The sentimental and mildly erotic lyrics of that song assure the incongruity. But even a more staid and pious melody, such as Watts's, makes a grotesque parody out of the poem. The problem is, of course, the repetition of the same melody for each stanza, which goes completely counter to the steady forward progress of the poem. Music appropriate to "Because I Could Not

Stop for Death" would have to be through-composed. Such compositions exist, but I have never heard one and am not much interested in doing so. The performance might honor Dickinson, but it could only detract from her own legitimate artistry. Celestial melodies that she may have improvised herself, or heard in the air as she wrote, vanished the instant she heard them, like thinnest mist, from the landscape of her poetry.

HUGHES

If in Whitman the musical context is remote, and in Dickinson undeclared, in much of the poetry of Langston Hughes it is conscious, insistent, purposeful, almost obtrusive. His adaptations of various kinds of blues and jazz, and to a lesser degree spirituals and hymns, declare themselves in the titles as well as the forms of many poems; like Dante's canzone, these poems, if not actually intended for music, are written as if they could be sung. We also see in Thomas Hardy's work poems written as if accompanied by music—poems that recall country ballads, jigs, and reels. Musical models assist in the cultural self-location of the poem for both poets: Hardy found his forms appropriate to his "Wessex" lyrics and narratives because they resembled the tunes he had fiddled and songs he had sung in his youth, and Hughes discovered, especially in the blues, structures and rhythms suitable to the African American experience.

To make yet another anachronistic comparison, some of the poems of Thomas Wyatt seem enfeebled by their too-near resemblance to songs, and the lyrics of Thomas Moore are vacuous without their melodies. But in reproducing the effect of the blues, Hughes keeps the language and situation direct and uncomplicated and the poems step forth from the implied melody with the candor we see in Burns. Not everyone approves of this forthright quality; James Baldwin, in the *New York Times Book Review* for March 29, 1959, writing on Hughes's *Selected Poems*, objected to what he called a "fake simplicity" and claimed that Hughes found "the war between his social and artistic responsibilities all but irreconcilable" (Gates and Appiah 38). It would be good to know more explicitly just what Baldwin meant by that last comment. Perhaps Hughes had made himself too accessible, to black as well as to white readers, and did not display a sufficiently fierce awareness of the overlapping ironies involved in playing simultaneously to multiple, and in many ways mutually antagonistic, audiences: black and white; poor rural black and sophisticated urban black; conservative whites (among whom one could find lively enthusiasm for "Negro" culture) and "enlightened" whites (among whom one could find those who disapproved of racial conciliation); neoprimitivists, both black and white, and those who wished to disburden contemporary African Americans of their African legacies. To judge from comments made in the *Voices and Visions* video segment on Hughes (PBS 1987), Baldwin felt that Hughes had exhausted himself in the effort to fulfill these conflicting commitments. The accusation of "fake simplicity," however, reminds me of the discomfort that some academics devoted to twentieth-century high modernism used to feel in the presence of Robert Frost's poetry, having been put off by Frost's faux-naivete, or even taken in by it. Hughes was less cunning, less deeply disillusioned, and perhaps more humane than Frost. Here is Hughes's "Acceptance":

> God, in His infinite wisdom
> Did not make me very wise—
> So when my actions are stupid
> They hardly take God by surprise.

Compare this with Frost's "Dear God, forgive my little jokes on thee, / And I'll forgive thy great big one on me." In both epigrams, the language is simple and colloquial, masking the depths of suffering and wisdom that have led to very different outlooks in each poet—reconciliation for Hughes and defiance for Frost. Hughes's simplicity, however, has something to do with his acceptance, among other things, of the folk song and the blues and the ways in which these expressed in unaffected language the truths of human experience, especially African American experience. Even as minute an example as "Acceptance" shows a looseness of meter that recalls the freedom with which folk music adapts words to measures—speeding up to accommodate extra syllables, or else slurring them together.

No one doubts that whatever the nature and magnitude of Hughes's achievement as a poet, a great deal of his poetry owe much to his musical experience—except when he is showing his Sandburgian free-verse or populist side, or his Whitman-style poetic emancipation. Recordings of Hughes reading his own work include copious commentary on its musical sources; even some verses that might seem conventionally patterned were intended by him to suggest what he called the "syncopated rhythms" of jazz (for example, "Midnight Raffle"). Musical models gave Hughes structures that were culturally authentic and freed him from the pentameters, from the quatrains and sonnets, that other Americans borrowed from British poets. Many another African American poet, from Dunbar to Cullen and beyond, had cultivated and would continue to cultivate those imported forms. Hughes's models included hymns, spirituals, ballads, and other kinds of popular music, but his greatest originality is in his adaptations of various blues rhythms and structures, and those of jazz that was evolving from the blues.

This is not the place, were I even competent to do so, to undertake a definitive discussion of what the blues is and where it came from. An extensive and controversy-ridden literature exists on these subjects; although discussion focuses mostly on pieces performed or composed in the United States in the last hundred years, and should therefore tend toward consensus, it has instead generated an obscuring fog comparable to that enveloping the medieval *conductus* or sequence. Even relations that at first seem clear-cut may end in ambiguity, such as the possible connection of blues with work songs. About 1950 I was taken out on a "pogy" boat operating from Fernandina, Florida, and spent the day watching a crew of twenty young black men set a quarter-mile-long net around schools of menhaden and then haul them in. A foreman led them in what I learned some forty years later was the "call-and-response" field and labor song that plantation slaves worked to and that some people think had origins in African chants. As best I can remember, at least some of the lyrics had to do with female companionship found or lost, and the singing seemed expressive of resignation to whatever life might bring, whether joy, sorrow, or exhausting labor. The singing coordinated the strain of hauling the net, pull by pull, and probably made the work a little easier and more pleasant. But it was done in a chorus—in answer to the foreman or song leader—and without instrumental accompaniment, and was really therefore more akin to spiritual or gospel singing than to blues. Indeed, spirituals have also been used as work songs. (A fine collection of authentic marine chanties may be found in the recording *Won't You Help Me to Raise 'Em* of the Menhaden Chanteymen [Global Village Music, 1990], led by bluesman Richard "Big Boy" Henry of Beaufort, North Carolina; these include "Lazarus" and "Sweet Chariot.")

Most definitions of the blues, however, insist that it is the expression of an individual singer and that instrumental accompaniment, usually guitar, or a small ensemble led by piano, is essential. So whatever sense of oppression, deprivation, and endless labor may have carried from work songs into blues singing, the form and occasion of blues seem to require performance for an audience; to see this variety of African-American music as a continuation of tribal chant and field-singing may be to construct a mythical history for it (not to dismiss the concept; myths are as real as anything else). James Weldon Johnson's belief, mentioned in the introduction to *God's Trombones*, that the preaching style in African American churches somehow reached back through the cadences of the King James Bible to something essentially African may not be provable, either, but the idea seems important. Thus to set about disproving W. C. Handy's account as to where he first located the blues seems to me to have little purpose, even if in making the following claim he may be exercising some imagination in identifying sources:

It was my good fortune to live for two years in the state of Mississippi and to hear the crude singing of the Negro down there. I also had experiences in my hometown, Florence, Alabama, where I carried water for the men who worked in the furnaces, who always sang when they worked. I heard bits of songs that they sang. Something like this:

Ay-Oh
Ay-Oh-Ooh
I wouldn't live in Cairo.

(qtd. in Tracy 91–92)

Steven C. Tracy explains with great tact and perception just how Handy made use of the authentic songs that he had encountered (91–94), not faulting Handy for having seen in them material that might be worked up into something performative and even commercially viable. Elsewhere, Handy put in a stronger claim for the folk song, rather than the work song, as a source for blues:

Each one of my blues is based on some old Negro song of the South, some folk-song that I heard from my mammy when I was a child. Something that sticks in my mind, that I hum to myself when I'm not thinking about it. Some old song that is part of the memories of my childhood and of my race. I can tell you the exact song I used as a basis for any one of my blues. Yes, the blues that are genuine are really folk-songs. (Scarborough 265; qtd. in Tracy 92)

Again my own experience may be useful, in considering how genuine folk singing evolves into commercial entertainment. I grew up hearing an almost-illiterate white woman hum and sing bits of songs as she cooked, sewed, or worked about the house, that were a blend, or alternation, of Protestant hymns and garbled and incomplete parts of Scots-Irish ballads or songs imitated therefrom ("The Old Barn Dance," "Old Joe Clark," and so forth). At exactly the same time (the 1940s) the Grand Old Opry was getting established over radio station WSM, operating out of Nashville, and I could recognize in what came over the airwaves on Saturday night or at 6 A.M. more regularized and perhaps in their way "arty" versions of this humming and half-articulated country singing. These Opry versions in turn generated songs that made their way eventually into the repertoire of such "country" singers as Brooklyn-born "Ramblin' Jack" Elliott (winner in late 1998 of a Presidential gold medal in arts and letters), with whom I passed a week of drinking and singing some years later (1959) in the dowdy tourist-class lounges of the Queen Elizabeth I. To me, this transformation of material transplanted to America from other

lands into native folk melody and thence into a more artificial and commercially successful form of popular entertainment seems comparable to what
happened to the blues.

The conversion of the simplest twelve-bar blues (which Hughes reproduced in "The Weary Blues," and which does seem to resemble a call-and-
response pattern) into something more complex and suitable for professional
entertainment is perfectly exemplified in Handy's "St. Louis Blues," which
got its classic performance in Bessie Smith's version. "St. Louis Blues" leads off
with a series of twelve-bar groupings and then launches into something more
akin to vaudeville rhythm with "St. Louis woman. . . ."

Other issues that arise besides the putative origins of the blues in African
American work and folk songs, and its development or exploitation in the
music hall and night club, are its possible sources in spirituals and its parallels in
ragtime. I mention these issues not to pronounce on them, but to emphasize
again the complexities that can cause confusion and turn discussions of the
blues into shouting matches between adherents of various theories or interpretations. On top of that, an accurate account of the origins and evolution of
the blues (to the extent that such a thing is even possible) is quite different
from an explanation of what blues meant to Langston Hughes. For him, it was
a cultural given. He first heard blues sung in Kansas City when he was about
ten years old, by a chorus of blind singers, and what he heard then came back
to him much later as his poem, "The Weary Blues." In later life, in Harlem,
New Orleans, aboard ocean liners, and in Paris, he experienced the various
transformations of the blues, against which he protested at times but which he
accepted along with the vicissitudes of his own life. Seldom did he give much
thought to its historical roots, though he did lay claim to the blues on behalf of
his race in a little essay that he wrote in 1940:

> The Blues and the Spirituals are two great Negro gifts to American music.
> The Spirituals are group songs, but the Blues are songs you sing alone. The
> Spirituals are religious songs, born in camp meetings and remote plantation
> districts. But the Blues are *city* songs rising from the crowded streets of big
> towns, or beating against the lonely walls of hall bed-rooms where you can't
> sleep at night. The Spirituals are escape songs, looking toward heaven,
> tomorrow, and God. But the Blues are *today* songs, here and now, broke and
> broken-hearted, when you're troubled in mind and don't know what to do,
> and nobody cares. (*Reader* 159)

In the same essay, it comes clear that as far as Hughes was concerned, the most
recent and sophisticated renditions of blues, including what Steven C. Tracy
calls the "vaudeville blues," which could be radically different from folk blues,

blended into the continuum of his own experience. His concept of the blues was, finally, not so much the idea of a form (although he certainly understood its formal structures) as it was the varying modes of expressing the singularity of black experience, the voice of the individual sufferer—either accepting or sardonically defining irremediable affliction and often erupting in laughter over the absurdity of life's predicaments.

In his autobiography, *The Big Sea*, Hughes describes his first big success as a poet, in which he made use of his recollection of the early encounter with blues:

> I sent several poems to the first contest. And then, as an afterthought, I sent "The Weary Blues," the poem I had written three winters before up the Hudson and whose ending I had never been able to get quite right. But I thought perhaps it was as right now as it would ever be. It was a poem about a working man who sang the blues all night and then went to bed and slept like a rock. That was all. And it included the first blues verse I'd ever heard way back in Lawrence, Kansas, when I was a kid.

> *I got de weary blues*
> *And I can't be satisfied.*
> *Got de weary blues*
> *And can't be satisfied.*
> *I ain't happy no mo'*
> *And I wish that I had died.*

> That was my lucky poem—because it won the first prize. (215)

"The Weary Blues" continues to be among the most-anthologized of Hughes's poems, and it illustrates perfectly his adaptation into a poetic form of his intuitive grasp of the then-current (mid-twenties) development of the blues into a more sophisticated kind of entertainment—already largely transformed into jazz. The poem provides a jazz-time envelope that enfolds the original blues (which he quotes in the excerpt above) within it, as if it were an embryo or controlling nucleus.

Of the nearly two hundred poems in Hughes's *Selected Poems*, about half are directly emergent from musical contexts in which regular, repetitive patterns prevail: songs, ballads, hymns, spirituals, and blues. A dozen are (or include) straight, classical, twelve-bar blues songs, some of them labeled as such. Many less regularly structured poems mention songs, or singing, or characterize themselves as songs, melodies, or boogies. Many others that one might be tempted to call free verse seem analogous to jazz improvisation and therefore constructive; most free verse has something iconoclastic about it, but Hughes, as a poetic artist, was not so much in rebellion against older metrics as in pursuit of new ways of writing that would be suited to his subjects. Even when his poetry showed what he had learned from Whitman, his mode of writing was also an affirmation of the Bible-based rhythms and intonations that he had heard in African American sermons, and which—as I have shown in *The Origins of Free Verse* (169–73)—black poets both earlier and later than Hughes, including Du Bois, had made use of. Everything he wrote, and all his ways of writing, were authentic parts of his actual experience, and that experience included a great deal of music.

The powerful and enduring appeal of Hughes's poetry can be explained in large part by its addressing itself to the ear rather than the eye; he escapes the dependence on the visual that is so much the heritage of twentieth-century imagism, or on the intellect, in the poetry of high modernism. Many students taking courses in modern poetry turn with blissful relief from Eliot and Pound (at least the later Pound) to the poems of Langston Hughes. And once again we have the same story that we have heard in connection with Wyatt, Burns, Blake, and Dickinson: directness and seeming simplicity of language mask a profound poetic originality. Hughes's originality does not just consist in treating subjects previously untouched in American poetry, in giving voices to those previously unheard, in cultivating a cultural local-colorism; it also involves reestablishing connections between the sister arts, and in so doing bringing into existence new poetries. As Howard Mumford Jones recognized in a review of Hughes's book, *Fine Clothes to the Jew*, in the *Chicago Daily News* of June 29, 1927, "In a sense he has contributed a really new verse form to the English language."

❧ 13

Some Moderns

Ne pas oublier . . . que nous sommes *contre* la musique. Apollon *contre* Dionysos.

—PAUL VALÉRY

THE POETS treated in this chapter—Thomas Hardy, W. B. Yeats, Paul Valéry, and T. S. Eliot—hardly exhaust the possibilities for considering relations between poetry and music in the first half of the twentieth century. One might take up the case of e. e. cummings, much of whose work seems very much the product of the Jazz Age; and in place of Yeats one might well consider Wallace Stevens as a continuation of nineteenth-century euphoniousness, at least in his serious poems (unlike Yeats he was often a whimsical titillator of the prosodic keyboard). Indeed, any poet working within the great accentual-syllabic tradition of poetry in English can be linked ultimately—usually through either British Romantic poetry or that of the Renaissance—to some distant musical context. Anne Sexton and Sylvia Plath (in their formal accentual poems) brought urgency and intensity to the old meter; W. D. Snodgrass continues to put the old colt through new paces. In the afterword that follows this chapter, I will mention other examples and explain briefly why, in this study, there is no attempt to deal with free verse other than that of Whitman. I have chosen these four poets because of their stature in modern literature and because in quite different ways the work of each invites commentary that takes music into account—and also because I am familiar with them. If I were at home in German or Italian, not to speak of Swedish or Russian, the choices might have been different.

Roughly and briefly, what is offered here is, with Hardy, a poetry that makes as immediate a break with music as any in the past—whether that of Dante, Wyatt, or Burns. With Yeats we have the triple distancing from actual music (in that, for example, one of Yeats's masters was Shelley, and one of Shelley's, in turn, was Milton). Paul Valéry solved the challenge to the Symbolists of nineteenth-century music, especially Wagner's, by increasing the structured density and intensity of poetic sound effects—the *musique naturele* of Deschamps—beyond that ever achieved in French before and possibly beyond anything ever written in any language. And Eliot wrote his way out of a chaotic post-Wagnerian iconoclasm into a pseudomusical structure that disguised his assimilation of every available English prosody and some from other languages, especially French. Like Eliot, Paul Valéry succeeded in freeing himself. He simply ceased to write verse for about two decades, and when he did resume he revealed himself as the complete post-Symbolist, having passed safely beyond the siren seductiveness of music and into a poetic that carried poetry further than ever from actual music. Eliot, on the other hand, gradually worked his way toward a reintegration and away from the *Götterdämmerung* of *The Waste Land*, the form of which poem may have owed as much to Wagner as did Mallarmé's *Un Coup de Dés*. Like Adrien Leverkuhn of Mann's *Doctor Faustus*, Eliot "took back the Ninth Symphony," retreating from the hallucinatory chaos of excessive poetic ambition, charming chaos away with the ruse of Beethoven's modification of the sonata form in his late quartets. What Eliot actually did in his *Four Quartets* had much more to do with a blending of every kind of poetry ever written in the English language than it did with a novel adaptation of musical form to poetic structure. It is easy—entirely too easy—to see the alternation of slow and fast "movements" in *Four Quartets*; the hard job is to explain the melding of earlier prosodic traditions.

Thomas Hardy, more than any other poet that I can name, recapitulated what had taken generations to accomplish in the past. Writing his way out of musical contexts, he authored a body of verse that acknowledged a deep indebtedness to music even as it broke free. The claims of these contexts enveloped Hardy, somewhat as necessitarian strictures trammel his fictional creations; the struggle to escape left its mark in the halting rhythms, the awkward locutions, the gnarls and whorls of his diction that may remind us of a handpost or railing sawed out of rough lumber, or of the oddities of attitude, comportment, and dress of his Wessex characters. The poems seem to reflect their own self-thwarting tendencies. Some readers of Hardy's poetry, including some very distinguished ones (especially those to whom his compassionate cheerlessness is not congenial), have been put off by the way it labors in such difficulties, finding the rhythms clunky. Hardy could tolerate extreme oddity in combinations of sounds much as he could chronicle in both his fiction and poetry characters and points of view that strike some readers as willfully perverse. Even after we take into account the many references to instrumental and vocal music in the novels, and its role as models for the poetry, we would not use the word "musical" to describe his verse—at least not in the sense that one would call Housman and much of Yeats musical. There is little euphony in Hardy and much dissonance, even cacophony. Yet musical it is, in a most profound and literal sense. Dave Townsend, a contemporary arranger of music that was known to Hardy, reminds us that

> the works of Thomas Hardy are full of music. Local traditional songs and music are part of the lives of his characters, and portraits of musicians and scenes of dancing abound. The Hardy family were noted local musicians. When they lived in Puddletown, Hardy's grandfather led the church band there and played the cello, and when they moved to Lower Bockhampton he and Hardy's father, playing violin, played for Stinsford church until the band was replaced by a harmonium shortly before Hardy's birth. They continued as before to play for local dances, and Hardy learnt the violin as a boy and played with his father and uncle. (4)

Hardy's metrics remain essentially faithful to musical paradigms while struggling against them, much as he retained a fundamentally pious outlook despite having worked himself away from the consolation and assurances of religion. The connections with liturgy are often evident; actual hymnal notation works well to account for the form of numerous poems. A good example is "The Darkling Thrush," which is written in Common Measure Doubled (CMD). Each stanza could also be described as two ballad stanzas run together; most readers of Hardy notice how often he borrows ballad meters, or writes in stanzas easily accompanied by jigs and reels of the sort that he played as a boy. The fact that he employs hundreds of nonce forms, invented for their particular poems and idiosyncratic to them, might seem to argue a positive inventiveness rather than an indebtedness, but even in these we may see an extension of the cranky irregularities that enlivened sacred as well as secular music of the West Country. Stinsford church choirs sang hymns in ways that a London congregation would have found amusingly countrified, adding flourishes, repetitions, and other gratuitous elegancies.

In Florence Hardy's *Early Life of Thomas Hardy*, which was written under the poet's own direction and much of the time in his own words, we read:

> Though healthy he was fragile, and precocious to a degree, being able to read almost before he could walk, and to tune a violin when of quite tender years. He was of ecstatic temperament, extraordinarily sensitive to music, and among the endless jigs, hornpipes, reels, waltzes, and country-dances that his father played of an evening in his early married years, and to which the boy danced a *pas seul* in the middle of the room, there were three or four that always moved the child to tears, though he strenuously tried to hide them. Among the airs (though he did not know their names at that time) were, by the way, "Enrico" (popular in the Regency), "The Fairy Dance," "Miss

Macleod of Ayr" (an old Scotch tune to which Burns may have danced), and a melody named "My Fancy-Lad" or "Johnny's gone to sea". (18)

We also learn that he was "wildly fond of dancing," that in old age he could recall Dorset versions of ballads that had long since ceased to be sung there, and that his "earliest recollection was of receiving from his father the gift of a small accordion" (25–27). He "loved adventures with the fiddle," and played for weddings and New Year's Eve parties, once receiving a hatful of pennies with which he was able to buy a book that he wanted (29–30). As a young man in London he bought himself a fiddle and practiced playing pieces from current Italian operas, another lodger joining him on the piano (56–57). In later years of his life, Hardy's annual stays in London always included much concert-going, and he preferred music to theater, on the whole, writing in a letter to Florence Henniker, "The history of the theatre is to my mind nothing to the history of the concert room" (*Letters* 2: 283). When his play *The Three Wayfarers* was produced in 1893, Hardy wrote offering to direct the dances himself and included "tunes & figures as they used to dance them" (2: 9). In 1907, writing to A. M. Bradley, he made plain his continuing interest: "I am looking for some old Dorset psalm-tunes—either composed by Dorset men, much sung in Dorset, or bearing names of Dorset places—for the Society of Dorset Men in London" (3: 285). And in 1908 he wrote to his wife Emma, "I miss the psalm & chant tunes very much on Sundays, never hearing a note of music now" (3: 347).

A hundred years earlier, British Romantic poets, nostalgic for the Middle Ages and feeling that native songs and ballads were the musical remnants of such times, employed late medieval meters, or variants of them, to add freshness or strangeness to their poems. Wordsworth's "Lucy" poems provide good examples of song stanzas, and Coleridge's "Ancient Mariner" and Keats's "Belle Dame Sans Merci" of ballads. As we have seen, the lyrics of Burns are consistent with the melodies that accompany them, or for which they may have been written—although, like Wyatt's more than three hundred years earlier, they are satisfactory purely as verbal art. In the Victorian period, Tennyson, Browning and many other poets occasionally wrote pieces designed to go with melodies, in which poetic complexities of rhythm and meaning are deliberately reduced; a good example is Browning's song that ends "God's in his heaven— / All's right with the world" (from *Pippa Passes*), which is sometimes taken as a summary of the poet's own outlook. In all these instances the relationship of poetic meter to music is much less complex than in Hardy's poetry. The meter is meant to be either reminiscent of a melody, or else accommodative to it. To the extent that numerous old ballads included ironic twists, betrayals, grisly or macabre incidents, and tragic consequences, one may say that Hardy, too, composed in a fashion in keeping with the folk traditions—as in one of his own favorites, "The Tramp-Woman's Tragedy," which recounts a murder, a hanging, and a stillbirth all brought on by an incident of foolish teasing. In that poem the form recalls the older ballads. More often, however, Hardy's subject offers a bleak counterpoint to the cheerful message of salvation or the lively dance tunes that the form of his stanzas may recall. That is, Hardy tells us in awkward words (the halting rhythms of which belie the transitory pleasures of the dance-floor, the happiness of a family group gathered around the piano, or the aspirations of a Christian congregation) that things do not, after all, turn out well.

Others have noted the ironic contrast between the form and the substance of Hardy's poetry. John Crowe Ransom, after comparing the stanzas of "The Subalterns" first to ballad measure and then with more conviction to the Common Measure of church hymns, says:

> But we come to the meaning, which is our major preoccupation, and Hardy's; and we quickly discover that there is such heresy in the theology that it would be unsuitable after all for being associated either with the Church hymnal or with the architecture of Christian churches. There are no churches, nor hymns, which can be expected to embody and publish Hardy's theological views. (176)

Another good example of incongruity (between form and tone), a disruption of an expected meter and its associations, is the early poem "Neutral Tones":

> We stood by a pond that winter day,
> And the sun was white, as though chidden of God,
> And a few leaves lay on the starving sod;
>   —They had fallen from an ash, and were gray.
>
> Your eyes on me were as eyes that rove
> Over tedious riddles of years ago;
> And some words played between us to and fro
>   On which lost the more by our love.
>
> The smile on your mouth was the deadest thing
> Alive enough to have strength to die;
> And a grin of bitterness swept thereby
>   Like an ominous bird a-wing . . .
>
> Since then, keen lessons that love deceives,
> And wrings with wrong, have shaped to me

> Your face, and the God-curst sun, and a tree,
> And a pond edged with grayish leaves.

We do not have to mark the scansion to hear a fundamentally anapestic rhythm (though, as even in mechanically anapestic limericks, most lines lead off with an iambic foot). Numerous serious poems, from "Lord Randall" to early Yeats and beyond, have employed anapestic meters, but this rhythm more often than not suggests spriteliness, levity, even frivolity, and is reminiscent of the jigging rhythms in songs and reels, dances and carols, that enlivened happy occasions or added a perhaps forced cheerfulness to the market days in Hardy's Dorchester. In "Neutral Tones" the meter constantly stumbles toward a prosaic flatness or an awkward reversal in the first three lines of each stanza, and, in the final line of each stanza the trimeter breaks down—nowhere more completely than at the conclusion:

> ★ ★ / ／ ★ ／ ★ ／
> And a pond edged with grayish leaves.

Here the triple meter reverses its accents and truncates itself so that the rising rhythm becomes a falling trochee, followed by an amphimacer whose two stresses further defeat the trimeter. In addition, groupings of consonants tend to lengthen out most of the unstressed syllables; the short vowel in "with" is surrounded by a total of seven consonants. Like the smile on the woman's face, the rhythm has just enough strength to die; the momentary upturn at the start of each stanza only increases the sense of disappointment, communicated simultaneously not only by the rhythms, but by the imagery and the connotations of the words—the washed-out colors and the winter-killed vegetation. Taken line by line, the poem reveals one instance after another where the accommodation of meter to meaning interferes with the fundamental anapestic rhythm—as in "some words played between us to and fro," where the stresses are batted back and forth like a shuttlecock. One can account for these effects simply by presupposing an anapestic template for the poem, but a new layer or level of irony may be preceived if we consider the poem a failed song— a tune not to dance to, but one that holds its subjects in strained, awkward, and painful immobility. The music has stopped, or run down, like the trailing off of an unwinded set of bagpipes or an interrupted ensemble; and there is no promise of any resumption—no anticipated gala or wedding.

As his own poems gained an audience, Hardy began to receive requests for permission to set them to music. At first he doubted whether this was possible, fearing that these would-be composers found "the work beyond them [and] do not, so far as I know, carry out their intentions" (*Letters* 3: 23). Subsequently not having found all such efforts pleasing, he became reluctant to allow just anyone to "melodize" his poems, as he put it with typically Hardy-esque awkwardness. But in his last years we see him eagerly corresponding with Ralph Vaughan Williams and Gustav Holst, pleased that well-known composers were interested in such projects (see *Letters* 3: 355, 358). It is doubt-ful that the poems gained anything from such settings, especially since Hardy did not compose them for that purpose. The poignancy—often the oddity—of the human situations, the peculiarity of emotion, or the philosophical impli-cations burden the poems, making them very unlike, say, Ben Jonson's "Drink to Me Only" or many lyrics by Schiller and Goethe. In the latter we find uncluttered sentiments that do not obtrude upon the music in performance.

As in most other respects, when we consider the relationship of Yeats's poetry to music we find that he makes a study in contrasts with Hardy. Yeats was completely tone deaf and could not carry a tune—yet the mellifluousness of his earlier verse did much to make him immediately acceptable to a genera-tion that grew up on the later Tennyson and on Swinburne. As if to compen-sate for his own bad musical ear, Yeats wrote poems as lyrics for established melodies (see his *Collected Poems*, Appendix B and notes), which Hardy almost never did. More poems by Yeats than by Hardy—at least two dozen—include the word "song" in their title; four others are called ballads, and others suggest the ballad form. Anyone familiar with Yeats's work will also think of nu-merous poems about dancing ("The Fiddler of Dooney," "To a Child Dancing in the Wind") as well as individual lines ("How can we know the dancer from the dance?" or "her feet / Practise a tinker shuffle / Picked up on the street."). Some of his plays include stage directions requiring the players to carry musi-cal instruments, and involve the playing of music and the singing of songs. Hardy took the musical grounding of poetry for granted, whereas Yeats was engaged in a typically romantic quest to put "music" back into poetry—along with magic, strangeness of all sorts, exotic and dreamlike landscapes, and so on. But actual music does not figure much in his poetry. Yeats's actual singing masters (in addition to himself) were the British Romantic poets that had enchanted him as a youth: Shelley, Blake, and to some extent Keats, par-ticularly the Keats that came to life again in Tennyson's early poetry. In the end, his incapacity to perceive musical intervals—or, perhaps, his capacity for perceiving no more than two or three very definite distinctions in pitch—proved a positive advantage, freeing him to concentrate on perfecting verbal patterns. Less innovative than Milton, Yeats carried the old accentual-syllabic metrics to new levels, welding together not only memorable lines, but entire stanzas, even entire poems, in a rhythmic and formal unity scarcely equaled by Donne or Keats, to name his chief rivals from the past in this respect.

Metrical analysis confirms what readers (at least those for whom auditory structure matters) experience in reading "Leda and the Swan."

```
★  /   ★   /    ★   /    /    /  ★  /
A sudden blow: the great wings beating still
★   /    ★   /   ★★  /    ★   /    ★  /
Above the staggering girl, her thighs caressed
★    ★    /   /    ★   /    /    ★  ★  /
By the dark webs, her nape caught in his bill,
★   /    ★    /    ★   /   ★ /  ★    /
He holds her helpless breast upon his breast.
 /    /    /    /   ★ /   /    /  ★   /            [or, ★ ★ / / ★ / / / ★ /]
How can those terrified vague fingers push
★    /    ★    / ★  ★    ★   /    ★  /
The feathered glory from her loosening thighs?
★    /    ★   / ★   /   ★    /   /    /
And how can body, laid in that white rush,
★   /    ★    /    /    /   ★   /   ★ /
But feel the strange heart beating where it lies?
★   /   ★ ★   ★ /   ★  /   ★   /
A shudder in the loins engenders there
★    /   ★  /    ★   /   ★   /    ★    /
The broken wall, the burning roof and tower
★   /   ★ /   ★    /
And Agamemnon dead.
                         /  ★   /   /     /         [?]
                       Being so caught up,
★   /   ★   ★  ★   /     /   ★  ★  /
So mastered by the brute blood of the air,
  ★   /   ★  /   ★  /    ★   /    ★   /
Did she put on his knowledge with his power
★   /    ★ ★ /  ★  ★   /    ★    /  ★   /
Before the indifferent beak could let her drop?
```

The first point to make is that, for all the expressive license of this short poem, Yeats keeps it firmly rooted in iambic pentameter. Lines 4 and 10 can be read no other way than as five consecutive iambs—and perhaps line 13 as well. The opening line is more regular than that of many of Shakespeare's sonnets, with a single substitution (the stress required by "wings"). Explication of the rhythmic effects that run counter to the template can easily impute to Yeats too much self-conscious cleverness, but it seems inevitable to notice that the extraordinary rhythmic uncertainty of "How can those terrified vague fingers push" makes the line hard to scan except in the context of the poem, and that this disordering of the meter makes us feel the useless gestures of a person frightened into submission, an effect continued in the "loosening" of the subsequent line. And surely something similar has already occurred in the "staggering" of the second line.

A scansionist with neoclassical leanings might be tempted to argue that some lines that seem hypermetric are actually ten syllables if we allow, in proper late-eighteenth-century fashion, for syncope ("stagg'ring," "loos'ning"), synaeresis ("being"), and a combination of elision and syncope in the last line ("Before th'indiff'rent beak could let her drop.") That the poem can be wrestled into fourteen ten-syllable lines, using such rationales, adds further strength to the underlying pattern. To do so is not altogether unnatural; syncope is often normal in the pronunciation of a word. There exists, therefore, even in the lines that seem most irregular, an adherence to the familiar underlying rhythm.

Intralinear rhythmic irregularity (or expressiveness), however strong, is overpowered by the breaks and enjambments with which Yeats disrupts entire lines, starting with the first phrase: "A sudden blow." The abrupt pause, of course, imitates the swooping collision, while the enjambed lines that follow suggest the irresistible progress of the assault. As the swan takes control, so does the meter settle into its underlying pattern: "He holds her helpless breast upon his breast." As in much of Yeats's greatest work, rhetoric comes close to supplanting poetry, its impassioned periodicities competing with the meter for dominance. Yeats recognized the dangers of writing this way, characterizing rhetoric as the will trying to do the work of the imagination, and asserting that rhetoric resulted from an argument with others, while poetry came out of an argument with the self. Sometimes rhetoric seems to move ahead of the poetry, as in the break that is typographical as well as rhythmic: "And Agamemnon dead." Here he invites us to review the huge scope of the interlocking myths just referred to, and after this dramatic pause, ends with a question that seems rhetorical, except that (to me, at least) it has no clear answer. From what Yeats writes elsewhere, we do know not only that he identified Maude Gonne with Helen, but that he considered Maud more willful and powerful than wise; Yeats may have considered that, as the offspring of this union, she did not put on his knowledge with his power.

Numerous effects on a more local scale can be pointed to. Notice, for example, the strongly stressed, long-syllable pairs of words associated with Zeus-as-swan: "great wings," "dark webs," "white rush," "brute blood." The initial sounds of the last are anticipated by "broken" and "burning" two lines earlier, but except for the first line, with its inverted reflection of "s" and "b" sounds, and the fourth line (which is in part simply repetition), alliteration and internal rhyme are not obtrusive. At least one line is enriched with a cumulative progression of sounds: "strange heart beating." And as we move into the sestet of this sonnet, the there/tower/air/power rhymes are reinforced by other sounds within the lines. In noting such things, though, we must again caution ourselves not to attribute our own analytical ingenuity to Yeats, who worked very hard on his poems, but by intuition and by ear.

In comparing Hardy and Yeats we are looking at examples of poetry that are as widely separated in terms of their relationship to music as they are by much else: Hardy's subjects—his characters and their circumstances—are closer to the actualities of existence than Yeats's imagination permitted him to approach, and Hardy's poems are much closer to musical sources than Yeats's. Yeats built on three hundred years or more of British prosody that had worked itself free from music in Chaucer's works and again in the sixteenth century. Prosodically, Yeats is a graft on the old trunk. Hardy is mostly new growth from the roots up: blighted and stunted, perhaps, by circumstance; rude and even archaic in rhythm; but full of life's actual vigor.

If the two poets can be said to share anything in terms of their prosody, it is an absence of self-consciousness about metrics (this is true, at least, of Hardy's best poems). At the same time that Coventry Patmore, Hopkins, and Robert Bridges were exploring new bases for British meter—or analyzing the older basis—and when George Saintsbury was busy codifying everything achieved up to that point by poets writing in English, Hardy and Yeats kept their attention fixed on the ultimate intentions of poems. Hardy, it is true, did interest himself in formal questions of prosody, at one time even corresponding with Patmore. Both Hardy and Yeats were saved from a preoccupation with prosody that was debilitating to others, especially to Patmore, but for entirely opposite reasons: Hardy by his profound immersion in the music of folk and church, and Yeats by his deafness to actual music but sensitivity to verbal nuances.

Samuel Hynes, in "On Hardy's Badness," argues that Hardy's worst poems are those in which he attempted to be consciously literary:

> The point, clearly, is that Hardy was two poets. One believed that poetry is an imitation of poetry, that it takes public and conventional forms, that it is, in short, *literature*. When Hardy wrote in this mode, when he consciously attached himself to the literary high culture of his time and became the Last Victorian, he was a bad poet: not just relatively unsuccessful, but awful. The other poet took poetry to be an ordinary but private activity, like meditation, or day-dreaming, or despair. This poet had no audience, and no immediate precursors: he wrote in an English tradition, but I think largely unconsciously, drawing on folk poetry and hymnology and the Bible, and on the

natural world, as other English poets had done before him, but not for literary ends, not to be a *poet*. His great precursors were anon., Hodge [a typical name for the English rustic], and God. (80)

Although Hynes says little about Hardy's prosody, we may take it that the risk he ran in that direction was adopting the self-conscious ingenuity that characterized much later nineteenth-century verse.

The risk to Yeats came from an entirely different direction: the hothouse aestheticism imported from France that lent the charm of "decadence" to his Rhymers' Club contemporaries but in some ways weakened their poetry. Yeats is often treated as an Irish manifestation of Symbolism—although, as Edmund Wilson pointed out long ago in *Axel's Castle*, he "found in Irish mythology . . . a treasury of symbols ready to his hand" (28). Wilson goes on to argue that Yeats's symbols were more satisfactory than those of Mallarmé because they were more rooted in ordinary experience and more accessible. For this reason as well as his tin ear, Yeats was not completely seduced by the magic of the musical word, even in his early years, and even though he had met Mallarmé in Paris and had assisted Arthur Symons in the composition of *The Symbolist Movement in Literature*. From first to last, of course, Yeats's poetry swarmed with symbols, some of which exhibit the personalized esotericism characteristic of much continental poetry. But the alchemy of Yeats's words did not include the creation of structures and effects intended either to challenge or to emulate the achievement of nineteenth-century actual music. The contrast implied here is with Symbolist doctrine and writings from Baudelaire to Valéry, and especially the theory and practice of Mallarmé.

The closest approach that Yeats made to French Symbolism was in his essay, "The Symbolism of Poetry," where he wrote:

> All sounds, all colors, all forms, either because of their preordained energies or because of long association, evoke indefinable and yet precise emotions, or, as I prefer to think, call down among us certain disembodied powers, whose footsteps over our hearts we call emotions; and when sound, and colour, and form are in a musical relation, a beautiful relation to one another, they become, as it were, one sound, one colour, one form, and evoke an emotion that is made out of their distinct evocations and yet is one emotion. (*Essays and Introductions* 156–57)

This passage is almost a translation of Baudelaire's poem "Correspondences," and certainly works as a reformulation of basic Symbolist doctrine. And there is scarcely any more succinct (certainly no more understandable) explanation of Symbolism than Yeats's sentence from "The Celtic Element in Literature":

The Reaction against the rationalism of the eighteenth century has mingled with a reaction against the materialism of the nineteenth century, and the symbolical movement, which has come to perfection in Germany in Wagner, in England in the Pre-Raphaelites, in France in Villiers de l'Isle-Adam, and Mallarmé, and in Belgium in Maeterlinck, and has stirred the imagination of Ibsen and d'Annunzio, is certainly the only new movement that is saying things. (187)

Although my argument for the rest of this chapter will be that two other great moderns, T. S. Eliot and Paul Valéry, owed their achievement to what they learned from poetry and not from music, I must first pause to consider just what did constitute Symbolism and the even more elusive question of the relation of Symbolism to music. A useful analogy for the latter might be the way that Romantic poetry (especially that of Wordsworth) was indebted to ideas that belonged more properly to painting. The Beautiful / Sublime duality that the seventeen-year-old Edmund Burke codified in 1757, which depends on the categories of scenes and objects chosen by painters of the seventeenth and eighteenth centuries as appropriate to the kind of painting they aimed for, reappears as Wordsworth's "ministries" of beauty (or love) and fear. A third aesthetic category, the "picturesque," betrays its source in the word itself. This is not the place to rehearse the history of the interaction between painting and poetry that continued on through the nineteenth century, of which the Parnassian school in French poetry was to some extent a continuation. But beginning with Baudelaire's infatuation with Wagner, music began to take the place of painting as the art to be considered in connection with poetry, at least in France. The painterly dimension of poetry proved more lasting in England.

To deal with the poetry of Paul Valéry, one must consider him as a post-Symbolist writer, and to do that, one must come to terms with Symbolism. Because the most important monuments of the Symbolist school belong to French poetry, and because Symbolist poetry is almost by definition gnomic, hermetic, even willfully obscure, the quest for an acceptable definition is even more problematic than for the word "romantic," itself a notoriously slippery term. Just as early discussions of Romanticism tended to be infected by the enthusiastic afflatus associated with that subject, what purports to be analysis of Symbolism often seems a discourse conducted by *poètes manqués*, who offer us nuanced, oblique, tangential, delicately suggestive interpretations that obscure more than they illuminate with the effulgent fog of their rhetoric.

My own approach may err in the direction of brusque oversimplification (though no more than Yeats's did), but at least the reader will know what he or she is disagreeing with. To me, Symbolism is perfectly continuous with Romanticism and with the drift toward subjectivity and claims for a uniquely personal artistic perspective that one finds in various forms—interrupted by repeated reactions—from the Middle Ages onward. Shelley's "Ode to the West Wind" is in many respects a Symbolist poem; Tennyson's "Mariana" even more so. Let us add the commonplace that Poe provided all the French Symbolists with both doctrine and examples to follow, and the unoriginal reflection that their difficulties in reading English made him all the more enchanting to them. Looking much further back, the simile of the soul as bird in Marvell's "The Garden" would not be out of place in a poem by Verlaine, while certain of Crashaw's tropes resemble inventions of the successors to the Symbolists, the surrealists. The difference between Symbolism and anything that came before is the frank abandonment of any pretense that the world reflected in the work of art is in any sense an imitation of or a comment on a durable world external to the artist. A Wordsworthian or Lamartinian landscape, which the poet interprets for personal purposes, is replaced by a *paysage intérieur.* This landscape of the soul is dreamlike and everything in it is symbolic of some feeling, impression, intuition; completely realized, such a panorama could be infinitely more satisfying (or more meaningful, at any rate, even if the artist found there images of pain and horror) than the rapid impersonal evolution and wrenching changes and displacements of the world outside the artist. Indeed, the subjective universe becomes the more real, permanent, and in some sense even classical refuge from the outrages offered to the spirit by shifting material circumstance and the increasingly obtrusive certitude of the natural sciences.

To say this is not to suggest that Symbolism is irresponsible escapism—although the emphasis on the efficacy of drugs, Baudelaire's reverence for hashish being an especially notable instance, might encourage one to see it that way. In some ways it is an insistence that varieties of human experience do exist that are indeed elusive, perhaps unavailable to most human beings, and that they must be valued. Mallarmé is much less read than Henry James, whose own audience remains limited to a small fraction of the population; yet few fault James for investigating the exquisite sensibilities of persons whose refinement at times stretches our credulity. We can excuse James because with his impressionistic emotional calculus he does seem to have discovered possibilities for human sentiment that might have escaped our attention, but which strike us as authentic and convincing when dramatized by his characters. If we make similar allowances for Symbolist poetry, we can see it as an enterprise of discovery of the possibilities of human perception. France, with its heritage of a confident classicism unmatched anywhere else in the world, provided a context within which such investigations of the human spirit could flourish without degenerating completely into egotism, eccentricity, or madness—even if the personal history of some *poètes maudits* may seem to argue otherwise. In the disdain for popular taste among these poets there remained a confidence in the validity of artistic standards, an aristocracy of sensibility. In the post-Symbolist work of Valéry we see a rebound from profound subjectivity toward neoclassicism, a rebound that owes much to an implicit acceptance of a beautiful but pitiless natural universe, affirmed by his own studies of mathematics. Valéry, as we will see, managed to poise on the threshold between the inner and outer worlds and to accept them as simultaneous aspects of the universe, contemplating both with a "dédain souverain."

For my purposes, the important thing is what Valéry did with the Symbolist notions about the music of poetry. By the time that Baudelaire experienced Wagner's music, the style and manner of his poetry were too completely developed to be much affected. His classical restraint and lucidity of language served to throw into darker relief the anguished and sometime macabre splendor of his images and themes. For Baudelaire, Wagner did seem to have achieved in his musical pageants a fusion of effects that poets could only dream of capturing with words on paper; added to this achievement was the celebrity commanded by Wagner, not to speak of the material success, none of which lay open to a *poète maudit*.

But Baudelaire's response to Wagner seems mainly to have been passionate admiration rather than envy or a desire to emulate him. For later Symbolist poets, however, and especially for Mallarmé, the example of nineteenth-century music was deeply troubling and challenging (see Pistone, "Symbolisme" 15–17). As Valéry put it, "Le problème de toute la vie de Mallarmé, l'object de sa méditation perpétuelle, de ses recherches les plus subtiles était, comme on le sait, de rendre à la Poésie le même empire que la grande musique moderne lui avait enlevé" [The problem of Mallarmé's entire life, the object of his perpetual meditation, of his most subtle investigations, was, as we know, to restore to poetry the same dominion that great modern music had taken away from it.] (1: 700). One can make the argument that Mallarmé's radical departure into the typographical free-verse fantasy of "Un Coup de Dés" represented a sudden rupture with the French poetic *esprit de géométrie* and an aspiration toward the asymmetrical grandeur of Wagner (see Herz 54). The words of the poem float across the pages, connected by tenuous resonances, echoes, and associations, interacting with the blank spaces, like the strains of an orchestra filling the opera house as the drama unfolds onstage. Prior to this final expansion (some would say, disintegration) of his poetics, Mallarmé had, after paying little attention to music for many years, come to see it as a model from which might be borrowed certain formal and rhythmic excellencies, a whole array of structural relationships, that poetry had never aspired to before, or at least not adequately (see Pearson 239–40; Balakian, *Symbolist Movement* 85). It was not so much a case of poetry aspiring to the condition of music as of poetry putting itself to school to learn from music what it ought to aspire to, with the hope of reclaiming what had been lost to the power of the word, and the hope of ultimately surpassing music. Most admirers of Wagner sense in his music Schopenhauer's and Nietzsche's expressions of the will to power, and of power achieved by new principles of organization in the music itself; this organization and this power, however, proved profoundly disruptive to the poetry of the earlier twentieth century. In some respects the emergence of poetry from music in the past century has been an escape from the entanglements of aesthetic confusion of the previous century, epitomized by Wagner.

A great deal has been written—much of it contradictory—about exactly how Mallarmé viewed Wagner, and especially about exactly what Mallarmé meant in his celebrated sonnet, originally entitled "Hommage à Wagner":

> Le silence déjà funèbre d'une moire
> Dispose plus qu'un pli seul sur le mobilier
> Que doit un tassement du principal pilier
> Précipiter avec le manque de mémoire.
>
> Notre si vieil ébat triomphal du grimoire,
> Hiéroglyphes dont s'exalte le millier
> À propager de l'aile un frisson familier!
> Enfouissez-le-moi plutôt dans une armoire.
>
> Du souriant fracas originel haï
> Entre elles de clartés maîtresses a jailli
> Jusque vers un parvis né pour leur simulacre,
>
> Trompettes tout haut d'or pâmé sur les vélins
> Le dieu Richard Wagner irradiant un sacre
> Mal tu par l'encre même en sanglots sibyllins.

(*Oevres* 71)

> [The already-funereal silence of watered silk
> Spreads more than one fold across the furniture
> Which a subsidence of the principal pillar must
> Cast headlong into memory's failure.
>
> Our old triumphant frolic from the book of spells,
> Hieroglyphics that enthrall the multitudes
> To flap their wings over such cheap thrills!
> Better throw that thing to the back of the closet.

From the original smiling crash detested
Among them by powerful lucidities spurt out
Even to a temple square born for their likeness,

Loud golden trumpets that swoon onto vellum
Richard Wagner, the god emblazoning a rite
That ink scarcely silences with sibylline sobs.]

In a general way, the poem says that Wagner's achievement appears to have relegated poetry to permanent storage in the dusty recesses of libraries; the implication, however, may be that this is not such a bad thing for poetry—to be supplanted, for a vulgar and spectacle-loving public, by Wagnerian opera. Or so I think. In a dozen pages laden with erudition and sparkling with intelligence, Graham Robb collates earlier explications of the poem and adds much of his own to elucidate the details and to draw the whole thing into some understandable configuration (110—22). Using a letter that Mallarmé wrote to his uncle, Robb interprets the poem as taking the point of view of a "sulking" poet. This fits well with my own concept in *The Origins of Free Verse* (263—72), of the French prose poem as a sulking rejection of popular taste that has learned to be satisfied with easily read prose fiction among other vulgarities. Another way to look at "Hommage" might be to see it as an attempt by Mallarmé to expel from his consciousness this intrusive clamor so as to make his way to the higher reaches of artistic achievement. In the essay "Richard Wagner: Reverie d'un Poète Français," Mallarmé's tenuous obfuscations dissipate as he explains:

> Singulier défi qu'aux poètes dont il usurpe le devoir avec la plus candide et splendide bravoure, inflige Richard Wagner!
> Le sentiment se complique envers cet étranger, transports, vénération, aussi d'un malaise que tout soit fait, autrement qu'en irradiant, par un jeu direct, du principe littéraire même. (541—42)

> [What unique defiance Richard Wagner inflicts on poets, whose duty he usurps with the most innocent and splendid valor.
> Feelings become mixed toward this foreigner, transport, worship, also an uneasiness that everything has been done, differently, by rendering radiant, with a sudden trick, the literary principle itself.]

Here (and elsewhere in the essay) we encounter words that stand out in the sonnet and that demand explication—"irradiant," for example—so that the poem seems in some sense a distillation or condensation of what he had to say in prose. Mallarmé speaks of the *Rêverie* that all art aspires to as "déité costumée aux invisibles plis de tissu d'accords" (544) [a god costumed in the invisible folds of a harmonic texture]—which reappears as "plus qu'un pli" [more than one fold] in the sonnet. The natural expectation is that a poem that purports to pay homage to Wagner ought to be interpreted as an honorific tribute, but I find myself siding with those interpretations that see it as more profoundly ambiguous than, say, Andrew Marvell's ode to Cromwell.

On the whole, the response of Symbolist poets to music, and to Wagner in particular, was to see the art and the composer as aiming in the same direction as poetry and as having achieved, possibly, a temporary advantage over poetry in moving the human spirit toward some exalting, dreamlike ecstasy. For many, Wagner's presence was overwhelming:

> Jamais les hommes d'aujourd'hui ne pourront absolument comprendre ce que Wagner, vers 1892, a été pour nous, l'immense zone de lumière que sa magie nous ouvrit, la lame de fond qu'il souleva dans nos âmes, le terrible dégoût qu'il nous imposa pour tout ce qui n'était pas lui. (Mauclair 222, qtd. in Pistone 5)

> [Men of these days will never completely understand what Wagner, around 1892, was for us, the huge zone of light that his magic opened for us, the blade that he sank deep into our hearts, the terrible disgust that he imposed on us with everything that was not he.]

Clearly, no poet could hope to surpass Wagner—or, in prose, Flaubert or Zola—in capturing the attention of the public who patronized the opera houses and the bookstores. These orchestrators of mass appeal (and even worse, popular journalists) must be allowed domination over the lower slopes of Parnassus. It remained for the Symbolists to continue upward to the peaks, lonely mountaineers to whom belonged the glory of solitary exploration while the throngs of tourists perambulated around the lower elevations.

Paul Valéry's adulation of Mallarmé and his complete submission to the elder poet as a master is well known and is evident in the seven different *Études Littéraires*, comprising nearly eighty pages, devoted to Mallarmé. From time to time his reflections on the poet lead him into comments on music that are relevant both to his and to Mallarmé's practice:

> Une oeuvre de musique absolument pure, une composition de Sébastien Bach, par exemple, qui n'emprunte rien au sentiment, mais qui construit *un sentiment sans modèle*, et dont toute la beauté consiste dans ses combinaisons, dans l'edification d'un ordre intuitif séparé, est une acquisition inestimable, une immense valeur tirée du néant. (*Oeuvres* 1: 676)

> [An absolutely pure musical work, a composition by Sebastian Bach, for example, which borrows nothing from feeling, but which *constructs a feeling*

that has no model, and the whole beauty of which consists of its combinations, of the building of a separate intuitive order, is an invaluable acquisition, and immense treasure created out of nothing.]

Valéry's familiarity with mathematics, in which possible but nonexistent relations are explored, could have suggested to him this idea of the invention, in poetry, of possible emotional states not previously realized—an imaginative calculus of feeling. Found also here is a lively apprehension of nonexistence, an area of speculation seldom ventured into by poets, which William James saw as the test of a truly philosophical outlook.

> Il faut choisir: ou bien réduire le langage à la seule fonction transitive d'un système de signaux: ou bien souffrir que certains spéculent sur ses propriétés sensibles, en développent les effets *actuels*, les combinaisons formelles et musicales,—jusqu'à étonner parfois, ou excercer quelque temps les esprits. (1: 650–51)

> [One has to choose: either just reduce language to the sole transitive function of a system of signs: or just put up with certain people speculating on its sensible properties, while producing *immediate* effects, formal and musical combinations—to the point of sometimes astonishing, or sometimes exercising their wits.]

Valéry understood that, for Mallarmé, music represented more a challenge and a source of intuitions about the formal possibilities of language than any sort of model. By the time he had completed *Le Cimetière Marin* he could state flatly (in *Lettre À Madame C . . .*): "La poésie n'est pas la musique." [Poetry is not music.] He then qualified this distinction, without much softening it: "Mais par le rhythme, les accents et les consonances, faisant ce qu'elle peut, elle essaye de communiquer une vertu quasi musicale à l'expression de certaines pensées. Non de toutes les pensées." [But with rhythm, with accents, and with repeating sounds, doing whatever it can, it tries to lend a quasi-musical power to the expression of certain thoughts. Not of all thoughts.] (2: 1262). Jean Hytier carefully documents his assertion that "Valéry's attitude with regard to music is ambivalent" (290). Hytier says that what attracted Valéry about music was (as for Mallarmé) the possibility of a purely formal system, but that he distrusted the emotional power that music exercised. Valéry's later writings include scattered remarks that make clear that he had long since come to consider the French language and French poetry as functioning in terms of its own system of sounds; indeed, he never seems that far away from the *musique naturele* of Deschamps, though one would not wish to suggest that the bluntness of the latter bore any comparison with Valéry's subtle and disciplined poetics. Hytier mentions with some regret Valéry's failure ever to engage in detailed analysis of the sorts of effects that he achieves in his own poetry—indeed, he conspicuously avoids using even the terms for assonance, alliteration, consonance, and so forth, which figure prominently in his verse. To me, it seems that the poet is already as self-conscious as one could possibly be as to what he was achieving—not a romantic self-consciousness, but rather an intense self-awareness, an Olympian detachment, that purges and purifies the personality of the poet.

Le Cimetière Marin cannot be translated. Even to say that is to make a play on words: the poem is rooted in the immobile suspension of the sea's continual renewal of itself, and in the acute sense of a particular place as well; to relocate the poem in another language is to move a cemetery. The title itself cannot be rendered satisfactorily: "Marine Cemetery" will not do, for several reasons; "The Graveyard by the Sea" sounds too sentimental; "The Graveyard of the Sea" sounds more appropriate for a poem about Cape Hatteras. "The Seaside Cemetery" comes a little closer, but still is not satisfactory. An early working title was "Mare Nostrum," which Valéry must have intended to mean our inner sea of consciousness as well as the Mediterranean; but this is no help in rendering the title satisfactorily into English. "Marin" suggests that which belongs to the sea, but it also designates a sea wind that blows up from the southeast and across the southern coasts of France, the wind that rises in the last stanza of the poem. The entire title implies the sea as the ultimate repository of all the transitory configurations of matter, including the human remains interred for the time being near the church—but also the repository and source of all consciousness. One can contemplate the title and discuss it at length, but no exact rendering is possible.

The same is largely true of the poem itself. Some passages, of course, lend themselves more easily at least to straightforward explanation in English, if not translation. Most accessible, perhaps, are the lines that render the pathos and anguish of our mortality. A rendering of the following, even in prose, must be loose and expansive in order to try to capture some of the emotion compressed into half as many words in the poem:

> Où sont des morts les phrases familières,
> L'art personnel, les âmes singulières?
> La larve file où se formaient les pleurs.
>
> Les cris aigus des filles chatouillées,
> Les yeux, les dents, le paupières mouillées,
> Le sein charmant qui joue avec le feu,
> Le sang qui brille aux lèvres qui se rendent,

Les derniers dons, les doigts qui les défendent,
Tout va sous terre et rentre dans le jeu!

(88–96)

[Where are the familiar turns of speech of the dead, their special ways
　of doing things, their individual souls? The graveworm spins its
　web where tears welled up.
The piercing cries of girls who are tickled—their teeth and eyes, their
　moist eyelids—the breast that sets one on fire—the blood that colors
　yielding lips—the last treasures—the fingers that defend them—it all
　goes into the earth and comes back into play again!]

This is about as simple as the meaning ever gets in the poem—and even here
there may be multiple senses of "la larve," which carries a second meaning of a
ghostly apparition from ancient times.

　Through most of the poem, multiple suggestions and cross-references of
image, symbol, and theme may stimulate commentary but defeat the transla-
tor. Wallace Stevens's "Sunday Morning" or "The Idea of Order at Key West"
provide examples of poems in English that might approximate some of these
difficulties if one were to try to produce a version in another language. Even
more than Stevens, however, Valéry demands to be experienced rather than
explicated; speaking for myself, I find that certain lines and passages communicate lucid impressions—I am to some extent changed by them and they
become part of my experience—but I am very hard put to find words for
this experience or understanding. To this degree Valéry may indeed have
achieved what Mallarmé sought in vain—the experiential immediacy offered
by music—though Le Cimetière Marin has in it also a Monet-like or Pissarro-
like impressionism, a pointillism.

　Take the first three words of both the first and last lines: "Ce toit tranquille"
[This calm roof]. Because the focus moves so rapidly to the surface of the sea,
some commentators hasten to give the "roof" that meaning at the outset. To
me, this is a mistake, especially since in line 18 the word "tuiles" appears.
Surely we are to see a tile roof with pigeons strutting ("marchent") across it—
whether the roof of a church, a house, or one of the mausoleums in the
cemetery across which the gaze extends. The idea of terra cotta, or baked
earth, with white forms interspersed across it reappears as a herd of sheep (61–
64), which perhaps also corresponds to a scattering of clouds in the sky,
further on in the poem. It may be that the problematic word "palpitent" seems
to require a more moveable surface, but as we soon learn, it is high noon of the
summer solstice, and the shimmering of heat from the tiles can easily account
for this effect in the middle ground. Throughout the poem Valéry employs

verbs that suggest movement, but movement that is cyclical, almost completely suspended, or at best transitional into some form or stage of existence
that is a precursor to its own self-renewal. "Palpitent," then, is more the
absence of progressive movement, like the "vibre" of Zeno's arrow further on.
At the beginning of the poem, there is no external foreground; that is supplied
by the rhythms of consciousness, of the perceiving mind. Of course the
"tranquil roof" does immediately become a metaphor both for the Mediterranean glittering in the sun and for the intense awareness of the percipient—
and both of those, metaphors for each other. There are six levels of reality
working at once: the unseen mind of the observer, the dimly sensed presence
of the graves and the gravestones, the roof with the pigeons, and the sea with
its scattering of white sails and the glints of light from its scintillating waves;
and the two steadier poles of this complex are the earth that has absorbed the
bodies of the dead beneath, and the sun at its zenith.

There is almost no forward movement in the poem. Indeed, that is the
point: the suspension of movement in the moment of perception—perception
too pure even to be called contemplative. Various kinds of mental discipline
have made possible the apprehension of the virtual, the power of pure being,
the "seul soupir" [single sigh] and the "point pur" [pure point]. From this lofty
eminence, this Apollonian elevation, however, the poet can survey the conditions of our changing world. He does not say as much, but mutability itself has
fostered a luminous detachment, a brilliant aloofness. Stevens's "Death is the
mother of beauty" seems somewhat crude and unfocused in comparison with
the confident lucidity with which Valéry surveys the limits of his own existence, acknowledging both the hollow resonances of our own vanity and the
horrid plenitude of the corpse-filled earth. Other formulations come to mind
from elsewhere—perhaps "Ripeness is all," or Spinoza's concept of immortality as a perfectly impersonal identification with one's own limited place in the
grand scheme of things. Valéry recognizes (and dramatizes in the poem) not
only the false promises of any eternal afterlife, with immortality personified as
a hideously costumed hag, but also the inability of consciousness itself to
persist in its lofty and somewhat disdainful apprehension of its own situation.

But what, one might well ask at this point, does all this have to do with music and poetry? In reply to an inquiry by Fernand Lot, Valéry wrote in 1929:

> Ce dont il me souvient, c'est d'avoir tenté de maintenir des conditions
> musicales constantes, c'est-à-dire que je me suis efforcé de soumettre à
> chaque instant le contenu significatif à la volonté ou à l'intention de satisfaire
> le sens auditif. Le rythme, les accents et les timbres doivent, à mon avis, êtres
> des facteurs *au moins* aussi importants que l'élément abstrait du langage

poétique. Je vais même jusqu'à penser qu'il ne faut pas craindre de sacrifier de "beau vers" isolés à la continuité en quelque sorte mélodique d'une phrase poursuivie au travers des rimes et des césures. (*Oeuvres* 1: 1675–76)

[What that reminds me of, is of having tried to maintain constant musical conditions, that is, I forced myself at every moment to make the meaningful content subsidiary to the will or intention of satisfying the auditory sense. Rhythm, accent, and pitch must, in my opinion, be factors *at least* as important as the abstract meaning of the poetic language. I even go so far as to think that one need not fear sacrificing some isolated good lines in favor of the continuity, in some respects melodic, of a phrase pursued across rhymes and caesuras.]

Elsewhere he tells us that when he began the poem, his intention was not to *say* something but rather to *do* something, and that, to start with, *Le Cimetière Marin* was no more than a vacant rhythmical framework, or one filled with empty syllables, with which he had been obsessed for some time (1: 1503–4). Other poets—Shelley and Eliot, for example, and probably Wallace Stevens—have worked in similar fashion; the difference is the intensity that Valéry achieved and maintained without, as Shelley did, allowing his imagery to rend itself into diaphanous shreds.

Valéry's auditory imagination settled on the ten-syllable line; at first such a line seemed to him somewhat impoverished in comparison with the generosity of the Alexandrine: "J'observai que cette figure était décasyllabique, et je me fis quelques réflexions sur ce type fort peu employé dans la poésie moderne; il me semblait pauvre et monotone" (1: 1503). [I observed that this pattern was decasyllabic, and I had a few thoughts about this breed mighty seldom used in modern poetry; it seemed impoverished and monotonous to me.] But then it struck him as a challenge to render the decasyllabic equal in power to the French classical line. Next he conceived a strophe made up of six of these lines, and a composition based on a certain number of such strophes, an arrangement of differing tones and functions. (In the end there were exactly two dozen stanzas—a dozen dozen lines—possibly a numerological reminiscence of the truncated Alexandrine.) These stanzas preserved a sufficient independence from one another to allow the poet to shuffle their order in various early versions of the poem, but his intention was that they should work together:

Entre les strophes, des contrastes ou des correspondances devaient être institués. Cette dernière condition exigea bientôt que le poéme possible fût un monologue de "moi", dans lequel les thèmes les plus simples et les plus constants de ma vie affective et intellectuelle, tels qu'ils s'étaient imposés à mon adolescence et associés à la mer et à la lumière d'un certain lieu des bords de la Méditerranée, fussent appelés, tramés, opposés. (1: 1503)

[Between the stanzas, some contrasts or some corresponding features must be established. This last condition soon requires that the poem, to be realized, be a monologue about "me," within which the simplest and most constant themes of my emotional and intellectual life, just as they were imposed on my adolescence and associated with the sea and the light in certain places along the shore of the Mediterranean, would be named, captured, set against one another.]

There exist various possibilities for determining the larger structural units of *Le Cimetière Marin*. If we simply divide the poem in half, we find that, thematically, the first half favors the Apollonian survey, the exhilaration of the self-sufficient intellect that has succeeded in living totally in the present moment as well as outside it; indeed, the last phrase of line 72 is "l'esprit clair," clear-headedness, the intellection that transcends mortal limitations. The second half carries us in quite another direction. Although satisfaction with self and resignation to the conditions of existence persist (the dead are seen as "well-off" where they are), in the ensuing stanzas the horror of physical and mental annihilation proves more and more distracting: death is a breast offered by the hag of immortality; the "beautiful lie and the pious deception" of belief gives way to the vacant skull and the mocking laughter of nothingness.

Also, the poem opens with a set of three strophes and concludes with a set of three. Stanzas four through seven are each so self-contained that one might be tempted to look for a point of division between any one of them, but Valéry's return to the word "Toit" at the end of stanza three, capitalizing it this time for emphasis, suspends the movement more than anywhere else. The "Non, non! . . . Debout!" of the twenty-second stanza is even more definite as an interruption and as the beginning of the conclusion. At that point the presiding intelligence of the poem has retreated into the absurd and sterile stasis of Zeno's mathematical paradoxes in an effort to renounce time and change, in particular the disintegration of the self. Nothing is left but to break out of this reverie of timelessness, to "try to live," to carry into life itself the momentary transcendence so briefly enjoyed.

I have been discussing the larger patterns in the poem thematically, but would argue that Valéry realized the same structure rhythmically—that one can certainly hear the ballade-like unity of the opening and the appropriately looser structure of the conclusion. It becomes more difficult to account for the two nine-stanza segments in the center. As I have said, beginning with stanza four there is much independence, with each unit making something close to a free-standing poem. This mirrors the freedom and detachment that seem to have been achieved at this point. At the same time, buried in each strophe is a hint of what will eventually challenge this too-complacent exhilaration. At first, all change seems delightful, or rather, change seems merely illusion, no more than a phase within a repetitive cycle, both the fruit that dissolves in one's mouth and the secret changes within oneself. "My shadow passes over the houses of the dead," he says in line 35, as if they were another race from himself, as if he were indeed in movement, as if movement were not an illusion. But then more ominous phrases occur: the sorrowful shadows implied by the light, the bony ground. He tries to resolve these feelings with a strangely unrealized metaphor of the distantly glimpsed sea as a faithful dog herding the tombstones, the "mysterious sheep," but the effort eventually becomes too great. The self-sufficiency of the stanzas gives way to a more continuous development; they are more closely linked, and they tend to answer one another.

Again, I acknowledge a tendency to stray from structural questions, which might have some bearing on whatever "musical" form can be found, to analysis of themes and images. But I have tried to suggest how the rhythms and tempos of the various segments of the poem differ, and how they are appropriate to the progress of the poem's argument. The tightness of the individual stanzas—with none of the lines really enjambed, even when punctuation is absent, and with each one pulling up sharply at the end of the sixth line—tends to obscure these changes, as does the lively, almost headlong, progress of the rhythm. Without claiming that Valéry has aimed at any sort of numerological symmetry of the sort found, say, in the *Vie de Saint Alexis*, one can assume that there is enough of the *esprit de géométrie* as well as *finesse* that we may go looking for symmetry. Such patterning is instinctive for the poet who has trained himself in mathematics as well as in prosody.

As in the couplet of classical prosody—the English heroic couplet as well as the French Alexandrine—Valéry's stanza observes a strictly repetitive form, but offers an interplay of rhythm and rhetoric that is infinitely various. The ten-syllable sesets rhyme invariably *aabccb*. Eleven of the twenty-four stanzas break in half with an end-stopped line, but this strophic caesura really follows no fixed pattern; indeed, five stanzas have no complete stops at all (although, as I have pointed out, neither is there any real enjambment even in the few lines where no punctuation appears). All one can say is that each strophe is rhythmically and rhetorically unique. Valéry makes abundant use of the exclamation point, the effect of which is to make a line into a self-contained vatic ejaculation, especially toward the end of the poem; in the concluding three stanzas most lines end this way with an effect that is distantly parallel to the way Coleridge wound up "Kubla Khan."

Perhaps the second stanza may do as an example of a typical stanza:

> Quel pur travail de fins éclairs consume
> Maint diamant d'imperceptible écume,
> Et quelle paix semble se concevoir!
> Quand sur l'abîme un soleil se repose,
> Ouvrages purs d'une éternelle cause,
> Le temps scintille et le songe est savoir.
>
> (7–12)

> [How purely these quick lightnings can consume
> Those diamond points of viewless spray and spume
> And how profound the peace that settles there!
> When the noon sun reposes on the depth
> Of that eternal source, achievement pure,
> Scintillant moment when the dream is truth.]

Here we see several things noted above: the division at the end of the third line, marked by an exclamation point; the independence of "Maint diamant d'imperceptible écume" as a phrase, even though it contains the direct object of the verb that concludes the first line; the rhetorical paralleling of "Quel . . . quelle"; the way in which the closed couplet that initiates the stanza opens up into the *cddc* pattern that concludes it. This last pattern seems to reinforce, throughout the poem, how a sense of a sharp focus, an intense moment of apprehension, dissolves even as we ourselves shall inevitably be dispersed in "l'ère successive," an untranslatable phrase that means roughly "the passage of time."

The effect of "Quel pur travail de fins éclairs consume" cannot be understood without reference to the opening strophe, where alliterative pairings and reflexive assonances and consonances accumulate almost to the point of overburdening the lines. In the line just quoted, such patterns evaporate suddenly, much as the spume of the distant whitecaps continually dissipates itself in the minute brilliance of the vertical sunbeams that play on the tops of the waves. Indeed, that is exactly what the next line says. But in that line, the density of sound reestablishes itself: the nasal of "Maint" and the sound of the vowel is first picked up with "diamant" and then repeated in "d'imperceptible," where the elided preposition echoes the "d" of the previous word. A liability in discussing *Le Cimetière Marin* is that one cannot easily separate its constituents for independent analysis. Valéry "feels his thought" more acutely than John Donne ever did; his imagery is a metaphor of its own realization—

that is, the actuality serves as a symbol of itself. And the rhythms of line and stanza, with the other kinds of auditory patterning, accommodate themselves to this feeling and this realization better than in any other poem I know. I have therefore—in an effort to single out one stanza for consideration in terms of its internal structure—already strayed into an account of intraline phenomena.

Basic to the muscular tautness of the poem is the quality of the rhymes. Because of lingering effects of grammatical gender and remnants of inflection, French offers a vocabulary enriched much beyond English with repetitive sounds. Even so, the percentage of lines that conclude with *rime riche* is surprising. (*Rime riche* occurs when the preceding consonant as well as the concluding vowel and consonant belong to the rhyme, as in "interne" / "citerne.") This particular augmentation might seem obtrusive and contrived, except that it scarcely appears until we are well into the poem, following the daringly identical rhyme of "toit" with "toi." But beginning with the fifth stanza, three-fourths of the rhymes are rich; some strophes contain nothing but such rhymes, and even when those are not found, pairs such as "arbres" / "marbres" produce much the same effect. So tactfully has Valéry allowed these to impinge upon our ear, however, that we may not notice them until we go looking for them.

More noticeable are the alliterating pairs: "Temple du Temps, qu'un seul soupir résume," which includes internal rhyme as well, and the "scintillation sereine sème" of stanza four are among more than a hundred examples that might be chosen from the poem. The latter phrase carries the effect of supercilious excess, the "dédain souverain" of the next line. Yet as common as they are throughout, the particular alliterating combinations are so varied as to produce a nearly subliminal suggestion of unity. They are, in any case, functional rather than showy, more like the way that Keats loaded his own rifts with ore in say, the opening of "To Autumn," than like the extrinsic decorativeness favored by Tennyson.

Some particular local effects might be singled out. "L'insecte net gratte la sécheresse" surely imitates the chitinous scraping of cicadas. The vowels of "Les cris aigus des filles chatouillées" distantly imitate those girlish shrieks, while "toute lourde de marbres" weighs down the line with an excess of proximate consonants. Sometimes there is something close to a pun: in "Comme le fruit se fond en jouissance," I cannot help hearing the word "jus" dissolved into the final word, while "mille tuiles" sounds almost comically suggestive of multiplicity. Most remarkable of all are the lines where a series of sounds rearranges itself like an aural anagram or palindrome: "O récompense après une pensée." All these things knit the poem together like the thread and designs of a Persian rug, or the incisions and reliefs of Moorish architectural decoration; unlike my analogies, however, the poem is replete with idolatrous detail and philosophi-cal insight—as well as abstract patterning.

In most respects, Valéry's poetic carries further than ever before all the kinds of verbal music discovered by earlier French poets. Verlaine may have called for "de la musique, avant toute chose," but with a few exceptions his lines are thin pipings in comparison with Valéry's chamber orchestra. If there is any way in which *Le Cimetière Marin* can be seen as directly emergent from music it might be that symphonic music had indeed suggested to poets the possibility of a structure and orchestration of sound that had not been attempted before. And that observation, a restatement of things said earlier, applies equally well to the work of T. S. Eliot, and especially to his *Four Quartets*, to which I now turn.

In considering the relation of Eliot's poetry to music, the best thing to do is to open his essay "The Music of Poetry" and read it through once a day for a week, if necessary stopping to read the poems to which he alludes. The latter recommendation could extend the period of study by some years, of course, since he mentions Mallarmé (in the same paragraph with Edward Lear's "The Dong with the Luminous Nose" and William Morris's "Blue Closet"). At the conclusion of the essay, he defines the relations of the two arts:

> I think that a poet may gain much from the study of music: how much technical knowledge of musical form is desirable I do not know, for I have not that technical knowledge myself. But I believe that the properties in which music concerns the poet most nearly, are the sense of rhythm and the sense of structure. I think that it might be possible for a poet to work too closely to musical analogies: the result might be an effect of artificiality; but I know that a poem, or a passage of a poem, may tend to realize itself first as a particular rhythm before it reaches expression in words, and that this rhythm may bring to birth the idea and the image; and I do not believe that this is an experience peculiar to myself. The use of recurrent themes is as natural to poetry as to music. There are possibilities for verse which bear some analogy to the development of a theme by different groups of instruments; there are possibilities of transitions in a poem comparable to the different movements of a symphony or a quartet; there are possibilities of contrapuntal arrange-ment of subject-matter. It is in the concert room, rather than in the opera house, that the germ of a poem may be quickened. (*On Poetry and Poets* 32)

Earlier I spoke, partly as a joke, of Eliot's "taking back the Ninth Sym-phony," retreating from the overweening ambition that would carry the hu-man voice and its poetry into a splendiferous pageant and spectacle that would overwhelm human sensibilities and transport the human spirit into ecstatic transcendence of all limitations. In truth, the self-deflating irony of Eliot's earliest poems kept him well distanced from such romantic presumption. One way of looking at *The Waste Land* is as a parody of such operatic pretension which repeatedly returns to earth with bathetic descents of diction ("Madame Sosostris, famous clairvoyante, /Had a bad cold"). In this essay, Eliot returns to what he learned from Mallarmé—and he may be the only poet writing in English who ever did learn anything from Mallarmé. And although he applied it in quite a different fashion, the lesson he absorbed sounds remarkably parallel to what we hear Valéry saying: "Il est né, comme la plupart de mes poèmes, de la présence inattendue en mon esprit d'un certain rhythme" (*Oeuvres* 1: 1674). [It was born, like most of my poems, from the unnoticed presence of a certain rhythm in my mind.]

Helped by his reading in Irving Babbitt, Eliot never came close to embracing any sentimental confusion of the arts; but he seems to share with Mallarmé and Valéry a desire to place poetry on an equal footing with music and, if possible, to reclaim some of the prestige lost to the other art. The "sense of rhythm and the sense of structure" are shared with music, though perhaps Eliot might also have allowed that these are inherited (as I would argue) from poetry's original intimate welding with actual music. In addition to these, however, Eliot is willing to allow other analogies—to permit a more sophisticated poetic structure that includes movements, counterpoint, thematic development, and transitions reminiscent of what composers had learned to do in music. And at this point we must remind ourselves that Eliot delivered the address for which this essay was the text just as he was completing his *Four Quartets*, so that in large part what we have here is an account of what he believed his intentions to have been in composing those poems.

As with most of his poetry, Eliot groped his way toward the final configuration of *Four Quartets* without knowing very clearly what his ultimate intention was. Louis L. Martz finds their structure prefigured in *The Waste Land's* five-part arrangement. (Others have noticed this as well; see, for example, Matthiessen 177.) Martz's argument seems entirely convincing, even when he points out what we all know about that poem's genesis: that the form owed as much to Pound as it did to Eliot. Martz says that "without Pound's editorial intervention, we would not have the short lyric, 'Phlebas the Phoenecian', appearing by itself as part IV of *The Waste Land*, and thus, presumably, we would not have the short lyrics constituting the four sections of all *Four Quartets*—the short movement that helps to create analogies with Beethoven's late quartets" (190). Seldom do discussions of *The Waste Land* consider it as a paradigm of organization—except for those that take Eliot's bait when he says that "the plan . . . [was] suggested by Miss Jessie L. Weston's book on the Grail Legend" and then goes on to mention *The Golden Bough* as well. To me, this has always seemed an invitation by Eliot for the reader to continue Pound's work of bringing organization to the poem—though as Eliot admitted many years later, the poem remained just as confused as ever despite that helpful intervention. Without going into a detailed recapitulation of Eliot's development from 1922 to 1934 (when "Burnt Norton" appeared), we can think of him as having gradually discovered that "the end of all our exploring / Will be to arrive where we started," and as having realized that the division of *The Waste Land* into five parts, and of those parts into segments with differing tempos, provided him with a formal model that could be refined into a quasimusical structure.

In an unpublished lecture delivered in 1933, Eliot mentioned what he was aiming at:

> [T]o write poetry which would be essentially poetry, with nothing poetic about it, poetry standing naked in its bare bones, or poetry so transparent that we should not see the poetry, but that which we are meant to see through the poetry, poetry so transparent that in reading it we are intent on what the poem *points at*, and not on the poetry, this seems to me the thing to try for. To get *beyond poetry*, as Beethoven, in his later works, strove to get *beyond music*. (qtd. in Matthiessen 90)

The iconoclastic chaos of *The Waste Land*, which may remind us of Stravinsky, or perhaps of a Wagner gone mad, is to give way to an art that transcends its own conventions—a seemingly retrograde step that actually carries the work outside of time itself.

I spoke irreverently above of critics who "take Eliot's bait" about *The Waste Land*, seeing in Eliot's own annotations a guide for further study. In a less mischievous way, it seems to me, Eliot intended his remarks in "The Music of Poetry" as a stimulus that might encourage students of his work toward analysis of the formal structure of *Four Quartets*. At the time that he was about to publish "Little Gidding," he wrote to John Hayward, discussing the use of the word "quartets" as part of the title for all four poems: "But I should like to indicate that these poems are all in a particular set form which I have elaborated, and the word 'quartet' does seem to me to start people on the right tack for understanding them ('sonata' in any case is *too* musical)" (qtd. in Gardner 26). Eliot was always a shrewd judge of what might attract the maximum amount of attention—and in this case, what could be more remarkable than that the former enfant terrible and iconoclast should emerge as a master of structure of a complexity never seen before in poetry? To say this is not to find fault either with Eliot or with his poem; I believe that *Four Quartets* is the greatest poetic achievement in English of the twentieth century and I believe that it will continue to be so regarded by many readers of the future. But I do think that the multitude of studies that undertake to demonstrate exactly how Eliot orchestrated his poems on musical principles, while they provide some readers and many authors with much diversion, are as misguided as those studies that repeatedly explicate *The Waste Land* in terms of the Fisher King and the Grail. Among the more cautious and intelligent applications of a musical interpretation is Matthiessen's:

> But he insists—and this has immediate bearing on his own intentions—that "the use of recurrent themes is as natural to poetry as to music." He has worked on that assumption throughout his quartets, and whether he has proved that "there are possibilities of transitions in a poem comparable to the different movements of a symphony or a quartet," or that "there are possibilities of contrapuntal arrangement of subject-matter," can be known only through repeated experience of the whole series. All I wish to suggest here is the pattern made by some of the dominant themes in their interrelation and progression. (183)

There is no denying that Eliot was from the first inclined to see his poems as suggestive of music—even if we consider the words used in their titles: "love song," "prelude," "rhapsody," "triumphal march." I would argue, however, that more relevant to what Eliot actually achieved in *Four Quartets* is his argument in an earlier paragraph of "The Music of Poetry":

> What I think we have, in English poetry, is a kind of amalgam of systems of divers sources [though I do not like to use the word 'system', for it has a suggestion of conscious invention rather than growth] [Eliot's brackets]: an amalgam like the amalgam of races, and indeed partly due to racial origins. The rhythms of Anglo-Saxon, Celtic, Norman French, of Middle English and Scots, have all made their mark upon English poetry, together with the rhythms of Latin, and, at various periods, of French, Italian, and Spanish. As with human beings in a composite race, different strains may be dominant in different individuals, even in members of the same family, so one or another element in the poetic compound may be more congenial to one or another poet or to one or another period. The kind of poetry we get is determined, from time to time, by the influences of one or another contemporary litera-ture in a foreign language; or by circumstances which make one period of our own past more sympathetic than another; or by the prevailing emphasis in education. But there is one law of nature more powerful than any of these varying currents, or influences from abroad or from the past: the law that poetry must not stray too far from the ordinary everyday language which we use and bear. Whether poetry is accentual or syllabic, rhymed or rhymeless, formal or free, it cannot afford to lose its contact with the changing language of common intercourse. (*On Poetry and Poets* 20–21)

Four Quartets is in fact just such an "amalgam." Anyone well read in English poetry, and in poetry in other languages, especially French and Italian, can pick out one instance after another where Eliot has borrowed from earlier prosodies. The eclecticism does not draw attention to itself as it does in *The Waste Land*, but neither is it much disguised by the conversational modern "voice," the "language of common intercourse," that pervades the poems.

The general rhythm of *Four Quartets* is accentual, except for those of the shorter movements that revert to accentual-syllabic meters. Julia Maniates Reibetanz's *A Reading of Eliot's "Four Quartets"* is unlikely to be surpassed as an analysis both of the meter itself and of the stages by which Eliot arrived at it. The only thing I have to add to her treatment is to point out some historical connections and to locate Eliot in a broader context of prosodic history. After introducing arguments and citing examples to show the dominantly accentual nature of the verse, Reibetanz tells us: "Neither the six-stress line nor the three-stress line was to serve as the principal vehicle for the verse in *Four Quartets*. Rather it is the four-stress line that stands as the norm." She also points out (as I had discovered for myself) that "it was in 'The Rock' that Eliot first settled into the four-stress line and used it in prolonged passages as the exclusive form of verse" (9).

Reibetanz comments perceptively on what the cultivation of an accentual meter did for Eliot: "[I]t allowed him to start from a different place, to feel free of the old metrical pressures, voices of the past which obviously haunted him deeply" (3). She is speaking in particular of the iambic pentameter that Eliot goes to such lengths to evade—though never escaping it—in his earlier work, particularly in "Prufrock" but also in *The Waste Land*. Where I differ with her—though I would prefer to think of it more as an extension of her arguments than as a difference—is that I see Eliot as reaching back toward something much older in the language even as he carries forward his own poetic evolution; to see his metric that way is perfectly in keeping with his well-known views about the use of tradition. As we all know, the four-beat line—which some prosodists now like to describe as a pair of dipodic units—is the ancient Anglo-Saxon rhythm. Neither is Eliot particularly in advance of his times in reviving the meter, though "reviving" is not the right word to describe what he did. One argument runs that submerged in every iambic pentameter line is a four-stress accentual beat, but we need not tax our ingenuity or endanger our credibility in trying to prove this. In fact, accentual meters are all around us, still, in versions of ballads, in songs, in nursery rhymes, and in the work of many other twentieth-century poets: Ted Hughes, Elizabeth Bishop, and Seamus Heaney, to name only three. Dylan Thomas's "Fern Hill" effects a complete divorce of the conjoined terms "accentual" and "syllabic"; Thomas counted out the syllables line by line in that poem, but it can only be read accentually.

In composing his later work in accentual meter, Eliot placed himself solidly in a line of poets who perceived that the pentameter overlay, especially as cultivated in the eighteenth century, could falsify their language. Even the eighteenth century was a great period of rediscovery of pre-Renaissance balladry, as we have seen earlier in this book, and further investigations into that period may turn up further examples of compositions imitative of the ballad rhythms. The best known early critical apology for accentual meter is Coleridge's introduction to "Christabel." Hopkins tried in his own way to "break the pentameter" (Pound's battle cry), but he remained fideistically attached to a five-unit line and to recognized patterns such as the sonnet. Coventry Patmore's theory and experiment with dipody resulted in lines that are closer to the tetrameters of Donne's "The Ecstasy" than to *Beowulf*, but at least he did seem to be reaching toward something more natural to the language. William Morris's "The Blue Closet" (of which Eliot was fond) can be considered as accentual meter, though Morris may have seen it as loosened or "substituted" iambics, if he thought about it at all:

> / / / /
> Lady Alice, Lady Louise,
> / / / /
> Between the wash of the tumbling seas
> / / / /
> We are ready to sing, if so ye please;
> / / / /
> So lay your long hands on the keys

(Some readers might wish to add a fifth stress [not beat] to the last line, or else force the meter into greater regularity by stressing "on"; the four-beat rhythm is already so well established that it overrides ordinary prose cadence.) Once one starts to cast about one pulls in numerous examples of accentual meters from the last century and a half: Arnold, Swinburne, Bridges, Graves, Auden, and many a minor poet. Even certain poems of Yeats are best accounted for by calling them accentual. There is, therefore, no reason to see anything very radical in Eliot's accentual meters—and no insult to Eliot in saying this. To do something that everyone else is doing, but to do it better than anyone else is doing it, is the greatest achievement of any artist.

Eliot does not, of course, aim at reproducing Old English meter as a tour de force, the way that various other poets have. When he first departed from iambic pentameter, he allowed an auditory palimpsest—his famous "ghost behind the arras"—of pentameter to glimmer across the lines. With the Germanic accentual line, he gives us the opposite effect, allowing the meter to stride sturdily forward, declaring its presence, but ready when necessary to halt, skip a step, turn aside, or even break into a jog or a sarabande, a Marvell-like tetrameter or a pseudosestina reminiscent of the French forms beloved of the poets of Eliot's youth.

Pulling the four-beat line in the other direction are the cadences of the Bible, particularly of the prophetic books of the Old Testament, and most particularly of Hebraic chanting as approximated in English by the translators of the King James Version. Sometimes the blend of accentual meter and biblical anaphora is so complete that one hardly knows which to call it, but more often (prefigured again by what he did in "The Rock") we find him over the space of a line or two sliding into a Whitman-like expansiveness. To call it "Whitman-like" is risky and perhaps tendentious. S. Musgrove's thorough treatment, *T. S. Eliot and Walt Whitman*, turns up numerous passages in which the two poets seem to parallel one another—and also documents copiously Eliot's aversion to Whitman and especially his dismay at the effect that Whitman had on the style of American poetry. In some sense, despite his many years of spiritual discipline, his genuine attempts to school himself in Christian humility, Eliot did place himself in competition with Whitman as the prophetic voice to be heeded, and he could not have helped realizing how much power Whitman gained by speaking to his readers in the familiar cadences of the Bible. I have argued elsewhere, however, that the most important connection between Eliot and Whitman is indirect, through the French vers-librists of the later nineteenth century who did indeed imitate Whitman. Even there, there is some confusion, since a "style biblique" tradition already existed in France before Whitman made himself felt there.

Many students of twentieth-century poetry consider *Four Quartets* the century's chief masterpiece; Eliot himself thought it his best work, and believed that "Little Gidding" was the best of the quartets. I will therefore treat that poem as the culmination of Eliot's constructive poetics, the end of a long journey that began with the profitable iconoclasms of his early work, a reintegration of English poetry. For anyone who cares to do so, it is easy to collect from Eliot's prose writings, both early and late, statements that make clear his belief that poetic structures have to be periodically broken and remade, always with reference to what has already been done with them; this sets him apart from those moderns who decree a state of permanent revolution or vatic transcendence—but also from those who "follow an antique drum."

Eliot's reliance on the fundamental four-beat line in "Little Gidding" is subtle but insistent; let us examine exactly what occurs in the first six lines:

Midwinter spring is its own season
Sempiternal though sodden towards sundown,
Suspended in time between pole and tropic,
When the short day is brightest, with frost and fire,
The brief sun flames the ice, on pond and ditches,
In windless cold that is the heart's heat.

Taken in isolation, or as part of an ordinary prose sentence, the opening line's cadence is ambiguous. Suppose it went like this: "Midwinter spring is its own season, given the unpredictability of meteorological events in the British Isles." Ordinary pronunciation would stress the first two syllables of "midwinter" about equally (we must always allow for quibbling, but in fact dictionaries mark both as strongly stressed). The same is true of "own season," at least as I hear it. Well, there are our four stresses, so what do we do for "spring"? Add another stress, evidently. That gives us enough stresses for a pentameter, but the way they are distributed makes that impossible. We must therefore wait for the second line to hear what we are into, although the alliteration in the first line is already urging us into the desired configuration.

The second line is close to being a perfect Old English alliterative line: four stresses, with one of the first two stresses echoed alliteratively in the third position. All it lacks is a more pronounced medial caesura. But even as the Anglo-Saxon begins to shrug its sinewy shoulders, Eliot is having some fun with it, balancing a highfalutin polysyllabic Latinate derivative with the past participle of an old German strong verb, "sodden," which, moreover, has longstanding associations that are both dreary and comical. Pairing the two words is a typical example of Eliotic hypsos-bathos, a step in the direction of the stylistic desideratum found toward the end of the poem. Here, the "formal word precise but not pedantic" is a little too much of the latter, and the "common word exact without vulgarity" might be stretched to suggest that toward sundown the day has had one too many pints of bitter. But in this line the rhythm is becoming well established:

      /   /   /   /
Sempiternal though sodden towards sundown.

The third line supplies the missing caesura, though here the alliterative coupling shifts to the second and fourth stress positions, while in the fourth line the third and fourth positions alliterate.

Line 5 comes close to destroying the pattern: "The brief sun flames the ice, on pond and ditches" reads most easily as iambic pentameter, with a spondee for the second foot and a hypermetric syllable at the end. Anglo-Saxon lines may be found that are as loose as this in terms of extra syllables, but they are exceptions.

> /　　/　　　　/　　/
> Windless cold that is the heart's heat

takes us back to Old English (more or less).

One can continue on to the first break (following "Zero summer") illustrating how Eliot continually challenges and then reasserts his Germanic line. This procedure (as I have already suggested) is the inverse of "Prufrock," which takes for granted the presence of the iambic pentameter as a norm, crossing and recrossing it in the course of that poem, reminding us periodically with perfect pentameter lines, even rhyming couplets, of what he is not doing. In "Little Gidding" the presumption is that there will be no iambic pentameter; in its place, the norm will be accentual meter—starting with a recollection of its most authoritative presence in Anglo-Saxon and Middle English alliterative verse. A recording of Eliot reading validates this conclusion; he introduces marked caesuras into almost all the lines, even where punctuation and syntax might not suggest that they would occur. Also, it comes clear that he employs a variant whereby the line actually begins at the caesura and concludes midway in the next (printed) line. By repeating words ("spring," "time") he anticipates the anaphora, and other kinds of repetition, that will dominate the remainder of Part 1. The alliteration intensifies and carries forward, also: "blanched," "blossom," "bloom."

After we have been pulled up short, however, by "Zero summer," Eliot shifts into his ecclesiastical mode, the range of gears being determined by cadences and repetitive patterns suggested mainly by the Bible and the Book of Common Prayer. For the next thirty-five lines (to the end of Part 1) the Old English rhythm might seem to have disappeared; less than a third of the lines can plausibly be scanned that way. (In fact, in his own reading, Eliot manages to give more of them four definite stresses than I would hear.) What we have is a gradual dilation that periodically draws back, an increasing exhilaration of spirit that expresses itself with prophetic urgency in cumulative anaphora ("If . . . If . . . If . . .") and other repetitions. The line not only expands, but breaks in the middle—and then returns to an isolated four-stress pattern:

> And turn behind the pig-sty to the dull façade
> And the tombstone. And what you thought you came for
> Is only a shell, a husk of meaning.

Beginning with the enjambment that pulls up short with "Zero summer," strongly enjambed lines are common. The culminating statement soars free of all metrical limitation—but see how it returns us to what might be better termed an ideal than a norm:

the communication
Of the dead is tongued with fire beyond the language of the living.
Here, the intersection of the timeless moment
Is England and nowhere. Never and always.

The last line is doubly alliterated (an initial open vowel counting for that purpose), a more-than-perfect Anglo-Saxon line made up of native words, and divided by a strong caesura. Within this one movement, to make an end is to make a beginning, and the end is where we started from.

Because the stanzas with which Part 2 opens consist of rhyming couplets, they give the impression of greater regularity, of a syllabic-accentual meter, that is not really there. Only one line can be scanned as perfect iambic tetrameter: "The marred foundations we forgot." Even there it seems a little unnatural to give "we" as much emphasis as other stressed syllables. Other lines sound as regular as many in Milton, Blake, Dickinson, or Auden—but require the "promotion" of a normally unstressed preposition or conjunction:

      /   /   /   /
Contending for the upper hand.

The real source of the rhythm in these lines, however, is not the cultivated octosyllabic or tetrameter (whether iambic or trochaic) used so commonly from Chaucer to the present, but rather the older, persistent, native meter of songs, spells, counting games, nursery rhymes—and contemporary rap songs. Using modern terminology, we might speak of implied offbeats and unrealized beats; using my Mother-Goose-trained ear, I can force an accentual scansion on the lines as follows, but this is not the way that Eliot read it himself:

    / /   /   /
Ash on an old man's sleeve
     /   /   /   /
Is all the ash the burnt roses leave.
    / /   /   /
Dust in the air suspended
   /   /   /   /
Marks the place where a story ended.
    / /   /   /
Dust inbreathed was a house—
    /   /   /   /
The wall, the wainscot, and the mouse.

/   / /   /
The death of hope and despair.
/   /   /
This is the death of air.

Some will see in this scansion merely a perverse determination to force a spurious regularity on the poetry. It may well be that. In his own reading of the poem, Eliot allows the shorter lines to sound as awkward trimeters, and Alec Guinness follows either Eliot or his own inclination in this and, as best I can tell, every other question of rhythmic emphasis in reading the poem:

/   /   /
Ash on an old man's sleeve.

Most likely the kind of poetry we have here is close to the ineptness that troubles the metrics of much Middle English verse (as in *Everyman*, for example), and to the cheerful abandon in John Skelton. To say this is not, of course, to apply the word "inept" to Eliot. His rhythms are more like the deliberate awkwardness of parts of Morris's "The Haystack in the Floods," where meter suggests the semibarbarousness of feudal times; if anything, I might be accusing Eliot of a lingering case of pre-Raphaelitism in his rhythms, though certainly not in his vocabulary. Whatever this "presto" movement of the poem may be, however, it is closer to a rustic native dance than to anything modeled on French or Italian. But it is a calculated awkwardness, unlike Thomas Hardy, whose metrical feet wore genuine clodhoppers.

The real model for this section, which Eliot's stanzas duplicate, may be Thomas Nashe's "Litany in Time of Plague" (ca. 1600). My suggestion for an isochronic interpretation of Eliot is a consequence of my having found that Nashe's poem is more satisfactory when listened to that way. All through Nashe's "Litany" I hear the tolling of church bells, epitomized in the line, "Come, come, the bells do cry"—a relentless and ominous regularity attained more surely in Henry King's "The Exequy." King's poem includes the lines

But hark! My pulse, like a soft drum
Beats my approach, tells thee I come.

Much of Nashe's poem could seem to be in trimeters, but it is surely impossible to read it entirely that way. Take the much-quoted third stanza:

Beauty is but a flower
Which wrinkles will devour;
Brightness falls from the air,
Queens have died young and fair,

> Dust hath closed Helen's eye.
> I am sick, I must die.
>> Lord, have mercy on us!

Yvor Winters used to intone this poem with lugubrious four-beat regularity (except for the refrain), introducing pauses, or as we might now say, implied offbeats, in order to keep the cadence going at that pace. I continue to find it most effective heard this way; otherwise it seems to stumble uncertainly. Since Nashe handled pentameters with passable skill, it seems unlikely that he was an auditory dummkopf who left us a random mix of imperfect lines. English poets on the whole were more at home in four-stress meters in the earlier Renaissance; for all we know, Nashe may have had some melody in mind for this lyric, the notes of which would automatically regularize the delivery. Eliot employs Nashe's form, or something very close to it, perhaps some kind of memento mori poem that carries him back to a time before the Renaissance, or to a popular mode that was so fixed that it resisted smoothing encouraged by continental, or even ancient quantitative, models.

For the rest of Part 2, as everyone recognizes, Eliot moves into a Dantesque mode, providing us with a better approximation of the real spirit of terza rima than any translation or adaptation of the *Divine Comedy* that I am familiar with. The great majority of the lines are hendecasyllabic, often terminating with an unstressed syllable, much like Dante's line. Some historians of English prosody have argued that Surrey's blank verse (his *Aeneid* translation) was imitative of Italian poetry; whether that is true or not, various poets from Chaucer on have been aware of how the Italian line worked, and have seen iambic pentameter as the closest thing in English. With Eliot's typography insisting on the similarity to terza rima, there seems little need to argue the point any further; the entire passage is about the length of some of Dante's shorter cantos. Once again, Eliot has carried us back to an earlier stage of English prosody—not with the jingling mechanical regularity of Longfellow or the fragile artificiality cultivated by the British "decadents" when they revived forms from Romance poetry of the Middle Ages, but by achieving what the sixteenth-century poets never quite managed: a real English equivalent to the eleven-syllable line, a five-beat accentual line that often ends with a weak syllable:

> In the uncertain hour before the morning
>> Near the ending of interminable night
>> At the recurrent end of the unending
> After the dark dove with the flickering tongue
>> Had passed below the horizon of his homing
>> While the dead leaves still rattled on like tin. . . .

I am a good deal less certain of the models for the opening of Part 3, though careful study of seventeenth-century sermons, especially those of Lancelot Andrewes, might turn up cadences, rhythmic patterns, resembling those first sixteen lines. The effect, after the long sequence of hendecasyllabics that came dangerously close to shading into iambic pentameter, is to expand the line away from five stresses, which we can in fact still hear:

There are three conditions which often seem alike

Yet differ completely, flourish in the same hedgerow:

Attachment to self and to things and to persons, detachment. . . .

But the next line after these has seven stresses, and the whole section concludes with a pair of lines which both seem to have six stresses. Perhaps one might call this a homiletic meter. Sermons by Donne and others often tend toward the biblical cadence and biblical anaphora, but this is something else. The rest of Part 3 makes a striking contrast; not only are all the lines very short, but every one of them can, with some effort, be heard as an accentual trimeter (rather rough in places, but trimeter not too different from "Rugby Chapel" or from some of James Dickey's more regular poems):

Why should we celebrate

These dead men more than the dying?

It is not to ring the bell backward

Nor is it an incantation

To summon the spectre of a Rose.

What we have, then, in the last segment of Part 2 and in Part 3, is an expansion or dilation well beyond the four-beat accentual referent of the poem, and then a contraction in the other direction to three beats. At this point there has been so much variation that we might imagine that the fundamental tempo has disappeared. If so, we may be surprised to be yanked abruptly back into tetrameter by the opening line of Part 4—"The dove descending breaks the air"—which along with most of these two stanzas is much closer to accentual-syllabic meter than the lyric that introduced Part 2. The tautness of these tetrameters (and trimeters) serves as a reminder of the meter that Eliot is breaking and reconstituting—and, of course, also serves as an agreeable "musical" variation, like the trio in the third movement of a classical sonata.

Part 5 reverses the structure of Part 1, beginning with a series of loosely structured lines connected by rhetorical repetitions and by anaphora, and, after the break, returning to a series of shorter accentual lines that alternate irregularly between four and three beats. The contrasts with "Prufrock" continue to hold—that is, the ways in which Eliot's strategy in "Little Gidding" is the reverse of "Prufrock." The latter ended with a rhyming couplet of iambic pentameter:

> By sea-girls wreathed with seaweed red and brown
> Till human voices wake us, and we drown.

"Little Gidding," finally, subsides in an almost structureless coda, as if in the moment of mystical reconciliation the human urgency to make a definite configuration no longer matters. Echoing, perhaps, the resolve of Tennyson's "Ulysses," this concluding segment of "Little Gidding" marches off to a firm four-beat cadence: "We shall not cease from exploration." From that point on, especially as Eliot begins to quote from Dame Julian of Norwich for the second time, breaking her phrases in the middle, it becomes very hard to mark any pattern of stresses with much certainty, though surely the dominant number of stresses is three. What, for example, do we do with "Quick now, here, now, always—"? To ask such a question is (of course) not to criticize Eliot, but rather to cast doubt on the usefulness of any scansion, even the most rudimentary, in explaining what occurs here. I think that his allowing the meter to subside and virtually disappear makes the most nearly perfect closure for "Little Gidding" and for the whole of *Four Quartets*:

> And all shall be well and
> All manner of thing shall be well
> When the tongues of flame are in-folded
> Into the crowned knot of fire
> And the fire and the rose are one.

In *The Waste Land*, Eliot not only borrowed from other languages but often enough from meters in those languages, sometimes approximating Latin hexameters or French Alexandrines, as well as many turns of phrase and rhythm from the Symbolists. Reminiscences from British poetry in *The Waste Land* tend to come from Jacobean playwrights, from Donne, from Marvell—indeed mostly from the seventeenth century except when he is parodying Pope. In "Little Gidding" the only foreign import is Dante, and the spirit in which Dante's meter is used is quite different from the jumble of fragments that he shored against his ruin in the earlier poem. Eliot seems almost mostly to have forgotten about the seventeenth century and to have made his peace with the ghost of Shakespeare. The tradition that he assimilates in this poem is both more ancient and more widely diffused throughout English poetry. Although I have not pointed to any particular alliterative work (such as *Beowulf, Piers Plowman,* or *Gawain*), I have insisted on the pervasive presence of the older accentual tradition; if in *The Waste Land* we are distracted by a multiplicity of specific and nameable sources, in *Four Quartets* the most important influences are nameless, or rather, known only to God. Even Dante is invoked only to allow Eliot and us to encounter a "familiar compound ghost," about whose identity or multiple identities scholars continue to argue. If this chapter were only about Eliot I would entitle it just that: "A Familiar Compound Ghost"— quite the opposite of the haunted meter of his earliest poems, which were escaping the familial specter of iambic pentameter. In my own efforts to discover other elements in Eliot's phantasmal compound, I have mentioned (in addition to the King James Bible and the Book of Common Prayer, which are themselves the work of anonymous committees) fifteen or twenty poets, mostly British, and have referred indirectly to many more. The poem, surely, is an amalgam of sources and of meters.

In an utterly different way than Valéry did for French poetry, Eliot carried the development of the music of poetry to a new level of sophistication in English. Valéry, in a fashion that is typical of the French love of abstraction, of "clear and definite ideas," of rationality and symmetry, took his poetic materials directly out of the language—a language that had been, for him, it is true, purified by Mallarmé from the "dialect of the tribe." Eliot, though English, is more catholic than Valéry, more metrically ecumenical, attached by a much wider range of connections to various manifestations of the English language and others as well. Valéry, in all his grandeur, is a little sparse; his is the spirit of limitations and perfection, of the instinct of the Académie Française for pruning away adventitious exuberance, of the espaliered pear and the pollarded plane tree. Enemies of Eliot might say that he rambles and muddles, but I find an amiable generosity and inclusiveness, and that includes his metric, which is a metric of compromise and assimilation in the best senses of both those words.

My purpose has been to illustrate persuasively (no one can ever "prove" such a thing) that neither of these great masters really took anything directly into their poetry from music except a passionate desire to accomplish in poetry what music seemed already to have done. Hardy came directly out of musical context. Yeats continued and in many ways brought to perfection the great Romantic revival of English prosody that was to some extent enriched by contact with surviving combinations of poetry and actual music. Valéry and Eliot carried their prosodies ever further *away* from actual music. It is easier to argue this point for Valéry than for Eliot, because Valéry does not try to give the appearance of building on a musical form. I realize that what I have said, and that what I am about to say, runs counter to some sensitive and intelligent commentary on Eliot, such as that by Harvey Gross in his chapter on Eliot and the music of poetry. But Eliot's appropriation of a Beethoven-like extension of the sonata form was in truth only a metaphor, of not much more real significance to his art than Whistler's "symphonies" or "nocturnes" were for his paintings. It is true, of course, that poetry is (at least for some poets, some poems, and some readers) an art with a temporal extension, and Eliot makes much of this, often wittily drawing attention to the progress of a poem while in the midst of the poem. But the medium of the poem is words, and such music as it really has is that of words, not of definite pitches, timbres, harmonics, or overtones produced by musical instruments, including the human voice when used for the performance of music. The illusion of a musical structure and of musical effects remains a pleasing one, however, a sort of aesthetic framework, like the illusion of a forest or a Greek temple in the background of a ballet. But *Four Quartets* is, after all, poetry—some of the best poetry ever written by any human being.

Afterword

I F W E A C C E P T the idea that all good poetry retains some connection with music, however distant and tenuous, there is no convenient stopping point for our discussion. In addition to all the examples mentioned so far, the work of many twentieth-century poets seems expressive of a delight in rhythm that goes beyond what mere words can express. Take, for example, one of the great favorites of our century, Theodore Roethke's "My Papa's Waltz." In it, Roethke manages to suggest a waltz rhythm, but when we look closer we see that it is really regular trimeters (with, perhaps, an implied extra beat at the end of the line, since most trimeters in English are really truncated tetrameters), and that it would not be possible to waltz to the tempo. Yet the inspiration for the poem is a lively musical memory, and as with many other poems by that poet it seems to contain not only irrepressible music but dance as well. Scanted also are marvelous pieces such as Yeats's "Fiddler of Dooney," Pound's "Dance Figure," Williams's "The Dance," and Stevens's "Peter Quince at the Clavier." The relation of Hart Crane's rhythms to various musical heritages could stand lengthy investigation, as, for that matter, could the connections between James Dickey's work and bluegrass and other kinds of country music. Much more remains to be said of other members of the Harlem Renaissance besides Hughes, and of other African American poets up to and beyond Nikki Giovanni, and their relationship to various jazz, blues, and gospel traditions.

This book might have taken many other directions. I have not, for example, tried to deal with the ways in which the different varieties of jazz may have affected poetic meter and form. "Jazz" denotes an array of musical subspecies that have already made their break with a musico-poetic context. In too many instances, poets who claim to be inspired by jazz, or working in a manner analogous to jazz, are really relying on some unaccountable inner prompting that has nothing to do with music. More persuasive is the idea that e. e. cummings, Langston Hughes, and Gwendolyn Brooks, who were immersed more unself-consciously in the musical currents of their times, can be profitably studied from that point of view. A second and perhaps better reason for my not essaying to account for a contemporary jazz-poetry connection is that

I know very little about jazz. Philip Larkin, who knew a great deal about it, seems utterly untouched by it as a poet. In retrospect, twentieth-century jazz may not seem to have any more connection with poetry than did nineteenth-century orchestral music with the poets who were contemporaries of Beethoven or Tchaikovsky.

Neither does it seem worthwhile either to justify or to question whatever analogies may have been proposed, or opposed, between Language Poetry and various kinds of music. Language Poetry is a somewhat played-out prolongation of Charles Olson's performative mode and Frank O'Hara's personalist improvisations—a continuation of a prosodic revolt that has transformed itself into a revolt against syntax and meaning. Much Language Poetry reads like an unmetrical translation of Mallarmé, perhaps alternating with some meterless Edward Lear.

Because it was part of the Imagist manifesto to call for a return to "the musical phrase," it might seem appropriate to account for various kinds of free verse in terms of their relation to a musical context. But, as I have argued extensively in *The Origins of Free Verse*, good free verse works contrapuntally to the established metrical conventions, even when it seems most distant from them. Free verse is therefore several times removed from music, taking for granted a metric that has long since set itself apart from an actual musical connection. The "music" of good free verse (including the Whitmanian biblical-anaphoric manner) is a complex interweaving of expected rhythmic recurrences of accentual-syllabic meter with the actual cadences—a more extreme example of the variety-amid-uniformity that one finds in the metrical variations, or substitutions, within lines of accentual-syllabic poetry. To say this is not to see free verse as a negation, but rather to situate it and give it meaning, a local habitation, within the long-established history of poetry. To say this is also to deny the egotism of the supposedly self-created poetic genius and to insist that poetry is shareable, learnable, and something we possess in common—including the free verse that has won lasting approval from readers. Modern free verse, though, reaches ever further away from music. Various experiments in free forms can be traced as far back as 1590, at which time poets were already feeling constrained by established meter and by forms, especially the sonnet. The best twentieth-century free verse remains that written by poets who were still close enough to the accentual-syllabic tradition (and competent to write in it, when and if they chose to do so): Pound, H. D., Mina Loy, Eliot, Williams, Yvor Winters in a few early poems, cummings, Sitwell, and a few others.

Although from time to time I have mentioned instances of poems being set to music, including some that were written so as to encourage the composition of settings, such recombinations do not fall within the scope of this study, even when they are as successful as Schubert's art songs. Neither have I tried to deal extensively with the effect on the rhythm or structure of a poem of its being intended for musical performance, as many have, with Byron's *Hebrew Melodies*, certain pieces by Tennyson, and many others from the Renaissance on. In the case of poems not specifically designed for music, the setting often falsifies the poem, although the fact of the poem's being set serves as a tribute to it. Mallarmé spoke for all true poets when, after Debussy told him that he was setting *L'Après-Midi d'un Faune* to music, he replied, "I thought I had already done that." He did not elaborate, but one may suppose that he had in mind the *musique naturele* appropriate to his own art.

As I confessed in my introduction, I make no pretensions of offering a complete survey. I have passed over numerous figures, even among poets writing in English, who may seem to cry out for attention. The lush "musicality" in much of Tennyson (which achieves a sickly overelaboration in Poe) could be the subject of an entire monograph, and the prosodic oddities that the theorizing of Robert Bridges and Sidney Lanier led them to produce could each stand a chapter—especially since Lanier made music the basis of his entire metric. With much regret I close this study with hardly a reference either to Baudelaire's poetry, which is for me the richest in functional (as opposed to decorative) verbal effects of anything written in French. Also, I make no more than a few casual references to Goethe.

Predicting the future of poetry is much like predicting the future of the stock market, except that it is less risky to one's financial security. Encouraged by that thought, I would venture to suggest that the future (like the past) belongs to the poets who delight in the way words sound. Much that gets printed now as poetry makes very dull listening; no auctioneer, salesman, or newscaster could make a living with as little sensitivity to the spoken word as what one finds distributed across the pages of various journals. As I have heard a distinguished formalist poet, Edgar Bowers, complain, "Poetry has become a commodity." One finds, however, among all the shoddy goods that glut the marketplace, some bolts of melody (to use the title invented for an early collection of Emily Dickinson's poems), some memorable sequences to which the ear attends. Every language offers endless opportunities for permutations and combinations of sound; it only remains for poets to discover or to invent new ways to make use of them. And even as I write, some new manifestation of *mousike*, or some newly-discovered musical analogy, may be waiting to invigorate poetry, or even to call it to a higher destiny.

Analysis of the Soractian Ode

For purposes of explaining what really occurs in the rhythm of the poem, a diagram of Horace's alcaic devised by George M. Lane in his great Latin grammar (1898) is by far the most helpful:

$$\text{⏑} : \acute{-}\,\smile \mid \acute{-}\,\rangle\ \#\ \acute{-}\,\smile\smile \mid \acute{-}\,\smile \mid \acute{-}\,\wedge$$
$$\text{⏑} : \acute{-}\,\smile \mid \acute{-}\,\rangle\ \#\ \acute{-}\,\smile\smile \mid \acute{-}\,\smile \mid \acute{-}\,\wedge$$
$$\text{⏑} : \acute{-}\,\smile \mid \acute{-}\,\rangle \mid \acute{-}\,\smile \mid \acute{-}\,\smile$$
$$\acute{-}\,\smile\smile \mid \acute{-}\,\smile\smile \mid \acute{-}\,\smile \mid \acute{-}\,\smile$$

The first two lines are in the eleven-syllable pattern called the greater alcaic; the third is an example of the nine-syllable alcaic; and the last is ten syllables, or the lesser alcaic—to give the individual lines, or verses, their names. The symbols above may be translated as follows.

⏑ This stands for an *irrational* syllable or foot in which, according to Lane, a "long syllable sometimes stands in place of a short" (2524). Lane also suggests that it may be somewhere between a long and a short. Note that in Horace's practice above the syllable is always long.

: This indicates an anacrusis, an isolated syllable at the start of a poetic line; such effects exist in English, as when Blake inserts the word "Could" at the start of the fourth line of his "Tyger" poem ("Could frame thy fearful symmetry"), and "Dare" at the start of the last line; these variations work against the regular trochaic beat of most of the poem: "Tyger, tyger, burning bright." Anacrusis comes from Greek, "a striking up." It is a sort of introductory half-measure to the first three lines; as Lane says, "It is often irrational" (2530).

/ Lane intends this to show where the *ictus* falls on a long syllable in each complete foot. He is using *ictus* in the Greek sense of the heavy beat, the Greek *thesis*. This marking is not meant to suggest anything like an English accentual beat, but it does suggest an emphasis created by the Greek meter, which overlays any residual stress in the Latin language itself.

⏑ This simply marks syllables that are quantitatively short.

_〉 An "irrational spondee." A normal spondee would be, of course: — —.

\# Lane uses this in place of the caesura marking (||) that I employed in my scansion of the entire poem. It indicates a metrical diaresis, a break in the line that coincides with the end of a foot. Lane apparently uses this mark to suggest a more natural pause than a foot-dividing caesura would produce (2542).

∧ This indicates a pause at the end of a line (2540).

But even in employing a system of such flexibility and specificity, Lane seems to have felt uneasy at the idea of constraining any single line to one of these patterns. At least that is one way to explain why, when he offers an example of the nine-syllabled alcaic, quoting the third line of the poem, he marks it differently from his own scheme, using an additional symbol (–̇). This seems to stand for a very light *ictus*, and its use seems to reduce the accent count from four to two. Here is an entire section from Lane:

> 2642. This verse consists of two complete trochaic dipodies, with anacrusis. The second foot is always an irrational spondee. The scheme is:—
>
> 〉̆ : ´– ⏑ | –̇ 〈 | ´– ⏑ | –̇ ⏑
>
> An example is—
>
> Sil | vaé la | bōran | tés ge | lūque.
>
> This verse occurs only in Horace, where it forms the third line of the Alcaic Strophe (see 2736).

Lane's inconsistency here, as noted above, seems only an effort at describing what he really perceives as the metrical character of the line. But his hesitancy over the question of *ictus* does provide an index to the delicacy of this entire issue. In other words, he feels the importance of the counterpoint at work in the poem and wants to indicate to what extent the Greek paradigm supervened over natural pronunciation, and perhaps even has induced a slight degree of accentualism into the Latin, an accentualism at variance with older pronunciation, current nonpoetic pronunciation, and subsequent pronunciation. Lane himself provides an excellent summary of the underlying situation:

> 2548. Although in all probability the Latin accent was mainly one of stress rather than of pitch, it seems to have been comparatively weak. Hence, when it conflicted with the metrical ictus, it could be the more easily disregarded. But accentual or semi-accentual poetry seems to have existed among the common people even in the Augustan age, and even in classical

Latin verse in certain cases (as in the last part of the dactylic hexameter) conflict between ictus and accent was carefully avoided. After the third century A.D. the accent exerted a stronger and stronger influence upon versification, until in the Middle Ages the quantitative Latin verse was quite supplanted by the accentual.

Lane here is assuming that what the Latin poets heard as *ictus* was something other than an increase in volume. Careful attention to recordings of modern poets who are well schooled in accentual-syllabic meters, such as Yeats and Frost, reveals that shifts in pitch can be an important part of the meter; perhaps the *ictus* coincided with a change in pitch.

At this point we must complicate the discussion even further by considering some ways in which the residual, natural stresses of Latin may have played against the alcaic meter of the Soractian ode. Using the Penultimate Law, accents or stresses might be placed on the words as follows; the markings suggest accent or stress, not pitch or quantity:

/ / / / /
Vides ut alta stet nive candidum
/ / / / /
Soracte, nec iam sustineant onus
/ / /
silvae laborantes, geluque
/ / /
flumina constiterint acuto?

/ / / / /
dissolve frigus ligna super foco
/ / / /
large reponens atque benignius
/ / /
deprome quadrimum Sabina
/ / /
o Thaliarche, merum diota.

/ / / / /
permitte divis cetera, qui simul
/ / / /
stravere ventos aequore fervido
/ / / /
deproeliantes, nec cupressi
/ / /
nec veteres agitantur orni.

$$\text{/ \quad / \quad / \quad / \quad /}$$
quid sit futurum cras, fuge quaerere et
$$\text{/ \quad / \quad / \quad / \quad /}$$
quem Fors dierum cumque dabit, lucro
$$\text{/ \quad / \quad /}$$
appone nec dulces amores
$$\text{/ \quad / \quad / \quad /}$$
sperne puer neque tu choreas,
$$\text{/ \quad / \quad / \quad /}$$
donec virenti canities abest
$$\text{/ \quad / \quad / \quad /}$$
morosa nunc et campus et areae
$$\text{/ \quad / \quad /}$$
lenesque sub noctem susurri
$$\text{/ \quad / \quad /}$$
composita repetantur hora,
$$\text{/ \quad / \quad / \quad /}$$
nunc et latentis proditor intumo
$$\text{/ \quad / \quad / \quad /}$$
gratus puella risus ab angulo
$$\text{/ \quad / \quad /}$$
pignusque dereptum lacertis
$$\text{/ \quad / \quad /}$$
aut digito male pertinaci.

It must be reiterated that the markings above are not offered as a scansion or even as a possible guide to a reading of the poem according to accents. The procedure has been to apply certain hypothetical rules of Latin pronunciation in order to see what sort of pattern would emerge. This entire approach is speculative, problematic, and may be in the eyes of some scholars irresponsible; but if the Penultimate Law means anything at all, it has to be applied more or less in this way. What does seem clear (*if* the law is correct), is that the natural reading of the words of the poem has been much changed by the meter. The incongruity would not be as remarkable as it is in English when quantities are attempted, because a quantitative overlay is next to impossible in English. But there must have been some tension even in Latin. Numerous commentators assert this. As William Beare puts it, "we shall find that the conflict between ictus and accents occurs in almost every line of Latin verse" (62). The question is: How does Horace's poem profit from this conflict?

In comparing the coincidences (of the accents marked just above) with the *ictus* or *thesis* marks introduced by Lane in his diagram of the alcaic, one finds some interesting instances both of reinforcement and of counterpointing. Lane counts *ictus* occurrences in each stanza: 5, 5, 4, 4. My counting of the coincidence of metrical *ictus* and accent (as determined above by applying the Penultimate Law) for each of the six stanzas is as follows. (These are the ratios between accent and *ictus*; note that the denominators for each stanza are all the same: 5, 5, 4, 4.)

Stanza	line 1	line 2	line 3	line 4
1	3/5	2/5	1/4	2/4
2	3/5	3/5	2/4	3/4
3	4/5	2/5	4/4	2/4
4	3/5	3/5	2/4	1/4
5	1/5	4/5	3/4	2/4
6	3/5	3/5	2/4	1/4

A further step in this analysis is to identify all lines in which the majority of *ictuses* are reinforced by accent as *resolute* [R]; those that fall slightly short of this as *neutral* [N]; and those where there is almost no reinforcement as *indefinite* [I]. Using R, N, and I to diagram the stanzas, then, we may see them as:

Stanza					coincidences [reinforcement of ictus by accent]
1.	R	N	I	N	8
2.	R	R	N	R	11
3.	R	N	R	N	12
4.	R	R	N	I	9
5.	I	R	R	N	10
6.	R	R	N	I	9

It is possible to argue that these patterns do make sense in terms of the psychological progress of the poem. We open in the first stanza with an exhilarating apostrophe to the wintry beauty of the mountain peak and the snow-laden forest; the rhythm seems loose and expressive, with the stresses and the quantities canceling one another out to some extent. Another way to put it might be to say that the spirit of the poet labors against the constraints of age and frees itself; one of the most remarkable incongruities of accent and *ictus* is "silvae laborantes." The greatest reinforcement occurs in the third stanza, where we find the central idea of the poem: "permitte divis cetera"— leave the rest to the gods! A relaxation characterizes the last three stanzas, which include two lines where there is a single reinforced *ictus*; the last line, especially, gives an effect of trailing off.

It will not do to stray too far in the direction of attributing to Horace what Yvor Winters called "the fallacy of imitative form." One must also emphasize that the structure of each stanza provides an iterative constant that frames and limits the progress of the poetic argument, but playing against this are the actual stress-rhythms of the words. Here is the poem's "music," which is due to the alcaic structure that supervenes over the natural impulses of the language. And here we may apply the familiar and often oversimplified concept of variety-amid-regularity to account for another pleasurable dimension.

If we consider the corresponding lines of each of the stanzas, using the criterion of *ictus*/accent coincidence again, additional interesting patterns emerge. The table below simply totals the coincidences for each of the four lines in all six stanzas:

Line	*stress*/ictus	*percentage*
1	17/30	57%
2	17/30	57%
3	14/24	58%
4	11/24	44%

What this tells us is that, on average, the interplay between accent and *ictus* is very nearly the same for the first three lines of each stanza, but that in the last line something odd happens; as a result, some expectation is established of a change in the last line. In terms of quantitative scansion, the fourth line—the lesser alcaic—is certainly the simplest and most consistent: a regular succession of two dactyls followed by a trochee and a spondee. The effect (for me) is of a metrical triumph, or resolution, at the end of each stanza where the deliberate metric overcomes the incipient irregularities offered earlier by the residual stresses. In a sense, the last lines are the most irregular in terms of agreement of *ictus*, or *thesis*, with accent; and yet they give an effect of closure, which is at the same time an intensification of counterpointing.

There are many other kinds of rhythmic imitation and metrical variation throughout the poem. Almost every stanza, for example, seems to contain one atypical line. In each stanza, the first three lines are a little indefinite when it comes to stress/quantity coincidence—especially the third; but in the third line of the third stanza, that line seems suddenly to jell into conformity with natural stress. Another pattern shows itself in that the regular division, by caesura or diaeresis, of the first two lines gives way, in each stanza, to a third and fourth line that maintain a more uninterrupted continuity. The three opening lines of the poem end with short syllables; after that, long-syllable endings predominate. These and other configurations can be tied to the meaning of the poem and the feelings motivated by it, as I have done above.

Bibliography and References

Allen, Gay Wilson. *The Solitary Singer: A Critical Biography of Walt Whitman*. New York: Macmillan, 1960.

Allen, Philip Schuyler. *Medieval Latin Lyrics*. Chicago: U of Chicago P, 1931.

Allen, W. Sidney. *Accent and Rhythm—Prosodic Features of Latin and Greek: A Study in Theory and Reconstruction*. Cambridge: Cambridge UP, 1973.

Alpers, Paul, ed. *Elizabethan Poetry*. New York: Oxford UP, 1967.

Anshutz, H. L., and D. W. Cummings. "Blake's 'The Sick Rose.'" The *Explicator*, 29.4 (1970).

Asselineau, Roger. *The Evolution of Walt Whitman: The Creation of a Book*. Cambridge: Harvard UP, 1962.

Attridge, Derek. *The Rhythms of English Poetry*. London: Longmans, 1982.

——. *Well-Weighed Syllables: Elizabethan Verse in Classical Meters*. Cambridge: Cambridge UP, 1974.

Balakian, Anna. *The Fiction of the Poet: From Mallarmé to the Post-Symbolist Mode*. Princeton: Princeton UP, 1992.

——. *The Symbolist Movement: A Critical Appraisal*. New York: New York UP, 1977.

Baldwin, Charles Sears. *Medieval Rhetoric and Poetic*. New York: Macmillan, 1928.

Barricelli, Jean-Pierre. *Melopoiesis: Approaches to the Study of Literature and Music*. New York: New York UP, 1988.

Barry, Kevin. *Language, Music, and the Sign*. Cambridge: Cambridge UP, 1987.

Bate, Walter Jackson. *John Keats*. Cambridge: Harvard UP, 1963.

Baugh, Albert C., et al. *A Literary History of England*. 2nd ed. New York: Appleton, 1967.

Bayly, Anselm. *The Alliance of Music, Poetry, and Oratory*. New York: Garland, 1970.

Beare, William. *Latin Verse and European Song*. London: Methuen, 1957.

Bédier, Joseph, trans. *La Chanson de Roland*. Paris: H. Piazza, 1937.

Beer, John. *Blake's Visionary Universe*. Manchester: Manchester UP, 1969.

Bentley, G. E., Jr. *Blake Records*. Oxford: Clarendon, 1969.

Bentman, Raymond, *Robert Burns*. Boston: Twayne, 1987.

Blake, William. *Complete Writings*. With variant readings. Ed. Geoffrey Keynes. London: Oxford UP, 1972.

Blodgett, Harold. *Walt Whitman in England*. Ithaca: Cornell UP, 1934.

Bogin, Meg. *The Women Troubadours*. New York: Norton, 1976.

Bonaventura, Arnaldo. *Dante e la Musica*. Livorno: Raffaello Giusti, 1904. Bologna: Arnaldo Forni, 1978.

Booth, Mark W. *The Experience of Songs*. New Haven: Yale UP, 1981.

Boswell, James. *The Life of Samuel Johnson*. New York: Modern Library, 1931.

Bowra, C. M. *The Creative Experiment*. London: Macmillan, 1949.

——. *Pindar*. Oxford: Clarendon Press, 1964.

Boyd, Morrison C. *Elizabethan Music and Musical Criticism.* Rev. ed. Philadelphia: U of Pennsylvania P, 1962.

Briffault, Robert S. *The Troubadours.* Bloomington: Indiana UP, 1965.

Bronson, Bertrand H. *The Ballad as Song.* Berkeley: U of California P, 1969.

——. "Literature and Music." Thorpe 127–50.

——. "Some Aspects of Music and Literature in the Eighteenth Century." *Papers Delivered by James E. Philips and Bertrand H. Bronson at the Second Clark Library Seminar, 24 October 1953.* Los Angeles: William Andrews Clark Memorial Library, 1953. 22–55.

Brown, Carleton, ed. *English Lyrics of the XIIIth Century.* Oxford: Clarendon, 1932.

Brown, John. *A Dissertation on the Rise, Union, and Power, the Progressions, Separations, and Corruptions, of Poetry and Music.* New York: Garland, 1971.

Brown, Mary Ellen. *Burns and Tradition.* Urbana: U of Illinois P, 1984.

Bukofzer, Manfred F. *Medieval and Renaissance Music.* New York: Norton, 1950.

Burns, Robert. *The Letters of Robert Burns.* 2 vols. Ed. J. DeLancey Ferguson. 2nd ed. G. Ross Roy. Oxford: Clarendon, 1985.

——. *The Merry Muses of Caledonia.* New York: University Books, 1965.

——. *The Poetical Works of Robert Burns, with Notes, Glossary, Index of First Lines and Chronological List.* Ed. J. Logie Robertson. London: Oxford UP, 1926.

——. *Robert Burns's Commonplace Book 1783–1785.* Facsimile. Transcr., introd., and notes by James Cameron Ewing and David Cook. Glasgow: Gowans and Gray, 1938.

Caldwell, John. *Medieval Music.* Bloomington: Indiana UP, 1978.

Caldwell, John, Edward Olleson, and Susan Wollenburg, eds. *The Well Enchanting Skill: Music, Poetry, and Drama in the Culture of the Renaissance.* Oxford: Clarendon, 1990.

Cattin, Giulio. *Music of the Middle Ages.* Trans. Steven Botterill. Cambridge: Cambridge UP, 1984.

Cazamian, Louis. *Symbolisme et Poésie: L'Exemple Anglais.* Neuchatel: Éditions de la Baconnière, 1947.

Celis, Raphael, ed. *Littérature et Musique.* Saint-Louis, Bruxelles: Facultés Universitaires, 1982.

Chambers, E. K., and F. Sidgwick, eds. *Early English Lyrics.* New York: AMS, 1973.

Chambers, Frank M. *An Introduction to Old Provençal Versification.* Philadelphia: American Philosophical Society, 1985.

Charters, Samuel. *The Poetry of the Blues.* New York: Oak, 1963.

Clinton-Baddeley, V. C. *Words for Music.* Cambridge: Cambridge UP, 1941.

Coker, Wilson. *Music and Meaning.* New York: Free Press, 1972.

Coleridge, Samuel Taylor. *Biographia Literaria with his Aesthetical Essays.* 2 vols. Ed. J. Shawcross. 1907. London: Oxford UP, 1939.

Commager, Steele. *The Odes of Horace: A Critical Study.* New Haven: Yale UP, 1962.

Comotti, Giovanni. *Music in Greek and Roman Culture.* Trans. Rosaria V. Munson. Baltimore: Johns Hopkins UP, 1989.

Conte, Gian Biagio. *Latin Literature: A History.* Trans. Joseph B. Solodow. Ed. Don Fowler and Glenn W. Most. Rev. ed. Baltimore: Johns Hopkins UP, 1994.

Daiches, David. *Robert Burns and His World.* New York: Viking, 1971.

Dante Alighieri. *The Banquet.* Trans. Christopher Ryan. Saratoga: ANMA Libri, 1989.

——. *Dante's Lyric Poetry.* Ed. and trans. Kenelm Foster and Patrick Boyde. Oxford: Clarendon, 1967.

——. *De Vulgari Eloquentia.* Ed. and trans. Claudio Marazzini. Milan: Arnoldo Mondadori, 1990.

——. *Il Convivio*. Ed. Maria Simonelli. Bologna: Casa Editrice Prof. Riccardo Pàtron, 1966.

Davidson, Donald. *Twenty Lessons in Reading and Writing Prose*. New York: Scribner's, 1955.

Davie, Donald. *The Eighteenth-Century Hymn in England*. Cambridge: Cambridge UP, 1993.

Delattre, Floris, and Camille Chemin. *Les Chansons Elizabéthaines*. Paris: Librairie Marcel Didier, 1948.

Demaray, John G. *Milton and the Masque Tradition*. Cambridge: Harvard UP, 1968.

Dent, Edward J. "Shakespeare and Music." Granville-Barker and Harrison, 137–61.

Deschamps, Eustache. *L'Art de Dictier*. Ed. and trans. Deborah M. Sinnreich-Levi. East Lansing, MI: Colleagues Press, 1994.

Dickins, Bruce, and R. M. Wilson, eds. *Early Middle English Texts*. New York: Norton, 1951.

Dickinson, Emily. *The Letters of Emily Dickinson*. 3 vols. Ed. Thomas H. Johnson. Cambridge: Harvard UP, 1958.

Doughtie, Edward. *English Renaissance Song*. Boston: Twayne, 1986.

Dryden, John. *The Works of John Dryden*. 20 vols. General eds. Edward Niles Hooker and H. T. Swedenborg, Jr. Berkeley: U California P, 1956–1994.

Edmonds, John Maxwell, ed. *The Fragments of Attic Comedy*. 3 vols. Leiden: E. J. Brill, 1957.

Eliot, T. S. *On Poetry and Poets*. New York: Farrar, 1957.

——. *Selected Essays 1917–1932*. New York: Harcourt, 1932.

——. *To Criticize the Critic*. New York: Farrar, 1965.

Erkkila, Betsy. *Walt Whitman among the French: Poet and Myth*. Princeton: Princeton UP, 1980.

Ewert, Alfred. *The French Language*. London: Faber, 1943.

Faner, Robert D. *Walt Whitman and Opera*. Philadelphia: U of Pennsylvania P, 1951.

Finch, Annie. *The Ghost of Meter: Culture and Prosody in American Free Verse*. Ann Arbor: U of Michigan P, 1993.

Finney, Theodore M. *A History of Music*. Rev. ed. New York: Harcourt, 1947.

Finney, Gretchen Ludke. *Musical Backgrounds for English Literature: 1580–1650*. New Brunswick: Rutgers UP, 1962.

Fisher, John H., ed. *The Complete Poetry and Prose of Geoffrey Chaucer*. New York: Holt, Rinehart, 1977.

Ford, Ford Madox. *Memories and Impressions*. New York: Harper, 1911.

Fowlie, Wallace. *Mallarmé*. Chicago: U of Chicago P, 1953.

Fox, John. *A Literary History of France: The Middle Ages*. London: Ernest Benn, 1974.

Freedman, Morris. "Dryden's 'Memorable Visit' to Milton." *Huntington Library Quarterly* 18 (1955): 99–108.

French, David P., ed. *Minor English Poets: 1660–1780*. 10 vols. New York: Benjamin Blom, 1967.

Gardner, Helen. *The Composition of "Four Quartets."* London: Faber, 1978.

Gates, Henry Louis, Jr., and K. A. Appiah. *Langston Hughes: Critical Perspectives Past and Present*. New York: Amistad, 1993.

Georgiades, Thrasybulos. *Greek Music, Verse and Dance*. Trans. Erwin Benedikt and Marie Louise Martinez. New York: Merlin Press, 1956. New York: Da Capo, 1973.

——. *Music and Language*. Trans. Marie Louis Gollner. Cambridge: Cambridge UP, 1982.

Gibbon, John Murray. *Melody and the Lyric from Chaucer to the Cavaliers*. New York: Haskell House, 1964.

Gleckner, Robert F. *The Piper and the Bard: A Study of William Blake*. Detroit: Wayne State UP, 1959.

Granville-Barker, Harley, and G. B. Harrison, eds. *A Companion to Shakespeare Studies*. New York: Macmillan, 1934.

Greene, Richard Leighton, ed. *The Early English Carols*. Oxford: Clarendon, 1935.

Gross, Harvey. *Sound and Form in Modern Poetry*. Ann Arbor: U of Michigan P, 1964.

Grout, Donald Jay. *A History of Western Music*. Rev. ed. New York: Norton, 1973.

Haar, James. *Essays on Italian Poetry and Music in the Renaissance, 1350–1600*. Berkeley: U of California P, 1986.

Halporn, James W., Martin Ostwald, and Thomas G. Rosenmeyer. *The Meters of Greek and Latin Poetry*. Norman: U of Oklahoma P, 1963.

Hammond, Eleanor Prescott. *English Verse between Chaucer and Surrey*. Durham: Duke UP, 1927.

Hardie, William Ross. *Res Metrica*. London: Oxford UP, 1934.

Hardison, O. B., Jr. *Prosody and Purpose in the English Renaissance*. Baltimore: Johns Hopkins UP, 1989.

Hardy, Florence Emily. *The Early Life of Thomas Hardy*. New York: Macmillan, 1928.

Hardy, Thomas. *The Collected Letters of Thomas Hardy*. Ed. R. L. Purdy and M. Millgate. Oxford: Clarendon, 1980.

——. *The Complete Poetical Works of Thomas Hardy*. Ed. Samuel Hynes. Oxford: Clarendon, 1982.

Harvey, Gabriel. *The Works of Gabriel Harvey*. Ed. Alexander B. Grosart. New York: AMS, 1966.

Havens, Raymond Dexter. *The Mind of a Poet: A Study of Wordsworth's Thought*. 2 vols. Baltimore: Johns Hopkins UP, 1941.

Herz, David Michael. *The Tuning of the Word: The Musico-Literary Poetics of the Symbolist Movement*. Carbondale: Southern Illinois UP, 1987.

Hollander, John, ed. *American Poetry: The Nineteenth Century*. 2 vols. New York: Library of America, 1993.

——. *The Untuning of the Sky: Ideas of Music in English Poetry 1500–1700*. Princeton: Princeton UP, 1961.

Horace. *The Odes and Epodes*. Ed. and trans. C. E. Bennett. Cambridge: Harvard UP, 1914.

Houston, John Porter. *French Symbolism and the Modernist Movement: A Study of Poetic Structures*. Baton Rouge: Louisiana State UP, 1980.

Hueffer, Francis. *The Troubadours*. London: Chatto & Windus, 1878. New York: AMS, 1977.

Hughes, Langston. *The Big Sea: An Autobiography*. 1940. New York: Hill and Wang, 1963.

——. *I Wonder as I Wander: An Autobiographical Journey*. New York: Rinehart, 1956.

——. *The Langston Hughes Reader*. New York: Braziller, 1958.

——. *Selected Poems*. 1959. New York: Vintage, 1990.

——. *The Ways of White Folks*. New York: Knopf, 1969.

Huot, Sylvia. *From Song to Book: The Poetics of Writing in Old French Lyric and Lyrical Narrative Poetry*. Ithaca: Cornell UP, 1987.

Hynes, Samuel. "On Hardy's Badness." Orel 72–81.

Hytier, Jean. *The Poetics of Paul Valéry*. Trans. Richard Howard. Garden City: Doubleday, 1966.

Jack, R. D. S., and Andrew Noble, eds. *The Art of Robert Burns*. London: Vision, 1982.

Jeanroy, Alfred. *Les Origines de la Poésie Lyrique en France au Moyen Age*. 3rd ed. Paris: Édouard Champion, 1925.

Johnson, James Weldon. *God's Trombones.* New York: Viking, 1927.

Johnson, Paula. *Form and Transformation in Music and Poetry of the English Renaissance.* New Haven: Yale UP, 1972.

Johnson, Samuel. *The Lives of the English Poets.* London: Everyman, 1925.

Johnson, Thomas H. *Emily Dickinson: An Interpretive Biography.* Cambridge: Harvard UP, 1960.

Jorgens, Elise Bickford. *The Well-Tun'd Word.* Minneapolis: U of Minnesota P, 1982.

Kahn, Gustav. *Symbolistes et Décadents.* Paris: Vanier, 1902. New York: AMS, 1980.

Keast, William R., ed. *Seventeenth-Century English Poetry: Modern Essays in Criticism.* New York: Oxford UP, 1962.

Keats, John. *The Odes of Keats and Their Earliest Known Manuscripts.* Introd. and notes by Robert Gittings. Kent: Kent State UP, 1970.

Kerman, Joseph. *The Elizabethan Madrigal.* New York: American Musicological Society, 1962.

Kime, Mary W. *Lyric and Song: Seventeenth-Century Musical Settings of John Donne's Poetry.* Diss. U of Denver, 1969.

Kirby-Smith, H. T. *The Origins of Free Verse.* Ann Arbor: U of Michigan P, 1996.

Knighton, Tess, and David Fallows, eds. *Companion to Medieval and Renaissance Music.* New York: Macmillan, 1992.

Lane, George M. *A Latin Grammar for Schools and Colleges.* Rev. ed. 1903. New York: Greenwood, 1968.

Langdon, Ida. *Milton's Theory of Poetry and Fine Art.* New Haven: Yale UP, 1924.

Leader, Zachary. *Reading Blake's Songs.* Boston: Routledge, 1981.

Le Huray, Peter. *Music and the Reformation in England, 1549–1660.* New York: Oxford UP, 1967.

Lewis, C. S. *English Literature in the Sixteenth Century.* New York: Oxford UP, 1954.

Lindberg-Seyersted, Brita. *The Voice of the Poet: Aspects of Style in the Poetry of Emily Dickinson.* Cambridge: Harvard UP, 1968.

Lobb, Edward, ed. *Words in Time: New Essays on Eliot's "Four Quartets."* Ann Arbor: U of Michigan P, 1993.

Lonsdale, Roger, ed. *The New Oxford Book of Eighteenth Century Verse.* Oxford: Oxford UP, 1984.

Lord, Albert B. *The Singer of Tales.* Cambridge: Harvard UP, 1960.

Low, Donald A., ed. *Robert Burns: The Critical Heritage.* London: Routledge, 1974.

de Machaut, Guillaume. *Le Jugement du roy de Behaigne* and *Remede de Fortune.* Ed. James I. Wimsatt and William W. Kibler. Music ed. Rebecca A. Baltzer. Athens: U of Georgia P, 1988.

——. *Poésies Lyriques.* Ed. Vladimir Chichmaref. Vol. 1. 1909. Geneva: Slatkine Reprints, 1973.

MacQueen, John, and Tom Scott, eds. *The Oxford Book of Scottish Verse.* Oxford: Clarendon, 1966.

Mallarmé, Stéphane. *Oeuvres Complètes.* Paris: Gallimard, 1945.

Marks, Harvey B. *The Rise and Growth of English Hymnody.* Philadelphia: Blakiston, 1937.

Marrocco, W. Thomas. "The Enigma of the Canzone." *Speculum* 33 (1956): 704–13.

Martin, John. *The Dance in Theory.* Princeton: Princeton Book Company, 1989.

Martz, Louis L. "Origins of Form in *Four Quartets.*" Lobb 189–204.

Matthiessen, F. O. *The Achievement of T. S. Eliot.* 2nd ed. rev. and enlarged. New York: Oxford UP, 1947.

Mazzaro, Jerome. *Transformations in the Renaissance English Lyric.* Ithaca: Cornell UP, 1970.

Mauclair, Camille. *Servitude et Grandeur Littéraires*. Paris: Ollendorf, 1922.

McColley, Diane Kelsey. *Poetry and Music in Seventeenth-Century England*. Cambridge: Cambridge UP, 1997.

McGuinness, Rosamund. *English Court Odes 1660–1820*. Oxford: Clarendon, 1971.

Messenger, Ruth Ellis. *The Medieval Latin Hymn*. Washington: Capital Press, 1953.

Meyerstein, E. H. W. Letter. *Times Literary Supplement* 22 June 1946.

Milton, John. *Complete Poems and Major Prose*. Ed. Merritt Y. Hughes. New York: Macmillan, 1957.

Morley, Thomas. *A Plain and Easy Introduction to Practical Music*. Ed. R. Alec Harman. New York: Norton, 1973.

Morris, Richard, ed. *An Old English Miscellany*. London: Oxford UP, 1927.

Morris, Timothy. "The Development of Dickinson's Style." *American Literature* 60 (1988): 26–41.

Mossé, Fernand. *A Handbook of Middle English*. Trans. James A. Walker. Baltimore: Johns Hopkins UP, 1952.

Mullen, William. *Choreia: Pindar and Dance*. Princeton: Princeton UP, 1982.

Musgrove, S. *T. S. Eliot and Walt Whitman*. New York: Haskell House, 1952.

Nauden, Marie. *Evolution Parallele de la Poesie et de la Musique en France: Role unificateur de la chanson*. Paris: Nizet, 1968.

Neubauer, John. *The Emancipation of Music from Language: Departure from Mimesis in Eighteenth-Century Aesthetics*. New Haven: Yale UP, 1986.

Nicholson, Lewis E., ed. *An Anthology of Beowulf Criticism*. Notre Dame: U of Notre Dame P, 1963.

Niles, John D. *Beowulf: The Poem and Its Tradition*. Cambridge: Harvard UP, 1983.

Nitze, William A., and E. Preston Dargan. *A History of French Literature*. 3rd ed. New York: Holt, Rinehart, 1950.

Opland, Jeff. *Anglo-Saxon Oral Poetry*. New Haven: Yale UP, 1980.

Orel, Harold, ed. *Critical Essays on Thomas Hardy's Poetry*. New York: G. K. Hall, 1995.

Paley, Morton D., ed. *Twentieth-Century Interpretations of Songs of Innocence and of Experience*. Englewood Cliffs: Prentice-Hall, 1969.

Paris, Gaston. *Histoire Poétique de Charlemagne*. 1905. Geneva: Slatkine Reprints, 1974.

Paris, Gaston, and Ernest Langlois, ed. *Chrestomathie du Moyen Age*. Paris: Hachette, 1910.

Pattison, Bruce. *Music and Poetry of the English Renaissance*. 1948. 2nd ed. London: Methuen, 1970.

Pearson, Roger. *Unfolding Mallarmé: The Development of a Poetic Art*. Oxford: Clarendon, 1996.

Peyre, Henri. *What Is Symbolism?* Trans. Emmett Parker. University: U of Alabama P, 1974.

Philips, James E., and Bertrand H. Bronson. *Music and Literature in England in the Seventeenth and Eighteenth Centuries*. Los Angeles: U of California P, 1953.

Pickard-Cambridge, Sir Arthur. *Dithyramb Tragedy and Comedy*. Oxford: Clarendon, 1962.

Pistone, Danièle. "Le Symbolisme et la Musique Française à la Fin du XIXe Siècle." Pistone, *Symbolisme* 9–51.

——, ed. *Symbolisme et Musique en France 1870–1914*. *Revue Internationale de Musique Française* 32. Paris: Honoré Champion, 1995.

Pondrom, Cyrena N. *The Road from Paris: French Influence on English Poetry 1900–1920*. Cambridge: Cambridge UP, 1974.

Pope, John Collins. *The Rhythm of Beowulf*. New Haven: Yale UP, 1942.

Preminger, Alex, and T. V. F. Brogan, eds. *The New Princeton Encyclopedia of Poetry and Poetics.* Princeton: Princeton UP, 1993.

Propst, Louise. *An Analytical Study of Shelley's Versification.* Iowa City: U of Iowa P, 1932.

Puttenham, George. *The Arte of English Poesie.* Ed. Gladys Dodge Wilcox and Alice Walker. Cambridge: Cambridge UP, 1970.

Raby, F. J. E. *A History of Christian-Latin Poetry.* 2nd ed. Oxford: Clarendon, 1953.

——. *A History of Secular Latin Poetry in the Middle Ages.* 2nd ed. Vols. 1 and 2. Oxford: Clarendon, 1957.

——, ed. *The Oxford Book of Medieval Latin Verse.* Oxford: Clarendon, 1959.

Ragg, Lonsdale. *Dante and His Italy.* 1907. New York: Haskell House, 1973.

Rampersad, Arnold. *The Life of Langston Hughes.* 2 vols. New York: Oxford UP, 1986, 1988.

Ramsey, Paul. *The Art of John Dryden.* Lexington: U of Kentucky P, 1969.

Ransom, John Crowe. "Thomas Hardy's Poems, and the Religious Difficulties of a Naturalist." *Kenyon Review* 22.2 (Spring 1960): 169–93.

Reibetanz, Julia Maniates. *A Reading of Eliot's "Four Quartets."* Ann Arbor: UMI Research Press, 1983.

Robb, Graham. *Unlocking Mallarmé.* New Haven: Yale UP, 1996.

Robbins, Rossell Hope, ed. *Secular Lyrics of the XIVth and XVth Centuries.* Oxford: Clarendon, 1968.

Roberts, Michael. *The Jeweled Style: Poetry and Poetics in Late Antiquity.* Ithaca: Cornell UP, 1989.

Roche, Jerome. *The Madrigals.* New York: Oxford UP, 1990.

Rollins, Hyder E., and Herschel Baker, eds. *The Renaissance in England.* Boston: Heath, 1954.

Rudenstine, Neil L. *Sidney's Poetic Development.* Cambridge: Harvard UP, 1967.

Russom, Geoffrey. *Old English Meter and Linguistic Theory.* Cambridge: Cambridge UP, 1987.

Rychner, Jean. *La Chanson de Geste.* Geneva: Librairie E. Droz, 1955.

Ryding, Erik S. *In Harmony Framed: Musical Humanism, Thomas Campion, and the Two Daniels.* Kirksville, MO: Sixteenth Century Journal Publishers, 1993.

Saintsbury, George. *A History of English Prosody from the Twelfth Century to the Present Day.* 3 vols. London: Macmillan, 1906–1910.

Santayana, George. *Interpretations of Poetry and Religion.* New York: Scribner's, 1921.

Scarborough, Dorothy. *On the Trail of Negro Folk-Songs.* 1925. Hatboro, PA: Folklore Association, 1976.

Scher, Steven Paul. *Music and Text: Critical Inquiries.* Cambridge: Cambridge UP, 1992.

Schleiner, Louise. *The Living Lyre in English Verse from Elizabeth through the Restoration.* Columbia: U of Missouri P, 1984.

Schnitzler, Gunter. *Dichtung und Musik.* Stuttgart: Klett-Cotta, 1979.

Sewall, Richard B. *The Life of Emily Dickinson.* New York: Farrar, 1974.

Shapiro, Marianne. *De Vulgari Eloquentia: Dante's Book of Exile.* Lincoln: U of Nebraska P, 1990.

Small, Judy Jo. *Positive as Sound: Emily Dickinson's Rhyme.* Athens: U of Georgia P, 1990.

Smith, David Nichol, ed. *The Oxford Book of Eighteenth-Century Verse.* Oxford: Clarendon, 1926.

Southern, Eileen, ed. *Readings in Black American Music.* New York: Norton, 1983.

Southworth, J. G. *Verses of Cadence.* Oxford: Blackwell, 1954.

Spaeth, Sigmund. *Milton's Knowledge of Music*. Ann Arbor: U of Michigan P, 1963.

Speirs, John. *The Scots Literary Tradition: An Essay in Criticism*. 2nd ed. London: Faber, 1962.

Spenser, Edmund. *Spenser's Prose Works*. Ed. Rudolf Gottfried. Baltimore: Johns Hopkins UP, 1949.

Steele, Timothy. *Missing Measures: Modern Poetry and the Revolt against Meter*. Fayetteville: U of Arkansas P, 1990.

Steinfeld, Frederick W. *Goethe and Music*. New York: New York Public Library, 1952.

Stevens, John. *Music and Poetry in the Early Tudor Court*. London: Methuen, 1961.

——. *Words and Music in the Middle Ages*. Cambridge: Cambridge UP, 1986.

Sutherland, John. *The Life of Walter Scott: A Critical Biography*. Oxford: Blackwell, 1995.

Swinburne, Algernon Charles. *William Blake: A Critical Essay*. London: John Camden Hotten, Piccadilly, 1868.

Tate, Allen. "Emily Dickinson." *On the Limits of Poetry*. New York: Swallow, 1948. 197–213.

Taupin, René. *The Influence of French Symbolism on Modern American Poetry*. Trans. William Pratt and Anne Rich Pratt. New York: AMS, 1985.

Taylor, Dennis. *Hardy's Metres and Victorian Prosody*. Oxford: Clarendon, 1988.

Tracy, Steven C. *Langston Hughes and the Blues*. Urbana: U of Illinois P, 1988.

Thompson, John. *The Founding of English Metre*. New York: Columbia UP, 1961.

Thorpe, James, ed. *Relations of Literary Study*. New York: MLA, 1967.

Thrall, William Flint, and Addison Hibbard, eds. *A Handbook to Literature*. Rev. and enlarged ed. Ed. Hugh Holman. New York: Odyssey, 1960.

Townsend, Dave. Sleeve notes for *Under the Greenwood Tree*. The carols and dances of Hardy's Wessex played on authentic instruments by the Mellstock Band. Saydisc CD-SDL 360.

Trotman, C. James, ed. *Langston Hughes: The Man, His Art, and His Continuing Influence*. New York: Garland, 1995.

Trypanis, C. A. *Greek Poetry from Homer to Seferis*. London: U of Chicago P, 1981.

Tsur, Reuven. *What Makes Sound Patterns Expressive?* Durham: Duke UP, 1992.

Valéry, Paul. *An Anthology*. Ed. James Lawler. Princeton: Princeton UP, 1976.

——. *Charmes ou Poèmes*. Ed. Charles G. Whiting. London: Athlone, 1973.

——. *Monsieur Teste*. Trans. Jackson Matthews. New York: Knopf, 1948.

——. *Oeuvres*. Paris: Gallimard, 1957, 1960.

——. *Poésies Choisies*. Paris: Hachette, 1954.

——. *Selected Writings*. Trans. various hands. New York: New Directions, 1950.

Walsh, P. G., ed. and trans. *Love Lyrics from the Carmina Burana*. Chapel Hill: U of North Carolina P, 1993.

Watts, Anne Chalmers. *The Lyre and the Harp: A Comparative Reconsideration of Oral Tradition in Homer and Old English Poetry*. New Haven: Yale UP, 1969.

Waite, William G. *The Rhythm of Twelfth-Century Polyphony*. New Haven: Yale UP, 1954.

Walpole, A. S. *Early Latin Hymns*. 1922. Hildesheim: Georg Olms, 1966.

Webb, Daniel. *Observation on the Correspondence between Poetry and Music*. New York: Garland, 1970.

Webbe, William. *A Discourse of English Poetrie*. Westminster: Constable, 1895.

Weinberg, Bernard. *The Limits of Symbolism*. Chicago: U of Chicago P, 1966.

Weinig, Sister Mary Anthony. *Verbal Pattern in "Four Quartets": A Close Reading of T. S. Eliot's Poem*. Troy, MI: International Book Publishers, 1982.

Whicher, George F., trans. *The Goliard Poets.* Norfolk: New Directions, 1949.

White, Newman Ivey. *Portrait of Shelley.* New York: Knopf, 1945.

Whitman, F. H. *A Comparative Study of Old English Meter.* Toronto: U of Toronto P, 1993.

Whitman, Walt. *The Gathering of the Forces: Editorials, Essays, Literary and Dramatic Reviews, and Other Material.* . . . 2 vols. New York: Putnam's, 1920.

——. *The Uncollected Poetry and Prose of Walt Whitman.* . . . 2 vols. Ed. Emory Holloway. New York: Peter Smith, 1932.

Wilhelm, James J. *Seven Troubadours: The Creators of Modern Verse.* University Park: Pennsylvania State UP, 1970.

Wilkins, Ernest Hatch. *A History of Italian Literature.* Rev. by Thomas G. Bergin. Cambridge: Harvard UP, 1974.

Williams, Gordon. *Tradition and Originality in Roman Poetry.* Oxford: Clarendon, 1968.

Williams, Miller. *Patterns of Poetry: An Encyclopedia of Forms.* Baton Rouge: Louisiana State UP, 1986.

Wilson, David Fenwick. *Music of the Middle Ages.* New York: Scherer, 1990.

Wilson, Edmund. *Axel's Castle.* New York: Scribners, 1931.

Wilson, R. M. *The Lost Literature of Medieval England.* New York: Cooper Square, 1969.

Wimsatt, James. *Chaucer and the French Love Poets.* Chapel Hill: U of North Carolina P, 1968.

Wimsatt, William K., Jr. Introduction to *Alexander Pope: Selected Poetry and Prose.* New York: Rinehart, 1951. vii–liv.

——. *Versification: Major Language Types.* New York: New York UP, 1972.

Winn, James Anderson. *John Dryden and His World.* New Haven: Yale UP, 1987.

——. *Unsuspected Eloquence.* New Haven: Yale UP, 1981.

Winters, Yvor. *In Defense of Reason.* Denver: Swallow, 1947.

Woods, Susanne. *Natural Emphasis: English Versification from Chaucer to Dryden.* San Marino: Huntington Library, 1985.

Yeats, W. B. *Essays and Introductions.* New York: Macmillan, 1961. New York: Collier, 1968.

Ziolkowski, Jan M., ed. and trans. *The Cambridge Songs (Carmina Cantabrigiensia).* New York: Garland, 1994.

Index

"Absolom and Achitophel" (Dryden), 171
accent
  in Greek, 47
  in Latin poetry, 15–19, 26, 29, 30–37,
    40–48, 126, 304–8
  in Romance languages, 45, 48
accentual-syllabic meter, 3, 7, 16, 49, 68,
    74, 100, 118, 119, 125, 129, 131, 134,
    150, 213, 229, 258, 264, 288, 296,
    301, 305
Acis and Galatea (Gay and Hughes), 182
Addison, Joseph, 178, 180, 183, 191
"Adonais" (Shelley), 150, 234
Aeneid, The (Virgil), 16, 83, 88, 295
African American poets and poetry, 251–
    57, 300
air, musical, 6, 7, 131, 132, 182, 196–99
Akenside, Mark, 191, 216
alba (Provençal form), 46
Albigensian Crusade, 58
Albion and Albanius (Dryden), 173–76
alcaic line, 29, 303, 304, 308
alcaic strophe, 19–21, 29, 46, 303–5, 308
"Alexander's Feast" (Dryden), 177, 178
Alexandrine, French, 46, 79, 279, 281, 297
alliterative meter, 3, 62–68, 73, 76, 77
"Amor, che nella mente mi ragiona"
    (Dante), 82
anacrusis, 303
Anatomy of Melancholy, The (Burton), 144
*Ancient and Modern Scottish Songs, Heroic
    Ballads etc.* (Herd), 197
apolelymenon, 145, 163
Apologie for Poetrie, An (Sidney), 43, 121
Arabic poetry, 48, 91
Arcades (Milton), 154–56
Arcadia (Sidney), 119, 132
Arcadian Rhetoric, The (Fraunce), 125

Aristophanes, 14
Aristotle, 11, 82, 128, 143
Arnold, Matthew, 100, 145, 157, 181, 289
ars metrica, medieval, 41, 42
Ars Poetica (Horace), 30
ars ritmica, medieval, 41, 42
arsis, differing meanings in prosody, 17, 18
Art of English Poesy, The (Puttenham), 126
Arthurian romances, 68
Ascham, Roger, 17, 121, 124
Astrophel and Stella (Sidney), 109, 110, 135
"At a Solemn Music" (Milton), 143, 145,
    147, 154
Auden, W. H., 46, 76, 147, 289, 293
Augustine, St., 31, 41, 42, 54, 96, 121
Avicenna, 83

"Baite, The" (Donne), 137
balada (troubadour dance song), 54
Baldwin, James, 251
ballad form and meter, 4, 7, 58, 71, 74, 89,
    102, 108, 170, 184–89, 200, 210, 214,
    219, 220, 232, 260–64, 289
"Ballad of Sally in our Alley, The" (Carey),
    188
"Ballad of the Dark Ladié, The" (Cole-
    ridge), 219
Barnes, Barnabe, 135
"Battle of Brunanburh" (anon.; trans.
    Tennyson), 65
Baudelaire, Charles, 268–71, 302
Bede, The Venerable, 42, 64
Beethoven, Ludwig van, 8, 100, 141, 198,
    259, 285, 286, 299
Beggar's Opera, The (Gay), 167, 188
Bentley, Richard, 18
Beowulf, 10, 62–69, 77, 80, 81, 101, 236,
    289, 298

Berryman, John, 189

Bible, the, 82, 119, 168, 240, 253, 267, 290, 292, 298. *See also* King James Version of the Bible

Big Sea, The (Hughes), 256

Bishop, Elizabeth, 288

Blake, William, 159, 169, 184, 186, 201–10, 213, 214, 240, 245–47, 257, 264, 293, 303

Blow, John, 178

"Blue Closet, The" (Morris), 284, 289

blues, as model for poetry, 184, 251–56, 300

Boccaccio, Giovanni, 86, 88, 97

Boethius, Anicius Manlius Severinus, 42, 54, 96, 121, 143

Book of Common Prayer, The, 7, 137, 292, 298

Booth, Mark W., 3, 102

Boswell, James, 171, 180

Bowers, Edgar, 302

Boyce, William, 167, 168, 180, 183

Brady, Matthew, 241

Brady, Nicholas, 178

Bridges, Robert, 267, 289, 302

Brienne, Jean de, 56

British Musical Miscellany, The, 204

Brogan, T. V. F., 1, 47

Browning, Robert, 235, 261

Brut (Layamon), 68

Burke, Edmund, 216, 225, 269

Burns, Robert, 2, 72, 169, 184, 186, 187, 195–211, 220, 237, 246, 250, 251, 257, 258, 261

Burton, Robert, 144

Byrd, William, 131

Byrom, John, 167

Byron, George Gordon, Lord, 49, 172, 195, 210, 215, 218, 224, 225, 231, 234, 302

Caedmon, 64

Cambridge Songs, the, 41

Camerata (Florentine musical circle), 164, 172, 175

Campion, Thomas, 3, 5, 7, 17, 116, 137, 144, 156, 169, 198

"Canonization, The" (Donne), 102, 129, 130

canso (Provençal form), 46, 86

cantata, musical and literary, 166, 176, 179–84, 190, 194

Canterbury Tales, The (Chaucer), 89

canzone, 82, 83, 86–88, 94, 105, 145, 156, 161, 162, 251

Carey, Henry, 188

Carmen Saeculare (Horace), 17

Carmina Burana (anon.), 26, 50, 51

carole (medieval French dance song), 54

Cary, Phoebe, 214

"Castaway, The" (Cowper), 189

Castelvetro, Lodovico, 143

Cato (M. Porcius Cato), 50

Catullus, Valerius, 32, 42

Cavalier poets and poetry, 110, 137, 141, 184, 210

"Cavalry Crossing a Ford" (Whitman), 240

"Celtic Element in Literature, The" (Yeats), 268

Certain Notes of Instruction (Gascoigne), 121

chanson de geste, 52, 62, 77–81, 88, 89

Chanson de Roland (anon.), 63, 77–79

Chapman, George, 2, 168, 225

Chatterton, Thomas, 219

Chaucer, Geoffrey, 6, 10, 16, 43, 52, 54, 68, 69, 73, 74, 85, 88–108, 125, 151, 212, 236, 267, 293, 295

"Cherrylog Road" (Dickey), 241

Childe Harold's Pilgrimage (Byron), 234

"Christians, to the Paschal Victim" (*Victimae paschali laudes*), 40

"Church Monuments" (Herbert), 112, 116, 117

Cibber, Colley, 204

"Cimetière Marin, Le" (Valéry), 275–84

Claudian (Claudius Claudianus), 50

Coleridge, Samuel Taylor, 76, 129, 161, 185, 190, 193, 210, 213, 215, 217, 219, 220, 225, 231, 282

Comédie Française, 46

Comus (Milton), 154–56, 169

conductus (medieval Church musical form), 26–28, 39, 253

"Congo, The" (Lindsay), 178

Congreve, William, 178

Convivio (Dante), 82, 83

Cooper, John Gilbert, 191
Corelli, Arcangelo, 141
Corneille, Pierre, 140
"Correspondences" (Baudelaire), 268
Coup de Dés, Un (Mallarmé), 271
Courtois d'Arras (anon.), 89
Cowley, Abraham, 136, 141, 163, 170, 171, 174, 177–79, 190
Cowper, William, 189
Crane, Hart, 300
Crashaw, Richard, 110, 270
Cullen, Countee, 252
Cunningham, Allen, 201
Cunningham, John, 180

"Dance Figure" (Pound), 300
Daniel, Samuel, 110
dansa (troubadour dance song), 54
Dante Alighieri, 2, 15, 43, 45, 79, 82–88, 94, 105, 156, 159, 162, 198, 223, 236, 237, 251, 258, 295, 297, 298
Davidson, Donald, 152
De Arte Metrica (Bede), 42
Debussy, Claude, 302
"Defence of Poetry, A" (Shelley), 221
"Demon Lover, The" (anon.), 232
De musica (Augustine), 31, 41, 59, 143
Denham, Sir John, 217
Deschamps, Eustache, 5, 6, 82, 85, 91, 94, 96, 97, 108, 127, 160, 161, 183, 259, 275
descort (Provençal form), 53
De speculatione musici (Odington), 59
"Deus creator omnium" (Ambrose), 34–37
"Devil's Thoughts, The" (Coleridge), 219
De Vulgari Eloquentia (Dante), 45, 86, 94
Dia, Countess of, 53, 54
Dickey, James, 241, 296, 300
Dickinson, Emily, 2, 3, 53, 131, 244–51, 257, 293, 302
Dido and Aeneas (Purcell), 178
"Dies Irae" (Thomas of Celano), 39, 40
dipody, classical, 36, 242
"Diverting History of John Gilpin, The" (Cowper), 189

Divine Comedy, The (Dante), 82–88, 162, 295
Doctor Faustus (Marlowe), 140
Donizetti, Gaetano, 239
Don Juan (Byron), 49
Donne, John, 6, 102, 110, 111, 129–31, 137, 139, 145, 161, 168, 194, 264, 282, 289, 296, 297
Dowland, John, 6, 7, 131
Draghi, Giovanni Baptista, 177
Drayton, Michael, 110
Drummond, William, 135, 145
Dryden, John, 136, 151, 166, 168–77, 180, 184, 198, 215, 224
Dunbar, Paul Laurence, 252
D'Urfey, Thomas, 178

Eccles, John, 178
"Ecstasy, The" (Donne), 137, 289
Eliot, T. S., 3, 18, 76, 100, 135, 136, 139, 145, 157, 160–65, 191, 198, 257–59, 269, 279, 284–99, 301
Elliott, "Ramblin' Jack," 254
Emerson, Ralph Waldo, 195, 203, 236, 238, 243
Enchiridion (Hephaestion), 12, 31
Endymion (Keats), 228
Ennius, 16
Essay on Criticism, An (Pope), 147, 168
Études Littéraires (Valéry), 274
Euripides, 14
"Eve of St. Agnes, The" (Keats), 225, 228, 232, 234
Evergreen, The (Ramsay), 197
Everyman (anon.), 140, 294
"Exequy, The" (King), 294

Faerie Queene, The (Spenser), 75
Faust (Goethe), 172
Fenton, Elijah, 185
Ferguson, Robert, 197
"Fern Hill" (Thomas), 288
"Fiddler of Dooney, The" (Yeats), 264, 300
Fine Clothes to the Jew (Hughes), 257
Fishburn, Christopher, 178
Flaubert, Gustave, 274
Foixà, Joifre de, 53
Ford, Ford Madox, 17, 95

Four Quartets (Eliot), 3, 76, 157, 259, 284–88, 290, 297–99
Fraunce, Abraham, 125, 126
free verse, 1, 3, 14, 31, 78, 118, 123, 131, 135, 139, 145, 149, 163, 164, 170, 174, 179, 213, 224, 236, 240, 256, 258, 301
Frost, Robert, 244, 252, 305

Galilei, Vicenzo, 164
Galliard, Johann Ernst, 183
Gascoigne, George, 30, 110, 111, 121, 123
Gay, John, 167, 182
Geoffrey of Monmouth, 68
Ginsberg, Allen, 243, 244
Giovanni, Nikki, 300
Giraldus Cambrensis, 28
"God Save the King" (anon.), 187
God's Trombones (Johnson), 253
Goethe, Johann Wolfgang von, 160, 172, 195, 264, 302
Goliardic poetry, 26, 33, 41, 47, 49, 50, 102
Gorboduc (Sackville and Norton), 140, 150
Gosson, Stephen, 121
Grand Old Opry, The, 254
Gray, Thomas, 190
Gregorian chant, 27, 38, 40, 134
Guinness, Alec, 294

Haley, Bill, 184
Handel, Georg Friedrich, 141, 156, 166–68, 177, 178, 182, 183
Handy, W. C., 253–55
Hardison, O. B., 5–8, 142, 160, 161, 164
Hardy, Thomas, 2, 3, 5, 49, 76, 189, 236, 244, 248, 251, 258–64, 267, 268, 294, 298
Harlem Renaissance, The, 255, 300
Harvey, Gabriel, 17, 121
Haydn, Franz Joseph, 139, 152
H. D. (Hilda Doolittle), 176, 301
Heaney, Seamus, 131, 197, 288
Henley, W. E., 189
Henry, Richard "Big Boy," 253
Hephaestion, 12, 31, 42
Herbert, George, 7, 112–16, 139
Herd, David, 197

Herrick, Robert, 2, 131, 137, 139
Hilary, Bishop of Poitiers, 33, 35, 37, 39
Hilton, John, 134, 135, 137
Hoccleve, Thomas, 107
Holst, Gustav, 264
Homer, 13, 15, 16, 30, 60–62, 69, 80, 225, 236
Hopkins, Gerard Manley, 76, 235, 267, 289
Horace (Quintus Horatius Flaccus), 3, 16–19, 21, 23, 29, 30, 32, 35, 36, 40, 43, 47, 50, 125, 143, 166, 174, 237, 303–8
Housman, A. E., 131, 189, 259
Hughes, John, 176, 181–84
Hughes, Langston, 2, 183, 251–57, 300
Hughes, Ted, 205, 288
Hulme, T. E., 4
Humphrey, Pelham, 137
Hunt, Leigh, 233
hymn
    Ambrosian, 34–39, 48, 83
    Blake's use of, 202, 203, 206
    Hardy's use of, as model, 244, 260, 262, 267
    irregular, eighteenth-century, 178, 190, 192
    medieval, 25, 28, 32–40, 42, 43, 46–51, 57, 60, 83, 102
    model for Emily Dickinson, 3, 245–47
    Protestant, 5, 100, 190, 193, 254
    religious, eighteenth-century and later, 184, 188–90, 249
    secular in regular forms, 191
    as used by Milton, 142, 145, 149, 150
    Vedic, 10
"Hymn Before Sunrise in the Vale of Chamouni" (Coleridge), 190, 217
"Hymn of Pan" (Shelley), 190
"Hymn to Adversity" (Gray), 190
"Hymn to Darkness" (Yalden), 190
"Hymn to Durga" (Jones), 192
"Hymn to Light" (Cowley), 190
"Hymn to Science" (Akenside), 191
"Hymn to the Morning: In Praise of Light" (Yalden), 190
"Hymn to the Naiads" (Akenside), 191
"Hymn to the Nymph of Bristol Spring, An" (Whitehead), 191

"I Care Not for These Ladies" (Campion), 137

ictus, 17, 18, 30, 43, 47, 115, 303–8

Iliad, The, 29, 61, 63

"Il Penseroso" (Milton), 139, 153

Imagism and Imagists, 3, 4, 164, 183, 301

"In a Prominent Bar in Secaucus One Day" (Kennedy), 105

In Memoriam (Tennyson), 189

Island in the Moon, An (Blake), 205

Ives, Burl, 184

James, Henry, 270

James, William, 275

jazz, and poetry, 237, 251, 252, 256, 258, 300, 301

Johnson, James, 196

Johnson, James Weldon, 253

Johnson, Samuel, 136, 145, 162, 168, 171, 172, 176, 178, 180, 183, 186, 189–91, 224

Johnson, Thomas H., 245

Jones, Howard Mumford, 257

Jones, Inigo, 141

Jones, Sir William, 192

jongleur, 55, 81

Jonson, Ben, 2, 127, 129, 151, 163, 168, 264

Julian of Norwich, Dame, 297

Juvenal (Decimus Julius Junialis), 50

Kavanagh, Patrick, 197

Keats, John, 2, 83, 102, 157, 176, 181, 186, 192, 197, 199, 210, 212, 224, 225, 228–34, 237, 249, 261, 264, 283

Kennedy, X. J., 105

King, Henry, 143, 294

King James Version of the Bible, 7, 240, 243, 244, 253, 290. *See also* Bible, the

kithera, importance to Greek poetry, 11, 13, 59, 63

"Kubla Khan" (Coleridge), 152, 219, 282

"La Belle Dame Sans Merci" (Keats), 181, 186, 231–33

Laforgue, Jules, 135, 145

lai (French form), 53, 77, 89, 91, 95, 97

laisse (French epic stanza), 77, 79, 80, 89

"L'Allegro'" (Milton), 139, 150, 151, 153, 191

Lamartine, Alphonse Marie Louis de, 270

Langhorne, John, 181, 191, 192

Langland, William, 71, 72

Language poets and poetry, 131, 222, 236, 301

langue d'oc, 32, 45, 58

langue d'oïl, 32, 45

Lanier, Sidney, 302

"L'Après-Midi d'un Faune (Mallarmé), 302

"L'Art de dictier (Deschamps), 94, 160

Lawes, Henry, 137, 140, 155, 156, 175

Lawes, William, 137

Layamon, or Lawman, 68

"Lazarus" (African American spiritual), 253

Lear, Edward, 284, 301

Leaves of Grass (Whitman), 239, 240

"Leda and the Swan" (Yeats), 265

Lehrer, Tom, 50

Leopardi, Giacomo, 135, 145

Lewis, C. S., 6, 104, 105

Lily, William, 143

Lindsay, Vachel, 178

Linnell, Mary Ann, 202

"Litany in Time of Plague" (Nashe), 294

"Little Gidding" (Eliot), 290, 292, 297, 298

Lives of the English Poets (Johnson), 168, 176, 191

Logan, John, 191

Longfellow, Henry Wadsworth, 30, 131, 235, 295

Longinus, 224

"Lord Randall" (anon.), 263

Lord, Albert B., 61, 64, 65, 80

Loris, Guillaume de, 54

"Love Song of J. Alfred Prufrock, The" (Eliot), 157, 288, 292, 297

Lowell, Amy, 165

Lowell, Robert, 189

Loy, Mina, 301

Lucan (M. Annaeus Lucanus), 50

"Lycidas" (Milton), 135, 136, 141, 145, 156, 158, 177, 180, 224, 231

Lydgate, John, 107

Lyrical Ballads (Wordsworth and Coleridge), 186, 213, 214

"Mac Flecknoe" (Dryden), 171
Machaut, Guillaume de, 90–92
MacLow, Jackson, 131
Macpherson, James, 196
madrigal, 7, 86, 100, 116, 118, 129, 131–
35, 140, 145, 155–57, 161, 167, 175,
181, 234
Magic Mountain, The (Mann), 259
Magoun, Francis P., 61, 63, 64, 80
Mallarmé, Stéphane, 1, 15, 259, 268–75,
277, 284, 285, 298, 301, 302
Mallet, David, 186
Malone, Kemp, 64
Manfred (Byron), 172
Mann, Thomas, 259
"Mariana" (Tennyson), 270
Marie de France, 89
Marlowe, Christopher, 110, 111, 137
Martial (Marcus Valerius Martialis), 30,
36
Marvell, Andrew, 110, 270, 274, 290, 297
Mason, William, 180
Maximus (Olson), 146
Mazzoni, Guido, 143
Medieval Hebrew poetry, 48
Menhaden Chanteymen, The, 253
mese, explained, 11
Metaphysical poets and poetry, 14, 110,
123, 130, 137, 141, 150, 172
metrici, 12, 41, 125
metron, 21, 34, 36
"Midnight Raffle" (Hughes), 252
Midsummer Night's Dream, A (Shakespeare),
76, 139, 140
Miller, James, 166
Milton, John, 96, 110, 113, 116, 118, 135–
71, 175–77, 191, 194, 201, 203, 206,
212, 215–17, 223–25, 237, 258, 264,
293
"Milton" (Tennyson), 20
minnesingers, 42, 55, 57
Minstrelsy of the Scottish Border (Scott), 210
modes, Greek musical, 10, 11, 59, 128
modes, medieval rhythmic, 59
monody, 136, 156–58, 175, 180, 181, 232

"Monody, Written Upon Avon" (War-
ton), 232
"Mont Blanc" (Shelley), 219
Montaigne, Michel de, 94
Monteverdi, Claudio, 141
Moore, Edward, 183
Moore, Thomas, 3, 210–12, 250, 251
Morley, Henry, Lord, 107
Morley, Thomas, 7, 131, 134
Morris, William, 19, 131, 284, 289, 294
Morte Arthure (anon.), 69, 71
mousike, 8, 9, 11, 13–15, 17, 18, 23, 54, 68,
121, 140, 159, 171, 183, 196, 302
Mozart, Wolfgang Amadeus, 40, 91
Murder in the Cathedral (Eliot), 76
"Music of Poetry, The" (Eliot), 139, 284,
286, 287
musique naturele, 95, 97, 108, 117, 121, 127,
161, 183
"My Last Duchess" (Browning), 235
"My Lute Awake!" (Wyatt), 108
"My Papa's Waltz" (Roethke), 300
Mystère d'Adam (anon.), 89
"My Sweetest Lesbia" (Campion), 116, 137

Nashe, Thomas, 294
"Neutral Tones" (Hardy), 262, 263
New Formalism, 12, 30, 131, 164, 236
Nietzsche, Friedrich, 272
"Night Thoughts" (Young), 217
Norman Conquest, effect on English
poetry, 10, 62, 67, 73
Norton, Thomas, 140
Notre Dame school of composers, 59, 84,
121

"Ode: Intimations of Immortality . . ."
(Wordsworth), 192
"Ode to a Nightingale" (Keats), 102, 225–
31
"Ode to the West Wind" (Shelley), 192,
270
Odington, Walter, 59
Odyssey, The, 30, 61
"Old Barn Dance, The" (American folk
song), 254
Old English meter, 3, 16, 62, 65, 66, 68,
69, 72–74, 76, 77, 151, 289

Oldham, John, 178
"Old Joe Clark" (American folk song), 254
Olson, Charles, 146, 193, 223, 243, 301
"On the Death of Dr. Robert Levett" (Johnson), 188
On the Morning of Christ's Nativity (Milton), 147, 149, 150
"On the Principles of Genial Criticism . . ." (Coleridge), 220
oral-formulaic theory of composition, 61–67, 69, 77, 80
organum (ninth-century singing style), 25
"Ossian" (pseudonymous author invented by James Macpherson), 192, 196, 242
"Ossian's Hymn to the Sun" (Logan), 191
Ovid (Publius Ovidius Naso), 30, 47, 50, 97, 125, 237
"Ozymandias" (Shelley), 224

Palladio, Andrea, 141
Paradise Lost (Milton), 118, 136, 141, 145, 158, 160–63, 169, 206, 224
Paris, Gaston, 57, 73
Parliament of Fowls, The (Chaucer), 99
Parnassian school in French poetry, 269
Parnell, Thomas, 190
Parry, Milman, 61, 63, 64, 80
Parsons, Theophilus, 178
Parthenophile and Parthenope (Barnes), 135
"Passage to India" (Whitman), 239
"Passion, The" (Milton), 150
pastorela, pastourelle (Provençal form), 46, 56, 57
Pater, Walter, 128, 131, 141
Patmore, Coventry, 267, 289
Penultimate Law, the, 15, 33, 305–7
Pepusch, Johann Christoph, 176, 183
Percy, Thomas, 184, 188, 197, 219
Persius (A. Persius Flaccus), 30, 50, 51
"Peter Quince at the Clavier" (Stevens), 300
Petrarch (Francesco Petrarca), 86, 88, 107
Pherecrates, 14
"Phoebus, Arise" (Drummond), 135
Piers Plowman (Langland), 43, 62, 65, 68, 71, 81, 120, 298

Pindar, 15, 136, 171, 174, 176, 178, 180, 192
Pindaric ode, genuine, 163
Pindarique (the pseudo-Pindaric ode), 136, 139, 141, 163, 164, 170, 171, 174–80, 185, 192
Pippa Passes (Browning), 261
planh (Provençal form), 53
Plath, Sylvia, 189, 258
Plato, 11, 82, 124, 128, 142, 144, 151, 154, 155, 158
Pleasures of the Imagination, The (Akenside), 216
Poe, Edgar Allen, 4, 131, 235, 242, 270, 302
Poems Chiefly in the Scottish Dialect (Burns), 196
"Poet, The" (Emerson), 236
Pope, Alexander, 2, 17, 18, 116, 136, 141, 147, 168, 171–73, 178–81, 185, 214, 215, 237, 297
Pope, J. C., 3, 66, 67
Pound, Ezra, 65, 67, 95, 162, 164, 165, 176, 257, 285, 301
Prelude, The (Wordsworth), 209
Prior, Matthew, 185, 186
Prometheus Unbound (Shelley), 172, 224
Provençal language and poetry, 24, 32, 37, 41, 46, 52, 53, 58, 78, 86, 210
Prudentius, Aurelius Clemens, 40
Psalms (biblical), 7, 16, 71, 138, 155
Psalms, versions of, 7, 138, 155
Purcell, Daniel, 178
Purcell, Henry, 166, 172, 178, 180
Puttenham, George, 126–28
Pythagoras, 83, 119

Qassida, The, 48
quantitative meter
    attempted in English, 5, 11, 17, 20, 21, 118, 119, 121, 124–26, 229, 306
    Greek, 3, 10, 11, 13–15, 49, 76
    Latin, ancient, 15–17, 19, 20, 30, 118, 305, 307, 308
    and Medieval Latin poetry, 32, 36, 37, 41, 43, 49–52, 59, 88, 95, 305
    in poetry of India, 10
    Sanskrit, 10

quantity, metrical
    possible effects in English, 11, 229, 230,
      244, 249, 295
    and stress in Latin, 30, 32, 36, 37, 40, 43,
      45, 49, 308
Quintilian (Marcus Fabius Quintilianus),
    87

Racine, Jean Baptiste, 140
Raleigh, Sir Walter, 6, 56, 110, 137
Ralph Roister Doister (Udall), 16
Ransom, John Crowe, 244, 262
"Rape of Lucrece, The" (Shakespeare),
    76
Rape of the Lock, The (Pope), 173,
    184
Red Book of Ossory, The, 26
Reliques of Ancient English Poetry (Percy),
    184, 188, 197, 219
Remede de Fortune (Machaut), 92
rhapsodes, 13
rhyme, origins and function, 46–53, 63,
    80, 93, 99
Rhymers' Club, The, 268
rhythmici, 12, 41
"Rime of the Ancient Mariner, The"
    (Coleridge), 220
Robinson, Edwin Arlington, 244
Roethke, Theodore, 244, 300
Roman de Brut, Le (Wace), 68, 78
Roman de la Rose, Le, 54, 91
rondeau (medieval French song), 54, 90,
    95
"Rose-Cheek'd Laura" (Campion), 144
Rowe, Nicholas, 179
"Rugby Chapel" (Arnold), 296
"Rule Britannia" (Thomson), 187
Ruskin, John, 19
Russell, Bertrand, 159

Sackville, Thomas, 140
"St. Louis Blues" (Handy), 255
Saintsbury, George, 170, 267
Samson Agonistes (Milton), 118, 136, 139,
    145, 162–65
Sandburg, Carl, 237, 252
Santayana, George, 243
sapphic meter and form, 41, 46, 120

Saturnian meter, 16, 76
Scholemaster, The (Ascham), 121, 124
School of Abuse (Gosson), 121
Schopenhauer, Arthur, 272
Schubert, Franz, 184, 302
Scots Musical Museum, The, 196
Scott, Sir Walter, 210, 211, 220
"Seafarer, The" (Pound), 65, 67
Seasons, The (Thomson), 187, 215
Select Collection of Original Scotish Airs for the
    Voice, A, 197
"Self-Reliance" (Emerson), 243
sequence (Latin *sequentia*), 25–27, 39, 40,
    50, 57, 253
Severus, Julius, 31
Sexton, Anne, 189, 258
Shadwell, Thomas, 178
Shakespeare, William, 2, 49, 76, 108, 111,
    130, 134, 137, 139, 140, 150, 168,
    170, 194, 212, 217, 224, 225, 229,
    265, 298
"She Dwelt Among the Untrodden Ways"
    (Wordsworth), 186
Shelley, Percy Bysshe, 91, 159, 172, 190,
    192, 210, 215, 219, 221–25, 231, 234,
    258, 264, 270, 279
Shepherd's Calendar, The (Spenser), 120
"Short Song of Congratulation, A"
    (Johnson), 187
"Sick Rose, The" (Blake), 203
Sidney, Sir Philip, 6, 43, 46, 109–11, 119,
    121, 122, 130, 132, 135, 141, 145
Sievers, Edouard, 3, 66
Singer of Tales, The (Lord), 61, 65
Sir Gawain and the Green Knight (anon.),
    62, 68, 72, 73, 298
Sitwell, Edith, 301
Smart, Christopher, 178, 205, 240
Smith, Bessie, 255
Smith, Edmund, 178
Smith, John Stafford, 187
Smith, John Thomas, 201
Snodgrass, W. D., 189, 258
Socrates, 11
Song for St. Cecilia's Day (Dryden), 177
"Song of Myself" (Whitman), 239
Songs of Innocence, Songs of Experience
    (Blake), 201, 207

Sophocles, 9
"Soractian Ode" (Horace), 20, 21, 305
Southwell, Robert, 110
Spanish Tragedy, The (Kyd), 140
Spenser, Edmund, 49, 75, 110, 119–21, 141, 145, 191
"Stabat Mater" (anon.), 39, 40
Stanyhurst, Richard, 17
State of Innocence, The (Dryden), 170
Statius, P. Panius, 29, 30
Steele Glass, The (Gascoigne), 110
Steele, Timothy, 123
Stevens, Wallace, 244, 258, 277–79, 300
"Subalterns, The " (Hardy), 262
Surrey, Henry Howard, Earl of, 7, 16, 58, 125, 212, 295
"Sweet Betsy from Pike," 105
"Sweet Chariot" (African American spiritual), 253
Swift, Jonathan, 50, 166, 180, 183, 185
Swinburne, Algernon Charles, 4, 5, 131, 264, 289
syllabism; syllabic verse, 3, 16, 37, 40–42, 45, 46, 49, 51, 52, 62, 72, 76, 78, 89, 91, 100, 107, 108, 118, 125, 165, 279, 287, 293, 295
"Symbolism of Poetry, The" (Yeats), 268
Symbolist movement (French), 4, 135, 258, 259, 268–74, 297

"Tale of Sir Thopas" (Chaucer), 99
Tasso, Torquato, 143
Tate, Allen, 244, 245, 248
Tate, Nahum, 71, 178
Tatham, Frederick, 203
Tea-table Miscellany, The (Ramsay), 197
Tempest, The (Shakespeare), 139
Tennyson, Alfred Lord, 11, 14, 20, 21, 33, 65, 131, 147, 161, 178, 208, 217, 225, 229, 235, 237, 240, 243, 244, 261, 264, 270, 283, 297, 302
Thebaid, The (Statius), 30, 83
thesis, differing meanings in prosody, 17, 18, 303, 306, 308
"They Flee from Me" (Wyatt), 107, 111, 129
Thomas, Dylan, 288, 289
Thomas of Celano, 39

Thompson, William, 183, 191
Thomson, George, 197–99
Thomson, James, 187, 215, 216
Three Wayfarers, The (Hardy), 261
"Thyrsis" (Arnold), 157, 181
Timotheus, 14
"To a Child Dancing in the Wind" (Yeats), 264
"To a Locomotive in Winter" (Whitman), 239
"To Autumn" (Keats), 225, 249, 283
Tomlinson, Ralph, 187
"To the Pious Memory of . . . Mrs. Anne Killigrew" (Dryden), 176
Tottel, Richard, 110, 112, 129
Traherne, Thomas, 240
"Tramp-Woman's Tragedy, The" (Hardy), 262
Troilus and Criseyde (Chaucer), 99
trope (medieval music), 25
troubadour poetry and song, 25, 26, 28, 41, 42, 46, 52–58, 73, 77, 83, 86–88, 90, 91, 94, 100, 108, 210, 237, 246
trouvère poetry and songs, 5, 26, 42, 55–57, 77, 88, 90, 101
tumbling verse, 16
Twain, Mark, 243
"Tyger, The" (Blake), 203, 303

"Ulysses" (Tennyson), 235, 297

Valéry, Paul, 117, 258, 259, 268, 269, 271, 274–85, 298, 299
Vaughan, Henry, 110
"Veni Creator Spiritus", 37, 38
Verdi, Giuseppe, 40
Verlaine, Paul, 270, 284
vernacular songs of the Middle Ages, 25, 26, 28, 29, 32, 33, 40–42, 45, 52, 59, 88, 94, 100
vers (Provençal form), 46
versus (medieval form), 26, 40, 46
"Vicar of Bray, The" (anon.), 188
Vie de Saint Alexis (anon.), 281
Virgil, 16–18, 29, 30, 32, 43, 62, 83, 86, 88, 97, 125, 159
"Voi, che 'ntendendo il terzo ciel movete" (Dante), 83

Wace, 68

Wagner, Richard, 9, 243, 258, 259, 269, 271–74, 286

Waller, Edmund, 168, 216, 217

Walter of Châtillon, 50, 51

Warton, Joseph, 180

Warton, Thomas, 179, 181, 217, 232

Waste Land, The (Eliot), 191, 259, 285–88, 297, 298

Watts, Isaac, 113, 203, 245, 247, 249, 250

"Weary Blues, The" (Hughes), 255, 256

Webbe, William, 17, 120, 121, 123–25

Wesley, Charles, 189

Whistler, James Abbott McNeill, 299

Whitehead, William, 191, 215

Whitman, Walt, 100, 193, 203, 236–44, 251, 252, 257, 258, 290, 301

Whittier, John Greenleaf, 242

Wilbye, John, 133

"William and Margaret" (Mallet), 186

Williams, Ralph Vaughan, 264

Williams, William Carlos, 136, 300, 301

"Windsor Forest" (Pope), 171

Winn, James Anderson, 1, 25, 26, 28, 35, 52, 90, 166, 169, 173–75, 177

Winters, Yvor, 129, 243, 245, 248, 295, 301, 308

Wordsworth, William, 14, 103, 168, 185, 186, 191, 192, 194, 198, 209, 210, 213–16, 218, 219, 224, 237, 243, 261, 269, 270

Wyatt, Thomas, 2, 5–7, 58, 103–8, 125, 129, 132, 134, 198, 200, 210, 212, 237, 246, 251, 257, 258, 261

Yalden, Thomas, 178, 190

Yeats, William Butler, 3, 19, 37, 131, 147, 208, 236, 244, 258, 259, 263–68, 289, 298, 300, 305

Young, Edmund, 217

Zola, Émile, 274